Murder in Trastevere

Murder in Trastevere

A
Roman Holiday
Mystery

Jen Collins Moore

LEVEL
BEST BOOKS

To my family

Praise for the Roman Holiday Mysteries

Praise for *Murder in Trastevere*

"Donna Leon beware, Jen Collins Moore is nipping at your heels. Moore exquisitely captures the sights, sounds and tastes of Italy, Rome to be exact. If you love armchair travel, then you will love *Murder in Trastevere*, where art and la dolce vita are the backdrop to expat infighting and murder in the Eternal City."—Tina deBellegarde, Two-time Agatha Award-nominated author of the Batavia-on-Hudson Mysteries

"Independent, fearless, and smart, expat Faye Masters lives an idyllic life… until a dinner party guest keels over in her home. When her friends turn against her and police scrutinize her, Faye takes matters into her own hands. In short order, she goes from a murder suspect to murder target, to an amateur sleuth determined to find a killer who's hiding in plain sight. Brimming with rich details and unforgettable characters, this engaging page-turner will keep you guessing till the very end. Italian history, cuisine, and culture are expertly woven into a fascinating and unpredictable mystery."—Lida Sideris, author of the Southern California Mystery series

"Filled with the sights, sounds, and tastes of Rome, Italy, *Murder in Trastevere* is the best kind of armchair traveling mystery. Jen Collins Moore masterfully transports the reader into each lush scene where art, culture, and mystery abound. An engaging cast of characters. A puzzling whodunit. A terrific book with an ending I didn't see coming."—Carol Pouliot, Author of The Blackwell and Watson Time-Travel Mysteries

i

Praise for Jen Collins Moore's *Murder in the Piazza*

"A dynamite new voice in cozy mysteries."—Abby Geni, award-winning author of *The Wildlands, The Lightkeepers,* and *The Last Animal*

"An enjoyably dramatic tale…[with a] mystery that delights."—*Kirkus Reviews*

"The streets of Rome come to life (and death) in this fresh, fun mystery that journeys through the intersections of art, travel, secrets, and delicious Italian cuisine. Jen Collins Moore is an outstanding tour guide."—Kristen Lepionka, Shamus Award-winning author of the Roxane Weary mystery series

"Delightfully clever romp through Rome."—J. C. Eaton, award-winning author of the Sophie Kimball Mysteries, the Wine Trail Mysteries, and the Marcie Rayner Mysteries

"Perfect blend of funny and smart!"—Molly MacRae, National bestselling author of the Highland Bookshop Mysteries and the Haunted Yarn Shop Mysteries

"Fans of Agatha Christie will enjoy this cozy and intelligent read."— Susanna Calkins, Award-winning author of the Lucy Campion and Speakeasy Murder Mysteries

Chapter One

Michelangelo Merisi da Caravaggio established a breakthrough technique of intensely contrasted light and shadow. The effect of one bright area in a painting mostly of darkness is, simply said, breathtaking.
—Caravaggio: Brash, Brutish, and Brilliant

What was Faye thinking, holding a celebration for a woman she despised? She should have cancelled when she had the chance. Faye Masters' problem wasn't the party itself. Faye adored them. She loved choosing the menu, planning the music, and sending out the invitations. She loved connecting guests with similar interests and bringing newcomers into the fold. Most of all, Faye loved being at the center of things. She would have people over every night if she could, and in the old days, she had.

Faye's problem was the guest of honor. Rowena Burke was a woman with a moral compass totally out of whack with the real world and a string of accomplishments that made everyone around her look inadequate in comparison.

It wasn't enough that Rowena was a corporate high flier with a handsome husband at her beck and call. She also regularly made time to run over a hundred miles (a hundred!) in weekend-long races and was some kind of up and comer in the sport. Not to mention being tall and slim with perfect teeth and a good sense of humor. All lovely qualities when they were your own. Not quite so nice when they were someone else's.

Faye straightened the glasses on the bar and told herself to buck up. She

1

had a full bank account, a foolproof recipe for *millefoglie* cake, and a memory for cards that made her a killer bridge player. Plus, her home was full of friends for the first time in a very long while. Life was good.

Faye moved through the crowd, urging food and drinks on the guests assembled in her penthouse apartment in the heart of Trastevere, a cozy neighborhood in Rome across the Tiber from most of the big tourist sites. It was close to everything and had charm coming out of its ears. The neighborhood wasn't exactly a well-kept secret, but the number of actual Italians still outweighed visitors, which was saying something in this city.

Faye joined a group of women who had been regulars at her weekly bridge parties for a year or two.

"We were stunned to hear George just up and left you," said Jessica, a rather short woman in her early forties, a few years younger than Faye. She was the cattiest of the bunch and could be relied on to report any gossip Faye hadn't heard first. Usually Faye enjoyed her juicy tidbits, but tonight she couldn't tell if Jessica's sympathy was genuine.

"How are you holding up?" another woman asked.

"Is it true George is already back in the States?" asked a third.

"Were you as surprised as we were?" asked another rather breathlessly.

The four women stared at Faye, waiting for her to respond.

This was harder than she'd expected. Faye swallowed. "Yes, he's back in California." She made an effort to hold a smile on her face. "You're sweet to ask about me. I've never been better. Really. The separation was a long time coming, but it's all for the best."

All lies, except the first part. Faye's soon-to-be-ex-husband George had moved back to the States three months ago. His new girlfriend was with him.

"I hope you can join the Caravaggio Società," she went on. "It's going to be a lot of fun." It was Faye's latest idea for a group outing: see all twenty-five of Caravaggio's paintings in Rome. She'd been reading about the Renaissance artist when she got the idea. If Rome was home to more of his work than any other place in the world, she should be taking it all in.

Faye had put together a list of museums and churches where Caravaggio's art was housed and proposed a schedule for visiting them. The first stop was Santa Maria del Popolo on Wednesday morning. No one had confirmed yet, but that was the way of the world. People didn't like to commit in case something better came along.

"I saw your note," Jessica said. "It does sound fun. I'm just so busy right now, I'm not sure." It was baloney. Jessica's husband was the one whose job had brought the couple to Rome. Jessica did some kind of freelance work, but it had never stopped her from joining any activities before.

Faye's guests tonight were all expats, twenty or thirty English speakers living here for a few years thanks to their employers. The gang ebbed and flowed as newcomers arrived and old hands moved on. Faye was the constant, clocking nearly ten years in Rome, and she made a point of welcoming everyone she could find. She loved doing it. She'd met loads of interesting people, and with the constant turnover, relationships didn't have time to get stale.

Faye forced a wider smile. "It's not nearly as hard as it sounds. We stick our noses into a few churches, see the art, then jet." Jessica seemed to be wavering, so Faye plowed on. "We'll stop for a glass of wine after. He's the bad boy of the Renaissance. How can you resist that?"

Jessica glanced around as if looking for someone else to talk to, and Faye had the uncomfortable feeling of being an interloper in her own home. "Think about it," Faye said. "It'll be fun. I need to dash. Hostess responsibilities."

Faye made a show of checking the buffet. She'd spent the last two days shopping and cooking, and her planning had paid off. Everyone was having fun. It was like old times.

Winnie, a banker who was much sharper than her frizzy hair and Midwest-nice demeanor suggested, came up and began filling a plate. "Tell me, are the rumors true?"

Faye's heart thumped, but she forced a laugh. "Probably. You know what I'm like. Which ones in particular?"

"That you're selling up. I can't imagine you anywhere else. It's not because of George, is it? You followed my advice?"

Winnie was well informed if she knew about Faye's plans to sell to Rowena's company, DiLorenzo Industries. Faye had only given verbal agreement to sell the building yesterday. Faye had been resisting the company's offers for years, and she would have kept on doing so if Rowena had not forced her hand.

"Do me a favor and keep it hush-hush until it goes through," Faye said. "I don't want to jinx it." Faye hadn't come to terms with the idea of selling, and the last thing she needed was for the gossips in the expat gang to start chewing over the news.

DiLorenzo Industries had been buying up Faye's block, building by building, over the last few years. They wanted to put an upscale hotel on the site, and Faye's corner location was the final piece of the puzzle. The massive conglomerate already owned everything in Italy from telecom to ice cream, and they were used to getting what they wanted. Faye just wished the hotel division didn't want her home.

The bells of Santa Maria chimed out the time. Rowena, the guest of honor, was now thirty minutes late. Faye moved through the crowd, offering compliments and accepting them in return as she moved between friends. Her apartment felt alive with sound bouncing off the exposed brick walls in a way that felt right. Since George left, Faye had taken to playing podcasts for company. This was much better.

Heather, one of the bridge regulars, waved a glass in Faye's direction. "We missed you at the *Toro Scatenato* on Tuesday. I ate tripe. Can you believe it?" Heather laughed. "How did I let Adam talk me into it?"

Adam was Rowena's husband and Faye's ostensible co-host tonight. They'd come up with the party a month ago to help Rowena meet some more people in Rome. That was back when Faye and Adam were still on friendly terms.

"I've been so busy helping Maggie, I just couldn't get away." Faye fibbed. She hadn't even heard about the outing. "If you like tripe, I know a really authentic place. We'll go soon, yes?"

"Did you hear that Rowena's buying art now?" Heather went on. "A gift for Adam. Talk about a happy couple, right?"

Faye frowned and looked for an escape. Hosting a party for Adam and Rowena was one thing, but listening to the gang wax on about them was another. She spotted Maggie White and excused herself. Maggie was sitting on a couch with three or four others. Faye perched on the armrest, letting the conversation wash over her as she waited for an opportunity to join in. "It's going well, thank you," Maggie was saying. "A new group is arriving tomorrow. I should really get back; there's still a lot to do."

Maggie ran Masterpiece Tours, a company offering painting experiences in Rome. There had been a flap when the company was forced to move out of their old offices on short notice. Faye had been happy to offer the ground-floor apartment in her building as a new home.

"Everything in the new location looks great," Faye said. She turned to the group. "I've been helping Maggie with the decorating."

"I was thinking about offering some insider tours of Rome myself," one woman said. "Did you know people will pay to have you take them shopping? It could be fun."

"I was talking with someone about managing their apartment as a vacation rental," put in another friend, Anna. "You know, doing all the bookings and making sure the cleaners have come. Just a little something on the side to stay busy."

Faye played with the links on her gold bracelet, wearing a smile but feeling on the outside of the conversation. Ever since Maggie took over Masterpiece Tours, the gang had flocked to her with entrepreneurial ideas. They all seemed to have forgotten that it was Faye who had landed Maggie the job in the first place.

"Speaking of busy," she said, "are you all joining the Caravaggio Società? I've even managed to get us a reservation at the Villa Aurora. It's very exclusive. A real coup."

There was a pause.

"You know I'd love to," Maggie finally said. "I'm going to try to come to a few when this group leaves."

"Well, not you, Maggie, obviously. I know you're busy with work. What about you, Anna? We're starting with Santa Maria del Popolo on Wednesday morning. It's where pilgrims first entered Rome back in the day, so it seemed a fitting beginning. Can you make it?"

Anna gave a noncommittal "mmm," then shifted the conversation to the challenges of inconsiderate houseguests, a constant complaint in the expat community. Faye found herself staring down at the floor with its intricate herringbone pattern of wood pieces arranged in alternating V shapes. It was worn in places, scuffed a little. How many feet had passed across it since the craftsman painstakingly laid it out all those years ago? It wasn't going to be easy to say goodbye to it, even if her time with the gang felt a little flat tonight.

The energy in the room changed, and conversation paused. Faye knew before she even looked that Rowena must have finally arrived.

The woman was physically imposing as she stood in the doorway taking in the scene. She was tall, blond, and muscular like one of those Norse goddesses. She had her assistant and boss with her, as if trying to make a big deal of the fact she was coming straight from the office on a Friday night.

"Is that Esta DiLorenzo with Rowena?" Heather asked.

"She looks great, doesn't she," Faye said. "We've had coffee a few times. She's a sweet old lady."

Esta was a minor celebrity. Her family's company was a household name in Italy, and the donna was a regular at theater openings and fashion shows, as well as the top dog in her family's hotel division. Esta had plucked Rowena from their Latin American office and gave her a high-profile job in Rome, grooming her to take over so Esta could finally retire.

Faye hoped she would look as good as Esta when she reached her seventies. The woman's posture was excellent, her gray hair cut in a neat stacked bob, and her clothes were stylish.

"How do you know her?" Maggie asked.

Faye stood and smoothed her skirt. "She's always on the hunt for real estate. She's been wining and dining me over the years."

Maggie frowned. "Are you thinking of selling? After we just got everything moved?" Maggie's voice sounded slightly panicked. She was still furious with her previous landlord for kicking Masterpiece out. She'd gone on and on about the importance of stability in a growing business ever since Masterpiece relocated.

Faye would have to break the news about the building's sale before it went public, but not yet. "You have nothing to worry about. Excuse me, girls, must greet the guest of honor."

Faye pushed her way through the crowd and made a show of air-kissing Rowena's cheeks. Faye had considered canceling the party when Rowena showed her true colors, but how? Explain to everyone why she wasn't speaking to the woman? No. It was better to play nice and save face.

Rowena turned to meet another guest, and Faye found herself alone with Esta and the assistant. "What a nice surprise," Faye fibbed. "Come in. Make yourselves comfortable."

Esta patted Faye's arm. "No, no. You are very kind, but I have another engagement." Her English was heavily accented, but fluent. "I did not intend to keep Rowena at the office so late, and Stefano and I, we only wanted to see Rowena safely here." She turned to the assistant. *"Andiamo, Stefano?"* Shall we go?

Stefano Ungaro was a gawky young man Faye had met at Rowena's office. Standing uncomfortably in the doorway, half inside the apartment and half outside in the hall, he reminded Faye of a baby giraffe trying to wobble on his legs after birth. Stefano would probably be handsome one day, but right now he was in those awkward early twenties when he was still growing into his adult shape.

"Would it be possible to use your restroom, Faye? A drink, it spilled on me. It is very sticky."

Stefano's shirt had a dark stain across the chest. No wonder he looked so uncomfortable. "Of course, there are towels under the sink. I'm sure I have a shirt you can change into. My husband left some here."

A look of relief spread over his face. "That would be *fantastico*. I'm afraid it is starting to itch."

George had done a terrible packing job when he left the matrimonial home. He left what seemed to be half his belongings, then he had the nerve to expect Faye to ship them to him. It was completely in character, and Faye didn't see any reason to rush to the nearest *Poste Italiane* to ship his things.

"Do not be long," Esta said in Italian. "We are already late."

Faye led Stefano to her bedroom, where she had eight boxes of George's belongings stacked in a corner. She began digging and finally found a shirt in the third one.

"This is very kind of you," Stefano said. "I will return it on Monday."

It was one of George's favorites. Faye had custom-ordered it for his last birthday, and it made her husband look ten years younger. "Keep it," she said. "My gift to you."

Faye left Stefano to change and returned to the party. Cliff Stewart, one of Rowena's running friends, cornered her. He worked in an auction house and looked completely normal apart from his slightly shaggy hair and tattoo on his forearm. You'd never guess he ran hundreds of miles for the sheer pleasure of it.

"Mind if I use your blender? I brought a smoothie jumpstart with me, just in case you didn't have anything high protein. I need to mix it up."

Faye frowned. "You don't have to do that. There should be plenty of meat on the buffet. I can refill anything that's missing."

Faye had set out bruschetta with cured meats, four types of salami from her favorite butcher, six cheeses, and a *Cassata Alla Siciliana* cake Faye had made the day before. The festive Sicilian dessert involved about thirty-seven steps and required mixing up her own pistachio marzipan and making two batches of sweet ricotta cream. Faye was proud of the finished result, with its liqueur-soaked sponge cake, candied fruit, and green icing.

Cliff clucked. "I'm vegan, Faye. All plant-based. Rowena's the same. You didn't get the message?"

Faye caught herself before she spat out an expletive. She and Adam had agreed on the menu when they discussed the party and he'd said nothing about vegan. "What about dairy?"

"No dairy, no eggs, no honey." He ticked them off his fingers. "Nothing that comes from an animal. End of story."

Faye mentally added another black mark next to Rowena's name. What was the point of running hundreds of miles a week if you weren't able to have a gelato at the end of it?

And why hadn't Adam told her? To make Faye look like a bad host, probably. A bean salad would have been easy enough to prepare. And Faye had a fantastic vegan chocolate cake recipe that George's one-time vegan stepson said was better than anything he'd tasted since giving up eggs, butter, and everything else that usually made baking such a joy.

Stefano poked his head into the kitchen, looking ridiculous in George's shirt, with its arms about two inches too short and waist about six inches too wide. "I am on a mission for Rowena. She needs food. High protein and not from animals." He winced, as if it pained him to say. "Do not shoot the messenger, please. I find the idea a mystery, but it is not my decision."

He seemed to notice Cliff for the first time. "No offense, Cliff. I know you do this, too. But to an Italian, it is very odd. You understand?"

"I'll share the shake," Cliff said. "We just need to make it stretch."

"Peanut butter, perhaps?" Stefano said. "Cinnamon? Those are the favorites of Rowena in the office."

"No problem," Cliff said. "I'll get it together." He pulled Faye's blender toward him and added a moss-colored sludge that smelled faintly of grass. "I know what it's like to be hungry after a big training day. Sustenance is on the way."

Faye had always written Cliff off as strange, but at least he was being useful. She handed him her last two bananas and a jar of peanut butter from the refrigerator. "Spices are right over there."

Stefano clasped his hands together in mock prayer and bowed slightly. "Thank you both. You have saved me." Poor Stefano. Catering to the needs of two bosses on a Friday night. And Esta had been in a hurry to leave.

Cliff's wife, Lilly, opened the door. "I've been looking all over for you, Cliff. You didn't really bring that awful stuff, did you?" She smiled at Faye. "I swear, my husband has the worst manners. Bringing your own food to a party. My mother would have been shocked."

Lilly wore a flowery peasant skirt and clunky leather sandals that reminded Faye of the hippie crowd in college. Not a woman Faye would have guessed had been raised by followers of Emily Post. Then again, it was impossible to predict how children would turn out. They were just as likely to rebel as they were to follow in their parents' footsteps.

Faye had no children of her own, but she had six sort-of stepchildren in her life: children of her husbands' former spouses. Some had turned out wonderfully, and others had been more of a challenge. The parents seemed, if not irrelevant, not the determining factor.

Lilly linked arms with Faye and led her into the hall. "I wanted to thank you for the invitation to the Caravaggio Società. It sounds like fun."

Lilly's chumminess was surprising. She and her husband had been in Rome for about a year and were really George's friends. Lilly and George worked at the same university, and Faye had always had the impression Lilly found her frivolous. She'd only invited the couple tonight because of Cliff's connection to Rowena. And as for the invitation to the Caravaggio Società, Faye knew people would be talking about it tonight and hadn't wanted the couple to feel left out.

Faye found herself being led across the room while Lilly kept talking. "I was also hoping for some advice about a day trip to the hills," Lilly said.

Travel advice was what Faye loved giving most. She launched into a description of Lake Bolsena, about two hours north of Rome. Faye was recommending restaurants in the area when Adam approached. "Rowena's asking for food. Do you have anything she can eat? Peanut butter? Apples? Nuts?"

He might have been talking to the waiter in a restaurant, not the co-host of a party where he'd mentioned not a single thing about his wife's special diet. "If I'd known, I would have been happy to—"

He held up his hand. "We can talk more later. I'll just grab something."

"Her assistant is already on it," Faye said, blocking his way into the kitchen. Adam didn't deserve to act at home in her apartment. "Cliff's agreed to share his smoothie." The sound of a blender began, as if to underscore her statement.

"Terrible stuff," Lilly said cheerfully. "Another sacrifice for that crazy hobby." She turned to Faye and made a gagging face. "One taste was enough for me, but Cliff says it replaces all of his lost nutrients." She shrugged. "At least he doesn't expect me to make it for him."

The whirring stopped. "I'll just go check in," Faye said. Stefano was gone, and Cliff was hunting through Faye's shelves. She plucked two glasses from a cabinet he hadn't yet opened and poured the frothy green liquid. It looked as unappetizing as before.

Faye handed one to Cliff. "Go on out. I'll just tidy up, then get this to Rowena." Faye gave the counter a wipe, enjoying a moment of peace away from the crowd, before delivering the glass to Adam. "For your wife."

He started to say something, but she caught sight of Esta and Stefano near the door and turned away to say goodbye. She was surprised they'd stayed this long.

Esta paused for the briefest moment in front of Faye, kissing the air around her cheeks. "We will be in touch about details soon, yes?"

So Esta knew about the sale. Rowena must have shared the news. Esta would be celebrating this weekend. How soon would DiLorenzo be able to get the hotel construction under way?

"*Grazie ancora* for the shirt," Stefano said. He made a show of pulling at the too-short sleeves. "It is very handsome on me, no?"

Faye laughed. "Better than a stain. Have a good weekend." George would be furious when he learned Faye had given away his shirt. She was glad.

Stefano pulled a face. "This job, there are no weekends. But I am learning a lot. I hope to see you again soon, Faye. *Buonanotte.*"

The pair waved to Rowena from the hall, then disappeared down Faye's wooden stairs. They were steep and narrow, and Esta wore dangerously high heels. Faye waited on the landing until she heard them arrive safely at the bottom.

The sound of a fork tapping the edge of a glass brought her back to the party. Adam stood with an arm around his wife, who smiled next to him. "A toast to Rowena and our many new friendships here. May they be long and rich. *Cin cin!*"

Faye surveyed the scene. The gang all seemed so cheery, toasting their friendship with this couple they barely knew. She wasn't too proud to admit that she had been jealous when Adam began changing some of their time-honored traditions and pulling everyone in with his own ideas. She'd tried resisting, but she saw the way everyone gravitated toward him. Her only option had been to hold on to his coat tails or risk being left out.

Looking at the gang crowded around the happy couple wasn't easy to stomach. Faye excused herself to refill the crostini platter, and that's when Rowena collapsed.

Chapter Two

Caravaggio produced an estimated ninety masterpieces. That productivity is stunning by any measure, and one must wonder if he was driven to perform because he sensed the grim reaper waiting.
—Caravaggio: Brash, Brutish, and Brilliant

Emergency services arrived in a matter of minutes, and the uniformed technicians whisked Rowena away with Adam at her side. It was Faye's first party since George left, and it was over in less than an hour.

It was just like Rowena to steal the show. Ridiculous, blaming a woman who had collapsed on the floor, face gray as she struggled for air. Faye couldn't help it.

Voices swirled around her.

"Heart attack, definitely. Classic case."

"It's always the fit ones. They run a marathon one day and collapse the next. Overuse. It's just as bad as french fries."

"Maybe she had bad genes."

"Does she have allergies? Does anyone know if she is allergic to nuts?"

On another night, Faye would know just the right thing to say to the guests, but Faye couldn't get the image of Rowena gasping for breath out of her head. *Pull yourself together*, Faye told herself. She needed to take charge. "I'm sure Adam will tell us when he knows something. The best thing we can do is send good thoughts." If only it were that easy.

She forced a light tone. "Don't forget, the first Caravaggio outing is

Wednesday. I'll send out some articles so we can all read up in advance, yes?"

The group seemed to take it as a cue to depart. Only Maggie offered to stay behind to help clean up. The apartment wasn't a wreck. Faye didn't throw those kinds of parties. But there were the usual dirty dishes and glasses, discarded napkins, and food needing to be dealt with.

"You're sure?" Faye asked. "Don't you need to be well-rested for the big day tomorrow?"

Maggie's tour guests were scheduled to arrive mid-afternoon the next day. "I don't mind helping, Faye, really." Maggie began stacking plates. "With the two of us, it won't take any time at all."

Faye felt her eyes threatening to tear up. She dug her nails into the palm of her hand. "Well, a little company might be nice. Thank you. It's all such a shock."

Faye began washing the blender, sticky with peanut butter from the smoothie. "Tell me about the plans for tomorrow. It'll get our minds off poor Rowena."

Maggie told her about the airport pickups and welcome packets at the hotel, the snacks the cook was going to make in the morning and all the other minutiae that went into making a tour feel special. It was well thought out. Faye was surprised to find she didn't have a single suggestion.

Maggie had Faye's storage containers out and was beginning the painful process of transferring bits of artfully arranged toasts and meats and cheeses into squashed quarters where they would become soggy and lose their distinctive flavors. "Where's your foil?"

Faye opened the drawer next to the sink and handed Maggie a new roll. She didn't remember running out of the old one. A week ago, she couldn't find a corkscrew, then it reappeared a day later in a drawer she was sure she'd double-checked. Another time she couldn't find her dishwashing gloves, then they turned up two days later. She was losing her mind.

"On second thought, just toss it all," Faye said.

"You're sure?" Maggie glanced at the cake that hadn't even been cut.

"Everything's been sitting out. Besides, I'm not feeling very festive right now, are you?"

14

"I don't know what I'm feeling," Maggie said. "I just can't stop thinking about Rowena. She didn't look good."

Faye hung up a dish towel. "She'll be fine. The medical system here is top-notch. She's probably sitting up in bed right now trying to decide if she can make her training run tomorrow."

Maggie shook her head. "I don't think so."

Maggie was usually a relentless optimist. Faye tied up the trash bag. "Come on. I'll walk you home."

Maggie stopped to change into a pair of extremely supportive, extremely unattractive shoes she'd stowed in Faye's bedroom. A month ago, Maggie would have worn the practical shoes at the party without a second thought. Maybe Faye's efforts to up Maggie's style were finally starting to work.

"They have a dog, don't they?" Maggie asked. Her gaze was focused on the laces of her shoes. She finished tying the second one and straightened.

"Who?"

"Adam and Rowena."

"Yes, she's called Daisy." A giant slobbering hound who, frankly, Faye found intimidating. "Why?"

"Adam's not going to be home anytime soon," Maggie said. "Someone needs to take her out."

Usually, Faye was the one who thought about things like this, bringing soup if someone was sick and remembering all the birthdays. To have forgotten Daisy wasn't like her. "I'll call Winnie Rogers. She and her husband have a dog. They'll know what to do."

"They live near the Vatican." Maggie struggled into a cardigan. "We can walk her. You know Adam and Rowena's door code, don't you?"

Faye did. Most of the expats had lockboxes or smart locks so visitors could let themselves in and out without their hosts rushing home to meet them. Faye had exchanged information with Adam when he'd first arrived. "I don't know. Maybe we should check with Adam first."

Maggie stopped buttoning and looked at her, hard. "Are you okay, Faye? For weeks and weeks all I heard was 'Adam this' and 'Adam that,' and now you're not even willing to go walk his dog?"

Faye smoothed her pixie cut and hoped Maggie didn't notice the flush spreading across her face. Faye had been swept up in Adam's energy along with the rest of the gang. He was an experienced expat and he'd entered their community seamlessly. It was only when he began bringing fresh ideas and changing their old routines that she began to pull away from his orbit. And then he'd betrayed her to his wife.

There was no way to explain any of this to Maggie without sounding like a teenager tangled up in a popularity contest, so Faye's only option had been to keep up the pretense of friendship. Putting on an act was something she excelled at.

"You're right," Faye said. "We should take care of Daisy. Let's go."

Faye locked the door and picked up the bag of garbage. The women made their way down the creaking stairs and onto Via Pecora, a little street just a block off a bustling restaurant row. It wasn't nearly as late as it felt. Twenty-somethings were still out in force, crowding the area's bars and restaurants, spilling over onto the sidewalk.

Faye was aware of how she must look to them, a middle-aged woman with nothing better to do on a Friday night than take out the trash. But collection had been inconsistent at Faye's building, and she was happy to clear out the detritus of the party.

The trash bin was nearly full. Faye pushed the bag in without bothering to sort out the recycling and led the way to Adam's. She paused in front of the lockbox. "You're a good friend, Maggie. Thank you."

"Think nothing of it. I need the exercise. What kind of dog is Daisy, anyway?"

"Something big and bouncy." All Faye knew was that the animal looked like the kind you saw on the Internet racing over jumps and moving sheep around in a field.

Daisy met them at the door, her tail wagging so madly even her rear end was wiggling. Maggie immediately got onto her knees and began cooing. Faye was happy not to have the dog slobbering over her. "I'll find the leash."

She located the dog's gear in the hall closet and found Daisy on her back enjoying a belly rub, tail whapping the floor, when she returned to the living room.

"This apartment is spectacular," Maggie said.

"I know. I heard Esta found it for them."

Adam and Rowena's apartment was freshly gutted, with new construction innards housed within a historic shell. The scale was large—the ceilings must have been over twelve feet—and double doors led out to a terrace bigger than Faye's entire apartment. And the outdoor space! Adam and Rowena had kitted it out with new wood decking, privacy greenery taller than Faye, and the type of furniture you'd see in a design magazine.

The apartment even smelled expensive, a mix of new fabric and leather, plus some understated floral notes. Adam had a great design eye and the resources—both time and money—to indulge them.

"They look so settled," Maggie said, looking around while she kept a hand on Daisy. "I still had boxes out at this point."

"Adam says he's got it down to a science, packing up one place, unpacking the next." Faye fumbled with the tangle of buckles and straps that made up Daisy's harness and tried to visualize how to wrap it all around the animal.

"Have you walked Daisy before?" Faye didn't need to see Maggie's expression to know her friend had doubts.

"I've walked with her." Not quite the same thing.

Faye got one loop around Daisy's neck and another around a leg, but there didn't seem to be a way to get it around the dog's middle. Daisy danced in place, making everything more difficult. Faye ignored the dog's warm breath on her face and tried again. This time she got Daisy's legs through the straps, but the dog stepped right out of it.

"Let me try." Maggie clipped the harness around the dog with an experienced hand, and they set off down the quiet street toward the main piazza. Daisy stopped to sniff the cobblestones and corners of buildings. Faye loved this neighborhood at night. Bars and restaurants echoing with the sounds of people enjoying themselves lined the narrow, winding streets. Someone was playing a guitar in the square that Faye and Maggie circled before steering Daisy back to her apartment.

Maggie gave Daisy a last belly rub while Faye started a text to Adam. *Daisy has been walked.* She paused before adding, *Hope everything is OK.* It was short and considerate. She hit send.

A moment later, her phone beeped the birdsong tone she'd assigned to Adam's contact. She read the message twice before it sank in, then handed it to Maggie to read.

Rowena died in the ER.

Faye hadn't liked Rowena. She'd wished the woman would just disappear and her husband along with her. But dead? She felt her eyes welling before she even registered the emotion as grief. Faye felt shaky as she reached for the phone Maggie held out to her.

Maggie's expression softened. "Daisy can spend the night with Burt and me. You'll stay, too, won't you?"

Faye felt a flood of gratitude. It wasn't that Faye was superstitious. She didn't think Rowena's ghost would come back to haunt her. But if a healthy, vibrant woman like Rowena could collapse in the middle of a party and die, what did that mean for everyone else?

Faye didn't even pretend to protest. She gave Maggie a hug. "Thank you." Being surrounded by people hadn't saved Rowena, but at least she hadn't been alone.

Chapter Three

Caravaggio's art shows life as it is, complete with torn clothing and dirty feet. This unsettling realism creates a connection between viewer and subject that was previously unknown and is, even today, totally captivating.
—Caravaggio: Brash, Brutish, and Brilliant

The Whites' guest room was totally adequate. Maggie rustled up a set of spare towels while her husband, Burt, removed all the bags and boxes piled on the narrow guest bed. They didn't stay up to talk. After telling Burt what had happened, there didn't seem to be much to say: life was unfair; Rowena's death was tragic; poor Adam.

Daisy took the change in locale in stride, sniffing every inch of the apartment before curling up on the rug next to Faye, which she found unexpectedly flattering. Faye focused on the dog's even breathing as she forced her mind toward sleep. It worked, and Faye was surprised when she woke to find it was daylight. Daisy was sprawled out in bed next to her, muzzle on the pillow and wide back snuggled right up against hers.

"Down, Daisy."

Daisy lifted her head and looked at Faye, then let it drop back down. Faye tried again, pointing at the floor this time, but Daisy didn't even bother to raise her head. Faye pushed the dog—gently—and Daisy seemed to glare at her for a moment before reluctantly getting to her feet, circling twice, then settling at the foot of the bed.

"Fine, have it your way." Now she was a woman who talked to dogs as if they could understand her. Wonderful.

Faye decided she might as well get up. She had cinnamon roll dough halfway through its first rise and a cake in the oven by the time Maggie stumbled into the kitchen an hour later. Her friend was a wreck: hair mussed, no makeup, and a nightgown in a style that did nothing to enhance her figure. "It's six-thirty, Faye."

"Do you have any cocoa powder? I thought we could all use some brownies today but couldn't find any. Oh, and you're out of milk. I'll pick some up when I'm out later."

"I'm going back to bed, Faye."

"Do you mind if I use your yoga mat?"

The mat was standing rolled up in a corner next to the television with two paperback books stacked on top of it. Maggie shrugged, which Faye took to mean "no problem."

Faye felt vaguely uncomfortable moving through her mix of strength exercises and yoga poses with Daisy's gaze on her, but she persisted. After thirty minutes, Faye did one final pattern, then went back to the kitchen to tackle the cinnamon roll dough.

She rolled it out and sprinkled cinnamon and sugar over top. She'd made this recipe so many times her hands worked without any conscious effort on her part. Faye shaped the dough into a neat log and found a sharp knife to slice it into even pieces. She set everything aside to rise again and made a cup of tea.

Faye inhaled and tried to focus on the aroma of her Earl Grey, but it was impossible. All she could think about was Rowena. Had she known what was happening as she collapsed? Did she have any regrets about her life? Probably not. Smug, self-righteous Rowena wasn't the type of woman to second-guess herself.

And how was Adam feeling? In shock, certainly, but maybe also a tiny bit relieved. Not happy. Faye didn't think Adam would wish anyone dead. But she wasn't sure that his marriage was as happy as he let on.

The fact of the matter was, he'd helped organize a party where there was nothing for his wife to eat. It could have been an oversight, it could have been an attempt to embarrass Faye, or it could have been intentional.

Whatever it was, there was no getting around the fact that it didn't show a particularly high degree of caring for his wife.

And then there was the whole situation with the job that he turned down. Adam gathered the gang less than two weeks ago to celebrate landing a position. He'd been wanting to get back into paid work after putting his career on hold to follow Rowena, and he'd finally found a company that wanted to hire him. The only catch was that the job was in Miami.

When asked how Rowena felt about it, he'd shrugged. "I've followed her around the world five times. We agreed the next move would be for me. She'll come when she can, and we'll make it work in the meantime."

Everyone had toasted his good fortune, and Faye hadn't wanted to question it. Adam was leaving, and that was good enough for her. She'd even bought a round of drinks, feeling warmer toward him than she had in weeks.

A few days later, though, Adam announced he was staying put after all. It wasn't exactly the right position for him and after so many years out of the workforce, he needed to choose his re-entry carefully. At least, that's how Heather reported it. Faye hadn't been with the gang that night, but it sounded like a load of hogwash.

Adam had finally found a company willing to hire him. What prospects did he have for something better? If Faye had to guess, she'd say Rowena hadn't liked the idea of being a long-distance couple and had convinced him to stay. It would be in character, that was for sure.

Faye put her cup down and shook herself from her reverie. Rowena was dead and Faye wasn't the type of person to celebrate someone else's misfortune. She put good karma into the universe and, most of the time, it came back to her in spades.

Some might argue Rowena's death was the universe's way of paying an unpleasant woman back for bad behavior. A little extreme, certainly. Not when lots of other, much worse people, continued to roam around enjoying their lives. But pretending it was a tragedy wouldn't help anyone.

There was still half an hour before the pastries would be ready. Faye picked up a sponge and prepared to clean the kitchen from top to bottom.

She was a tidy cook and hadn't made a mess, but it must have been several weeks since either of the Whites had given their kitchen a deep clean.

By the time Faye had everything spotless, the cinnamon rolls were out of the oven and ready to be iced. Faye packed the cake and half the rolls for Adam, then managed to get Daisy into her harness with a minimum of struggle. However Adam was feeling about Rowena's death, he would want his dog's company. And no matter how much Faye resented Adam, she wasn't about to show up at a house of mourning without food for the family.

Faye left a note for the Whites and picked up the spare key Maggie had pressed on her the night before. The heat enveloped her the moment she stepped outside. It was still bearable, but it was going to be oppressive later in the day. Faye hoped Maggie's guests were ready for it. June was one of those months that could go either way. One day might feel like early spring, another might feel like the depths of summer.

The streets were quiet, as they always were early on Saturday mornings. Window boxes bursting with flowers decorated the iron balconies, and the air smelled earthy and floral. A few pigeons shook their feathers in a puddle, and a young man was busy unlocking his scooter. Otherwise, Faye felt like she and Daisy had the street to themselves.

Faye walked slowly, enjoying the moment. Daisy seemed content to amble along, stopping for a smell here and there, but never tugging on the leash. She wasn't a bad dog, really. Faye shifted the leash and carrier bags to the opposite hands. The cake and cinnamon rolls weren't heavy, but her gait was unbalanced. Faye made an effort to stand tall and be conscious of the weight, the way she practiced in her Pilates classes. She would view this walk as an exercise in conscious posture.

But as much as she tried to focus on a strong core and long limbs, Faye's mind returned to the party. She'd been off her game, even before Rowena's collapse. She'd been trying too hard to make a good impression on the gang, as if she had something to make up for after George's desertion.

When the shock of Rowena's death passed, Faye would get the regular bridge games going again. They'd fallen by the wayside when Adam refused to play, and Faye realized now it had been a mistake to let them go. The challenge of pitting your wits against someone else, the puzzling out of the cards your opponents held, the pairing up with a lively partner. These were things she missed. In the meantime, the Caravaggio Società would bring everyone together. Faye would study so she could speak knowledgeably when the group gathered.

Adam's building didn't look like much on the outside, just the usual centuries-old narrow four-story building that dominated the neighborhood. The front door was old and wooden and used a simple key code: 1-2-3-4. Adam had complained about the security but said the building's older residents had difficulty remembering anything more complicated.

Adam didn't answer his buzzer when Faye arrived. He was probably sleeping off the first effects of shock. She would get the key, drop Daisy and the food, and get out without disturbing him.

Faye let herself into the vestibule and opened Adam and Rowena's lock box. The code was their street number, hardly more sophisticated than the main door, despite Adam's grumbling about his neighbors.

Daisy practically pulled Faye up the stairs and wiggled madly outside her apartment door while Faye put the carrier bag down and did a few shoulder rolls to rebalance herself while Daisy snuffled every inch she could reach. Faye tapped lightly, then slipped the key into the lock. There was a shout as Daisy took off through the door.

Adam was standing in the living room. "God, Faye! What are you doing here?"

He looked awful. His eyes were bloodshot and had dark circles and bags beneath them. From the appearance of his hair, he hadn't yet showered. His t-shirt and jeans, at least, didn't look slept in.

Adam knelt and buried his face in Daisy's fur, then looked up. "How did you get in?"

"Lockbox." Faye held out the bag. "I baked." He looked at her as if she had offered him a bag of dead rats. "And I thought you'd want Daisy back."

There was a long pause, and Faye wished she had called before coming. She was used to welcoming newcomers, being the first on the scene with soup when someone was sick. She never thought that she might be intruding. "I'm sorry."

She hovered in the doorway, not sure if she should stay or go. The Burkes' apartment occupied the entire floor. The hall gleamed. There wasn't even dust in the corners near the doorjamb, which cleaners often overlooked. "Do they have any idea what happened? A heart attack? Something from all that training?"

He shook his head. "They're doing an autopsy."

She felt for him despite everything. He looked older, beaten down. A far cry from the fun man-about-town who'd hijacked the expat gang. "How soon will they have the results?"

"I have no idea."

If it had been George who collapsed, Faye would have asked. She'd have dug into the reputation of the team performing the autopsy and learned exactly what tests they were going to do and when the results would be back.

"You should ask. The family has the right to know."

"I was up half the night talking to the police, Faye." He got to his feet and came to the door. "They said it's routine in situations like this."

"Situations like what?"

There was the sound of footsteps on the stairs, and an elderly couple appeared on the landing. Adam greeted the pair and exchanged a few pleasantries about the weather before they continued downstairs. Were they wondering what an attractive woman was doing at the door of a married man so early in the morning? For Adam's sake, Faye hoped not.

When the door to the street clicked closed, Adam jerked his head in the direction of the stairs. "Not here."

Faye thought he was inviting her inside, but instead, he took Daisy's leash and led the way down the marble steps, each one worn in the middle from generations of feet.

Daisy wagged her tail at the unexpected extension of her walk as Adam led them down the street. "They asked about Rowena. What her life was like. What her mood was. Who her friends were. Any enemies. They were acting like it was a suspicious death."

"She just died. It's got to be routine."

"It wasn't routine, Faye. They were acting like they thought someone killed my wife. Me, maybe. I didn't like them."

Adam was prone to exaggeration and hyperbole. It was one of the things that made him fun. He could tell a great story, embellishing details as needed to up the hilarity. That wasn't Faye's style, but she understood the appeal. People liked the positive energy. But right now, it was misplaced.

"I'm sure they were just doing their jobs. There's paperwork for everything here. You said yourself they don't have an autopsy yet. This is going to be one of those tragic things that just happens. Wrong draw of the genetic hand."

"You weren't there, Faye. Don't try to tell me what happened."

His words stung. She'd been so friendly to Adam when he and Rowena had arrived. She'd stayed civil after he'd betrayed her to his wife, even hosting that damn party for them. He hadn't even thanked her for taking Daisy last night, let alone for bringing cinnamon rolls.

Faye focused on pulling in her stomach and lengthening her spine. He was in shock. He clearly wanted to talk. She would be the bigger person and humor him. "What did you say?"

"I told them the truth. I loved my wife." He cleared his throat. "She was a good woman, on the verge of getting everything she'd been working for. She was up for a big promotion at work. She'd just qualified for the Valtellina 100." His voice shook a little. "We were going to take some time out after that. Really reconnect with each other. We've been so busy…."

"Is that why you didn't take the job in Florida?"

He frowned. "You didn't like Rowena, Faye. You were jealous of her success. Fine. But there's absolutely no reason to mock my grief."

He was right. That was the problem with Adam. As over-the-top as he was, he was also smart and understood her a little too well. That's what had hurt so much about his betrayal. "I'm sorry."

Daisy snuffled the ground next to Adam, presumably catching the scent of something delectable, because she began rubbing the side of her head against the pavement. Adam jerked the leash and Daisy gave him a "what's wrong with you?" expression.

Adam ran a hand through his hair. "I didn't tell the police about the bank accounts, Faye. They asked if anyone had a reason to want her dead, and I said no."

Faye stumbled over a curb. "I never wanted her dead."

"You threatened her, Faye. I'm just saying I haven't told anyone, including the police." Faye had never been punched in the stomach, but she guessed this is what it would feel like.

She had made a silly mistake. It happened when Adam and Faye were the last ones left at the dinner celebrating his new job. She'd had an extra glass of wine and was cheery about the prospect of his departure from Rome.

Faye had replayed the scene in her head over and over again. "Whatever happens with Rowena, don't lose sight of the money," she'd said. It was the type of advice she gave all the time. Go to this grocer, not that one. Stay on top of paperwork from this government agency, don't worry about that one.

Adam had looked blank. "What do you mean?"

"If you and Rowena divorce." He'd shaken his head a bit, as if he still didn't understand. "Don't let her control the money, Adam. She's liable to hide it in bank accounts you'll never find, and when the lawyers are dividing everything up, there'll be a whole lot less than you think. If you're not on top of things, it'll be gone before you know it."

He'd leaned back in his chair and laughed. "You watch too much television. Regular people don't do things like that."

"Of course they do." Faye remembered taking a bite of the chocolate dessert she'd told herself she would eat just half of. "I did."

"You didn't."

"Oh, but I did. Four bank accounts George will never find without an excellent forensic accountant who knows how to follow a trail that crosses three continents."

He'd laughed, like it was all a joke. "How on earth did you pull something like that off? What kind of people do you know, Faye?"

26

"Bankers. Good ones." She'd run her spoon around the edge of the bowl, finishing the last bite. "I can make an introduction if you like."

"I'm fine, thank you very much. But if things change, it's good to know."

They'd paid the bill, and he'd walked her home. There was never anything romantic between them. Hardly even a friendship. But that night, she was enjoying Adam's company. "Congratulations again about the job," she'd said when they reached her door. "We'll miss you." It was a lie, but the right thing to say.

"You're a good friend, Faye. A terrible wife, but a good friend."

"I was an excellent wife. It was George who cheated and then left me. I'm the wronged party."

"Just balancing the scales, right? Fair enough."

And that should have been the end of it. A fun night out, a little too much personal information shared, but that was how connections were built. Then, a few days later, Rowena contacted Faye and threatened to tell George about Faye's deceit unless she came clean herself. Faye didn't want Rowena dead, but she definitely disliked the woman, and Adam, too, for sharing her story.

And what could she do? Tell everyone she was angry with Adam for telling his wife she was hiding money from George? No, that wasn't an option. Faye took the whole thing as a life lesson and moved on.

Faye took pride in her self-control, but if Adam expected her to be grateful because he hadn't told the police he'd spilled Faye's secrets to his wife, he was sorely mistaken. "And did you tell them you hated the hours your wife worked? Or that you resented all the time she spent running? Or that you'd given up your career to follow her around the world, and she couldn't care less about your sacrifice?"

Adam didn't respond. They had come to a church, and a few parishioners were going inside. Most were elderly and dressed in dark colors, the devoted few who still went to church every day. "No? I didn't think so. Don't go playing the saint here, Adam. We both know what kind of man you are."

Adam looked away. "Hiding money in your divorce isn't exactly ethical, Faye. The police will be calling you. I'd think about what you're going to say."

Daisy's gaze was on Faye, as if she were telegraphing her sympathies. Faye bent over to rub the dog's ears. At least Daisy liked her.

Chapter Four

Caravaggio rose from tragic roots. The bubonic plague wiped out his family, leaving him destitute and alone. Could he have achieved success without that childhood adversity? One suspects not.
—Caravaggio: Brash, Brutish, and Brilliant

T he police did call. An Inspector Nardelli asked to meet Faye at 10 Via Pecora at her earliest convenience. This morning, preferably. Faye agreed to meet in an hour, then began stripping the Whites' guest bed.

Maggie and Burt had already left for the day. Maggie would be at the tour office absorbed in the final preparations for the guests arriving that afternoon, and Burt had said something about an early tee time.

Faye shook a pillow from its case. What would the police ask? Questions about the Burkes' marriage? About Faye's meeting with Rowena?

Faye paused, pillow still in her hand, and replayed her conversation with Adam. He was naturally shaken up, but also hostile. Her divorce was nothing to do with Rowena. Except that Rowena had known about the things she was hiding.

Faye swallowed. Maggie and Burt had said to stay as long as she liked. There was no need for Faye to spend the night alone. She spread the top sheet back on the bed and pulled the blanket tight, tucking the corners square before folding the comforter across the foot. She'd get through this meeting with the police before making any decisions about when to go home.

There were still twenty minutes before Faye needed to leave, but she found herself unwilling to linger at the Whites' alone. She locked up and headed to Via Pecora, forcing herself to stroll to her apartment instead of striding along in her usual efficient pace.

The tasteful Masterpiece Tours sign Maggie had affixed to the ground floor door looked good. The red and gold lettering was understated and upscale. Maggie would not be happy when she learned Masterpiece needed to move again.

DiLorenzo Industries would probably want to start construction on the new hotel immediately. Regular people might face years of permits and red tape before they could undertake a renovation on an entire city block, but the DiLorenzos were connected. Maggie and Masterpiece would be out on the street as soon as the deal went through.

Faye knocked on the Masterpiece door, but there was no answer. Maggie and her assistant, Thomas, were probably out buying last-minute supplies. Faye was tempted to let herself in to inspect the progress, but instead she climbed the narrow staircase to her third-floor apartment. The treads were uneven, and the lighting was poor. Bringing them to modern code had been on her list of things to do when she'd inherited the building from her grandparents, but George always said people had been climbing those stairs safely for hundreds of years, and she'd never gotten around to it.

Faye hesitated at her door. It was heavy, with polished wood and decorative paneling. It was silly to feel anxious as she slipped her key into the lock. Yes, someone had died here less than twenty-four hours ago, but over the centuries, countless people had probably died here as well. Before modern hospitals, dying at home was common practice. And death rates were much higher then.

Faye bit her lip and swung the door open. Everything was fine. The apartment was tidy, just as she and Maggie had left it.

Faye had remodeled the apartment a few years ago, and she loved it. It was clean with modern lines, with some of the building's history preserved in exposed beams and polished floor. She hated to think of it being torn apart to make way for tourists on vacation.

The kitchen was double the original size, but still compact by American standards and closed off from the main living room. While everyone today seemed to want an open concept, Faye insisted on separation, putting it down a hall with a door so that she'd had peace to cook and bake while George took over the living room to watch sports and classic movies.

The police would expect refreshment. Faye filled a kettle and set about preparing coffee. The beans were in the cabinet, but where was the grinder? Faye checked the cabinet twice, sure she'd put it away when she'd made coffee yesterday morning, but it wasn't there.

She opened the four other cabinets before finding it on the wrong side of the sink. She must be losing her mind. For the last few weeks, things had been out of place. Some missing for good, others turning up a day or two later. In the old days, she would have accused George of moving them.

Faye was relieved when the buzzer signaled Inspector Nardelli's arrival. Faye opened the door and put on a wide smile to greet the two officers who came to the landing. They introduced themselves. Inspector Nardelli was a woman in her late thirties, and Officer Piras was a man who looked barely out of college.

Faye led them into the apartment. "I'm just making coffee. Can I offer you anything else? Cookies?"

"Just coffee, thank you." Inspector Nardelli didn't take a seat the way a normal guest would. She wandered to the bookcase while Officer Piras opened the doors to the terrace and whistled at the view.

"I'll just be a minute then." Faye put together a tray with coffee cups, cream, and sugar. Piras was looking at Faye's collection of china birds while Nardelli was inspecting the family photos on the mantle when she returned. Were they gathering information about her? "It's such a nice day. Shall we sit on the terrace?"

Faye took her usual seat, the one with its back to the building and view opening up in front of her. Inspector Nardelli took the seat opposite. It was George's spot. Typical of him, turning his back on the city.

Officer Piras took out a notebook and sat a little further away from the table than was normal. His suit showed off his broad shoulders and narrow waist. He was a man who cared about his appearance. Nardelli's suit was a little boxier than was fashionable, and her dark hair was pulled back in a tight ponytail. She radiated experience and competence.

Nardelli took a sip of the coffee. "Delicious, thank you. It's been quite a morning, and I needed that."

The inspector seemed to have all the time in the world, so unlike the usual brusque Italian authority figures. Faye relaxed. She was in good hands.

Faye put on her hostess smile. "I'm happy to help in any way that I can. It's so good of you to come out on a Saturday morning. I understand that the cause of Rowena's death is still unknown?"

Someone down the street turned on some pop music and a familiar melody filled the air. Inspector Nardelli smiled. "Death, sadly, does not pay attention to the calendar."

"Of course not. I just meant coming out when it might be for nothing. We all wondered if Rowena's death might have been a tragic result of over training."

Nardelli frowned. "I understand what you are saying. But I am afraid that will not be the case. Rowena Burke was poisoned."

Faye took a sip of her coffee and found she had a hard time swallowing. Adam was right. Rowena had been murdered. Here, in Faye's home.

"Tell us about your relationship with Rowena Burke, please."

"She was a friend. Well, more like the wife of a friend. Adam, Adam Burke, and I, we're friends. Just the way so many of us expats are. It's a group, you know? And Rowena is his wife."

It was a simple question, and Faye was coming across as a bit of a dimwit. She hadn't expected to feel so nervous. But Nardelli simply nodded encouragingly. Perhaps everyone was nervous in these interviews. It wasn't the type of thing you got experience in.

"You must have been good friends to host a party, no?"

"Rowena and Adam haven't lived here long, but I've become quite friendly with them. At least, with Adam. I do my best, you see, to welcome newcomers. I've lived in Rome for ten years now, and I know how hard it can be for new arrivals to adjust."

Faye turned to Piras, the note taker, and added, "I have dual citizenship, in case you need that. My grandparents were Italian, and so it was—"

"That is fine, Signora Masters." Nardelli smiled. "We are not concerned about immigration status. We can focus on the important things, yes?"

It was refreshing to meet an Italian official not interested in dotting Is and crossing Ts. Faye felt herself smiling back.

"The party was your idea?"

"I'm not really sure." Faye forced herself to slow down and take her time. These officers were on her side. She and Adam had been at a cafe near the Borghese one afternoon, waiting for the gang to join them. He'd complained Rowena was working all the time trying to make a good impression with the people in DiLorenzo headquarters. It was impossible to get her to break free from her desk for anything except training.

Faye had suggested a bridge party, she remembered that clearly, but Adam had shot it down. He and Rowena had no interest in learning what Adam called an old person's game. A cocktail party had been the logical next step. "Everyone loves a party, don't they?" Faye said.

It was just a week ago that Rowena had called Faye and demanded that she come clean with George. Faye had called Adam immediately, but he'd dodged her calls and didn't answer his door when she rang the bell. When she finally cornered him out walking with Daisy on Monday, Adam looked harassed and said they could just cancel if Faye was so angry with him.

Faye refused. Was he seriously suggesting that she call everyone and say her first big party since George left was on hold because she'd had a falling out with the new golden boy and his wife? Absolutely not.

Nardelli finished her cup of coffee and shook her head when Faye suggested a second. "And the menu, you determined that?"

"Adam and I put it together." Faye paused. "I had no idea Rowena had gone vegan. It's popular among these ultra runners, I understand. I would have planned something completely different if I'd known. But I think it must have been a recent change, and Adam has been so busy it probably didn't even occur to him to mention it to me."

Nardelli nodded, as if this was what she was expecting to hear. "And what did Rowena eat and drink?"

It really was just like on television. "Not much."

Piras didn't make a note, so this answer must have been insufficient. "I'm not sure, exactly. As I said, I didn't know about her new diet, so the menu wasn't a good fit, I'm afraid. Her friend Cliff made her a smoothie in the kitchen. You know about Cliff Stewart? He and Rowena are great friends, and I'm sure he'll be able to help you much more than I can. They spend hours and hours together every week. They probably know each other's darkest secrets. What else is there to talk about out there, right?"

Rowena's running friends were a strange crowd. People from all walks of life brought together with a single, bizarre interest. And a lot of them had complicated histories and used their running to stay grounded, or so Cliff said.

"We understand Signora Burke ingested the drink, as you say, and also an energy bar."

"An autopsy's already been done?"

Nardelli shook her head. "Emptying a stomach is the first treatment when a patient presents symptoms such as Signora Burke's."

Faye fought the image of Rowena lying on her floor. "You should talk with Cliff about the other runners. There was a big race last weekend. Maybe she fought with someone there."

Nardelli didn't smile this time. She probably thought Faye was trying to tell her how to do her job. "How would you describe Signora Burke?"

Nardelli seemed intent on ignoring Faye's questions. Was it a power play? Show Faye who was in charge? Faye liked the woman less and less.

"I'd say she was hard driving. Competitive. She liked to win." As soon as the words were out, Faye realized her mistake. This wasn't a word association game. "I'd also call her successful and brave."

That was better, complimenting the dead woman. "Rowena was prepared to upend her life for better opportunities for herself. Most of the expats here take these positions because they want to live abroad. They want to enjoy everything Italy has to offer. With Rowena, it seemed different. She was here for work and to make a success of it."

Moving to Italy was a sort of fantasy come true for most couples, one that added so much to their joint happiness that they were both delighted to be there, even if the trailing partner's career suffered a temporary slowdown. It was a price they were both willing to pay.

But Rome was Rowena's fifth international assignment, and rather than enjoying the Eternal City as a couple, she left Adam set up their life on his own, while she dove into work. If Rowena was concerned about the impact on her husband's career, Adam never mentioned it.

"Other than these runners, is there anyone who would want to harm Signora Burke? Someone who would have a grudge against her?"

The honest thing to do would be to say, "Why, yes, I did. Rowena Burke was threatening to share information that I didn't want made public. I didn't kill her, but I did have a motive."

Getting it all out in the open would be the smart thing to do. There were no secrets in a murder investigation. That's what they always said. Even if Adam hadn't told the police about the bank accounts yet, there was every reason to think he would. The best thing for Faye to do would be to get out ahead of it and explain everything from her point of view.

"Signora Masters?"

Faye couldn't do it. "Rowena was so busy with work and her hobby, the ultra running, I didn't have the chance to really get to know her."

Inspector Nardelli uncrossed her legs as if getting ready to depart, and relief flooded through Faye's body. It hadn't been easy, but the interview was coming to a close. She could play up the drama of the experience when she called some of the gang to tell them about it.

Faye was so caught up in her thoughts, it took her a moment to register that Nardelli didn't stand. "Signora Masters, it is early in this investigation. We do not have the official reports. But it appears very possible that poison was involved. Poison that Signora Burke consumed here. Tell me about yourself, Signora Masters."

Nardelli had a stain of something white on her shoulder. Faye had been friends with plenty of mothers over the years and recognized it as a baby's spit-up. An infant at home would explain Nardelli's tired eyes and eager acceptance of the coffee. Perhaps Nardelli was just back at work, eager to make a good impression. She might be digging into Rowena's death to show she was still in the game, chasing every lead. They didn't have the autopsy results. There was still a chance Rowena's death had been natural. Tragic, but nothing more.

"Faye, please. I'm not sure what there is to say. I'm an ordinary woman with lots of friends and no complaints."

"You are, I believe, in the middle of a divorce."

Nardelli and Piras were thorough. It was only a few hours since Rowena had died, a Saturday no less, and the police already seemed to know all about her. Italian inefficiency was one of the gang's most frequent complaints about life in Rome, but they were wrong. These two had been busy.

"That's true. It's never easy, but we're making the best of it. My husband was the one who called an end to a marriage we both knew was over."

Piras made another note.

"Most women in your situation are not able to be so generous, Signora Masters," Inspector Nardelli said.

Her situation. Faye felt her face flush. The police knew she'd been dumped.

"Did your husband have any particular reason for ending the marriage? Jealousy, perhaps?"

Faye tucked a strand of hair behind her ear. "As I said, he is the one who ended the marriage. If there was any jealousy, it would have gone the other direction. You've heard about his new girlfriend?"

"It is natural in those situations to want, what is it? Revenge? Signor Burke is an attractive man. His wife works long hours and is away on her hobby even more. Nothing would be more natural than to take mutual comfort."

Faye felt herself bristling. Comfort? An old-fashioned term. Or a function of the language. Nardelli was fluent, but there was always an odd turn of phrase when speaking outside your mother tongue.

"Absolutely not." Faye liked to flirt. She appreciated the attention. But that was as far as it went. Had someone in the gang told Nardelli otherwise? "Did someone say something?"

The sun had crept higher in the sky. Maggie and Thomas must be racing around with the final preparations for the guests.

"I understand you and Signora Burke had a business relationship, in addition to social, yes? You are involved in the sale of this building?"

This was it. One final chance for Faye to come clean about her relationship with Rowena. She could own up to Rowena's threats and move on. She could tell them that Rowena pressured her to sell. For all Faye knew, the police wouldn't even ask for the details of the bank accounts. As they'd said earlier, they weren't concerned about paperwork.

The sun angled directly into Faye's eyes, and she shifted her chair. She couldn't bring herself to do it. "DiLorenzo Industries is interested in developing this block. Esta and I have been discussing it for years, and Rowena was simply trying to make her boss's case."

The inspector leaned forward. "And what did you say?"

Faye had been blindsided when Rowena invited Faye to her office, then calmly announced she knew Faye was withholding information in her divorce negotiations. Rowena said she would tell George's attorney if Faye didn't do it first. It wasn't any business of Rowena's, and Faye said so. But Rowena just shook her head and said she didn't like to see people breaking the rules. She believed society broke down when people just looked out for themselves or some similar rubbish.

It didn't feel like a blackmail attempt. Just a self-righteous woman causing trouble. But still, Faye offered to sell in exchange for Rowena's silence. It was the only thing Faye could think of.

Faye shifted, remembering how Rowena had pursed her lips as she considered the offer. It was last Friday morning, and Rowena said she needed the weekend to think it over. And when Rowena called Monday to say they had a deal, Faye took grim satisfaction in knowing that even holier-than-thou Rowena had her price.

"I said I'd think about it." Faye would have to tell Maggie eventually. But without knowing DiLorenzo's plans, it didn't seem right to throw a curveball right before a tour started.

"You did not accept the offer?"

Faye's heart thumped. That was a stupid lie to tell. Nardelli would find out from Esta that Faye had agreed to sell. She needed to backpedal. "I'm sure the deal will go through eventually. It's Esta's passion project."

"And yet Signora Burke, she died in your home before concluding what was many years of discussion?"

Faye flushed. "Rowena's death won't have an impact." She pushed her chair back. "I've promised a friend that I would help with something this morning. I'm afraid I'm already late."

Maggie had, in fact, said she didn't need any help, but now that Faye was lying to the police one more fib wouldn't make things any worse.

"Certainly. Just one last question, if I may?" Nardelli's tone was mild enough, but there was something about the woman's body language that put Faye on edge. "Last night after the party, you cleaned. That was strange, no?"

Faye finally understood. The police weren't here for a friendly chat to learn more about the victim. Faye was a suspect. She almost laughed at the absurdity of it all. If she was going to kill anyone, it would be George. Maybe his girlfriend. But Rowena? She was not a woman worth going to prison for, let alone face eternal damnation.

At least Faye could answer this question truthfully. "I like things clean. It's a quirk of mine. Ask anyone."

Not everyone kept their homes as neat as she did, and Faye noticed some people felt defensive about it, as if she were judging their housekeeping. Maggie, for one, was always apologizing for the laundry left out or the stacks of books.

Nardelli made an "mmm" sound, the way a therapist did when waiting for you to keep talking, but Faye wasn't about to take the bait. She would wait for a question. Faye sat with both feet firmly on the tile floor. She knew she looked like a stereotypical American expat to this woman: time to exercise and eat right; time to get her hair done; money to live in a really nice area without holding down a job.

Nardelli's boxy suit was probably covering a few pounds of baby weight she hadn't had the time or energy to shed. Her mother-in-law was probably always on her about her housekeeping. And from the dark circles under her eyes, the inspector probably stayed up late just to keep up with her children's laundry.

Errant husband aside, Faye's life must look too good to be true. Maybe it wasn't a surprise that this woman thought Faye was hiding something.

Finally, Nardelli nodded at Piras and got to her feet. "Thank you for your time, Signora Masters."

Faye closed the door behind the officers. She avoided looking at the spot where Rowena had collapsed, focusing instead on the small table by the front door.

The black and white photos in silver frames were out of order. The one of a puddle reflecting an ancient column was in the back, while the one of gelato was in the front. Faye pushed back a feeling of unease as she moved them back into place.

Chapter Five

One of Caravaggio's first jobs was filling in the fruit and flowers in another artist's work. Caravaggio's thoughts about his employer outsourcing in this manner have not been recorded.
—Caravaggio: Brash, Brutish, and Brilliant

Faye found Maggie in the private courtyard that was supposed to be the heart of the Masterpiece Tours experience. It was an oasis in the middle of the city. Big enough for twelve painters to set up easels—Faye had helped test layouts—plus a dining table, casual sitting area, and plants galore. Faye had found ones with big leaves, white flowers, and even some with fruit growing on them. The effect was practically tropical.

Maggie sat at the table, deep in conversation with Thomas Evans, the tour's twenty-five-year-old painting instructor. Maggie looked up from her notepad. "We're breaking for lunch soon. You'll join us, won't you?"

"Is Ilaria cooking?" The tour provided guests with lunch and dinner, and Ilaria DeMarco's cooking was a highlight of the tour.

"She's in a group meeting," Thomas said. He was English, and everything sounded posh when he said it. "Again."

Thomas and Ilaria were dating, and he'd convinced her to stay on at Masterpiece when she announced she was starting graduate school.

"We're picking up some *pizza al taglio*," Maggie said. "And then we want to hear all about everything. You're okay, aren't you?"

On another day, Faye would have insisted on making lunch. Crusty bread, good cheese, some sliced fruit, maybe a pasta salad. It would have been easy to assemble, but she couldn't muster the energy this afternoon. "Pizza sounds perfect."

"Give us ten more minutes," Maggie said. "I want to finish going over the logistics for tonight, then we're all ears."

Faye wandered into the apartment-turned-tour-office while they wrapped up. With Faye's help, Maggie and Thomas had transformed the former master bedroom into an art studio, complete with paint-splattered tables and cabinets from the old studio. The need to clear out the old location was a shock, and the owner's name was mud around Maggie these days.

Faye had overseen the decoration of the sitting room, with the groupings of comfortable chairs and sofas to encourage guests to mingle. She knew it was the personal connection that would make Masterpiece Tours stand out. With any luck, the furniture would fit in whatever new location Maggie found.

"Smashing, isn't it?" Thomas pulled the door to the courtyard closed behind him. "I'm rather bullish on this whole endeavor. Maybe old Neddy pulling the rug out from under us wasn't all bad. Forcing us to stand on our own two feet and all that."

Thomas was a few years out of Oxford and, by all accounts, had been drifting until he found his niche teaching hobbyists to improve their painting.

"You've worked marvels," Faye said. "And now that you've done it once, next time you can find a location that's really perfect for the tour."

Thomas gave her look. "You must be mad if you think we're doing all this over again. Maggie has tours scheduled nearly back-to-back for the next year. The job now is for her to sell them."

"Just stay flexible."

He shrugged. "Maggie told me what happened. Ghastly. How are you holding up?"

"You're sweet to ask. Never better."

"Really?" His eyes crinkled at the corners with genuine concern.

She looked away. Some of the accent pillows had been placed on the wrong sofas. Faye swapped them out. "Well, maybe not really, but good enough."

"It's really sobering when someone dies. Reminds you of your own mortality and all that." He rubbed his hands together. "Maggie's sorting through some last-minute messages. Let's get lunch sorted, yes?"

They walked a few blocks to Pizzeria Ridente. The sun was out in full force, and heat bounced off the buildings in these narrow streets, making it feel even warmer. Italians were relaxing at the cafe tables outside while tourists were packed into the air-conditioned interiors.

"How's the husband holding up?" Thomas asked.

"I can't tell. I thought Adam was in shock this morning, saying that the police were treating it like a murder investigation. But then the police came to interview me."

They had come to an intersection, and Thomas stopped. "Murder investigation? I thought Maggie said it was a heart attack."

"They were talking about poison." Faye stepped aside as a woman on a scooter angled her bike for a turn. "They even seemed to suspect me, if you can believe it."

Thomas frowned. "They do that." He had been a prime suspect in an investigation himself. "Just stay on your toes, all right?"

The counter staff greeted Thomas by name and told him the *suppli* were fresh from the fryer. Thomas ordered six of the fried rice balls and stood debating in front of the counter loaded with rectangular slabs of pizza. There were eight different pans with different meats and vegetables covering a blanket of cheese, fresh red sauce and a chewy crust. Each and every one looked delicious.

Faye waited while Thomas dithered over the selections as long as she could, then pointed to several pizzas. The *sportellista* cut the pieces and weighed them out. Just like at a butcher or green grocer, everything here was sold by the gram. Faye and Thomas waited while the slices were heated in the oven.

"Did I tell you about my Caravaggio Società?" Faye asked. "Some of us are on a mission to see all the Caravaggios in the city. I was hoping to ask for your advice."

"Changing the subject from murder? Fair enough. When did you become an art fan?"

"I have a book. Caravaggio seems to have been quite a character." The *sportellista* boxed the slices, and Thomas carried them as they made their way across a piazza toward home. "Besides, it's as good a project as any."

There was something about Thomas that made Faye drop her guard. She would have told everyone else Caravaggio was the key to understanding Baroque art or some such highly erudite thing. The truth was, she was bored and lonely and thought the club would be an activity the gang could get behind.

"Well, he's not my cup of tea," Thomas said. "Important as all get out, but hardly full of sunshine and unicorns. Pay attention to his use of light, and your friends will all think you're an expert."

A group of American tourists was relaxing on the fountain stairs eating their own pizza and debating what made it so much better than the stuff at home. One was arguing it was the cheese from happy European cows. Another said the vegetables were fresh, not from some big foodservice supplier. The third said Italians weren't afraid to load the sauce with olive oil. All three were right.

"My advice is check Caravaggio's paintings off to say you've seen them, then go see some modern stuff," Thomas said, turning down a cobbled street barely wide enough for a car to pass. Faye had the momentary feeling of walking through a tunnel of green. It felt fifteen degrees cooler than out in the piazza thanks to the climbing plants hanging off the terra-cotta walls and large planters bookmarking doorways. The space had a secret garden feel, and Faye wished they could linger all day.

The street ended at Via Pecora. Faye could understand what the DiLorenzos saw in her block. It was made up of eight buildings with walls that touched and whose top floors had views extending over the city in all directions. The block was charming but in need of some love. Three windows were boarded up on one building and a metal security door rusted at another.

The DiLorenzo plan was to build a luxury hotel spanning the entire block.

They would keep the individual building facades intact and as many of the interior elements as possible to give it an old-world feeling with all the modern luxuries. At least, that's how Esta described it. The company had bought up all the other buildings over the years, and Faye's was the final piece in their development puzzle.

She had inherited 10 Via Pecora from her Italian grandparents and had treated it as an investment until George got the position that brought the couple to Rome. Over the years, Faye remodeled the top-floor apartment to suit her taste and had installed friends and acquaintances as tenants on the lower floors.

The DiLorenzo terms weren't terrible. Faye could use the proceeds to buy a place like Adam and Rowena's and still have plenty of money left over. But at the end of the day, she didn't want to move. She didn't want to displace Maggie, and she didn't want to figure out what to do with her life now that George was gone.

Maggie put her notebook aside when Faye and Thomas returned. She poured iced tea while Thomas doled out *suppli* and pizza.

"Tell me everything," Maggie said. "How's Adam?"

"Grieving," Thomas said. "The homicide police were here this morning, and Faye's on their list of suspects."

"Murder?" Maggie turned to Faye. "Tell me Thomas is exaggerating."

"I wish he were. The police were asking about my personal life. It was, I don't know, unsettling." Faye took a sip of tea. "Oh, and Adam didn't bother to thank me for the cinnamon rolls. I should have saved them all for you and Burt."

"The man's in shock," Maggie said. "But they were delicious, and another time I'll have to get the recipe. But why murder? And why suspect you?"

Faye took a bite of her pizza. Burrata cheese and pesto. The pesto was fresh and bright, and the nuggets of soft cheese were almost buttery. The *sportellista* left it lukewarm so the cheese wouldn't melt. So simple, and something they'd never get right at those brick oven restaurants in the States despite charging a fortune for their attempt.

Faye wiped her fingers on a napkin. "The police don't know anything yet. They're being thorough, exploring every angle, I guess. The inspector impressed me." Or Nardelli had until she directed her questions to Faye's life. "But if you wouldn't mind putting me up for a few more nights, they thought it might be for the best. Just in case."

Nardelli certainly would have said that, if Faye had thought to ask. She hadn't consciously made the decision to stay over again, but Faye had found herself tossing some essentials into a duffel bag after the police departed.

"Of course, as much time as you need. We're happy to have you."

"And I changed the code to the lockbox before coming down."

It might have been a bit like closing the barn door after the horse had gone, but she'd felt a spark of liberation when she changed it from her wedding anniversary to her own birthday. It was as if she was setting herself free from George as much as she was putting safety measures in place. "You still have your key, don't you?"

Maggie nodded. "Did you tell them about George, Faye?"

"What about him?"

"Well, you're in the middle of a divorce. Divorces get messy."

"You think George is involved?" He was six thousand miles away in California. Besides, Maggie knew as well as anyone how incompetent George was.

"I'm not saying anything. It just seems wise to tell the police everything so they can sort through it."

"Well, they knew all about him, goodness knows how. They seemed to think I was after Adam on some kind of rebound from George." Faye laughed, then stopped when she saw Maggie's reaction. "Not you, too? There was nothing between Adam and me. We were friends. Are friends."

"What am I missing?" Thomas said. "The husband?"

"You're not missing anything other than some gossip, which apparently I've been the subject of," Faye said. "If I were on the rebound, which I'm not, there's an entire city of men here. I don't need to go after someone's married husband. Who said there was something going on?"

Maggie took a bit of *suppli*, but Faye refused to let her off the hook. She waited until her friend swallowed. "Well?"

45

Maggie shook her head. "I'm not sure, really. It's just, you're normally so friendly to newcomers, but you've been sort of on edge about Adam. Someone wondered if there might be anything romantic between you two. I can't remember who." Maggie leaned forward. "If the police have heard things, it wasn't from me."

Faye's cheeks burned. Her friends had mistaken her jealousy for misplaced attraction. She was more out of the loop than she realized. Faye's phone chirped, and she was glad to have an excuse to step away from the table. It was Olivia, George's stepdaughter. Faye moved inside to answer it.

"Faye, Tim told me what happened. Are you all right?"

"I'm fine. It's good to hear your voice. How did Tim find out?" Tim was Olivia's younger brother.

"Social media, I guess. Is it true someone died at your house? Are you a suspect?"

Faye sighed. "Someone died, and they're looking into it. They have to consider all the possibilities."

Faye glanced outside at Thomas and Maggie. Maggie had a notebook out and was writing something as the two talked.

"It was that runner, right?" Olivia went on. "Rowena something? I'd have thought it was her heart. They give out all the time if you push too hard. I was at school with the U.S. champion, and he said…."

Faye loved Olivia, but the woman considered herself an expert in all subjects thanks to her high-power social circle. There wasn't a person Faye could mention who Olivia couldn't find a second-degree connection to.

Faye had six stepchildren. Well, not really stepchildren. They were her husband's steps. George had four stepchildren from his first two marriages. Olivia and her brother, Tim, as well as their two half-brothers, Ronnie and Paul. Faye's first husband also had two stepchildren from his wife's prior marriage.

It wasn't as complicated as it seemed. Faye's two husbands had been in the children's lives to varying degrees while the kids were growing up, and she had stayed connected after those marriages dissolved.

The children had all been in college or beyond when Faye came on the scene, but she felt a fondness for them, and they had all seemed to enjoy her the way you did a doting aunt or older cousin. She would take them out to nice dinners and shows, send lovely gifts at Christmas and birthdays, and exchange the occasional text message about their lives.

She liked them, and they liked her. In many ways, being a sort-of-stepparent was the perfect role for Faye. She could be interested and supportive without carrying the burden of actual parents or stepparents. "You're sweet to call, Olivia."

"I'm sending you chocolates," Olivia said. "Really good ones from that chocolatier in Paris. They're from all of us. Or they will be, if I can get ahold of Ronnie."

Ronnie was a free spirit, turning down his family's suggestion that he go to law school or take a high-powered banking job. He'd stayed with Faye a month or so ago and was the worst type of houseguest: he cleaned out her pantry, left wet towels on the bathroom floor, and walked off with her spare key. Plus, he'd asked for seed money to transition from his career as a professional gambler in Budapest to being a social media influencer. She had suggested that he earn the money instead.

"Have you checked Ronnie's social media channels?" Faye asked.

Olivia laughed. "Did he hit you up for money, too? I told him I could get him a job interview at a well-funded startup social platform, but he wasn't interested. Keep an eye out for him. I don't think he ever wants to leave Europe. Tim and Paul send their love, though. We're having dinner at the club tonight. We'll toast you, okay? Call if you need anything." And Olivia was gone, probably to check the next item off her daily task list.

Maggie set the notebook aside when Faye returned to the table. "Everything all right?"

"The stepchildren send their moral support. And chocolates."

Faye focused on her *suppli*. Crunchy on the outside, with a melted bit of mozzarella on the inside. It was one thing to swear off cheese out of concern for animal welfare or environmental sustainability, or any of the other things vegans talked about. But to do it in hopes of getting a better time in an insanely long foot race like Rowena? It seemed too big a sacrifice for a hobby.

"I should let you get back to your meeting. I can take this inside."

"Don't be daft," Thomas said. "We were talking about the murder."

Maggie handed the notepad to Faye. There were two columns headed *Rowena* and *Faye*. "It seems just as likely that you were the intended victim as Rowena. The food came from your house, didn't it?"

"The police aren't even certain it was murder," Faye said. "It's a theory, nothing more." Maggie and Thomas didn't say anything. Faye waited a beat, but then gave in. "Rowena didn't eat anything." Then she thought of the disgusting smoothie. "You don't think it was in the energy drink Cliff made?"

"I have no idea," Maggie said. "But you need to be prepared. And you're going through a divorce. That's always a red flag."

Faye had thought Rowena must have done something to bring her own death on. If Maggie and Thomas thought it possible that Faye was actually the intended victim, then that meant they thought she had done something worth killing over.

"If George were going to bump me off, he would have done it before filing for divorce. He's about to get everything he wants: freedom, a young girlfriend, and half my money. Killing me doesn't improve his situation at all."

At least, not from his point of view. He knew nothing about those bank accounts. She'd put enough money there to be worth killing over, but George had never involved himself in the details of the couple's financial situation. As long as Rowena had kept quiet, George wouldn't have any reason to believe Faye had been withholding information.

"Who gets the other half?" Thomas asked.

"Divided equally among the stepchildren." Faye took another bite of pizza, but it had cooled off. The idea of eating tepid pizza on a hot day was too much, and she pushed it away.

"Does it change with the divorce?" Thomas asked. He often came across as a bit of a lightweight, but he was zeroing in on details that the police hadn't asked about.

"Of course not." Faye pushed her chair back. "If you're thinking one of them snuck over here to kill me for one-twelfth of my estate, you're wrong. These are college-educated young professionals. One-twelfth of my money isn't going to change their lives, even if they were the homicidal types, which they are not. In general, they are delightful individuals who enjoy my company as much as I enjoy theirs."

Maggie and Thomas exchanged a glance, and Thomas put down the pen. "Just trying to help, Faye."

"I know. I'm sorry. I appreciate it. What do you have for Rowena?"

He passed the paper over. Under Rowena's name was written:

Adam?

Work issue?

Personal issue?

Running issue?

Under Faye's name was:

George?

DiLorenzo Industries?

Not exactly a breakthrough.

"We didn't write Adam's name down in your column," Maggie said. "But we didn't think we should have just one item, so we added DiLorenzo Industries."

"It was my idea," Thomas said. "If they've been buying up the block and you're the last holdout, it means they benefit from your death, right?"

Faye flushed, and Thomas went on. "I know it's a bit of a cheesy cliche to have an evil company behind the whole thing, but when I heard Esta was there last night, I thought, why not? We're brainstorming, no bad ideas and all that, right?"

Thomas was eating his piece of potato and salami pizza folded in half, like a sandwich with the crust on the outside and fillings on the inside.

"Maybe it was some kind of crazy attention seeker," Faye said. "Like that Tylenol case. Someone poisoned something, and Rowena got unlucky."

Faye was usually very careful about tamper seals. She had thrown away brand-new jars of food if she didn't hear the satisfying pop of a vacuum being broken. Not everyone was as careful as she was.

Maggie wrinkled her nose. "I don't know, Faye."

Thomas drummed his fingers on the table. "It's important to be prepared in case the police veer off in a direction that you don't like. If it's some kind of crazy person, great. But if not, well...."

"What do you suggest?"

"We start with Rowena. She's the victim." The idea of doing the police's job for them was nonsense, but she'd play along. He made it sound like they were a team, and that felt good.

"Question one: why kill Rowena at Faye's house?" Maggie said. "Slipping something into her food at a party seems awfully complicated." She took a bite of her mushroom-and-something slice and chewed thoughtfully. "There have to be a hundred easier ways to kill someone."

Thomas shrugged. "She didn't eat any party food, though, did she? That's why Cliff had to share his smoothie with her."

Thomas wasn't part of the expat gang. His friends were younger, more likely to be in Italy on their own nickel. But he had worked at an auction house before coming to Masterpiece. Rowena's running partner, Cliff, still worked at one.

"Did you cross paths with Cliff at your old job?"

Thomas drummed his fingers on the table. "We worked together. He wasn't my biggest fan. The feeling was mutual."

"What's wrong with him?" Maggie asked.

Faye's phone rang before Thomas could answer. *"Pronto."*

"Faye, this is Stefano Ungaro. I am sorry to disturb you on a Saturday, but Esta wished me to phone."

The DiLorenzo offices would have been thrown into turmoil by Rowena's death. "It's no problem, Stefano. I'm so sorry about Rowena. You must all be in shock."

Maggie and Thomas gave Faye a questioning look, and she shrugged. Thomas pointed at the remaining *suppli* and she nodded.

"Yes, it is terrible." Stefano said. "Are you available to see Esta tomorrow? She apologizes, but she would like to see you to discuss the details of the sale."

Faye flushed and stepped away from the table, saying a silent prayer that Maggie and Thomas weren't able to hear the other end of the call. "Where?" She got the details, and Maggie and Thomas were clearing the plates when she returned.

"Everything all right?" Maggie asked.

Faye should tell them about the sale. She should get out ahead of it. But the tour guests were arriving in just a few hours, and the two needed to focus. "Absolutely," Faye said. "I should leave you to it. Good luck this afternoon. Call if you need anything."

She wished she could be part of the team Thomas had talked about, but Faye needed to face Esta on her own.

Chapter Six

Caravaggio was just another artist selling paintings on a street corner until friends introduced him to influential collectors. Without his social network, Caravaggio might have disappeared from history, unknown and unappreciated.
—Caravaggio: Brash, Brutish, and Brilliant

Burt White invited himself along on Faye's visit to Esta DiLorenzo's the next day despite Faye's best efforts. One minute she was telling him she was going for a walk; the next minute, he had his canvas hat on and was standing next to her on the sidewalk.

"Maggie told me to keep an eye on you, just until the police know more," Burt said as he checked the front door lock for a second time. He had been solicitous about her safety after Maggie told him about the police interest. Burt's concern was touching last night. This morning, though, she needed to get to Esta's alone.

"It's broad daylight," Faye said. "I'll stay on busy streets. And if I see George, I'll keep my distance. Fair?"

"Nothing doing," he said. "Maggie was quite clear. 'Don't let Faye out of your sight,' so that's what I'm doing. For today, at least. I do need to be in the office tomorrow."

Faye laughed. "I wouldn't expect anything else."

Burt held out his elbow like a gentleman from another era. "So where are we going? North or south?"

"North." Esta lived in a tony neighborhood beyond the Vatican. The walk would give Faye an hour to lose to Burt. They ambled companionably

52

through the narrow streets, sticking to the shade whenever they could find it.

When Burt's shirt began to cling to his back, she made her move. "It's such a hot day. Why don't you head back? There are some shops I want to see up near Balduina that would bore you silly."

He moved off the sidewalk to make room for a family pushing a stroller. "I don't mind."

"Really? It's one of your precious days off, and you want to spend it shopping?" George would have been off in a flash.

"And miss meeting Esta DiLorenzo? Not a chance."

She flushed. She hadn't told him where she was going. "What?"

"You have a terrible poker face, Faye. Stick with bridge. You've said before that you don't believe in shopping on Sundays, and you've checked an address about three times on your phone. I realize I'm just a corporate suit, but I know you pretty well."

"And Esta?"

"The DiLorenzo family business has connections to one of our clients. They mentioned Esta lives in Balduina. It's not a leap to think that you might want to talk to her after what happened to Rowena."

"I'm not playing amateur detective, if that's what you think. I have every confidence the Italian police have this all well in hand."

He studied her, then nodded. "Okay, not investigating. But you must have an appointment; otherwise, when I said I was coming, you would have just gone tomorrow when I'm at the office. When's the meeting?"

The light changed, and they crossed. A scooter ignored the light and zipped through the crosswalk in front of them so close Faye could feel the heat of the exhaust. "In twenty minutes," she admitted. "Esta's interested in my building. She's been trying to buy it for years."

"And George gets half of everything in the divorce, so you need to keep the fair market value as low as possible."

Sweet Burt. Faye could have hugged him for giving her this cover story. Her attorney already had a tentative agreement with George's side that included the building and the assets she'd disclosed. Faye was the one who was dragging her feet. "Exactly. You know how lawyers are."

"So, what's our game plan?" Burt asked. "Did she call the meeting, or did you? That affects the power dynamics."

"Rowena was pushing hard for the sale. To be honest, she was acting as if it was a done deal."

They stopped at a light, and Burt gave her a look. "Why would she think that?"

Faye shrugged. "I think she thought the deal was inevitable. Esta's used to getting her way. I think Rowena wanted to be the one to lock in the sale. To look good for Esta and all that. With my divorce, well...."

Faye let it dangle, and Burt seemed to accept her story.

"I understand Esta's grandfather built the business from nothing," Burt said. DiLorenzo Industries was still family owned. No small task when you get a generation or two away from the founder. "The family is supposed to be ruthless. It takes a certain will to expand as successfully as they have."

Esta's older brother took over the organization thirty years ago, when it was primarily in the hotel business. He diversified into some of Italy's fastest growing industries. His sons, Esta's nephews, took over when he died.

"How important is your building?"

"In the big scheme, nothing. Esta's in charge of hotels, and that's supposed to be a tiny piece of the corporate pie." Faye had read that analysts expected the company to sell its hotel division sooner or later. "But to Esta, it's the finishing touch on a plan she cares deeply about." It couldn't be fun to be in charge of a business your family didn't want.

"Don't discount emotion," Burt said. "If Esta's motivated, she'll find a way to make you sell. It's too bad she knows about the divorce. The less she knows about your personal life, the better. Still, with her resources, expect her to know everything and to use it."

Faye had never seen this hard-charging side of Burt. Maggie said he did something dull involving finance. Was he like this at work, too?

"Nothing's done until you sign the paperwork," he went on. "Don't let her steamroll you."

Faye thought about her conversation with Rowena. Had the woman told Esta why Faye had finally decided to sell? Right now, answering that question was the only thing that mattered.

They passed a crowded cafe. If it weren't for Rowena, Faye could be enjoying an espresso and cookie in the shade of the large umbrellas instead of preparing to walk a tightrope with Esta. Because that's what this conversation was going to be. Chances were, Rowena hadn't told Esta why Faye had agreed to the sale after all these years. Rowena would have positioned it simply as a triumph of her negotiation skills.

Faye felt a tiny charge of excitement. If she was right, then the whole reason for Faye's decision to sell had disappeared when Rowena died. Esta would be in the dark, and Faye could keep her home. For the first time since Rowena died, Faye felt the knot in her stomach loosen. Just an inch, but enough so that she felt like she could breathe. She would tread lightly with Esta. Managing social situations was Faye's superpower.

They found Esta's building. There were no gates around it or any of the other trappings that would signal to the world that a Very Important Person lived there. Just a single black buzzer next to an old wooden door. The house must have been built several hundred years ago, but the finish on the door was freshly applied, and the white-washed wall around it didn't show a hint of decay.

"If she offers you food, take it," Burt said. "Same goes for drinks. Get the opponent into the habit of giving you things. It's one of Cialdini's principles of persuasion. Except alcohol. That's off limits."

"We've got this," Faye said.

"Maggie would understand if you decided to sell, you know," Burt said.

"I'm not here to take an offer, Burt."

"I know, but no one is going to be more motivated to buy the property than Esta if she already owns all the other buildings on the block." He caught her gaze, and the corners of his eyes crinkled in genuine concern. "And, well, you might want a fresh start."

At least ten members of the gang had told Faye to treat George's departure like a fresh start, as if it was a good thing. Faye liked her old life just fine, thank you very much.

Esta answered the door herself. She wore some sort of soft summer-weight suit with high heels. Weekend or not, Esta was an old-school Italian *donna*. Esta looked older, though. Her face was gray beneath a layer of foundation, and her posture was less upright than it had been two nights before. Elegant or not, she was in mourning.

"Come in, come in. You are so good to be here. Rowena's death, it is such tragedy." Faye caught a whiff of Esta's perfume. Light and floral.

Burt held a hand out to Esta. "I'm a friend of Faye's. I'm sorry for your loss."

Esta clucked. "I heard your marriage ended, Faye. Single life, it is a good thing?"

Burt turned pink. "Oh no, nothing like that. Faye's married to one of my best friends. That is, I'm married to one of Faye's best friends. Faye's staying with us, and I'm keeping her company. The shock, you know."

So much for Burt being a cool hand. There was nothing romantic about their friendship. Balding, middle-aged men in love with their wives were not her type. But Faye liked him, and he liked her.

They followed Esta down a long hall lined with paintings of all styles and colors, some vibrant and modern, others dark and old. They didn't seem hung according to size or content. A large painting of a hippopotamus hung over a sketch of a nude, while a colorful painting no larger than a hardcover book hung on its own.

Faye stopped for a closer look. The painting had appeared to be of an insect on a leaf from a distance, but now that she was closer, she saw that it was of a child in a sailboat.

Esta tapped the frame. "This artist has a sense of humor, no? This is one of his early works. I bought it before he was famous." She mentioned a name that Faye didn't recognize, but then how many living artists could Faye name? She drew a blank as she tried to come up with anyone besides Banksy.

"I read something about him." Burt's forehead furrowed as he appeared to run through his mental microfiche. "There was a bidding war in London

56

a few years ago. A Saudi prince and tech billionaire both wanted something for their wives?"

"Girlfriend, in the case of the billionaire. Said the piece matched her new rug." Esta laughed. "I am just happy to have discovered the artist before the rest of the world. And that auction spectacle increased the value of my little picture more than you would like to know. I have thought about selling it many times, but I cannot do it. It is too precious to me."

The hall opened into a conservatory across one end of the building, one wall nearly all glass and the other three walls painted white and hung with just one work on each. It was a relief after the crowded hall.

The paintings were different sizes and colors, and there was no unifying theme in the subjects. One used just a few blue lines, but it was clearly a woman swimming. Another was a heavily detailed and realistic cityscape. The third was an enormous painting of a donut. They were all lovely, but unconnected. Nothing Faye would think to hang in her own home, but here they worked.

"What shall we drink? Orange juice? Tea? Soda? Prosecco? The tastes of Americans are difficult for me to anticipate."

Faye had been invited to Esta's office several times over the years, and a succession of handlers had always escorted her from the main lobby to the executive floor to a holding area outside Esta's office before finally being invited into the inner sanctum. Today they seemed to be all alone.

A tray with olives, flatbreads, and cookies sat on the coffee table in front of them. Daisy would have devoured it all in the time it took Esta to answer the door.

"Orange juice sounds great," Burt leaned forward for a cookie. "I'll help. You'll have some too, Faye?"

Esta was setting this up as a social call, and Faye wasn't sure what to make of it. While Esta and Burt were getting the drinks, Faye stood to take in the art. Thomas had said Esta collected modern pieces, and he was right. It wasn't the random paint splotches she'd been prepared for, though. These were fresh but accessible, all different styles. The cohesive element simply seemed to be that Esta liked them.

The glasses clinked on the tray. "Here we are," Burt said, setting it down.

"*Grazie*," Esta said. "I can manage myself, but one gets used to having help. My guards, they do not let me do anything."

Faye wondered, briefly, what use bodyguards were if they all had the same days off. Wouldn't it be a simple matter for someone with ill intentions to learn their schedule? Perhaps Esta's were for show more than anything else.

Their host took a sip of juice and continued. "You like my collection? I do not have the budget of the Saudis and tech stars, but I like to make the discoveries before they are known, yes?" She gestured at the painting of the swimmer. "This is by Costantini. Exquisite, no? Some of her older works are in DiLorenzo hotels around the world. Others are at our office. The collection there is quite remarkable. I will give you a tour, yes?"

Esta had taken a seat opposite Faye. The chair was modern with a firm seat. Probably easy to get up from. Faye's own seat on the sofa was so soft she couldn't move without jostling Burt on the cushion next to her.

Esta tapped her fingers on the arm of the chair. Her nails were painted dusty pink, and she wore heavy rings on each hand, with a slim gold watch on her left wrist. It was as if Esta had run out of small talk and was getting herself together to talk about the real purpose of the visit. Faye braced herself. *Please don't let her tell Burt about the bank accounts*, she prayed. *Please, please, please.*

"The police, they are hinting that Rowena's death was not natural. That someone was involved, and I cannot understand it. She always seemed so confident at work. You were her friend. Did she tell you anything about trouble? Someone bothering her? Anything at all?"

Faye felt a wave of relief. Esta was trying to understand Rowena's death, just like everyone else. "I wish we'd been closer." It was a lie, but it was what polite people said. "I really don't have any idea what was happening in her life."

"But you had a party for her. She was looking forward to it, a chance to get to know more people, yes?"

"I try to be helpful, to be welcoming of new people," Faye said. "Maybe her husband would know more. Or her running friends. Did you meet Cliff at the party?"

Esta shrugged. "The man with the green drink? He comes to the office sometimes, to run with Rowena. He was the one who made her drink, yes? What did he put in it? It looked like water from a very old pond."

"He's the one. I'm not sure. He brought something from home, some sort of mix."

"Ah, those energy boosts. Rowena kept energy bars in her bag. Vile things. I tasted one once. Not even food. But at least she only ate them when running. Never as a snack. He put nothing else in?"

"Bananas, I think," Faye said. "Peanut butter and cinnamon. It can't have helped the taste."

Esta nodded. "A sad last meal. Rowena worked too hard. She hadn't eaten since breakfast."

Faye glanced around. From the outside, the building looked like nothing special. Maybe even a little down-at-the-heel in the way these centuries-old houses often did. But the interior was a masterpiece, blending remnants of the old beams and floors with fresh walls and clever lighting.

One wall had floating shelves with an assortment of family photos. Faye recognized Esta as a much younger woman standing with a handsome man. The photographer captured her looking up him, as if she'd said something and was waiting for his answer. Judging by the family resemblance, it had to be the brother whose sons now ran DiLorenzo Industries.

"Ah, you see the family photo? My brother and I made quite a pair." Esta stood and handed the photo to Faye and Burt. "To believe we were once young, yes? My brother, he was a powerful force in my life. The most powerful force, perhaps, even more than my husbands. He grew DiLorenzo Industries in ways my grandfather would never have imagined."

Esta took the picture back, and her hand shook slightly as she set it on the shelf. "Now, the new generation is taking over. I have no children to stand up for the hotels when it is time for me to retire. I had hoped Rowena might fight for them. Now? I do not know what will happen. All I can do is continue moving forward."

Faye thought of the expectation that the hotel division would be sold. Was it the nephews, Luca and Matteo, driving that?

Esta removed an invisible piece of lint from her sleeve, then met Faye's gaze. "I would like to be open with you, Faye."

Faye's heart thumped. The woman knew. She knew why Faye had agreed to sell, and Burt would know it, too.

"Look, Esta—"

But Esta cut her off. "Rowena surprised me when she said you agreed to sell. Even more so when she told me the purchase price. A fraction of what I am prepared to pay."

Faye swallowed. She felt Esta's gaze on her and shifted her weight, fighting the soft cushion that was steadily rolling her closer to Burt.

"Rowena was very optimistic in her outlook," Esta went on. "A very American trait, perhaps, to confuse something that you wish to happen with something that will certainly happen. I believe Rowena thought she could manifest anything she desired with hard work. A good quality in many ways, but it is dangerous, no?"

Faye looked away. From Esta's living room, she could see across the river to the heart of the old city. She couldn't make out specific buildings so much as the colorful jumble of rooftop tiles and balconies and patches of green.

Faye felt her heart pounding and wondered if Burt could hear it too. Esta was giving her the very lifeline she had hoped for.

Esta leaned forward. "Was Rowena telling the truth, or was she just hoping, when she said you would sell?"

Esta didn't know how Rowena had gotten Faye's agreement. Esta didn't even believe Faye had agreed to sell. Faye was free.

She maintained a neutral expression, the one she used in bridge tournaments when she saw her partner's dummy hand and knew they had the game clinched as long as she played it right. And Faye always played it right.

"I appreciate you asking, Esta. I can't pretend that I understood Rowena, but no, we had no agreement." Strictly speaking, that was the truth. They hadn't discussed any of the details or signed any paperwork. As Burt said, without her signature, there was no agreement.

Esta sighed. "I am disappointed, but not, I am afraid, very surprised."

Esta's voice caught. "This quality of hers. It is not, I hope, related to her death."

Burt cleared his throat. "From what I understand, it's not entirely clear that Rowena was the intended victim. The food, after all, came from Faye's house. It's possible that Faye was the target all along."

"I don't know that I'd go that far," Faye said. "There were a lot of guests at the party. Any one of them could have been the intended—"

"And you are here for protection," Esta interrupted. She rubbed her thumb against her middle finger. Faye noticed the polish was chipped. "Faye is lucky to have good friends."

Faye was aware of the padding of feet, and a fluffy white cat barreled down the hall toward them. It stopped in front of Faye and meowed twice. Faye looked at Esta. She had no idea whether the cat was asking to be picked up or telling Faye to get out of its seat.

Esta murmured to the cat in Italian and reached down to pick it up. "Don't mind Micio. You are not allergic? *Va bene.* Animals, they love me." The cat settled on her lap and leaned his head into her hand as she stroked him.

"And you, Faye, you will be careful? I, myself, I do not know what to believe. I wonder, you know? The police, they see the DiLorenzo name related to the case, and they think 'ah, this is my opportunity to be in the newspapers, to get a step higher up.' That woman, that Nardelli, she asked me if Adam was happy with Rowena's career. Would she have asked that of a man? No, I do not think so."

"What did you tell her?" Faye asked.

Esta adjusted her watch. "I said that I do not manage the relationships of my employees. But was Adam happy? No, I do not think so. He did not even go to her race, the one last weekend. Did you know that? I do not pretend to understand her interest in all that running, but it was important to her, no? And Adam, he did not go to cheer her on. It was an important one, too. She qualified for some big race."

"The Valentina 100," Faye said. Adam had talked about it for weeks beforehand. He'd intended to go and do whatever supportive things spouses did while their wives and husbands put themselves through voluntary torture.

"Rowena pretended she did not mind, but she said it was the first race of hers he had missed." Esta shook her head. "You are divorcing, Faye. You know what it is like. These missed events, they are the first signs of trouble, no? Rowena was a woman who willed the world to be what she wanted it to be, but a woman can do only so much to hold onto a husband who does not want to be held. I know that as well as anyone."

Faye had told George she could look past the cheating. She said they could stay together if he broke it off with the girlfriend. But it hadn't worked. He'd left her anyway. "There was nothing at the office?" Faye asked. "Nothing that could have led to this?"

"Of course not." Esta sank back in her chair. "I do not suppose I can convince you to change your mind, Faye? I do know that divorces are ugly things, and we make decisions that are not always in our best interests. I have been through it three times, so I know, yes?" Esta laughed. "And my mistakes cost me more than one building. Anyone would advise you to sell now. You will not get a higher price."

"I have a tenant on the ground floor," Faye said. "A tour business, just getting established. I need to consider their interests."

"I saw something about that as we passed by on Friday. What do they do?"

"Masterpiece Tours," Faye said. "Bringing the best of Rome to discerning travelers. Guests get lessons and spend their mornings painting all kinds of things. Streets. Trees. It's under new management and off to a promising reboot. I've been consulting, actually."

Esta leaned back in her chair. "That is very interesting. We are always looking to expand the experience of our hotel guests. Perhaps there are partnership opportunities, yes?"

"One just started yesterday."

Esta clapped her hands. "Then that is perfect. I will send Stefano tomorrow. What is their schedule? Are they at the building all day, or do they go out and see the city?"

"They start each day with painting instruction in the studio—that's in the apartment—then they go apply it. Tomorrow is the Vatican Museum."

Maggie would be over the moon.

"Perfect. And you, you said you consult for the tour. You will be there, too, of course."

"Absolutely." Faye could give Stefano one-on-one attention while Thomas led the tour and Maggie managed the guests. "I'm an integral part of the business."

Faye's phone buzzed. She pulled it from her bag to mute it and saw the call was from George. She turned the sound off. She would talk with her husband later.

"This project, it is important to me," Esta said as she walked them to the door. "Taking an old block of buildings and transforming it into something new and vibrant, that is the lifeblood of our city. Some people, they would have us mummify the old, and that leads to erosion of the spirit. Rome cannot live as a museum to the past."

Micio curled around Esta's ankles, and Esta picked him up and nuzzled her face in his fur. "Just promise me you will consider the sale, yes?"

Faye nodded. They kissed cheeks at the door, and Faye was reminded of her grandmother, the woman who had given her the building in the first place. They were both tough Italian ladies who were more sentimental than they let the world see.

"That was instructive," Burt said. "She wants your building, and she's prepared to pay for it. What are you going to do?"

Esta was supposed to be an expert negotiator, but she'd shown her hand with the sale. Why? Faye decided it didn't matter. She'd learned what she had come for. Esta knew nothing about her secrets.

"I'm staying put." For the first time in days, Faye felt genuine relief.

Chapter Seven

Caravaggio's peers made detailed drawings before beginning to paint. Caravaggio rejected this methodical approach and began his work directly on his canvases. Contemporaries labeled this reckless, but historians agree it gave his paintings a spontaneity virtually unknown at the time.
—Caravaggio: Brash, Brutish, and Brilliant

Mornings were a difficult time in the White household. There was just one bathroom, and there'd been some confusion over shower schedules on Monday. Faye had jumped in after her morning run, not realizing until she emerged that others were waiting.

Faye dressed quickly and found Maggie at the kitchen table in her bathrobe, gaze bouncing between the closed bathroom door and her watch. "I was hoping to get in early. Instruction starts at nine and I wanted to review some new ads before the guests arrive."

Faye pushed a plate of scones toward her friend. Current and orange zest, a batch Faye had made the night before to thank the Whites for their hospitality.

Maggie took one and seemed to eat it mechanically while she kept her gaze on the bathroom door. "I'm really not sure you should have gone out running on your own, Faye. I wish Burt could stay home today to keep you company."

Faye savored her first bite. Tender and citrusy, with just the right amount of flakiness. Maybe a tad more salt next time. They'd be even better with a pat of butter, but the Whites had run out.

"Then it's a good thing I'm coming on the tour. I'll be perfectly safe with you and Thomas and all the guests."

Maggie bit her lip. "You know I appreciate you renting me the apartment and all the decorating you've done."

"And the web design."

"And the web design. And telling Esta about us. I'm just not sure how professional it looks for you to come on a tour."

They'd been through it twice last night. "I've taken hundreds of visitors through the Vatican over the years," Faye said. "I might not have been an art major like Thomas, but I know what people like. Plus, I know where the best bathrooms are."

"We're fine, Faye. Thomas and I have it covered."

"I know you do. And the tour group will love it. But Esta specifically asked if I'd be there."

The bathroom door opened before Maggie could respond.

"Looks like it's all yours," Faye said. "I'll be ready when you are." Maggie opened her mouth but closed it again without arguing, and Faye considered it settled.

Once she was sure Maggie was out of earshot, Faye made a call. She had arranged for two friends-of-friends to be on the tour at Faye's own expense to serve as supportive customers. Nan and Paul Foster had promised to do their darndest to make sure everyone had fun, and Faye hadn't seen the need to mention her financial arrangements to Maggie. Nan answered on the first ring.

"Everything is so nice." Nan's voice came through the phone with a little background static. She must have put Faye on speaker. "Everyone's so friendly, and the hotel is perfect. Paul's here. Paul, it's Faye."

Nan's husband's voice was in the background, as if he were a few feet away from his wife. "Hi, Faye. Will we see you today?"

"I'm still working on it. But you have a special assignment. There's a VIP named Stefano joining the tour this morning. He's considering whether it complements his hotel's operations. It could be an excellent opportunity for Maggie."

"Understood," Paul said. "We'll make sure he knows how great it is."

"It won't be hard," Nan added.

Burt, now fully dressed, waved to Faye as he raced through the living room, briefcase bag on his shoulder and sport coat over one arm. A businessman in a hurry. She heard him thump down the apartment building's steps as Nan continued. "It really is lovely. I'm sure he'll see that for himself."

Faye kept watch on Maggie's bedroom door. She didn't want her friend to find out her most enthusiastic guests were being paid to be boosters. "I just don't like to leave things to chance."

"Smart woman," Paul said. "We'll take care of it."

"Thank you," Faye said. "I appreciate it."

She was about to click off when Nan's voice came through again, a little hesitant this time. "Faye? Maggie told us there had been a death in the building. That there might be some police in and out, and to not worry about it. Is everything all right?"

Faye swallowed. She wouldn't have told the guests what had happened, but Maggie must have thought it was for the best. "It is, thank you. A tragedy, but it'll be okay."

"You tell us if we can help," Paul said. "We're standing by."

Faye bit her lip. "You're sweet. Just focus on having a good time on the tour. Thanks again."

Faye pushed her scone away. The tender pastry had lost its appeal. She picked up the Caravaggio book she'd been reading last night, instead. The Caravaggio Società wasn't scheduled to visit the Vatican for a few more days, but it wouldn't hurt to get a sneak peek if she was going there anyway.

Faye was reading about Caravaggio's troubled childhood when Maggie returned to the kitchen. She wore a tan skirt that hit at just the wrong place on her calves and a brown blouse whose tucks and seams stretched in a way the designer had never intended.

Faye took a sip of her coffee. "It's a big day. Did you want some help choosing an outfit?"

"No, I'm ready." Maggie glanced down. "Why? Is something wrong?"

Faye folded her napkin. "Of course not. You look wonderful, Maggie. I

ny longer. She wandered into the kitchen to wash the cups and
e guests left out. Ilaria wasn't due until lunchtime, and she'd want
tchen waiting for her.

ne glasses clean and dry, Faye stuck her head into the tiny bedroom
was using as an office. Her friend wore a pained expression.

t's wrong?" Faye asked. "If it's the pants, the waistband just takes a
etting used to."

not that. I just opened this."

ggie handed over an official-looking letter with a lot of legal language
t forms and missed deadlines.

kes. What's it about?"

have no idea." Maggie ran a hand through her hair. "My lawyer says to
down and find out as soon as possible. Would it really be okay if I left
and Thomas to handle the tour? I'll make it up to you."

had been a long time since someone had truly needed Faye. She smiled.
"They'll be in good hands, I promise."

After Maggie had left, Faye still had at least ninety minutes before it
was time to leave. She moved through the sitting room fluffing pillows.
There weren't any snacks set out for the guests. They were supposed to
eat breakfast at the hotel, but Faye had corralled enough groups to know a
steady supply of food was key.

The pantry was sparse, but there were oats and some spices. Faye decided
to make a batch of her coconut cardamom granola. The guests could
snack on it with yogurt so it would be healthy without being in-your-face
nutritious.

It was nice having the apartment's tiny kitchen to herself. It was more
orderly than the Whites' messy space, but with the pleasant hum of voices in
the studio down the hall. The recipe was simple enough—just oats, honey,
coconut, and a mix of nuts and spices, all of which Ilaria had in the cabinets.
The cardamom, Faye realized, was actually her own bottle. She'd told Maggie
to help herself to anything they needed, and Faye was glad her friend had
taken her up on the offer.

Faye mixed the ingredients and had a batch in the oven in less than fifteen

---

just thought, on a tour, you might want to be more colorful so everyone
can spot you. What about your red linen blouse? It looks so nice with your
hair."

Five minutes later, Maggie wore a flattering blouse, and the pair of striped
wide-legged trousers Faye had given her a month ago. She found them
still in their tissue paper wrapping when she rummaged through Maggie's
dresser looking for outfits. Maggie looked perfect, even if she did refuse
the lipstick Faye proposed.

Faye walked Maggie to 10 Via Pecora and somehow never left. If
possession was nine-tenths of the law, then occupation was nine-tenths of
the argument to accompany the tour to the Vatican that day.

Thomas was arranging easels when they arrived, and Faye was surprised
by how much she appreciated his bear hug. "Glad to see you safe and sound.
No one lurking in the shadows as you walked over?"

"The Whites are a good protection squad," Faye said.

"Well, keep it that way. No word from the police?"

"Not a peep."

The guests trailed in from their hotel, which Maggie had booked just a
few blocks away. Nan gave Faye a big American-style hug when she and
Paul arrived. "I've heard so much about you, Faye. It's great to meet you in
person."

Paul gave her a big wink as he shook her hand. "I feel like we've already
met. Nice to make it official."

The other guests introduced themselves while Faye helped get everyone
set with coffee and tea while they waited for the morning instruction to
begin.

"Are you the one who saw the murder?" one of the men asked before his
wife kicked him in the ankle.

Faye nodded.

"How is the family doing?" asked his wife.

"As well as can be expected," Faye said. "I saw the husband yesterday, and
he was still in shock. No children, thank goodness."

"Do they have any leads?" an elderly woman asked. "They say the first forty-eight hours are the most important, otherwise, poof! The odds it will be solved go right down the toilet."

"Oh, be quiet, Betty," a round, white-haired woman wearing a World's Best Grandma t-shirt said. "Ignore my friend. She watches far too much television."

There was a tap at the door, and Stefano came in. He was dressed in the uniform of the wealthy young Italian male: open collar shirt, pressed pants, leather shoes, and expensive sunglasses. Today, at least, his clothes were clean and well fitting. Still, his long arms and legs were slightly uncoordinated, giving the impression of someone about to knock over a table.

He air-kissed Faye. "I am grateful for the invitation. I could not think on a day like this, no? The paintings, they will be a welcome distraction."

Faye introduced him to Maggie, who said the usual things about being sorry about Rowena's death.

"It feels unreal," he said. "The police, it is all hush-hush so we do not even know what they are thinking. Everyone is so upset, nothing will be happening at the office for a few days."

"We are honored you could come and experience the Masterpiece magic," Maggie said, leading him toward the studio. "Our guests begin each day with a painting tutorial, then they experience one of Rome's sights through the eyes of an artist."

Faye trailed behind the two. Stefano was nodding along. "The light here is really good. It is all right if I make some notes?"

Nan waved him over to the empty easel between her and Paul. "You're going to love this. We just arrived on Saturday and already are learning so much."

"It's a really nice change from the trips we usually take," Paul added. "We like to stay in high-end hotels, but sometimes they don't have activities that suit active travelers like ourselves. We've often said we just want a hotel to make it easy to pursue the activities we like, isn't that right, Nan?"

His delivery sounded a little scripted. Faye hoped Stefano didn't notice.

"That's right," Nan said. "And don't worry if you haven't done a lot of

painting. There are people of all skill leve feel like I've made friends for life already."

The World's Best Grandma snorted. "I u. experienced artists. My friends, the Alberts, to have a very nice picture up over their mantle."

"Advanced students get as much out of the tour as said. "Accelerate your learning under the skilled guida isn't that what the brochure said?"

"I sincerely hope so," said the man who had asked Faye i the murder. "I nearly flunked out of preschool because I cou paint."

Thomas gave what sounded like a genuine laugh that seeme everyone in the room. "I love nothing more than a challenge. A few tricks up my sleeve that will change the way you think about yo The act of creating art is transformative. I truly believe that. The that goes up on the wall is secondary. Shall we get to it?"

Faye and Maggie lingered for a few minutes while Thomas began lecture. He sketched two triangles on the easel facing the group, one abou three times the size of the other "Think about the weight of an object. Larger objects have more visual weight than smaller ones, so how do you balanc them?"

He picked up a brush and painted the smaller one red. It was striki how much it changed the impression of the two shapes. "Color is k He sketched out more small triangles. "Or more objects. I also like to negative space." He painted in a background around the objects, leav tight margin around the larger triangle and a wider one around the c of smaller ones. The large triangle looked dwarfed in the scene.

Faye had never given the subject much thought. You saw a pictu it looked right or it didn't. Maybe she would learn something on t today, too.

"When we're at the Vatican, I want you to watch for balance and masters created it," Thomas said. "But first, let's do some exercis

Maggie went into the office, and Faye didn't feel like she had

to linger
glasses t
a clean
With
Maggi
"Wh
ttle
"It
M

just thought, on a tour, you might want to be more colorful so everyone can spot you. What about your red linen blouse? It looks so nice with your hair."

Five minutes later, Maggie wore a flattering blouse, and the pair of striped wide-legged trousers Faye had given her a month ago. She found them still in their tissue paper wrapping when she rummaged through Maggie's dresser looking for outfits. Maggie looked perfect, even if she did refuse the lipstick Faye proposed.

Faye walked Maggie to 10 Via Pecora and somehow never left. If possession was nine-tenths of the law, then occupation was nine-tenths of the argument to accompany the tour to the Vatican that day.

Thomas was arranging easels when they arrived, and Faye was surprised by how much she appreciated his bear hug. "Glad to see you safe and sound. No one lurking in the shadows as you walked over?"

"The Whites are a good protection squad," Faye said.

"Well, keep it that way. No word from the police?"

"Not a peep."

The guests trailed in from their hotel, which Maggie had booked just a few blocks away. Nan gave Faye a big American-style hug when she and Paul arrived. "I've heard so much about you, Faye. It's great to meet you in person."

Paul gave her a big wink as he shook her hand. "I feel like we've already met. Nice to make it official."

The other guests introduced themselves while Faye helped get everyone set with coffee and tea while they waited for the morning instruction to begin.

"Are you the one who saw the murder?" one of the men asked before his wife kicked him in the ankle.

Faye nodded.

"How is the family doing?" asked his wife.

"As well as can be expected," Faye said. "I saw the husband yesterday, and he was still in shock. No children, thank goodness."

"Do they have any leads?" an elderly woman asked. "They say the first forty-eight hours are the most important, otherwise, poof! The odds it will be solved go right down the toilet."

"Oh, be quiet, Betty," a round, white-haired woman wearing a World's Best Grandma t-shirt said. "Ignore my friend. She watches far too much television."

There was a tap at the door, and Stefano came in. He was dressed in the uniform of the wealthy young Italian male: open collar shirt, pressed pants, leather shoes, and expensive sunglasses. Today, at least, his clothes were clean and well fitting. Still, his long arms and legs were slightly uncoordinated, giving the impression of someone about to knock over a table.

He air-kissed Faye. "I am grateful for the invitation. I could not think on a day like this, no? The paintings, they will be a welcome distraction."

Faye introduced him to Maggie, who said the usual things about being sorry about Rowena's death.

"It feels unreal," he said. "The police, it is all hush-hush so we do not even know what they are thinking. Everyone is so upset, nothing will be happening at the office for a few days."

"We are honored you could come and experience the Masterpiece magic," Maggie said, leading him toward the studio. "Our guests begin each day with a painting tutorial, then they experience one of Rome's sights through the eyes of an artist."

Faye trailed behind the two. Stefano was nodding along. "The light here is really good. It is all right if I make some notes?"

Nan waved him over to the empty easel between her and Paul. "You're going to love this. We just arrived on Saturday and already are learning so much."

"It's a really nice change from the trips we usually take," Paul added. "We like to stay in high-end hotels, but sometimes they don't have activities that suit active travelers like ourselves. We've often said we just want a hotel to make it easy to pursue the activities we like, isn't that right, Nan?"

His delivery sounded a little scripted. Faye hoped Stefano didn't notice.

"That's right," Nan said. "And don't worry if you haven't done a lot of painting. There are people of all skill levels here. So many nice people, I feel like I've made friends for life already."

The World's Best Grandma snorted. "I understood this tour was for experienced artists. My friends, the Alberts, took this tour a year ago and have a very nice picture up over their mantle."

"Advanced students get as much out of the tour as beginners, Jean," Thomas said. "Accelerate your learning under the skilled guidance of our gifted tutor, isn't that what the brochure said?"

"I sincerely hope so," said the man who had asked Faye if she had witnessed the murder. "I nearly flunked out of preschool because I couldn't even finger-paint."

Thomas gave what sounded like a genuine laugh that seemed to include everyone in the room. "I love nothing more than a challenge. And I have a few tricks up my sleeve that will change the way you think about your skills. The act of creating art is transformative. I truly believe that. The picture that goes up on the wall is secondary. Shall we get to it?"

Faye and Maggie lingered for a few minutes while Thomas began his lecture. He sketched two triangles on the easel facing the group, one about three times the size of the other "Think about the weight of an object. Larger objects have more visual weight than smaller ones, so how do you balance them?"

He picked up a brush and painted the smaller one red. It was striking how much it changed the impression of the two shapes. "Color is key." He sketched out more small triangles. "Or more objects. I also like to use negative space." He painted in a background around the objects, leaving a tight margin around the larger triangle and a wider one around the cluster of smaller ones. The large triangle looked dwarfed in the scene.

Faye had never given the subject much thought. You saw a picture, and it looked right or it didn't. Maybe she would learn something on the tour today, too.

"When we're at the Vatican, I want you to watch for balance and how the masters created it," Thomas said. "But first, let's do some exercises."

Maggie went into the office, and Faye didn't feel like she had an excuse to linger any longer. She wandered into the kitchen to wash the cups and glasses the guests left out. Ilaria wasn't due until lunchtime, and she'd want a clean kitchen waiting for her.

With the glasses clean and dry, Faye stuck her head into the tiny bedroom Maggie was using as an office. Her friend wore a pained expression.

"What's wrong?" Faye asked. "If it's the pants, the waistband just takes a little getting used to."

"It's not that. I just opened this."

Maggie handed over an official-looking letter with a lot of legal language about forms and missed deadlines.

"Yikes. What's it about?"

"I have no idea." Maggie ran a hand through her hair. "My lawyer says to go down and find out as soon as possible. Would it really be okay if I left you and Thomas to handle the tour? I'll make it up to you."

It had been a long time since someone had truly needed Faye. She smiled. "They'll be in good hands, I promise."

After Maggie had left, Faye still had at least ninety minutes before it was time to leave. She moved through the sitting room fluffing pillows. There weren't any snacks set out for the guests. They were supposed to eat breakfast at the hotel, but Faye had corralled enough groups to know a steady supply of food was key.

The pantry was sparse, but there were oats and some spices. Faye decided to make a batch of her coconut cardamom granola. The guests could snack on it with yogurt so it would be healthy without being in-your-face nutritious.

It was nice having the apartment's tiny kitchen to herself. It was more orderly than the Whites' messy space, but with the pleasant hum of voices in the studio down the hall. The recipe was simple enough—just oats, honey, coconut, and a mix of nuts and spices, all of which Ilaria had in the cabinets. The cardamom, Faye realized, was actually her own bottle. She'd told Maggie to help herself to anything they needed, and Faye was glad her friend had taken her up on the offer.

Faye mixed the ingredients and had a batch in the oven in less than fifteen minutes. Still more than an hour to kill. She should go up to her apartment and pick up some more clothes. Instead, Faye settled on a sofa and took out her book on Caravaggio. He'd moved to Rome as a young man and almost immediately began getting into regular trouble with the police. The book listed a series of drunk and disorderly charges and lots of fights. The behavior continued even after he began getting commissions from the Catholic church.

Here was a man paid to bring the stories of the bible to life, who everyone knew was trouble. Why not choose someone more virtuous to spread the good word and enjoy those fat commissions? Maybe as a sinner, Caravaggio understood the world better than his more virtuous counterparts.

Chapter Eight

Caravaggio's art is so exact in its details that modern botanists can identify the individual cultivars in his work. One must wonder if this attention to detail helped him sell the reality of the notably unreal elements of his paintings: namely, angels and other heavenly messengers.
—Caravaggio: Brash, Brutish, and Brilliant

Faye intended to make the most of her time with Stefano on the ride to the Vatican. She took the seat next to him in the spacious van.

"Masterpiece Tours has a long track record, but its new management is actively focused on growth," she began. "If a partnership with DiLorenzo Hotels makes sense, we would work together to arrange custom tours for your clientele."

Belatedly, Faye realized her use of the word "we." However Faye had presented herself to Esta, she needed to remember that she was helping Masterpiece as a friend, nothing more. It wouldn't do her any good to get too invested in someone else's project.

Stefano nodded. "Of course. It is all very impressive."

"We can put together some projections once we know more about what Esta might be interested in."

"For now, my assignment is to experience the tour, yes? To be a visitor."

"Of course." They rode in silence for a moment or two and Faye listened to the chattering of the guests behind her. They were talking about grandchildren and past careers, hometowns, and other tours they'd taken.

They were passing the Porta San Pancrazio, a stone building with an arch in the middle of it that was one of the remaining gates from a wall that once surrounded the city. This building was relatively modern, at least by this city's standards. The one from Roman times had fallen to the Goths in the 500s, and this structure was from the 1800s. It was hard to imagine the city with such a clear line between inside and outside, but for centuries, on and off, residents had attempted to control access with gates like this.

Faye turned her attention back to Stefano. "Have you worked at DiLorenzo Industries long?"

He smiled. "Esta was kind enough to take me in about one year ago."

"Take you in?"

"Ah, you do not know. My family and the DiLorenzos are close. Esta is a sort of godmother to my mother. She and my grandfather, they are friends. My family said I needed to get experience outside our own company. Esta took me in as a favor."

He lowered his voice. "A bit of a last chance, you know? They think I was not serious about learning the business, so this is their solution. They tell me to see what it is like to start at the bottom so that I appreciate my work when I return to the family. If prove myself, they will consider giving me another chance."

"Goodness."

He laughed. "It is all good. I am doing well. Esta and I, we get along. It is a good match."

They paused at a traffic light and a mob of pedestrians crossed. They were in the thick of the high season, when tourists flood the streets and museums. Some of the expats grouched about summer here, but with glorious weather, long daylight hours, and plenty of places to escape the crowds, Faye loved it.

"But you worked for Rowena?"

"Ah, yes. I did. Esta thought I could help Rowena understand the company, navigate the politics, as you say."

"How did that work out?"

He grimaced. "I could have done more if she had let me. I grew up with Luca and Matteo. Esta's nephews, they are in charge now, yes? They were like older cousins to me. I know how they think. But Rowena, she did not accept my advice."

"How so?"

He glanced around the van, but the other guests were occupied in their own conversations. "She wanted to get a position at the headquarters, away from the hotel division. She approached them straight on, very American. They refused, of course. She was brought here to work for their aunt. Why harm that relationship for a—" he paused, as if to hunt for the right word. "For a nobody."

He coughed. "I mean no disrespect. Rowena was very capable. But there are many capable people in this world, yes? Rowena was not as special as she might have believed."

Faye felt a pang for Esta. She'd said yesterday that Rowena was supposed to take over when she retired. But Rowena had been angling to switch lanes. "But why would Rowena want to change positions? She'd only been here a few months. Wasn't she happy?"

He shrugged. "She said the real power was with Matteo and Luca. She wanted to be closer to them."

It didn't paint a very attractive image of Rowena's professional life, and Faye felt a flicker of satisfaction. Between Rowena's superstar career and running accomplishments, not to mention handsome, doting husband, the expat gang had put the woman on a pedestal. There was something nice about knowing she hadn't been quite so perfect after all.

"Maybe she was afraid that you'd tell Esta if she asked for help."

"Maybe. I don't hide my family. Or that Esta is my ticket out of this peasant purgatory."

Faye laughed. "Is it so bad, being an assistant?"

He smiled. "You mean making sure the kitchen is full of Rowena's vegan snacks and high-protein meals? It is fine, but I was raised to do more, you understand?"

For the first time, Faye noticed the young man's expensive watch and the cut of his shirt. It had not been purchased off the rack.

"I want to make a bigger contribution," he went on. "Soon enough, Esta will tell my family I am reformed, and I can return to our businesses."

The van swung away from residential streets and drove next to the high walls that circled the Vatican. They were almost to the museum.

"Tell me," Stefano said. "Why did Esta send me today? This tour may be very good, but it is not something Esta would involve herself in. The marketing department, they handle things like this."

Faye was wondering that herself. She was prepared for Stefano to try to convince her to sell the building. Burt would say it was a negotiation strategy, showing an interest in Faye's friend's business in hopes of getting something in return. "I have no idea. Maybe she wants to give you a nice day out."

Thomas led them through to the museum entrance. "It would be a Herculean feat to see everything in this museum in a day, even in a week, so we will not try. We are artists, and our focus is on the masterworks here that will help us in our craft, yes? We'll leave the historical bits and bobs to the tourists."

They were behind a small group of South Americans, and Thomas gave them a meaningful look as he spoke. "When we get through the turnstile, we will make a beeline for the classical statues."

Thomas led them at a brisk pace past relics from Ancient Egypt—as well as Roman copies—past a balcony and into a formal courtyard complete with trees in giant pots, a fountain, and classical sculptures galore. Some guests were breathing hard, but they all managed to keep up.

Thomas finally stopped in front of one sculpture. It was a naked young man with a cape hanging off his outstretched arm. "When it comes to composition, there's no better teacher than looking to the Greeks. This is *Apollo*, a Roman copy of a Greek sculpture."

The guests gathered round. Stefano and Faye hung back while Thomas began his lecture. "The Greek Golden Age lasted only fifty years. Think about that for a moment. Those ancient Greeks who we hold in such esteem were at their peak for just half a lifetime. But the Romans were sharp enough to recognize a good thing when they saw it, and they copied a lot of the art, including this statue."

Thomas looked the dapper professor today in a button-down shirt open at the collar and his sleeves rolled up to his elbows. "The folks in the Renaissance came along fifteen hundred years later and were just as dazzled as the Romans. They did the same: they copied the art. And that's what we are going to do in the studio tomorrow."

A family approached with two teen girls who looked as if they'd like to be anywhere but there. The children glanced at the statue, then moved on.

Thomas gestured around the room with a rolled-up sheaf of notes. "What I want you to notice today is how alive these sculptures are. The artists captured their subjects in motion. See how Apollo's weight is on his back leg? It was a revolutionary idea."

"Fascinating," Nan said. Her voice was unnaturally loud. "Such a clear explanation. I feel like I have a new understanding of art history now. Thank you, Thomas."

Thomas grinned. "Connoisseurs in the Renaissance considered this sculpture to be the most perfect work of art in the entire world. They loved its balance, its lightness. All important things. And totally different from this next piece."

He led them to a monstrous statue of a muscled man fighting a hopeless battle against a giant snake. The beast was twisted around the man and seemed on the verge of crushing him. Two boys were in the scene looking just as hopeless.

"*Laocoön and His Sons,*" Thomas said. "It's the Trojan priest who said beware of Greeks bearing gifts. What do you see?"

"My worst nightmare," one of the guests said.

Thomas grinned. "You and Indiana Jones, right? This sculpture's all about motion and power. It's terrifying."

Jean, in her "World's Best Grandma" shirt, nudged Barb. "How about painting something like that for your daughter's living room?"

"Perish the thought."

Thomas shook his head. "This is a masterwork. Pliny said it was the greatest of all art works, but then it was lost for more than a thousand years. When it was discovered in the fifteen hundreds, they actually carried it through the streets. Can you imagine?"

Faye couldn't.

"People had read about it in the ancient texts, and then they actually found it," Thomas continued. "We know Michelangelo saw it and a lot of his work, and that of so many others, is directly influenced by this very piece."

Faye tried to appreciate the sculpture. Laocoön did look tortured. And the marble was perfectly smooth. But it didn't move her. And she wouldn't want it in her living room, even if someone offered to carry it up all those stairs.

Nan raised her hand. "How does a sculpture like this get lost?"

It was a good question. The massive sculpture wasn't the sort of thing you could misplace.

"Tastes change," Thomas said. "I'd say we should be grateful it was forgotten rather than taken to bits and used for parts, which happened to so much of the art and architecture of the time."

"It was buried at the palace of Emperor Titus," Stefano said. "The conquerors did not have the same appreciation for art. It was discovered with other statues that had the same burial. Michelangelo, he was at the excavation."

Stefano hadn't struck Faye as an art fan. Perhaps a knowledge of art was part of the upbringing for a rich young man here.

Thomas nodded his approval and led them past objects from the Etruscan era, waving a hand as he strode by. "Nice art. Important people. Not our focus today."

Barb stopped a moment to look at a sarcophagus of a long-dead nobleman. "Amazing, isn't it? Looks like the super at one of my old apartments."

"It's a shame we're not doing an in-depth tour." Jean's lips were pinched, giving her the expression of a pig who'd tasted lemon juice. "The collection here is priceless. And the idea we're breezing past it all just pains me more than I can say."

Stefano leaned over to Faye. "There is always one person who wants to see everything, no?"

Faye laughed, and Stefano went on. "Thomas is very good. It is not always easy to bring the old works to life. My grandfather, he collects art and likes to tell me the stories behind them. His passion, that is what makes it interesting."

"He's a collector like Esta?"

"No. He likes old things that everyone already agrees are valuable. Esta, she likes to discover new artists. She is a gambler. She has made some very good discoveries."

They rejoined the group, which had gathered around a giant fresco depicting clusters of white men milling about in a remarkably three-dimensional building.

"Look at the lines in the painting." Thomas said. "Notice how the tiles are arranged, their focus leading your eye straight to the center. And the columns are all pointing to the middle. Every sightline is drawing our attention to the main action in the center."

"Someone said that Rowena was interested in collecting art," Faye said. "Was that Esta's influence?"

"If it was just for the wall, she would have had no problem. But if she wanted it to pay off like Esta's purchases, she would need to be very lucky." Stefano made a dismissive gesture. "I do not believe she made a purchase yet. She was talking with a dealer."

"Cliff Stewart?"

"Her running friend? No, she asked for the name of Esta's dealer."

Faye was having trouble getting a clear image of Rowena. Stefano said she was trying to land a job away from Esta, yet she was trying to imitate her mentor's hobby.

"Did Esta and Rowena get along?"

He hesitated. "Of course. Esta chose Rowena as her protégé. Her successor."

"But Rowena was trying to get a job with the nephews."

Thomas was guiding the guests away to the next masterpiece, but Stefano stayed anchored in his spot. "I do not want to give you the wrong impression. Esta and Rowena worked very well together. Rowena was confident, without fear. When we faced issues, she said they could be solved, and many times, they were."

"What kind of issues?"

Stefano shrugged. "Anything. Everything. The advertising was behind schedule because of a delay in approvals. Rowena said they would hit their deadline, and they did. There was an issue with supplies for the housekeeping department. A price increase from a supplier. Rowena said that they could get the costs down, and they did."

It was what Esta had said. Rowena had a confidence that seemed to manifest things into being. And most times, she was right. How annoying. "No disgruntled employee issues?"

"Ah, you are looking for a motive. I am afraid not. There were management things. Important to the turnover, but boring to everyone else."

Faye tried not to feel disappointed. She hadn't consciously realized she'd been casting around for an explanation. But Stefano was right. Annoyances at a workplace were irritating, but not worth killing over.

"No wonder Esta wanted Rowena to take over when she retired. Rowena must have been a very positive energy in the office. And she was working hard to secure Esta's legacy with my building."

Another group entered the room, and Thomas moved down the hall. "When we talk about sight lines in your sketches, think about how this work draws your attention, and consider what you can do. Now for the real masterpiece…."

"You seem like a nice woman," Stefano said. "I shouldn't say anything, but Esta does not want your building."

"I'm sorry?" Esta had been chasing Faye's building for years.

"It is, as you say, her legacy. And when the project is complete, she has agreed to exit, to leave the company. If the project is not completed, she does not have to retire. It makes sense in a tangled way, no?"

Stefano's explanation was a modern version of Penelope, the patient wife of Odysseus who promised to remarry when she finished her weaving. She ripped her work out each night so the deadline would never come.

Esta was a rich woman with a powerful pedigree, passed over in favor of the younger generation when her nephews were selected to lead the company. If she was being forced out, delaying her final project would be a reasonable way to hang on. Perhaps that was why Esta had not pushed harder for Faye's building yesterday. The older woman said she wanted to buy, but she'd also given Faye an out.

Faye's expression must have changed, because Stefano hurried on. "She has not said any of this to me. It is just my suspicion, yes? I may be wrong. I am, as my family reminds me, just a small, unimportant piece of the DiLorenzo machine. After all, what does an assistant know?"

Everything, Faye thought. If you want to know what is going on in an organization, you ask the assistants. They are the invisible hands who anticipate their boss's desires before they are even aware of them. They understand the politics in a way few others recognize.

Stefano was right. Poor Esta.

"If you would like my advice, Faye, take whatever the last offer was on your building. Luca and Matteo are losing interest in the hotels very fast. There is more money to be made elsewhere, and it may be Esta does not have the time she thinks. If they turn her money off, your building will not sell to DiLorenzo. And I do not know anyone else would value it as much."

Here was the sales pitch she'd expected. And yet, Faye believed Stefano was telling her the truth about Esta. George's defection aside, Faye was an excellent judge of character. This awkward young man struck her as trustworthy. At least, she hoped he was.

Faye put her hand on his arm and squeezed. "*Grazie*, Stefano. I hope you get back to your family business soon."

He smiled. "I will soon enough. But for now, this is not so bad, even if I am working on the weekends."

"Is that typical?"

"Yes, but Esta is very considerate. When she realized how late it was, she insisted we leave for the party immediately so Rowena would not be very late. Maybe I need to come up with more of a social life, no?"

"Just don't go around opening any more drinks in the car."

He grinned at her. "The price of being an assistant to an American. A good Italian would never drink in an automobile. I was opening it for Rowena."

He shook his head at the memory. "It does not feel real, does it? That Rowena was alive on Friday and dead today."

Faye was feeling the same way.

Thomas had gathered the group outside the Sistine Chapel. The museum didn't allow talking inside the famous room, so he was telling them what to look for in advance.

"We're nearly done, aren't we?" Barb rubbed her forehead. "I'm approaching art overload."

Even Jean, who had wanted to see the entire museum, was looking less keen than she had at the start of the tour. Even great art gets tedious.

Thomas led the way into the Sistine Chapel, where Michelangelo had single-handedly painted the history of the world over nearly six thousand square feet. Breathtaking, mind-blowing, and a bit over the top.

They oohed and aahed, then Thomas led them to the exit reserved for tours. It would save the fifteen-minute walk back to the main entrance. "Ready? There's no going back if we exit."

Stefano made a mock bow. "I must return to the office and prepare my report. I will get a taxi outside. This has been most delightful and informative."

Faye's chaperoning duties were complete. Ilaria would have a delicious lunch waiting for the group. Faye was about to follow along, when she thought of the Caravaggio painting inside. If she saw it now, she could really soak it in. Then, when she came back with the Caravaggio Società, she'd be able to express the artistic appreciation they would expect from the Società's champion.

"Go on without me," she said. "I have a few more things to see here."

"You're sure you want to be alone?" Thomas asked.

Maggie had probably told him to keep an eye on her, same as Burt. But in all of Rome, Faye couldn't imagine a more secure place than the Vatican Museum.

Chapter Nine

*Caravaggio's contemporaries grudgingly agreed that he did an excellent job of
capturing the grime, gore, and brutality of everyday life. However, there was no
consensus that these subjects constituted fine art.*
—Caravaggio: Brash, Brutish, and Brilliant

Faye dodged a group of women taking selfies as she made the long
walk back toward the main museum. She crossed a courtyard and
passed through an arched doorway with red letters spelling out
"Pinacoteca" in mosaic tiles. The Vatican's picture gallery had all the greats:
Raphael, Leonardo da Vinci, Giotto, and, most important for Faye that day,
Caravaggio.

Most of the art inside the grand hall was not to Faye's taste. It was the
old-fashioned two-dimensional stuff that's important to art historians, but
not particularly attractive to modern eyes. It would probably look nice in
some Medieval church with candles flickering and parishioners who had
never seen anything any better, but it wasn't exactly stuff you'd want on
your wall.

Just as bad, the triptychs and other religious paraphernalia were all
crammed together without an altar or stained-glass window in sight. It was
like having a gorgeous designer couch in a tiny room scooched up next to
a Gehry chair on one side and a Ming vase on the other. All very nice on
their own, but too much right next to each other.

Moving through the hall was like moving through time. Pieces started
to have a different feeling. More vibrant, more alive. Faye was in the

Renaissance area. She must be getting close to the Caravaggio.

She studied the picture labels as she moved along, looking for Caravaggio's *The Entombment of Christ,* when she noticed Cliff and Lilly Stewart in the middle of the hall. Rome really was a small place. The couple was in front of the picture Faye had been hunting for.

The painting itself was massive, and it showed Christ's body being carried by his friends. It was a subject Faye had seen from different artists more times than she could count. This one was a standout.

Caravaggio had painted most of the scene in darkness, with a spotlight focused on Christ's body. The effect was like one of those gorgeous modern-day black-and-white photographs where the subject is laid bare and painfully human.

The figures in the picture were rather ordinary. Just regular people caught up in something they hadn't signed on for. For the first time, Faye thought about the people who had lived alongside Christ. What had they thought as the events unfolded? They couldn't possibly have imagined their stories would be told and retold thousands of years later.

Cliff took a step back. "Faye! What a surprise. We couldn't face going to work today. Are you taking your solace in art, too?"

Rowena's running partner wore his hair in a ponytail and Lilly wore a peasant skirt. They had the air of latter-day-hippies about them which Faye always found slightly off-putting.

Lilly wrapped Faye in a hug. Her arms were soft and surprisingly comforting. "How are you? I mean, Rowena dying in your house. It's too awful."

Faye had always had a feeling this woman didn't like her very much. Probably because she was such good friends with Faye's soon-to-be-ex-husband George.

"I'm staying with the Whites for now. I was just here with Maggie's tour, and it felt like a shame leaving the museum without seeing a few more paintings." There was no need to mention wanting to get a jump on the Caravaggio Società.

"Great art is humbling," Cliff said. "Reminds us of our place in the world."

Faye nodded. The characters in the painting did seem real. Maybe that what was so special about it.

"I've known a lot of death in my life," Cliff went on. "You can't be an addict without loss. But it doesn't ever hurt any less."

Ah, yes, Cliff and his addiction talk. There was nothing wrong with being a former addict. Staying sober was admirable. But Cliff had a way of bringing every conversation back to his recovery, as if he were somehow a deeper person because he'd been through a hell of his own making.

"It was my idea to come see the Caravaggio," Lilly said. "Your email about celebrating the work of a master seemed like a good distraction right now.

The point of the Caravaggio Società was to see all the pictures as a group, but this wasn't the time to say so, at least not directly. "I hope you'll come with everyone on Wednesday to Santa Maria del Popolo. Experiences are so much deeper when they're shared with others. I know I read that somewhere, and it's true, isn't it?"

"That's what I tell Lilly about the importance of races," Cliff said. "You could run a hundred miles alone, but to be out there with others achieving the same goal, that's where you really feel like you're doing something."

Faye's phone buzzed with a local number. "Excuse me just a minute."

She stepped to the side and answered. It was Inspector Nardelli. "Would you have an objection to a search of your home?"

"Search?" Faye was aware of Cliff and Lilly standing a few feet away. She lowered her voice. "Of course not, that's fine." What else would a person say when involved in a police investigation? "But why now?"

"We have the toxicology report, Signora Masters, confirming Rowena Burke was poisoned. Now, we look to where it came from. You understand?"

This was really happening. Rowena really had been murdered. Faye hadn't realized she was holding onto some hope that it was a mistake. That the police were overreacting. That they'd come back with an undetected blood clot or weakness in her heart. But no. Someone had killed Rowena, and the police thought it might be connected to her.

Faye swallowed. If she were behind Rowena's death, as Nardelli seemed to have hinted the other day, she would hardly have been foolish enough to keep the poison in her home, but the inspector wouldn't appreciate her pointing it out. Faye would just have to go along with it.

"I appreciate your diligence. Just tell me if there is anything I can do."

"Is everything all right?" Lilly asked when Faye returned to them. The museum was so quiet they wouldn't have had any problem hearing her side of the conversation.

"It was the police," Faye said. "They know for sure now. Rowena was poisoned."

"Oh, God," Lilly said. "It just doesn't make any sense."

Faye was aware of a family standing near them. A child of about ten seemed to be listening to every word. Faye angled her head toward the exit and the Stewarts followed her.

"The police were at our house on Saturday morning," Lilly said. "They were asking about the smoothie Cliff made. Where did the ingredients come from? Who else handled it? It was as if they suspected him of slipping something into it."

"They're just doing their jobs," Cliff said. "They were really interested in Rowena's running. She just qualified for the Valtellina 100, you know. It was what she'd been working toward for the better part of two years. Just knowing she'd finally gotten her points is a solace."

"It's the biggest race on the European ultra circuit," Lilly said. "One hundred miles up in the mountains. It's a brutal event, so you can't just sign up for it. You've got to prove you can handle it by completing a bunch of other races. Cliff finally qualified in the same race Rowena did last weekend. It's one reason they made such good training partners. They were both just a few points away from a shared goal."

"Gosh." Faye didn't know what else to say. She enjoyed running more than any of her friends. She liked the rhythm and the repetition of it. But ten miles was about where she maxed out. "How do you train for something like that?"

"A lot of hours on the trail," Cliff said. "It's been a great way to explore the countryside, but it means Lilly puts up with me being gone a lot on the weekends."

"And falling asleep at six every night," Lilly said. "He sometimes goes out at 3 a.m. just to get used to running with a headlamp."

The three made their way toward the exit, not stopping to look at any of the other art. Was this what it had been like to walk these halls when this palace was private, off limits to ordinary people? Its denizens would have taken the art for granted, considering it just part of the decor.

"It's about learning to run when your body's telling you to sleep," Cliff was saying. "The Valtellina can take thirty to forty hours to complete. That's running through two nights. It's insane."

Faye agreed, but Cliff's excitement made it clear he considered the Valtellina to be the good kind of crazy.

"I can always one-up the women complaining that their husbands spend too much time playing golf. At least those men never play through the night." Lilly's tone was affectionate.

Cliff gave his wife a squeeze. "It keeps me clean and sober. And I'm going to take a break after the Valtellina."

Faye remembered Adam saying the same thing. "Rowena, too, right?"

"That's news to me," Cliff said. "She was getting some really good times. Rowena was talking about dialing it up after the next race, not back."

"Rowena was buying a new watch to help with training," Lilly said. "She wanted one like Cliff's and came by to see it last week. The things they can do with GPS are amazing. She wanted to see all the functions."

Cliff dodged a tour group wearing headphones that had stopped right in front of him. He moved lightly on his feet. Faye could imagine him jumping from stone to stone down a rocky path. "I've promised Lilly at least six months of a normal life," he said. "Though I'm not sure I even remember what that's like."

"What would you do, Cliff?" Lilly said. "Sleep until six?"

He laughed. "Let's not get crazy. Maybe five."

Faye blinked in the sunlight when they finally stepped outside. A silence had settled over them, and it was the natural time to part ways, but Faye found herself wanting to stay with these two. They were company. More than that, she was actually enjoying them. She shouldn't have written them off so quickly before.

"I heard Rowena was buying a picture," Faye said to keep the conversation going. "Was she doing it as an investment, hoping to find new artists like Esta?"

"You didn't say anything about that, Cliff." Lilly put on the sunhat that had been dangling from her wrist. It was pink with yellow poppies. It made her look younger.

With his job at the auction house, Cliff played the local art expert when members of the gang were purchasing art. It should have been a softball question to get the conversation rolling again, but he frowned.

"Nothing like that. She thought Adam could use a little cheering up and I suggested she buy a piece of art."

"What kind of cheering up?" Faye asked. The three were walking toward Trastevere. The crowds had thinned a few blocks from the Vatican, and they were able to walk in the shade of the trees along the Tiber.

"A job he was hoping for fell through. She said he was feeling down about not getting it, and I said a new hobby might help."

Faye stopped. "Fell through? Adam said he decided not to take the job."

Cliff shrugged. "People tell themselves all kinds of stories to make their realities more bearable."

"Cliff and Rowena talked about everything on those runs," Lilly said. "He was her spiritual guru."

Cliff shook his head. "No one's an expert on life, but I'm happy to share anything I've learned on my journey."

Rowena hadn't struck Faye as a tortured soul. "What kinds of things?"

"Everything. Like this weekend, she was worried about some ethical issue," Lilly said. "She was asking Cliff what you should do if you find out someone's been lying: should you get involved or stay out of it?"

Faye flushed. Rowena had been talking about Faye and the bank accounts she was hiding from George. If Rowena had mentioned Faye's name, Cliff wasn't letting on.

"Other times, it was to complain Stefano hadn't bought the right type of almond milk," Lilly continued. "She was all over the place."

"She didn't meditate," Cliff said. "It helps focus the mind, but Rowena said she was too busy. She didn't realize slowing down would help her do more. It's the curse of modern life."

"I toured the Vatican with Stefano this morning," Faye said. "I liked him."

"He only has the job because he's practically a member of the DiLorenzo family," Lilly said. "If Rowena could have hired her own assistant, she would have. She felt like his loyalties were to Esta instead of to her."

So Stefano was right. Rowena hadn't trusted him.

They walked along in silence, and Faye wondered if the police were still at her apartment. She imagined bins of sugar spilled on the counter and her jars of spices ransacked. *Be reasonable*, she told herself. They would be looking for poison, not turning everything upside down.

Cliff's kitchen might be getting the same treatment since he'd been the one to bring the smoothie mix. "It sounds like the police are focused on the things Rowena ate at the party," Faye said. "Did they take anything from your home?"

"Because of the smoothie?" Cliff said. "It was a mix another runner gave me. I've drunk loads of it, and I'm fine."

"Not at the party, though," Lilly said. "Cliff put it down and didn't get a chance to drink it. The police were really interested in that, as if it were suspicious."

Cliff coughed. "They're just doing their job."

Faye felt a glimmer of something. Relief, she realized. Maybe this wasn't about her, or about Rowena. If the smoothie was involved, it could be about Cliff. The former addict was sure to have a complicated history.

"The police asked if there were any runners Cliff didn't get along with," Lilly said. "Can you imagine someone wanting revenge for cutting the line to a porta potty or taking the last massage table in a recovery tent?"

Cliff laughed. "People go crazy during the races, but it's usually in the form of grouchiness toward their support crew. And once the race is over, anyone with an ounce of courtesy apologizes and moves on. Tensions run high in the moment. Our loved ones get that."

Lilly squeezed his hand. "You're a perfect gentleman out there, always have been."

"Anyway, the police picked up the rest of my green juice for testing, just in case. I'm not going to sweat it in the meantime."

"I'm just so grateful that Cliff didn't drink it," Lilly said. "I don't even like to imagine what would have happened."

Faye thought back to the party. Cliff had made two glasses of the green stuff. "It was lucky you put it down." She tried to remember washing the glass, but couldn't.

Cliff shook his head. "Didn't get the chance."

"Cliff crushed it in that last race," Lilly went on. Faye didn't remember her ever being so chatty. "He beat Rowena by a good hour last weekend. Rowena was used to beating Cliff, and she wasn't happy when he passed her. What did she expect? That you would hold off and finish alongside her just because you were friends?"

Cliff shot his wife a look like the ones George always gave Faye when she said too much about office politics at cocktail parties.

"She was disappointed, but she got over it." Cliff kicked a stone out of their path like a professional soccer player making a winning goal. It landed at least twelve feet ahead of them. "Rowena was very competitive. I think she liked ultras because it's one of the few sports where women can win races outright, not just the female division."

"Was Rowena good enough to have a shot at winning?"

Cliff snorted. "Not even close. She was getting a lot better, though. Who knows? Maybe with more time and focus she could have been." Cliff pulled a folded baseball cap from his back pocket and put it on. "In these races, the only thing that matters is not getting a DNF, that's a Did Not Finish. I've been in enough therapy to know I use running to replace my old addictions. Rowena was running to prove something to herself."

"What?"

He shrugged. "Tough childhood. Father in jail, mother ditched and left her with a string of relatives. Rowena probably wanted to show herself she still had what it took to be a survivor."

"I had no idea." Rowena had an Ivy League pedigree. Faye hadn't ever wondered what Rowena's life had been like before that.

"She didn't talk about it much. Didn't want people to label her a victim." Cliff smiled. "She would have been royally pissed to have died like this."

"If this all turns out to be a stupid accident, I don't know if that's better or worse." Lilly flushed. "I'm sorry, Faye. I didn't mean to sound crass. I'm still struggling with the idea of Rowena's death being murder. I just think she must have taken something by mistake."

"It wouldn't matter to Rowena," Cliff said. "She'd still be dead."

Faye's phone rang. It was George. She couldn't dodge him forever. She accepted the call and let herself fall a few feet behind Cliff and Lilly. "Yes, George, what is it?"

His voice came through as it always did on the phone, low and hushed, as if he were having a conversation in a quiet room and didn't want to disturb anyone. "This is ridiculous, Faye. My lawyer says you're asking for more time. What's the problem?"

"My lawyer is checking some records. I want to be thorough."

George's voice was pleading. "I'm burning through money, Faye. I need this to be done."

Faye had heard George's girlfriend had expensive taste. It would serve him right if she bankrupted him.

"And what about my things?" George went on. "You said you'd send them and—"

"If they were so important, you should have taken them when you left."

"I want all this to end. Do you understand?"

"It's not a good time, George. One of the gang died last night, at my home. The police are involved."

There was a pause, and Faye heard a babble of voices in the background. Where was he calling from? It didn't sound like a California backyard.

"I didn't know that," he said finally. "I'm sorry."

"You should be. And while we're talking about death, please stop telling the kids I'm cutting them out of my will. When Ronnie was here, he said you told him I'd changed it. Aren't the kids a little old for you to be trying to win them over?"

90

"He was looking for money for some hair-brained venture," George said. "I told him to ask his rich stepmother before it was too late, that's all."

Faye was the wronged party here. George was the one who left the marriage. But Faye was aware of Cliff and Lilly listening, and was careful to speak in her most polite, most calm voice. "Just stop calling me, George. And stop telling the kids things that aren't true."

Faye clicked off. She hated that her heart was pounding. "I'm so sorry. That was George, and we've been playing phone tag."

"How is George?" Lilly asked in an artificially cheerful voice. She wasn't very good at pretending she hadn't heard every word. "We miss him at the university."

"Enjoying the weather, I believe. He always loved California."

George's preference for the West Coast had been one of the many unfathomable things about her husband. They lived in paradise here in Rome, and instead George kept pushing for the couple to return to the States.

"Have you talked with Adam?" Faye asked. "How is he holding up?"

"I left a message," Cliff said. "He's probably in shock. I think we all are."

Faye was reluctant to say goodbye when they reached her building. It had felt good to have company. "Will I see you on Wednesday at Santa Maria del Popolo?"

Lilly looked as if she was going to say no, so Faye plowed on. "The distraction will be good for everyone. What did you say, Cliff, about great art reminding us of our place in the world?"

"I'll try," Lilly said.

Faye stood on the step and watched Cliff and Lilly walk hand-in-hand down the flower-lined street. It was Faye's favorite type of summer day: hot enough to wear your prettiest sundress without being so miserable you needed to take refuge in an air-conditioned cafe. She should be out there enjoying everything the city had to offer. Instead, she was alone, bracing herself for the havoc the police had wreaked on her apartment.

Chapter Ten

Caravaggio gave as much attention to the fruit and flowers in his paintings as to the human figures. The artist's homage to the traditional still life, widely considered the lowest of the artistic genres, was despised by many contemporaries.
—Caravaggio: Brash, Brutish, and Brilliant

The door to the Masterpiece Tours office was open, so Faye stopped in. She was in no rush to get upstairs to see the state of her home. The large sitting room was empty, but Thomas was in the courtyard talking with Barb and Jean. The guests were stationed at easels, laughing at something Thomas said. Two other guests reclined on lounge chairs, eyes closed and books open on their laps. Faye wandered into the kitchen and found Ilaria slicing onions.

"Thomas told me about the death. *Mi dispiace.*" The cook was in her mid-twenties and wore her long brown hair tied back in a ponytail. She had the dark good looks Italian women were known for and was dressed in stylish jeans, colorful top, and a chunky white beaded necklace that Faye instantly coveted.

"What security have you taken?" Ilaria's movements were fast and neat, one slice after another. Her tone was as casual as if she'd been asking Faye about the weather.

"Security? I took a self-defense class back in college, but that's not—"

Ilaria put her knife down. "Thomas said it is possible that you were supposed to die, not this other woman. You must be careful, Faye."

Faye was not entirely clear on Ilaria's life outside of school and Mas-

92

terpiece Tours. Her family ran a business, which Maggie had hinted was connected to illegal operations, the mafia even, but Faye had always assumed her friend was exaggerating. Now she wasn't so sure.

"I'm staying with the Whites," Faye said.

Ilaria tsked. "That is not security. I can make a phone call and have someone here in the hour. Yes?"

"No." At any other time, Faye would have loved walking around with a handsome bodyguard at her side. She imagined the gang ogling when she ran into them, and she'd whisper casually that her escort had once been a member of the Italian Special Forces.

But with a real threat hanging over her, the idea left a sour taste in her mouth. It would be tantamount to admitting that Faye had been the target after all. And if that was true, that would mean Faye was someone who was so awful someone thought she deserved to die.

"You're really sweet, Ilaria, but no, thank you."

"You are in denial, maybe. But you can call me if you change your mind. Day or night, yes?"

"What are you making?"

"*Ragù alla bolognese.*"

"Lucky guests." Ilaria would serve the meat sauce the traditional way with an egg-based tagliatele. "Did Maggie sort out her paperwork issue?"

Ilaria reached for a bunch of celery and began dicing. "She was told to go to another office, then another. All to do with the change in address. Red tape like that, it will take weeks to complete."

Ilaria pushed the celery into a tidy pile and began chopping carrots into tiny cubes. "She said she'd like to see Neddy in his grave for selling the old place without telling her." Faye blanched and Ilaria hurried on, "Not that she is not grateful for this new location. Just the work to set it up."

Faye hoped Burt would keep quiet about Esta's offer.

"Would you like a biscuit?" Ilaria asked. "There are some left from lunch." Ilaria pointed to a plate of cookies. They were a mix of American-style chocolate chip and peanut butter. Faye shook her head.

Ilaria moved the vegetables to a sauté pan on the stove and reached around

Faye for some salt. The granola Faye had left out to cool had been packed into two glass jars.

"Thank you for putting the granola away for me. I thought the guests might like it with yogurt as an afternoon snack. It's *cardamomo*, a specialty of mine."

"You found the spice here? I borrowed it, thinking it was cinnamon. The words are very similar, no? *Cannela* for cinnamon and the English cardamom. I was rushing and took the wrong one. I am sorry I did not yet return it."

Faye waved off the apology. "Can you use the granola?"

Ilaria shook her head. "No more American food, please. The biscuits, they were bad enough. I had to make them so they would be ready for the guests. And the ingredients, they were not so easy to find. Guests come here for Italy, yes? Not their favorite peanut butter cookies. I had to take from your kitchen for that recipe, too." Ilaria's tone softened. "I do appreciate the idea, but no."

"It's no problem. Maggie and Burt will eat it."

Maggie thought of Adam, home alone with Daisy. When someone was in mourning, you put aside any other issues and offered them support. Rowena's close friend Cliff said he'd only bothered to leave a message. Faye hoped the rest of the gang had stepped up and done more. She texted Jessica and Heather.

Have you checked in with Adam? How is he?

She waited a few minutes, but there was no reply.

They probably hadn't. That was the problem with the gang. They were all perfectly nice, but not, well, reliable. That was why Faye was always the one organizing parties and setting up dinners. Without her, they didn't happen.

Faye looked again at the two jars. She'd drop one at Adam's, just to let him know people were thinking about him.

If anyone asked Faye why she was bringing baked goods to a man who'd betrayed her, she'd have said it was just the way she was raised: when something bad happens to a neighbor, you help, no matter your personal feelings. But part of her also wanted to see him again. Give him a chance to apologize for selling her out to Rowena. He might not, but there was no harm in trying.

Adam didn't answer when Faye buzzed his apartment from the street. She waited a minute and tried again. Still nothing, so she used the 1-2-3-4 code to get into the building. She climbed the stairs and knocked on his door. There was no response, not even Daisy. The pair must be out on one of their walks.

Faye let herself in and put the granola on the counter next to the cake and cinnamon rolls she'd brought on Saturday. It didn't look like Adam had eaten anything. Grief was taking its toll.

Faye let herself out and sent Adam a text. *Left granola at your house. Let me know if you need help with anything.*

Officer Piras called while Faye was at the market picking up goods to restock the Whites' pantry. "Inspector Nardelli requests that you come to the station right away."

Faye's heart thumped. "Is there news?"

"I cannot say."

Faye walked straight there and was relieved to be taken to Nardelli's office immediately. Nardelli and Piras sat at a desk with papers spread out on it. They were hard workers, and they had gotten results if they were already calling her in.

"Thank you for coming," Nardelli said. "Please have a seat."

Faye put the groceries on the floor and sat. The chair legs were uneven, and she rocked unsteadily when she leaned back. Faye forced herself to sit at attention.

Nardelli opened her folder. "We have received the results of the laboratory tests from the items in your home."

It had been just a few hours. Nardelli must have the clout and the political capital to get results so quickly.

"I really appreciate you calling me in to share the results in person. All clear, I assume?" Faye gave a small laugh, but a knot had developed in her stomach.

Nardelli shook her head. "The *burro di arachidi* in your kitchen contained poison."

"My peanut butter? I'm sure the tamper foil was intact when I bought that jar. I'm very careful about things like that."

Faye's mind was racing to catch up. Cliff's green sludge wasn't the source of the poison. Cliff hadn't been the target. This was about Faye.

She had bought the jar a few months ago to make Buckeye candies, which George adored. She used to make them for him at least once a month. A fact she was sure he hadn't bothered to mention to his lawyer. Faye had been a devoted wife, no matter how his memory was changing things.

"It doesn't make sense. I used peanut butter from that jar already. George and I were both fine."

Nardelli tapped the paper, which looked highly technical and, besides, was upside down. It could have said anything. "We believe the tampering occurred in your home, after you had opened the jar. When did you last use it?"

Faye tried to think. She leaned back and the chair wobbled with a small thump. "Two months, give or take." It wasn't very helpful, but she was having trouble focusing. Her peanut butter had been poisoned. Her's. Not Cliff's smoothie jumpstart. Not Rowena's drink. Faye's peanut butter. It made no sense.

Officer Piras handed Faye a cup of water and she took a sip. It didn't help. "You're saying the poison was intended for me."

"The evidence supports that, no?"

Faye stared at the woman across the table. The inspector probably faced all kinds of hardened criminals every day. Her bedside manner with victims, if that was what she was suggesting Faye was, was lacking.

Faye gripped the paper cup. "I'm having trouble wrapping my head around all this."

It was one thing for Maggie and Thomas to suggest that Faye had been the target. It was another for the police to find evidence of it.

"Who has access to your home? Does anyone have a key?"

"Everyone. All the expats in the gang, at least. They know the code to my lockbox." Faye had thought she was being so careful, changing the code after Rowena's death. Too little, too late.

Nardelli frowned. "We will need to speak with anyone who might benefit from your death."

"Of course." Faye mechanically wrote out George's contact information and phone numbers for the stepchildren.

"George gets half whether we divorce or if I die." She meant for her tone to be cavalier, but she found herself catching on the word die.

Nardelli glanced at the paper, then handed it to Piras. "Did you have any friction? Anything we should know?"

Faye thought of her call with George earlier that day. "Divorce is never easy."

Nardelli angled her head, but at least she didn't throw Faye's words about a happy, well-needed divorce back at her. "He would like it over and done with, that's all."

It sounded bad, even to her ears. Damn George. If he were still here, none of this would have happened.

"And where is Signor Masters?"

"California." At least, she'd assumed that's where he was calling from. The truth was, he could be anywhere. "But it couldn't hurt to double-check."

Did she really suspect George now? Bumbling, incompetent George? Faye couldn't believe it. But from what the police were saying, maybe this was a case of incompetence. The wrong woman had died. What was more incompetent than that?

Nardelli nodded. "Is there anyone else who would have a motive?"

"No one." Faye was vanilla. She made things better, but nothing to get excited about on her own. "I don't know what to say. I just, I can't believe this is about me."

Nardelli shook her head, as if everyone said this. Maybe they did. Maybe everyone walked around thinking their life was perfect until suddenly it wasn't. "Please tell me about your relationship with Adam Burke."

"Adam?" Faye struggled to follow Nardelli's line of questioning. "He's a friend."

"A close friend?"

"No, I wouldn't say that." Certainly not anymore.

"Some of your friends, they told us you and Adam were close. You hosted a party for his wife. But now you say no, you were not close?"

Faye shifted in her seat. "I suppose it's a question of semantics. If you want to know about his relationship with Rowena, I can tell you what I know, but—"

Inspector Nardelli held up her hand. Surely an officer shouldn't interrupt a victim. Faye wanted to be supportive of a fellow woman who had achieved a position of authority, but she was losing patience.

"Signor Burke says your behavior is extremely attentive. He did not file an official complaint, but he said that you have entered his apartment without permission. Taken his pet. Left unwanted gifts...."

Faye suddenly wanted nothing more than to be out of this room, with its dull green paint and scuffed floor. Old movies made being a woman in distress seem glamorous. Not this. The fluorescent lighting was cheap, and the room held an odor of onion that was going to cling to her skin all day.

"I really don't understand what's happening here. You said I might have been the intended target. Now you're suggesting I've done something wrong? Isn't it a little out of fashion to blame the victim?"

Faye could feel herself getting wound up, but she didn't stop. "I don't know what you're getting at, but I am a nice person. A person who other people like. I don't go out of my way to annoy anyone. I don't stand in the way of anyone getting what they want. I don't go around threatening to reveal secrets, and I don't get into relationships with people with a tendency toward violence or desperation. I am a nice, normal, middle-aged woman doing the very best she can, and I do not appreciate your line of questioning."

Nardelli opened her mouth as if to say something, but Faye kept going. "You'll just have to look harder at the Rowena side of things. Just because there was poison in my kitchen doesn't mean it was for me."

She hated the blank expressions on Nardelli and Piras' faces. "Rowena and her running friend Cliff were a little too chummy. Did anyone ask if there might be something more going on there? He's the one who made the smoothie. He could have poisoned the peanut butter to throw you off the scent. And he's a recovering addict. Who's to say he hasn't fallen back on his old ways?"

They didn't write anything down, so she kept going. "And why was her assistant Stefano even at the party in the first place? Has anyone asked that question? And Adam, who was so kind as to tell you I've been too attentive. What do you think that indicates? Someone who is trying to divert attention, maybe? Poison in my home doesn't prove anything."

Faye didn't know if what she was saying made any sense, and she didn't care. She wanted out of this room. She pushed her chair back and stood. Her shirt clung to her back, her pants were wrinkled, and she didn't care. "I'm sorry, officers. I really am. But you will have to look into Rowena's life before you come pointing fingers at mine."

Inspector Nardelli didn't stand but looked up at Faye. "It is always interesting, Signora Masters, when victims do not wish to help the police. It is natural for them to want justice, yes? But you are not being helpful. It makes me wonder why."

Faye noticed the smile creases on Nardelli's face for the first time. Perhaps in another life she was fun and outgoing, laughing all the time, but Faye had trouble imagining it.

"I understand you are depressed," Nardelli went on. "Your husband is gone. You perhaps developed an interest in Signor Burke. This, it is very common."

Nardelli couldn't have come up with this alone. The gang must have painted this picture of Faye. She flushed.

"The poison was in your home," Nardelli went on. "I have to consider if you put it in the *burro di arachidic* yourself. Seeking attention, yes? Perhaps you did not intend to do actual harm, but poison is not so easy to control. Did it go further than you expected?"

Faye laughed without thinking about it. From victim to killer? Were these people mad?

"I'm sorry, but this is too much. I appreciate your time and attention. If anything else occurs to me, I will let you know. But I'm afraid I must go."

She didn't even have the police on her side now. Wonderful.

Chapter Eleven

Caravaggio was pragmatic in his approach to art. He reused models' clothing, employed bland, easy-to-produce backgrounds, and frequently used himself as a cheap model.
—Caravaggio: Brash, Brutish, and Brilliant

Faye walked back toward Trastevere in a daze. She was crossing the Piazza Santa Maria when she heard voices calling her name. Nan and Paul Foster, her undercover promoters, sat at easels facing the octagonal fountain that dominated the square. Paul had sketched the fountain. Nan had drawn fifteen lines in what appeared to be random directions.

"I'm not feeling inspired, I'm afraid." Nan fanned herself with her sketchpad. "It's been such a nice day, but it's got to be almost time for cocktails."

"Nan's just jealous," Paul said. "Thomas called my sketches promising, and I told myself I'd make ten more before dinner. Here, look." Paul proudly passed a stack of drawings to Faye. He had captured one of the giant shells anchoring the fountain's design and was working on the ornate shield nearby.

"These are excellent, Paul. You're getting a nice balance in."

As fountains went, this one wasn't one of Rome's best. The water didn't move with much force, and there weren't any of the lunging serpents or striding gods that lent drama to many of the city's other water displays. But it was beloved for its role as a giant community bench. Wide steps wrapped around it, and neighbors often settled on them to catch up as they watched children play nearby. A few years ago, Faye had even joined the crowd here to watch a soccer match someone had projected onto a public screen.

"The tour was wonderful this morning," Nan said. "I hope that young man came away with a positive report."

The tour of the Vatican felt like it had been a week ago, not just a few hours. At that point, Faye had still been holding onto hope that it was all going to be a tragic accident. The police investigation was now real, and there didn't seem to be any doubt it was connected to her.

"I'm glad you're learning something." It was amazing, really, how you could talk about one thing and still be so worried about another. Faye must be a better actor than she'd ever given herself credit for. "I really appreciate you both coming on the trip and helping to boost everyone's experience."

"Are you kidding?" Nan said. "Paul's having the time of his life. No artifice required. Seriously, Thomas is really good. And the food! You've got to include a warning about the potential for weight gain."

Nan zipped her pencil into a case. "That said, I can't look at this piece of paper for one more minute. I've been eyeing that church over there. Want to join me?"

The Basilica of Santa Maria anchored one edge of the square. Like so many churches in Rome, it was squashed in the corner between two other buildings, totally unlike the church-on-a-green style at the heart of so many New England towns. But the insides were always impressive.

"I'd love to." The visit would be a good distraction.

It was cool inside the church, and the women stood in the entry for a moment, soaking it in. It reminded Faye of lingering in the dairy aisle of her grocery store back home on a hot day. "Let's sit in a pew," Faye whispered.

They took one right in the middle, and Faye enjoyed Nan's look of amazement as she took it all in. Unlike the fountain, the church was truly impressive.

Faye pointed up. "See the columns? They came from the Roman Baths of Caracalla, but they're from different places in the ruin, so there're all mismatched."

Some of the tall pillars were capped with the fancy scrolls of Ionic column capitals, while others had the highly decorative leaf-and-scroll toppers of Corinthian capitals. The lack of cohesion was out of place in this highly designed building with its glittering mosaics, coffered ceiling, and gilt-covered everything.

"Amazing." Nan kept her eyes up as she spoke.

"It is, isn't it?" Faye lived so close to it, yet not gone inside for at least two years. Faye loved Rome, but wondered if she really appreciated it anymore.

She thought of the old bit with the fish who's asked how the water is, and he answers, "What water?" You take your surroundings for granted.

Without George's job, what was she doing here? She might be the official welcoming committee, but she didn't have any close friends. The gang was too transient for that. Even Maggie and Burt, who were being lovely and supportive, were new friends. The expats who had known Faye the longest hadn't even bothered to check in. It was probably just a matter of time before Maggie and Burt drifted away, too.

Something about her tone must have caught Nan's attention. "How are you holding up, Faye? We saw the police going up to your apartment this afternoon."

Two tourists took seats behind them, so Faye got up, and she and Nan moved slowly around the perimeter of the church.

"It's a little stressful, actually. My jar of peanut butter was laced with poison, apparently." Faye forced a laugh. "If I'd been in the mood for peanut butter toast for breakfast, I'd have been the one to die, not Rowena."

And that was the real issue. Faye could have died.

"Oh, my dear." Nan patted her hand. "Paul was supposed to be on a friend's plane that crashed. He quit his job and left his high school girlfriend. That brush with death changed his life."

Faye bit her lip. "I'm glad there was a happy ending."

"I'm sorry, that was thoughtless of me," Nan said. "Paul says I'm always a Pollyanna. It's not the same thing at all. How terrible for you, to think someone wants you dead."

They stopped in front of the semi-circular dome with all the magnificent mosaics. It was what the church was known for. The style wasn't her taste—it was those old paper-cut-out style characters—but she did admire the sheer detail work involved. How did anyone piece together those tiny bits of color to create a cohesive picture? It was beyond her.

"It just makes no sense. Anyone who knows me knows I would never eat peanut butter." Faye forced a laugh. "My palette is a little more sophisticated than that, thank you very much."

Nan paused by a column and looked up. "Goodness, they are big, aren't they?"

They were. Faye had read that some of the columns had carvings of Egyptian gods at the top, which the Christians had failed to remove before installing them in the church. Probably because they didn't know what the pictures were, the same way the early Christian invaders in Greece did their best to obliterate the Olympian gods in the Greek temples, but left winged figures intact because they thought they were angels.

"What did the police say about the peanut butter?" Nan asked.

"They weren't explicit. I got the impression the inspector thought I might have poisoned the peanut butter myself."

Nan put her hand on Faye's arm. It felt warm and motherly. "I had nothing to do with this, Nan."

"That's a very good thing. I think highly of the Thompsons, and would I hate to think they introduced us to someone with such a bloodthirsty streak. But people will be saying it, Faye. You do see that, don't you?"

Faye swallowed. Nan was wrong. The people who knew Faye—Winnie, Heather, Jessica, and all the other regulars in the gang—they wouldn't think Faye had a hand in Rowena's death. Sure, the police had to investigate every angle. But no one who really knew Faye would believe it. There had to be another explanation, and the police would find it.

"Let's go find Paul," Nan said. "We should liberate him from the easel."

Paul had produced six more sketches, each with a slightly different centerpiece. His head gleamed with sweat as he passed them around. With all the stones retaining the heat of the day and no breeze to speak of, the piazza was baking.

"Let's get a drink before you head back to the group," Faye said. "There's a wonderful enoteca around the corner. You can fill me in on the tour so far."

Paul packed up the couple's gear and chatted about Thomas's instruction. Faye knew Nan would tell him about the state of the investigation soon enough, and Faye treasured this time while he was still treating her like a normal person. Not a victim, not a suspect, just a new acquaintance on the road to becoming a friend.

Glass-fronted, wood-paneled Enoteca Collina was two blocks away. It was just five o'clock on a Monday evening, and there were still plenty of tables indoors, where the air conditioning was going full blast by Italian standards.

Nan and Paul ordered local wines from the list on a blackboard, and Faye asked the waiter for his favorite. There was the usual buffet of house-made bites set up in the rear. At two euro a plate, it was a bargain.

Faye spotted Jessica and Heather filling their plates. Faye had introduced the two women when Jessica first arrived in Rome, arranging a dinner party with George and their husbands. It had been a fun night, and she'd been glad when she heard the two couples started doing things together.

Faye waved at her friends now, and they waved back but didn't approach. Faye took a sip of wine and watched as the two returned to their table. Could either of these women have given Nardelli the idea that there was something more to the relationship between Faye and Adam than she let on? Faye pushed the thought aside. Nardelli had been spitballing, that's all. And Faye had made the mistake of taking it personally.

Faye turned to Nan and Paul. "Come meet my friends. You'll love them." She pushed herself to her feet and waited while the couple followed more slowly. "Girls, girls, so nice to see you! Meet Paul and Nan, two dear friends visiting from the States. I'm making sure they get a dose of local culture before returning them to Maggie's tour. We'll join you."

Faye borrowed a chair from a nearby table, then organized some more nibbles. She looked around the table and smiled. *See?* she tried to telegraph to Nan. *These women like me. They trust me.* But Nan just reached for a potato chip, seemingly unwilling to catch Faye's eye.

104

"Have you lived in Rome long?" Paul asked.

"Almost two years," Jessica said.

"Nearly three for me," Heather said. "My husband's company is asking if they'll ever get him back in the States. We're living on borrowed time."

It was always sad when someone moved on, but maybe Faye's group had gotten stale, and what she needed was some fresh blood.

While Paul and Nan talked about a shared alma mater with Heather, Faye moved her chair closer to Jessica. "Have the police been talking to you? They've seen me twice now, and between you and me, they're coming up with some wild theories. I hope they're up for the job."

Faye wanted Jessica to say the police were treating everyone like suspects, that everyone knew Faye couldn't possibly be involved. But Jessica just shrugged. "They seem pretty thorough to me."

Faye took a sip of her wine. She'd followed the waiter's recommendation to try a dark one, but it tasted like a barnyard. "They were asking me about my friendship with Adam. I got the feeling that someone told them there was something between us."

"Oh, Faye." Jessica glanced away, then came back to meet Faye's gaze. "You don't have to do this. We all know you had a crush on Adam."

Faye felt her cheeks flush. "There was no crush. We were friends. He was closer to you than to me. I didn't even get an invitation to that dinner where you ate tripe."

Jessica shook her head. "I get it, Faye, I do. George treated you like garbage. You were in a slump, and Adam was there. He's fun and handsome. People get those crushes all the time. You wouldn't be the first woman to make a fool of herself over a man who wasn't interested." Heather made a shhshing movement, but it was too late. Jessica's suggestion was clear: she thought Faye was some sort of pathetic stalker.

Faye reached for her glass again, careful to keep her hand steady. "I think there's been some kind of misunderstanding." Nan caught her gaze, but Faye looked away. "I welcomed Adam and Rowena the same way I do everyone. That's all."

"I didn't mean anything," Jessica said. "You know me. Just too much wine."

"Have you seen Rowena and Adam's dog?" Heather's tone was bright, and it was clear she was trying to change the subject. "She's great with a frisbee. I must have watched Adam throw that thing at least two hundred times last weekend, and she caught every one."

That was the weekend of Rowena's race. Esta mentioned it was the first one Adam missed. Why?

"Our dog is terrible with a tennis ball," Paul put in. "Strips the fuzz off, then leaves the rubber carcasses all over the yard."

The conversation moved to cats and hamsters, and Faye tried to act a part of it, smiling and laughing when the others did, but she could feel Jessica and Heather looking at her. Nan had been right. Faye's friends suspected her, and they weren't trying very hard to hide it.

She should be grateful the pair didn't know about the bank accounts Rowena had been holding over her. If they knew she had an actual motive for wanting Rowena dead—something other than their vague gossip about jealousy—if would be the final nail in her coffin.

What hope did Faye have that the police would clear things up? Not much, given Nardelli's line of questioning. If Faye wanted her old friends back—her old life back—she'd have to find the solution herself.

Chapter Twelve

Caravaggio set out to snag the attention of Francesco Cardinal del Monte, a career-making collector. The artist produced two paintings of men being tricked out of their fortunes and displayed them where his mark would walk by. The collector appreciated the allusion and took Caravaggio under his wing.
—Caravaggio: Brash, Brutish, and Brilliant

I*f you want something done right, you need to do it yourself* was a mantra Faye lived by. She would like to believe the police would find Rowena's killer and get a conviction, but this was not the time to put her faith in others.

Faye dropped Nan and Paul at Masterpiece Tours and headed to the Whites'. Her mistake had been waiting on the sidelines, she realized. Now that she'd decided to take charge, Faye's outlook changed. She was not a pawn in someone else's game or a victim of circumstance. She would see this through.

Faye waved to the owner of a cafe and chatted for a moment with an elderly Italian neighbor who shared her passion for baking. Life felt, for a moment, almost normal. She had the apartment to herself. Burt was working late, and Maggie would be with the tour for hours. Faye settled down on the sofa with a notepad and pen. Understanding the victim was the key to understanding any crime. What she needed to do was learn more about Rowena's personal life.

Faye tapped the pad with her pen twice, trying to decide what to write. A list of what she knew about Rowena would probably be best. Faye tapped the pen again, then began.

Hard childhood

Good-but-not-great runner

Trying to cheer up Adam

Liked by her boss

Secretly trying to get job at HQ

She thought about listing "struggling with moral dilemma" but decided against it. If Faye showed this list to anyone, they'd want to know why she wasn't following up on the moral dilemma angle, and Faye could hardly explain that she already knew what Rowena had been struggling with, and that it was Faye's offer to swap the building for Rowena's silence. Besides, the issue was resolved. Rowena had taken her up on the offer.

Instead, Faye wrote:

Switched to high-protein vegan diet

It probably wasn't important, but it was the reason she'd drunk the smoothie in the first place.

Faye's phone rang. It was Maggie. Faye put the papers aside. "I'm so glad you called. I just met with the police. You're not going to believe it. They found poison in my kitchen. In the peanut butter, of all places. They're saying I might have been the target all along." She took a deep breath. "It's what you and Thomas said, but I'm not convinced. I'm—"

"Faye, I need a favor." Maggie sounded excited. "Thomas and I just got called about doing an interview on a U.K. television program. It'd be great publicity."

"Congratulations!" Faye bit her lip. Maggie hadn't called to check in on her. "Do you want some help finding an outfit? Green would look great on camera, and I think there's—"

"No. Well, yes, please, thank you. But that's not why I'm calling. The interview is tomorrow morning. It's called 'Tuesday Travels,' and someone canceled at the last minute. They want Thomas and me to sub in. I hate to ask, but is there any way you could take the tour in the morning? The guests love you, and I know you're probably busy, but...."

Faye smiled into the phone, an old trick to force a cheerful tone. "I'd be happy to. What's the tour of?"

"The Capitoline Museum. Thomas has arranged for a friend to do an 'artist in residence' talk in the studio first thing, so the art instruction will be covered. But if you could take them on the tour, I'd be so grateful."

"I love the Capitoline. You're doing me a favor by asking me to go."

The Capitoline was Faye's favorite museum. Unlike all the places in the city stuffed with Renaissance and Baroque art, this museum was mostly statues, and mostly from the ancient period. Attractive pieces with interesting stories about a time in history that had played out like a soap opera. Plenty of love affairs and villains and complicated family histories.

"I really appreciate it, Faye. I need to get back to the guests. But I'm sorry about the police. We'll talk about it tonight. You'll be careful, won't you?"

Maggie wasn't like Jessica and Heather. Her friend was busy, but she was concerned. "Of course." Faye said. "I'll get some outfits ready for you."

Faye spent forty-five minutes putting together some options from Maggie's closet. She wished she'd thought to ask if the interview would be standing or seated. Either way, she'd found some good choices.

Faye fussed over Burt when he came home, making him a plate of leftovers. He had only taken a few bites when Maggie arrived. They both listened as she told them about her conversation with the police.

"The thing is, anyone who knows me knows I don't eat peanut butter. They could have chosen a hundred and one other things in my kitchen and been successful. The police are going at this all wrong. Whatever's going on here, I wasn't the target."

Faye and Burt exchanged a look.

"Humor me, all right?" Faye showed them her notes.

"Not much to go on." Burt handed it back. "Why did Adam need cheering up?"

"Cliff said Adam was feeling down because his job fell through. But he told everyone he'd decided against taking it."

"So you've caught Adam in a lie," Maggie said. "That's promising. It's always the husband, isn't it?"

"Hmph." Burt tapped the paper. "Just to play devil's advocate, where is

George in this whole mess?"

"We're not talking about Faye right now," Maggie said. "This is about Rowena. It's about building theories. We're not narrowing down to one solution. Think broadly."

"Fine. Then I say Adam laced Rowena's smoothie with poison, then put some poison into your peanut butter to confuse the situation." Burt leaned back, arms crossed, looking pleased with himself.

"Oh really, Burt," Maggie said. "That's a little complicated, don't you think?"

"Not at all. He handed the drink to her, right?" Burt said. "All he'd have to do was turn his back and drip something into it, then slip into Faye's fridge another time. Easy as can be."

Faye took a sip of her wine. The Whites' home was small, but it had a lived-in feeling that was surprisingly comfortable. Burt's briefcase was on the kitchen counter, and Maggie's shoes were by the sofa where she'd kicked them off earlier. Even the stack of mail on the coffee table, which would have driven Faye crazy in her own home, seemed to add a warm feeling.

"I can't accept that poisoning a drink is as simple as that," Maggie said. "Get a glass and try."

Burt obliged, and the two women laughed as he cradled the glass next to his body with one arm so that he could use both hands to pretend to unscrew an imaginary cap from an imaginary jar.

"That's hardly fair," Burt said. "Adam would have practiced. Like those young men who put Rohypnol into people's drinks. It must be possible."

"Possible, but not the only option," Maggie said. "Cliff had easy access. I'm not saying he did it, but he was in the kitchen alone with her drink, wasn't he? He'd have had all the time in the world, no practice necessary. And he's an addict. That speaks to a troubled past."

"I told the police he could have fallen off the wagon," Faye said. "They didn't take me seriously."

"I don't think it's called a wagon when it's drug use," Burt said.

"It's not?" Maggie asked. "I thought it was. Has he been acting erratically at all? Anything strange?"

Faye thought about Cliff and Lilly at the Vatican. Cliff had seemed himself. Perfectly normal, no bloodshot eyes or shaking hands. He was the picture of health. "I don't think so. But maybe there was something from his past that Rowena found out about and didn't like. She was like that. Sanctimonious."

Maggie cocked her head. "Why do you say that?"

Hell. She couldn't very well tell them because she'd experienced it firsthand. "It was something Cliff said."

"Was Rowena worried about anything?" Burt asked. "Been causing trouble for anyone? What really was the state of her marriage? Maybe we need to go back to basics."

"And I need to get some sleep if I'm going to nail the interview," Maggie said.

"I'll come up with a plan," Faye said. "Thank you both. For everything."

"You're welcome to stay as long as you like," Burt said. "It's the safest thing."

Faye lay in bed, trying to think what to do next. Adam was the obvious person to talk to. Even if she could get him to speak with her, would he tell her the truth? She'd just have to do her best.

Faye picked up her Caravaggio book to try to clear her mind. The artist had been the suspect in a murder investigation. Well, not really a suspect. More like the clear perpetrator. He'd been convicted and done a runner before they could put him in jail. Was it that easy to disappear nowadays? Probably not.

The next morning, the Masterpiece guests greeted Faye with genuine pleasure. They nodded along as she guided them into the Capitoline Museum. They paused in a courtyard, and Nan took a photo of Faye in front of the massive fragments from the statue of Emperor Constantine. Faye smiled as she posed in front of a seventy-two-inch foot. Wouldn't George be surprised if he found this tagged on a social media page? Happy and confident, moving on with her life.

"Where's the rest of the statue?" asked Jean, the woman who had been wearing the "World's Best Grandma" t-shirt earlier.

In addition to the foot, there was a huge elbow joint, a hand making a number-one gesture, and a few bits and pieces Faye couldn't identify. Knees, maybe. Or possibly thighs. "Only part of the statue was marble," Faye said. "The arms and legs and head. They made the rest of it out of wood and bricks, then covered it with bronze. Those don't survive as well."

Jean looked skeptical. "Why not do it all from marble? The emperors had plenty of money, didn't they."

Faye felt her smile fade. Jean was right. Money wouldn't have been an issue for Constantine. Why *not* make it all out of marble? It would have looked nice and been sturdy.

"I believe the statue was quite tall," Paul said. "I read forty feet? That would have been awfully heavy if the entire piece was made from marble. It probably couldn't stand up safely."

Faye shot him a grateful look. "That's right." The information had come back to her. "The Colossus of Nero was made of copper, too, which is much lighter. That statue was as big as the Statue of Liberty and is what that the Colosseum was named for. It was originally at his palace, but after he died, they made some changes to it and announced it was now a statue of the sun god."

"That's quite practical," Jean's friend Barb said. "No point in dumping an entire statue just because the subject's fallen out of favor. But I don't remember a sun god."

It was hard to keep track of the Olympian gods, they all had so many different jobs. Which one drove the chariot behind the sun? Faye was drawing a blank and needed to get back on solid ground. "Nero's statue—the one that was rebranded—is completely gone. Probably taken down by an earthquake in the four hundreds, then people just scavenged the pieces. Copper would have been valuable in the Middle Ages. Now, if you'll follow me, there's much more right through here."

"Well done," Nan said in a low voice. Then, louder, "You've got me thinking about all this in a new way, Faye. Imagine something so big just disappearing. It's rather humbling."

Barbara and Jean lagged behind as Faye led the group up a flight of stairs. Faye paused on the landing so they could catch up. Barbara gripped the metal handrail as she made her way to the group. "What are these?"

"Reliefs," Faye said. "From, ah—" She scanned the wall for a helpful label with identifying information. "The reign of Marcus Aurelius." She had an excellent memory, but the emperors often ran together for her.

Faye resumed her climb, but the group didn't move, as if waiting for her to elaborate. When in doubt, put the question back to the group. "Let's think about your lesson with the artist in residence this morning. What do you notice here?"

After a moment's silence, Paul said hesitantly, "Balance?"

"Yes, exactly."

"It doesn't look balanced to me." Jean stepped closer to the relief depicting a figure driving a chariot pulled by four horses. A figure hovered over him, holding two wreaths.

She was right, and Faye remembered the history. "Excellent catch. Someone else was originally in the chariot with Marcus Aurelius. He was originally with his son Commodus, who turned out to be one of the crazy emperors they ended up assassinating."

"That doesn't sound very civilized," the man with the beard said. "Wasn't Rome supposed to be the model for our legal system?"

It was sometimes difficult to square the ideals of the Roman empire with reality. The period before the crazy son had been known as the "Five Good Emperors," probably because they were so rare. Faye had read that a whopping fifty percent of Roman emperors ended up being assassinated. A daunting statistic by any measure.

"Commodus was one of the truly awful ones. When he was twelve, he ordered an enslaved person killed because his bath wasn't hot enough. Not that killing an enslaved person was a particular crime back then. They were considered on the same level as cows and horses from a legal perspective. But it shows a short temper on Commodus's part."

"Spoiled," Barb put in.

Faye nodded. "In the worst way. He went around dressed up as Hercules so people would treat him like a god. He liked to play gladiator in big spectacles. Of course, it was all rigged to make sure he didn't get hurt. And what really bothered the upper classes was that he ordered some senators put to death so he could take over their estates. It took at least three attempts before someone finally killed him."

"Good riddance," said Barbara with gusto. "No wonder they scrubbed him out of the picture."

"Such a shame," said Edward, one of the quieter guests. "My book group read Marcus Aurelius' *Meditations* last year. Terrible for him to have had a son who turned out like that."

The best families could produce terrible children, and terrible families could produce outstanding ones. Just look at Faye's stepchildren: some superstars, others asking for money to get their social media influencer careers going. Fortunately, her sort-of-stepson Ronnie was no Commodus, just a man who'd always looked for a shortcut and didn't think about the consequences. But there were also success stories like Rowena. Her childhood had been rough, and she'd overcome it.

"Yes, and Rome went downhill from there," Faye said. "Three emperors in one year, martial law, devalued currency. You can't blame one person for it all, but if I had to choose, Commodus would get my vote. Now, there's an important statue up here Thomas wants you to see."

Faye led them through two rooms to the sculpture of the *Boy Extracting a Thorn*. Compared to the religious drama of the Vatican art, this statue was a breath of fresh air: a child sitting down to pull a thorn from his foot. No gods. No moment of religious awakening. Just a human being performing a human task.

Four young women jockeyed in front of Faye's group, so she stepped back toward the windows to make room until they passed. "This is a Roman copy of a Greek sculpture. There are lots of these *Spinarios* around the world. You can find them in Florence, at the Met, who knows where else."

Another group had entered the room, and Faye realized they needed to move on. The museum was a former palace. And while the rooms were large by the standards of any home, they weren't big enough for many tour groups to linger together. "The *Capitoline Wolf* is just this way."

They had about forty-five minutes before the van would pick them up.

After viewing the famed wolf who had suckled young Romulus and Remus, Faye moved the group through a few more rooms with priceless objects that were, frankly, beginning to blend together.

Faye came to a stop when they reached a bust of a curly-haired man wearing a lion's head. He looked chunkier than most of the figures they'd seen that day, and his eyes had the heavy lids of a man who was slightly hung over. Not someone she'd want to spend any time with. "Allow me to introduce Emperor Commodus."

"I thought they destroyed all the images of him," the bearded man said.

"They were supposed to. Folks found this one hidden in an underground chamber in the 1800s, tucked away with some other important pieces of art."

"And just forgotten?" Nan asked. "It reminds me of that sculpture at the Vatican."

"The man with the snakes," the bearded man said.

"Exactly. It all seems so sad, doesn't it?"

"You hear about it all the time, though," Paul said. "Some farmer finds a treasure in his field that someone must have buried and forgotten."

"You do? I don't," Nan said. "Aren't farmers all riding around half asleep in programmed GPS tractors?"

"Don't mind my wife," Paul said. "She has strong opinions about American agriculture subsidies. These stories are usually from Europe. I'm sure it's different here."

Nan snorted, but so affectionately Faye had no doubt the two were in love. She missed that back-and-forth banter of marriage. Though in later years, it had been more back than forth with George. Her husband had tuned her out long before he found his graduate student.

Not that it excused his behavior, not one bit. If he'd been a better man, he would have come to her and told her he was unhappy while there was still time to do something about it instead of waiting until his bags were packed and he had a one-way ticket back to the States.

"It's always rich people who think the rules don't apply to them," Jean said, still standing in front of Commodus. "Here's this terrible man whose image everyone agrees should be erased, and some aristocrat says, 'That can't apply to my property. I'm special. I'm keeping it.'"

The force of her comment took Faye by surprise. "Very insightful, Jean."

"Maybe they didn't condone censorship," the bearded man said. "Erasing an image doesn't erase his errors. Maybe they'd have done better to keep his memory alive so they could learn from it."

It was the type of argument a certain type of man always made. He'd argue any point, good or bad, just to have the satisfaction of having the last word.

"Nonsense," Jean said, her tone indicating the discussion was closed. The World's Best Grandma was growing on Faye.

"Now, there are just two paintings we want to see on our way out," Faye said. The day's tour was supposed to focus on sculpture and what it showed about positioning the body, but the museum had two Caravaggios that Faye wanted to see. The Società was scheduled to visit the following week, and Faye wanted to be prepared.

It was a longer walk than Faye expected to the picture gallery on the second floor, and she was grateful the guests seemed too tired to ask about any of the art they passed. Finally, the group arrived in an airy room that felt more like a traditional museum than the converted palace where they'd spent most of their tour.

An enormous picture dominated the space; even the ceiling was bumped up into a dome to accommodate it. But the work Faye wanted was to its right: a young woman holding a man's hand in *The Fortune Teller*.

It was one of Caravaggio's most famous paintings. It was fine, but it was hard to see what the fuss was about. Not dark and gory the way the painting of Jesus at the Vatican had been. But all the same, just a picture. The couple looked neat and tidy—more than Faye would have imagined anyone in the 16th Century actually was. It must have been a dreary time to be alive, no showers, little laundry, lots of dirt around. The Romans, with their baths, would probably have smelled much nicer.

"Well, here's the first one," she said. "A painting by the great Caravaggio." They all stood back and looked at it for a moment. "What do you see? Any ideas?"

"It's a nice use of light," Barbara said a little hesitantly.

"And the background is interesting," Paul said. "It's so plain. That makes it Baroque, doesn't it? Thomas gave us a cheat sheet. Bland background and sense of motion equals Baroque."

"I think he said Baroque was more about capturing a snapshot in time, while Renaissance was about showing stability, didn't he?" a quiet woman said hesitantly.

"Very good." Faye would have to remember that bit for when she returned.

"My goodness, is the woman stealing from the young man?" Jean laughed. "I thought it was a romance taking place. How clever."

"Not so clever for the young man," the bearded man said.

Faye looked at the couple in the painting. The girl was the one breaking the law, but the artist had made her look like the hero, while the victim, a foppish young man, appeared the fool. Faye waited for some deeper feeling about the picture to strike her, but she was coming up short. Maybe she just wasn't in the right mindset.

She led the group to the other painting, *St. John the Baptist.* She knew from her reading that she was looking for a naked young man with his arm around a sheep, and it was easy to spot.

"The light's nice," the quiet woman said.

"Definitely Baroque," Paul added. "Nothing balanced there."

Faye had read that the notable thing about the painting was the subject. It was supposed to be about a big religious moment, but instead Caravaggio had celebrated his subject, a gleeful-looking young man with thighs Faye couldn't help but covet. Caravaggio's commission might have been for a biblical story, but he'd painted it the way that he wanted.

What allowed this artist to live life on his own terms? Was it pulling himself up from the devastation of his childhood that allowed him to behave as he liked? Maybe anyone who'd overcome the impossible would do the same. Maybe that was why Rowena had threatened to tell George about the bank accounts. Being on the straight and narrow gave her a sense of control.

Rowena's death was sad and tragic and nothing to do with Faye. Someone had made it impossible for Faye to gloss over, and for the first time, Faye was angry. She was tired of being pulled into this. She was tired of being in limbo. She needed to find Rowena's husband and get some answers.

"Light and landscape, we've learned a lot, haven't we? Let's go find the van."

Chapter Thirteen

Caravaggio was fortunate to be working at a time when the Catholic Church was fighting to woo the faithful back from Protestantism. Popes were on a spending spree, enlisting artists to create enormous quantities of work that confirmed the power and dominance of their faith.
—Caravaggio: Brash, Brutish, and Brilliant

Faye sent Adam a text on the van ride back to the tour office, and her phone vibrated a few minutes later. It was only Olivia, George's stepdaughter, checking in. Faye tapped a few words back and sent Adam another message. He was usually tied to his phone. He must be ignoring her intentionally.

Maggie and Thomas met the group at the door, bubbling about the interview's success. "The producer loved us," Thomas said. He'd dressed up for the TV interview, and with his button-down shirt and open smile, he could have been a model in a housewares advertisement. "She's referring us to some of their sister programs. Who knows, I might have a future as an arts presenter."

"It was great publicity," Maggie said. "With any luck, we'll get the next few tours sold out. Thank goodness you got us settled here so quickly, Faye. This wouldn't be possible if we were in the middle of a move."

How would Maggie have reacted if Faye had been forced to tell her DiLorenzo Industries was buying the building in the middle of all these tours? Faye didn't want to see an upside to Rowena's death, but being able to stay put—and save face with her friend—was a relief.

"Can you stay for lunch?" Maggie asked.

Faye shook her head. "I need to track down Adam and figure out what was going on with Rowena."

"You sure that's a good idea?" Thomas ran a hand through his hair. "He's the husband and all that. Sort of suspect number one. I'll come with you."

"Having a stranger along won't make him very chatty," Faye said.

"I'm the easiest person in the world to talk to," Thomas said. "It's part of my charm."

"Maybe so, but not today." Faye intended to ask Adam why he'd told his wife about her bank accounts, and she didn't need Thomas to be part of that conversation. Having Burt tag along on her meeting with Esta had been stressful enough. "Don't worry, I'll stay in public places."

Adam was a creature of habit, and he went to the *Mercato San Cosimato* every Tuesday afternoon. If she was lucky, she could find him still there. Faye's phone buzzed. She waved goodbye as she turned to check the ID, hoping it would be Adam. "Another time, I promise." It was George. She rejected the call.

Faye could hear guests laughing inside the apartment and, for a moment, wanted to go back and tell Maggie and Thomas she'd changed her mind. She could bring Thomas with her and enjoy his support. But if she did that, she'd risk Adam telling all. She had to go alone.

Faye walked the short blocks to the *Piazza San Cosimato*. It was bustling. Vendors filled the space with tables loaded with wares, and giant white umbrellas provided shade for the shoppers moving between the stalls. Faye usually came to the market when it opened at six-thirty, so she could have her pick of produce and time to catch up with the grocers. She scanned the square, but didn't see Adam through the crowd.

"Faye! We've been wondering where you'd gotten to." Gabriella, who ran a cheese stall, greeted Faye in Italian. "You missed my special taleggio. We are out, but I have the provolone George loves."

Faye glanced around to make sure she hadn't missed Adam. There was a man with a straw hat who might be him. He turned, and she saw she was wrong. "Just a small bit today. George is watching his waistline. You know how men are."

"Ah, he's just trying to stay handsome for his beautiful wife. You make him something delicious with this, and he will be happy, yes?"

It was the same thing each week, with Faye taking home a block of provolone she didn't want because she didn't have the heart to tell this woman that her husband had left her. Faye moved through the shoppers, keeping one eye out for Adam while still greeting her favorite grocers. Without consciously planning it, she purchased two eggplants and three containers of strawberries.

She was loading her bag when she spotted Adam. Or, more accurately, she spotted Daisy. The dog had her nose inside a shopping bag, wolfing down something that, judging by the wag of Daisy's tail, was delicious.

"Daisy, no!" Adam caught her too late and was attempting to pull his dog away, but Daisy had locked her legs, tail wagging even more furiously.

Faye watched as Adam apologized to bag's owner and handed over a fistful of bills. Daisy, finished with her treat, caught sight of Faye and tugged in her direction.

Faye waved. "How much did that cost you?"

"You saw that? More than I want to think about. Daisy's done it before, and I've learned to pay up and move on."

Faye bent to rub Daisy's head. "It's not your fault, is it, Daisy? It's not fair for people to leave yummy food where you can reach it."

Adam gave Faye a look, and she realized how she must sound, talking as if Daisy could understand. She was as bad as Maggie.

Daisy looked up at Faye and leaned her head against Faye's thighs, so Faye rubbed the dog's ears.

"She's after your food," Adam said. "She has a nose like a scent hound but without the speed. What is it? Sausage?" He didn't look as gray this afternoon as he had before. He must have finally gotten some sleep. Or food. Maybe both.

"Cheese. Yours." Faye held the packet out to him. "I thought you might like some provolone. Gabriella's is the best in the city."

He frowned. "I don't want anything from you." His tone was sharp, and she felt the gaze of the nearby grocer on her.

"Fine, no problem." He either had something to hide, or he agreed with the gossip that Faye did. Either way, it was going to be a difficult conversation. "I've spoken to the police, Adam. Twice. I need to understand what's going on."

"What's going on? My wife is dead, and the poison was found in your kitchen. Now you show up looking for me. What am I supposed to think?"

"They didn't find a vial of poison in my kitchen, Adam. Someone poisoned my peanut butter."

"Or you just want it to look that way." He wouldn't be the first man to try to cover his guilt by pointing a finger at someone else, but Adam's anger seemed genuine.

"I just want to talk. Let me buy you lunch." Faye set her purchases on the bench next to Adam. "Watch these for me. This bakery makes the best sandwiches. I'll be back in a minute."

She didn't give him a chance to argue. All those years of marriage to George had given her a thick skin. Keep up a cheerful attitude, and eventually people will come around. That principle had served her well in life.

Adam shrugged and sat, and Daisy curled up at his feet. When Faye returned, she handed him a sandwich. They were in the shade, and it was as good a place to talk as any. She sat next to him and unwrapped her sandwich.

"What is it you want, Faye?"

"I want to know why you told Rowena about my bank accounts." It wasn't what Faye planned to open with, but she realized it was what she really wanted to know.

"I've asked myself that a thousand times." Adam looked down at Daisy's leash, rubbing the strap between his fingers before looking up again. "It just came out. If I could take it back, I would."

Faye wanted to believe that Adam was genuinely sorry, but she couldn't. "How does something like that just come out? 'Oh, by the way, did I mention Faye has some interesting bank accounts? Ones she hasn't told George about?'"

Adam sighed. "Rowena and I were discussing ethics, and I told her everyone stretches the truth. She argued the opposite. Your name came up as an example in my defense." He spoke as if it were the most natural thing in the world.

"Why were you talking about ethics?"

"I'd prefer not to say." Adam unwrapped his sandwich and lifted the top piece of bread to look inside. She'd chosen the one with really good prosciutto. He set it down again.

"For goodness sake, if I poisoned your sandwich, there'd be nothing to see," Faye said. "And you don't get to pull this 'prefer not to say' business. This is a murder investigation."

"The police are investigating, not you."

Daisy yawned and rolled onto her side, as if bored with the discussion. Faye reached down and rubbed the dog's belly. There was something comforting about her soft fur. It was thinner than on her back, and Faye could make out the pink of the dog's tummy.

It was hard to picture this animal having the energy to catch two hundred frisbees. "Why didn't you cheer Rowena on last weekend?" Faye asked, remembering Heather's story of seeing Adam and Daisy at the park.

"What did Cliff tell you?"

"Cliff? He told me Rowena was struggling with an ethical issue." Faye took a bite of her sandwich, mind racing as she tried to put the pieces together. "I thought it was about my offer to sell Via Pecora if she stayed quiet about the bank accounts. But that wasn't it, was it? The ethical issue she was struggling with was you."

Adam pushed his sandwich away. "Rowena had very high standards." He spoke slowly, as if choosing each word. "I don't just mean doing a good job. I mean in ethical areas. The world was black and white for her. No middle ground."

"Cliff said the same thing."

"You have to understand. When you grow up in a family like Rowena's, you need a moral compass so clear that you can hold onto it for dear life. And it worked for her. She made a success of herself beyond her wildest dreams."

"It was that bad?"

Adam shrugged. "She didn't like to talk about it much. Dad sold drugs. Mom walked out. Rowena bounced from place to place."

"I'm sorry." And Faye meant it. No one should grow up like that. Faye should have cut the woman a little slack. Still, a criminal father and wandering mother could be important in a murder investigation. "Was she still in touch with her family?"

"Both dead. No siblings, either." Adam leaned forward. "The thing was, she didn't just believe that she should follow the rules, she wanted everyone else to do the same. Even for little stuff. If a vending machine dropped two candy bars instead of one, she'd turn the other in at the building's front desk. Fine. A little unnecessary, but no harm done. It was when she tried to put that on everyone else that things got sticky. My sister told her once about entering a different email address when buying something online to get a discount for new customers, and Rowena made such a big deal out of it my sister didn't speak to her for a year. In college, Rowena told the dorm monitors if someone snuck in a keg. It's hard to be friends with someone like that."

Faye wondered why he was telling her all this. If Adam suspected Faye of being involved in his wife's death, he wouldn't be here having a heart to heart. But it seemed like he needed to talk. "And you crossed the line? That was her moral dilemma?"

Adam nodded, his expression grim. "I exaggerated my work experience. I was perfect for the job, and the HR people were just checking a few boxes, so I made it easy for them to hire me. It was an inconsequential detail, the sort of thing everyone does and no one thinks twice about."

"How did Rowena find out?"

"She didn't believe I could land a job. When I told her I'd gotten the offer, she demanded to read the description and said I wasn't qualified. She flipped when I told her I'd fudged it."

It had been years since Adam had worked. It was the usual story. When Rowena's career took off, Adam said his own just seemed less and less important. So, when they moved from place to place, he'd stopped looking for positions and focused instead of making a comfortable life for them.

Faye had experienced the same thing. So had many of the expat wives. Did she regret it? She wasn't sure. It wasn't helpful to look back on decisions you've already made.

"I want you to understand that I didn't set out to tell Rowena about the bank accounts," Adam went on. "It slipped out, and I'm sorry. But the fight wasn't a big deal. These are the things that happen in marriage. They don't mean anything."

Maybe. Couples argued, then they got over it. They made compromises. It was part of being human. "But you didn't take the job."

He shrugged. "I couldn't take it with her judging me. I told them I changed my mind."

"And she was buying you a picture to cheer you up?"

"Apparently, my wife thought a nice painting would make up me missing out on the one opportunity that would get my career out of the deep freeze." His tone was bitter. "I put my career on hold to follow Rowena around the world, and she and her friend decide a painting will cheer me up." Adam took a bite of his sandwich. "Forget I said that last bit. This is really good."

The secret was the prosciutto. The shop got it from a local butcher, and it was head and shoulders above anything Faye had found elsewhere. "How long was Rowena a vegan?"

"You too, Faye? The police already asked me about the menu. I have no idea. She left for work before I was up every day and crashed before the sun went down. We hadn't been enjoying many romantic meals lately."

"Stefano knew about her diet," Faye said. "He says keeping the kitchen stocked is one of his special skills."

Adam took another bite, then wiped his fingers on a napkin. "Good for him. It didn't earn him many brownie points with Rowena."

"What do you mean?"

"Nothing. He just wasn't making her life any easier. If Rowena had a plan, he'd tell Esta about it. He wasn't trying to steal her ideas or anything like that. It was more that he was keeping Esta informed every step of the way.

It wasn't particularly empowering for Rowena."

"Stefano was never alone with the smoothie." Cliff had hinted that there were issues between Rowena and Stefano, as well. Faye hadn't taken it seriously. "He came in as Cliff was making it."

Adam gave Faye a look. "I wasn't suggesting Stefano poisoned Rowena."

"So, who do you think did?"

He glanced around, then leaned in. "Faye, you and I both know that you said you'd do anything to stop George from getting your money. Rowena threatened to tell him about it. I don't know what else there is to say."

A horn sounded, and Faye was suddenly aware of the surrounding crowds. What a place for two prime suspects to be having a heart-to-heart. She plowed on, anyway. "I didn't need to kill your harpy of a wife. I agreed to sell my building. And you know what? She took the deal. Rowena might have thought she was above the rest of us mortals, but in the end, she had her price just like everyone else."

Chapter Fourteen

Cheating is a common theme in Caravaggio's paintings, with cunning thieves pulling fast ones on their aristocratic betters. Was Caravaggio poking fun at his benefactors' giant payments for his work? We will never know.
—Caravaggio: Brash, Brutish, and Brilliant

Faye found Thomas and Ilaria outside 10 Via Pecora when she returned from her encounter with Adam. The cook laughed at something and gave Thomas a kiss on the cheek, then waved goodbye. He stayed in place for a moment watching Ilaria walk away.

"Back to school?" Faye asked.

"Lecture this afternoon, then back for dinner, then some group project tonight. I'm not sure I did her any favors convincing her to stay on with Masterpiece. She's being pulled a thousand different directions."

"This tour will be over soon enough," Faye said. "Then maybe Maggie can find someone new. I'll keep my ears open."

"You missed a smashing lunch. Minestrone and a strawberry salad. Did you find Adam?"

Faye thought of her sandwich. She'd only been able to stomach a few bites of it before throwing it in the bin. "I did. All was not sunshine and light between him and Rowena."

Thomas whistled. "You got him to talk. Was one of them cheating or something?"

An expensive black car cruised past and pulled to a stop a few doors down the road. Two men emerged from the rear doors dressed in the sport-coat-

and-open-shirt uniform of the successful man who is never off duty. They were speaking loudly in Italian. "It's not as bad as I expected," one said.

"Ci fai o ci sei?" the other one answered. *Are you stupid?* "We need to polish the hotels and sell them as fast as we can."

"I think those are Esta's nephews," Faye whispered. "Matteo and Luca."

The one talking about selling was stout for an Italian. He must be Matteo, the older of the two siblings. He was the one who had gotten the top job when Esta's brother died three years earlier.

"What are they saying?" Thomas asked. His Italian was serviceable, but not fluent like Faye's.

"Shh. I'm trying to listen." She and Thomas were across the street, and the pair seemed totally unaware they were being watched.

"Father promised Esta she could finish the project," said Luca. The younger brother was fair-haired, tanned, and slim. He had a golden boy look about him. Had it rankled him that his brother had been picked to lead the organization, or did he accept it as the natural order?

"And he's not here," Matteo said. "This is a business. If Aunt Esta needs a pet project, she can serve on the boards of some museums, no?"

"They're talking about the idea of a DiLorenzo hotel on this block," she said to Thomas. "It doesn't sound like they think it's a good investment."

Another black car pulled up, and Faye recognized Esta's driver before the old woman stepped out.

"That's Esta?" Thomas asked as Esta kissed her nephews.

"Le mie caramelle," Esta said. "It is so good of you to make time to come to Roma to see my little project."

"Yes, and she just called them her butterscotches. I guess you never do grow up."

Faye stepped back into the doorway. She wasn't exactly hiding, but she didn't want to be caught eavesdropping, either.

"It will be magnificent," Esta went on. "Imagine this entire block restored to its grandeur. We will be playing up how we're redeveloping this quarter, bringing our trademark style to a street in need of attention. It will give a boost to the entire collection. An upmarket retreat for the upmarket clients we have lost over time, yes?"

"What's the projected turnover?" Matteo asked.

Esta named a number that was staggering.

"It's a waste of your time," Matteo said. "It will have no effect on the bottom line. A rounding error."

"It sounds like the nephews aren't on board," Thomas said. "That's good news. None of us want to be next door to a construction site. A project like that would take years."

The buildings on the block had remained empty since DiLorenzo Industries had acquired them, and it showed. They hadn't been wonderful when they were sold, but they'd gone downhill since. As much as Faye hated the DiLorenzo pressure to sell, living in the only occupied building on a vacant block wasn't ideal.

Esta pursed her lips. "It's about more than the revenue, Matteo. The hotel brand is going down, thanks to all the budget boxes you insisted we build in the middle of nowhere. This is a marketing push as much as anything else. Your papà understood that. It is why he championed this as much as I did."

Faye had always longed for siblings. She wished for playmates every year when she blew out her birthday candles as a child, and as an adult she thought how much easier life would be if she had a confidante who would love her no matter what. Watching Matteo and Luca, Faye wondered what their father's relationship had been with Esta. Had he really been supportive, or had he treated her with the same disdain this younger generation showed?

Esta's tone was fierce. "I understand you want to sell the division on which your great-grandpapa built the business. I disagree. Reinforcing the flagship shows the world we're not just chasing easy money."

This was a different side of Esta: defensive and brusque. Her charm and warmth seemed to have evaporated around these men.

But then, everyone is different when they are with different people. Faye could be bubbly with one friend, serious with another. Maggie would call it being fake, but it was more about adapting to your environment. Faye had learned how to do that when she moved around as a child. The star athlete in one town, scholar in another. No one exists in a vacuum.

"And the death of Rowena Burke, what will that mean for your project?" Luca asked. "When she asked for this meeting, she said there was news about the construction to share."

Faye glanced at Thomas to see if he'd caught this. No one had mentioned Rowena calling a meeting with the brothers.

Esta shook her head. "She should not have asked you to come all this way. There has been no progress. There is still a holdout."

Luca sniffed. "The building on the corner? It is a simple matter. Let the wrecking ball begin smashing and don't be too careful about where the debris falls. After a week of that, they would take five euros to make it stop."

"These are not nice people," Thomas whispered.

"I'm sure they're exaggerating," Faye said, but her stomach churned. Luca was talking about extortion.

"I understand your approach," Esta said. "I think we may need more finesse. Just a little more time, yes? Let's go back to the office."

"I hope Stefano has the coffee ready," Matteo sniggered. Clearly, the brothers thought it was funny their family's friend was at the bottom of the corporate hierarchy.

"You were always hard on him," Esta said. "He's working hard."

Luca sniffed. "That is hard to believe. Do you remember when he broke my mother's vase and hid in the closet all afternoon? Then at university, he disappeared for an entire semester after failing two courses and not wanting to tell anyone. He's spoiled and irresponsible. I can't see that changing."

"He's doing much better now," Esta said. "I'm sending him back to his grandfather soon."

"Good riddance," Matteo said. "Better there than messing about in our business."

"What's this all about?" Thomas whispered. "I'm only getting bits and pieces."

"I'm not sure," Faye whispered back. "Something about Stefano having a checkered past. The brothers don't like him."

Esta had reached her car, and the driver had the door open for her. "I'm sorry you came all this way for nothing."

Matteo shrugged and said something to his brother that Faye didn't catch.

"*Vabbè, non importa.* I'm always happy for an excuse to come to the city," Luca answered before climbing in.

"It must be nice to have so much free time." Matteo said. He followed his brother, slamming the door without a word of goodbye to his aunt.

Esta stayed a moment watching them go, then got into her own vehicle.

"Well, that was something," Thomas said after the cars departed. "Poor Esta, being related to those two. Are you coming inside?"

Faye shook her head. "I'm heading back to the Whites. I want to call Stefano and find out what all this was about."

"Wait a tick. I'll walk you over. Better safe than sorry and all that."

"The more I think about this mess, the more sure I am that I wasn't the target," Faye said. "The poison in the peanut butter was a plant to throw the police off. I'm sure of it." At least, mostly sure. Faye would know if someone wanted her dead. And as much as George might be angry with her, he hadn't come all the way back to Italy to do this.

Faye was unloading her groceries onto Maggie and Burt's counter when Stefano returned her call. "What can I do for you, Faye?"

"When is construction starting on the Via Pecora project?"

He coughed. "Why do you ask?"

"Because I just saw Matteo and Luca outside my building, and they told Esta to start demolition to make my life miserable."

"Ah."

"Yes, ah." Faye had made a mistake putting her confidence in this boy. Cliff and Adam said Rowena hadn't liked him, and it was clear Matteo and Luca didn't respect him either. Only Esta seemed to defend him, and she probably just had a soft spot for the little boy he'd once been.

"I am sorry, Faye. That is not something that I anticipated. Luca and Matteo, they are—" He paused.

"Bullies?"

"Difficult. It is very much their way, to arrive and put pressure on people. When I was a child and they were teenagers, they were not so nice. As adults, they are still not so nice."

131

"So, is the construction happening?" Faye picked up a knife and began slicing an eggplant using long, clean cuts. The knife was sharp, and every slice felt like a release.

"Truly, I do not know. Esta is a practical woman. She values her relationship with her nephews, and she values her independence. My guess? Yes."

Faye moved the diced eggplant into a big bowl and drizzled it with a hefty pour of olive oil. She gave it a good sprinkle of salt and transferred the pieces to a baking sheet and then into the oven. "You can't just decide to start a massive project on a dime."

"Rowena had already begun the process. She had the lawyers begin the paperwork."

"What kind of paperwork?"

"I do not know. Permits. Title verification. Construction details. I cannot say. I am a secretary, no?"

Faye had thought she had control in this situation with the DiLorenzos. Refuse to sell, and the project would stay on hold. She didn't love the vacant buildings, but they were better than a construction site. Now, though, she realized she had been naive.

This would happen with or without her. She'd tied herself up in the decision to swap the building for Rowena's silence. She hadn't realized what a good deal she'd made. Rowena could have told George everything, and in the end, Faye might still need to sell if she didn't want to be caught up with the DiLorenzos.

"What about you? What will you do when Esta retires?"

"I will be not be here. Esta should be giving her report to my grandfather any day. By fall, I should be back where I belong."

Faye began to assemble dessert: a zabaglione custard with strawberries. She cracked egg yolks into a bowl and mixed in Marsala and sugar.

Stefano cleared his throat. "I understand they found your food had been poisoned. It is a relief to know that Rowena was not the target, but it must be worrisome for you. Be careful, yes?"

Faye paused and let the whisk rest against the side of the bowl. The tool's heavy handle caused it to overbalance and tip onto the counter. If Faye were in her own kitchen, she'd be using a bowl with higher sides and this wouldn't have happened. Now she'd have to wash it and dry it extra well so that water didn't disturb the custard mix. "I'll do my best."

"Get in touch with Esta soon, yes? It is no good to draw things out."

It was like something George had said when he announced he was leaving Faye. That he was tired of being in limbo. He just wanted to move on, even if he was making a mistake.

Faye finished the custard and poured it over the strawberries. She ran a finger around the mixing bowl. It was sweet and creamy. She wished she'd made more. After tidying the kitchen, Faye was at loose ends, and it felt like ages until Burt came back from work.

"It smells good in here," he said when he finally walked in the door. "More baking?"

"Just dinner. I thought we could save dessert until Maggie gets home. It shouldn't be too late."

"Fine with me. How was your day? Anyone suspicious trail you?" It was a weak joke, but she was touched.

"Only a group of Masterpiece guests."

Faye told him about the tour while they ate the roasted eggplant salad. She'd tossed the vegetable with mint, pomegranate, and *freula*, an Italian couscous. It was the type of recipe she loved in the summer: not too fussy and loads of flavor.

When Maggie came home, they took bowls of strawberries and zabaglione out onto the terrace.

"I've been thinking about the lethal smoothie," Burt said. "It's the key, isn't it? Who had access to it?"

Motive and opportunity were the pillars of any investigation. Faye had been failing on the motive side. Opportunity was their only hope.

"We need to look at it two ways." Maggie licked the custard off her spoon. "One, that the smoothie itself was poisoned, and the peanut butter jar was just to throw the police off." Maggie made it sound like a breakthrough. It was what Faye had been saying all along.

"And two?" Burt asked.

"And two, that the peanut butter was poisoned in advance by someone who knew that it would be used for the smoothie."

"So we're going to ignore the possibility that it was intended for Faye?" Burt said.

"It's like Faye's been saying, no one who knows her well enough to want her dead would poison something she doesn't eat."

Faye was grateful that Burt and Maggie didn't suggest a third possibility: that she'd laced the food with poison herself in a bid for attention. Or Revenge. Or who knew what else. Faye shot her friend a smile. "Cliff was the one who made the smoothie," Faye said. "And he knew Rowena's diet best."

"Was it his idea to share it with Rowena?" Maggie asked. "I thought he brought it for himself."

"Back up," Burt said. "If Cliff shared the smoothie and didn't get sick, doesn't that mean only Rowena's glass was poisoned?"

"I wish it were that simple," Faye said. "Cliff didn't drink his. He said he didn't get a chance." She'd thought back to that night and had no memory of pouring out Cliff's drink when they were cleaning up. "Maggie, did you wash his glass?"

"I don't think so," Maggie said. "I'd remember a full glass of green stuff."

Burt steepled his fingers. "The police must be looking into this. A man brought the poisoned drink and didn't have any? That's Class A suspicious."

"But why Cliff?" Maggie asked. "What conceivable motive could he have?"

"That's what we need to find out." Faye realized she knew little about him beyond his stories of recovery and racing. "From the way he talks, he was her spiritual guru, but Rowena seemed to be pretty independent to me."

"You think he's lying about their relationship?" Burt said.

"He could be," Maggie said. "Trust but verify."

Faye should have asked Adam about Rowena's relationship with Cliff when she had the chance. Now she'd burned that bridge.

"I still say Adam is the prime suspect," Burt said. Faye had given her friends the highlights of their conversation, sidestepping questions about how she'd gotten him to admit to the fight with Rowena. "He wasn't happy. His wife put her career ahead of him. She put her hobbies ahead of him. She even gave him a hard time about getting a job."

"You get a divorce if you're unhappy," Maggie said. "You don't need to kill the woman. Just look at George. Oh, sorry, Faye."

Faye studied her hands, unwilling to meet Maggie and Burt's gaze. Her fingers were long and thin. She'd always been proud of them, even if they were the result of the genetic lottery rather than any effort on her part. She still wore her wedding ring. Faye had tried taking it off a few times, but her hand looked bare without it.

Burt coughed. "I just didn't get the idea that Adam really wanted to work. Maybe he was relieved when Rowena told him not to take it."

"I don't think so," Faye said. "His career was a casualty of Rowena's success. As she climbed the corporate ladder, his income became less important, his time less important. He said he wanted to get his career back on track."

"It's the same old story, isn't it?" Maggie said. "Even without children to manage, when a dishwasher needs fixing, someone has to be the one to stay home for the service appointment. Someone's putting mental energy into meals. Into holidays. Even vacations. People don't intend to step aside; they just drift further and further from the fast track."

"You didn't," Burt said. "You were a vice president at the old place."

Maggie patted Burt's hand. "I wasn't talking about us. It's just a pattern you see. Usually, it's the wife, but not always."

It had been like that for Faye and George. Not that he was a high-powered executive, but he traveled all over the world lecturing about his arcane academic specialty. To everyone's surprise, he'd gotten a book deal, then a second. That book somehow caught on with the public and he'd had a brief moment in the spotlight. Faye had been proud of him, but it was hard not to feel like an afterthought when you were the spouse holding everything together behind the scenes.

"Maybe this is about money, plain and simple." Maggie ran a finger around the rim of her dessert bowl thoughtfully. "A life insurance payout would be a nice start to a new life."

"Much better than half of whatever a divorce judge would give him," Burt said.

"I don't have a life insurance policy," Faye said. "Just in case you're thinking about George. He gets the same amount in the divorce settlement as he would if I died."

"Oh Faye." Maggie exchanged a look with Burt. "We don't think that." But they did. Why else would they keep reminding Faye to be careful? They must think there was at least a good possibility that this was all intended for Faye.

She took a sip of her wine. Crisp and dry, perfect for the warm night. The drink may have been part of Italian life for millennia, but Faye had read it would be a mistake to believe the ancient residents drank the same stuff she had in front of her.

Archaeologists or anthropologists, or some other people who were supposed to know these things, said the old version was a very sweet drink that was diluted with water—sometimes even seawater—to make it more palatable.

"I don't see money as the motive," Faye said. "The Caravaggio Società meets tomorrow. I'll try to learn more about Cliff there."

Maggie stretched. "I'm fading." She was still in the outfit she'd worn for the TV interview: the green jacket and navy pants Faye had laid out. It had been a good choice. Maggie looked polished and professional. "Chin up, Faye. We're making progress."

Chapter Fifteen

The Catholic Church commissioned Caravaggio to decorate their places of worship, but was the artist devout? One may consider his response to a question about why he gave a horse center stage in a painting about the conversion of St. Paul. Caravaggio's answer: "Because the horse stands in God's light."
—Caravaggio: Brash, Brutish, and Brilliant

F aye stayed up late searching for information about Cliff. She found posts online about his last race. The event had been a big deal, just as Cliff and Lilly had said. Faye found a slew of blog posts and articles and comments from fellow runners about it. She clicked on the names of the most active contributors and sent the same private message to each: *I was a friend of Rowena's. I know running meant the world to her. Do you have a few minutes to talk?*

Maybe no one would reply, but there was no harm in putting some ticklers out there. With any luck, someone would answer and tell her something about Rowena and Cliff's relationship.

Faye left early for the Caravaggio Società the next morning to stay out of Maggie and Burt's way. She opted to walk but still arrived at the Piazza del Popolo fifteen minutes before the scheduled meeting time.

Faye planted herself on the stairs of Santa Maria del Popolo and checked her messages. No runners had reached out. No one from the gang had responded to her Società reminder. She put her phone away and tried to enjoy the setting.

The piazza was Rome's grandest square. It had the same elliptical design as the piazza at St. Peter's and was home to not one, not two, but a whopping three churches. And all dedicated to Mary, the mother of God. Faye tried and failed to imagine a time when three churches of the same religion—dedicated to the same saint, even—had enough parishioners to stay busy.

In addition to the churches, the piazza was home to massive statues, two large fountains, four mini-fountains, and a host of attractive four-story buildings, not to mention a burst of greenery thanks to its location at one corner of the Borghese Gardens. As if that weren't enough, a giant Egyptian obelisk stood smack in the middle of it all. The piazza designers had wanted to impress everyone who passed through it, and they'd succeeded.

Faye thought she saw some members of the gang approaching, but they turned out to be commuters. Faye checked her phone again. No messages. They'd probably arrive in one big group full up on pastries from a breakfast stop at a cafe. Faye often skipped breakfast, so they wouldn't have invited her along. When they arrived, she would use the time to learn more about Rowena, especially her relationship with Cliff. Faye had to be subtle, but that was what she was good at. Finessing conversations and making it easy for people to talk.

Faye leaned back, enjoying the sunshine. She couldn't ask for a more pleasant place to wait. Usually she was busy, hustling from place to place. It had been a long time since she had just sat and enjoyed the city.

At one time, this piazza was the place where travelers entered the city. What would those visitors from all over Europe have felt passing through the massive three-arched Porta del Popolo, a stone gate so elaborate it looked like a building in its own right? Relief at having their journey behind them? Awe at the grandeur of this Catholic city? Fear of the new life ahead?

God, she was getting maudlin. Everything would work out. It always did. She'd see when the gang showed up. Things would be like old times. Heather and Jessica had shared some gossip the other day, but her friends wouldn't be so quick to indict her.

Young people hustled through the piazza on their way to work. Two older men talked energetically about something while a mother pushing a stroller stopped to tie the shoe of the toddler next to her.

Faye made a conscious effort to distract herself, and her gaze settled on the obelisk. If her memory was correct, the ancient Romans had sailed it all the way from Egypt, then carried it to a place of honor in the Circus Maximus racetrack. The city fell into squalor in the Dark Ages, and the obelisk had languished until some pope ordered it moved as part of the urban renewal projects of the Renaissance.

What a life that piece of stone had led, if you could say an obelisk had a life. It was humbling to think about that monument, which had been carved well over three thousand years ago, then hoisted into a place of pride in the middle of a desert where it stood for a thousand years before someone had the idea to load it onto a boat and sail it to another continent. It had been parked in the middle of an entertainment complex, then after another thousand years, give or take, it was moved again to smarten up another part of the city. And today, people just walked past, never giving it a second thought.

There had to be a message there about her own problems, but before Faye could decide, she spotted a woman moving purposefully across the square, long flowered skirt billowing behind her.

It was Lilly, and she was slightly breathless when she reached Faye. "I'm so sorry for being late. It was a nightmare getting out this morning. Everyone already inside?"

Faye winced. Here she was, sitting all alone when she'd invited at least thirty people this morning. She almost wished Lilly hadn't come so she didn't have a witness to her humiliation. But Faye would make the best of it. She'd wanted to learn more about Rowena and Cliff, and who would know more than Lilly? With just the two of them, Faye would learn more than she could with an entire group listening in.

"I'm not sure first thing in the morning was the best choice for a meeting. We can get started, and any stragglers can jump in."

"I'm glad to have an excuse to visit the church," Lilly said. "I've never been."

Faye hadn't either. Only in Rome would Santa Maria del Popolo be considered a minor church. In addition to the Caravaggios, it housed sculptures by Bernini and features by Raphael. And yet Faye had never entered.

It took a moment for Faye's eyes to adjust when they stepped inside. It was beautiful in the way all these Renaissance churches were: gilt everywhere, tons of marble, oil paintings, statues, and side chapels. No expense had been spared.

Lilly trailed behind, typing on her phone. "Sorry," she said when she finally looked up. "Wow, this is amazing."

Lilly drifted away, head angled up as she began a circle around the church. Faye followed in her wake, murmuring now and then to show appropriate appreciation.

"How is Cliff doing?" Faye asked. In the hush of the church, the question sounded too loud. She lowered her voice. "It seems like he was Rowena's closest friend."

"He's pretty shaken up," Lilly whispered. "It's bad enough without the police grilling him about that smoothie. They're treating him like a suspect, so they're casting around for a motive."

Faye felt a surge of relief. She and the Whites weren't the only ones wondering if there was more to Cliff than he let on. "That's terrible," Faye said. "Did they say why?"

Lilly shrugged. "That's where they're stuck. They asked if he and Rowena were having an affair."

It was an idea Faye had considered. Cliff wasn't her ideal match, but Lilly had married him, so some people must find him desirable. "But you don't think so."

"No way. Besides being madly in love with me, responsibility is a key part of Cliff's recovery, and he'd never do anything to jeopardize that. I told the police all this, and you know what they did? They asked if he might be using again."

"No!" Faye was pretty sure she did a good job of sounding shocked at the idea.

"It's typical," Lilly went on. "Someone dies. Blame the addict."

They came to an ornate chapel to the side of the altar. Three paintings dominated the alcove. Two were moody, dramatically lit works that Faye immediately recognized from her reading as the Caravaggios. They flanked a colorful, almost cheerful picture in the middle. "*Crucifixion of St. Peter,*" Faye whispered to Lilly. "The one with the horse is the *Conversion on the Way to Damascus.*"

The crucifixion was agonizing to look at. It showed St. Peter being nailed to a cross. The man's feet were higher than his head, and Faye's stomach turned as she looked at the nails driven through his extremities. She'd seen crucifixion imagery thousands of times, but this one felt more real.

The conversion, at least, should have been a happy occasion. Caravaggio had painted a man lying on the ground next to a beautiful horse. The man, St. Paul, didn't look particularly excited. The horse was nice, though.

"I always like animals in this old art," Lilly said. "They look just the same as they do now. Sometimes, with the people, I get caught up looking at their clothes and hairstyles and can't really connect, you know? Animals feel more timeless."

"You and me both." George's co-workers had always made Faye feel lowbrow. It was nice to know she wasn't the only one who viewed art this way. Maybe Faye had misjudged this woman. If Cliff was involved in Rowena's death, Lilly would need a friend.

They moved on. "I don't feel like I got to know Rowena," Faye said. "Not really. I know she was great at her job, that she was a great runner, that she and Adam had the perfect marriage, but nothing more."

Lilly gave her a look. "Perfect marriage? I wouldn't say that. I stopped over on Monday to drop off something and they were in the middle of a huge fight."

"What about?"

"I couldn't really hear. Adam was saying something about the rest of the world not living by the same rules Rowena did."

It fit with the story Adam had told Faye the day before. The couple had been arguing about Adam's application for the job, and he'd had the idea to use Faye's name to help his case. "I understand Rowena had a thing about rules. Impossibly high moral standards."

"That's an understatement," Lilly said. "There was an issue when a runner took water from someone cheering him on. That's technically against the rules about outside support or something. Anyway, Rowena was one of the runners who signed a petition saying the runner's finish should be erased."

"Lovely."

They finished their circle of the church and stepped outside. Faye fumbled for her sunglasses. "I feel more cultured already. Should we get a coffee?"

"I'd love to, but I need to get to the university. But I'll see you at Palazzo Barberini. I'm looking forward to it."

"I'm headed your way," Faye lied. "We can walk together."

They crossed the square and down the Via del Babuino, one of Rome's elegant shopping streets with clean cobblestones and, in some places, wide sidewalks. "I know Cliff wouldn't ever have cheated on you, but could Rowena have had a relationship with anyone else? One of the other runners? Someone at work?"

Lilly shook her head. "No way. Esta was her only close tie at the office, and I wouldn't call them friends. And anyone who suspects romance is happening out there on the trail has never been to an event. Cliff comes home filthy, exhausted, and totally drained. I love him, and I'm proud of him, but trust me, there's nothing sexy about it."

A delivery van blocked the sidewalk ahead. Faye and Lilly waited for a car to pass, then dodged into the street around it and back onto the sidewalk.

"What about Adam? You must have gotten to know him pretty well at all the races."

"You'd think so, but no. He's easy to be around, telling a funny story or remembering what you talked about the last time you were together, but I never got any deeper with him. Some people are like that. They're so focused on putting up a great appearance you never get to know them."

Poor Adam. What was wrong with trying to be entertaining or a good listener? No one wanted to hear your problems.

"I think Rowena took her husband for granted," Lilly went on. "Cliff says Adam had been wanting to look for a job, and Rowena belittled him for it, saying it wasn't worth his time because he'd make so much less than she did."

Two office workers strode past, deep in conversation. "I don't know if Rowena was necessarily a bad person, but she was self-absorbed," Lilly said. "Maybe she and Adam were well-matched. They both cared a lot about appearances. About being right."

Lilly's words stung. When George announced he was leaving, he had described Faye the same way.

"Do you know why Adam missed this last race?"

"Rowena said he was sick, but judging from that fight, I don't know if I believe it. The situation wasn't ideal. Rowena rode with us, and she was sort of a pill on the way back."

"She wasn't happy about the race? It was a big milestone, wasn't it? She got the points she needed to qualify for the next big event, didn't she?"

"The Valtellina 100. Cliff couldn't understand her mood. Apparently, she thought she'd beaten him because they'd gotten separated at an aid station, and she'd gone ahead and didn't see him pass her. When she saw him there ahead of her, she couldn't get over it."

"She must have been distracted."

"Cliff said she had things she was trying to work out. I don't know if it was Adam or what, but it got to her." Lilly fluffed her hair. "I'm used to tension on the course. I always try to go and help Cliff out at the aid stations, and it can be ugly there. Tears. People wanting to quit or being really rude to their support crew. I mean, no one's at their best when they're going through hell. But when they finish, they're so happy to be done, it's all in the past, and they're just giddy to have accomplished something amazing. But not her."

"You're nice to help out."

"I like it. It's a giant tailgate. We bring tents and chairs and talk about how glad we are that we're not the ones running. Later our loved ones tell us how great we are for showing up."

Faye hadn't thought about the logistics of cheering someone on for a hundred-mile race. She'd been to marathons before and there was always a lot of racing for the spectators to get from point to point to see people several times. "You go all that way and don't see much of the actual race?"

"It'd be impossible. Other than the aid stations and a few checkpoints, the runners are alone out there."

"How do you know where to find him?" In a race that long, a few minutes off pace could translate to hours behind in hitting checkpoints.

"I use an app. It's not perfect, but I can see where he is."

They had come to *Il Babbuino*, quite possibly the city's ugliest fountain. It depicted a lecherous creature with the head of an old man and hirsute body of a goat reclining in front of a trough of water. He was nicknamed "the baboon" because of his appearance. At one time, the wall behind him had been covered with graffiti much beloved by locals, but city officials decided to cover it with anti-vandalism paint to present a tidier impression.

"Listen to me, going on and on," Lilly said. "I talk too much when I get nervous. How are you doing?"

"Oh, you know me, I'm doing just fine." Faye thought about what Lilly's complaint that Adam never opened up. "It's hard living alone sometimes, especially after being with someone for so long. You start to imagine things."

"What kinds of things?"

"I keep losing track of stuff. Nothing seems to be where I left it. Not a break-in, nothing valuable is missing. Just things put back on the wrong shelf. A tea towel folded wrong. When George was home, I would blame it on him. But now I wonder if I'm just going a little crazy."

She hadn't told anyone about it. They would say she was taking George's departure hard and ask if maybe she'd had too much to drink. "Ignore me. Just old age. Have you made any plans for Lake Bolsena yet?" Lilly's expression was blank. "The weekend getaway not far from Rome you were asking about."

"Oh, right. No, we haven't. I don't know what will happen now." Lilly cleared her throat. "Have you talked with George? I get the sense he's really sorry about how things ended between you two."

"What gave you that idea?"

"He said something about it yesterday. He's in town for the big conference, and I think he'd like to find a way to smooth things over."

"What?" George was here, in Rome? Faye's mind raced. Inspector Nardelli hadn't said anything about it. Did the police know?

"Not repair the marriage," Lilly said quickly. "Just, you know, be more amicable."

How many other things had Faye missed? George, the man who wanted nothing more than to be away from her, was in Rome. George, who had access to her apartment. George, who had motive, despite what Faye had told the Whites. Faye felt sick.

"I'm sorry. I thought you knew," Lilly went on. "He's here for that big conference that we put on every year."

There was no way George had anything to do with the poison in Faye's home. He wasn't that type of person. If he were, what would it say about Faye's judgment, being married to someone capable of murder? And worse, being a woman whose husband wanted her dead? That wasn't Faye. "I guess I've been distracted."

Lilly paused to take a picture of *Il Babbuino*. "For Cliff. This beast reminds me of him the morning after a race. He's always hobbling around like an old guy." Lilly softened her tone. "It sounds like the negotiations with George have been pretty rotten, Faye. I'm sorry about that."

It meant a lot coming from Lilly, who was George's friend. "I just never expected to be fighting over something as silly as sending him a few boxes of clothes," Faye said. "He's the one who left, and now he wants me to do him the favor of sending his belongings to him. It's just so petty."

"It's hard to be our best selves when we feel attacked," Lilly said.

"I meant George."

Lilly stopped and took a breath. "Look, I told George I wouldn't get involved, but you might feel better if you gave them back. Just put it all behind you and move on."

Faye braced herself for what was coming next. Right on cue, Lilly added, "Get a fresh start, you know?"

Faye gritted her teeth. "He'll get the boxes when my lawyer says it's all over and not a minute sooner."

They walked a few more blocks before Lilly stopped again. "This is my street. Thanks for organizing this, Faye. You're not at all how I thought you'd be." Lilly gave a little laugh. "If I'm honest, you've always intimidated me."

"Me?" Faye was the least intimidating person she could imagine. She was nice, average. Nothing out of the ordinary.

"You've always had this perfect life," Lilly said. "You're so connected to everyone. You have these brilliant parties. You're an amazing baker. You always look put together." Lilly blushed. "I don't know. You just seem to have your life together."

"My husband left me."

"Well, yes, there's that. It makes you a little more human."

Lilly waved goodbye before Faye could think of a response. She walked home through the heart of the old city, preferring the winding streets to the more direct route along the river.

The morning had not been a waste. The gang hadn't bothered to come, but she'd learned more about Rowena. A picture was emerging of an impatient woman who didn't like to lose, and who was not always considerate of her husband's own wishes.

Faye tried to ignore the fact that it felt uncomfortably like a picture of herself.

Chapter Sixteen

Caravaggio frequently produced multiple paintings of a single subject. Modern viewers might wonder what drew the artist back to the theme again and again. Caravaggio's rationale was more pragmatic: there were collectors willing to buy.
—Caravaggio: Brash, Brutish, and Brilliant

Thursday was hot and sticky, the type of weather Romans don't typically see until August. Sightseers would be wilting by noon and gelato sales would spike by two p.m.

Faye checked her messages, but none of Rowena's ultra friends had gotten back to her yet. She went for a run while the temperature was still bearable, then called Nan to check in. Maggie had said the night before that she had everything under control, but Faye wanted an actual guest to confirm things were going smoothly.

"Do you think I should come help out today?" Faye asked. "Just to help make sure everyone's having a good time."

There was some background noise on the other end of the line; Faye could make out Nan's muffled voice saying, "It's my daughter. I'm going to step outside."

"Sorry about that," Nan said. "I needed to get somewhere private. I told them it was a call from home." Nan would make a terrible secret agent. It was barely three a.m. on the East Coast. "Everything's going really well," Nan went on. "Jean was saying last night how much she's learned, which is something coming from a battle axe like her. One of the others said his sister and brother-in-law have already sent a deposit for a tour this fall."

"That's great, Nan. I know you and Paul have been working hard."

"No work necessary." Nan's tone was warm. "It's been a delight. Thomas's lecture is starting soon. I should run."

"I could come in, just to make sure the transition to the tour goes well."

"Maggie and Thomas have it." Nan paused. "Are you all right, Faye?"

"I'm fine. Great, actually." Faye glanced out the window. One of Maggie's neighbors greeted a friend, and Faye watched as the pair proceeded down the street, arms linked. "If I'm not needed there, I'll use the time studying up for the next meeting of the Caravaggio Società. It's this afternoon."

It was unlikely the gang would show, but there was no reason not to immerse herself anyway. Faye settled in with a cup of tea and her book and tried to focus. She learned that Caravaggio's productivity outpaced any other artist of the time. He worked quickly, and his contemporaries said he wasn't playing by the rules when he skipped steps that everyone else considered critical. The author suggested the complaints came from envy. Faye wasn't sure. Caravaggio was quarrelsome and violent. The other artists probably just didn't like him.

She put the book aside and stretched. It wouldn't do to sit inside all morning. Maggie had forbidden her from baking, something about waistlines and unnecessary calories. A walk would be the pick-me-up she needed.

She was not going to let the fact that George was in Rome change her life. The police knew he was here. She'd called Inspector Nardelli with the news and learned the detective had already interviewed him. The police were on top of things. That should be enough for her. Faye would just stick to busy streets the way she had on her run, and it would be fine.

The heat enveloped her as soon as she stepped outside. It must have been twenty degrees warmer than when Faye went out earlier, and she felt like she was standing in front of an oven. She would be better off indoors with a glass of cold lemonade and a good book. Not the one on Caravaggio, though. She needed a break from her self-imposed art history study.

There was an excellent English-language bookstore a few blocks away, and Faye arrived just as the owner unlocked the door. Faye let the air conditioning wash over her as she chatted with the owner. She was still talking about the man's Canadian boyfriend when the door squeaked and Heather walked in.

Faye waved. "Heather!"

A look that passed over Heather's face that Faye couldn't read. "Oh, hi, Faye." Heather glanced around. "What are you up to?"

Faye held up the paperback the owner had recommended. "I needed something new. We missed you yesterday. Are you coming to the Basilica di Sant'Agostino this afternoon? We can walk over together."

Heather shook her head. "No, I can't make it."

Faye waited for Heather to elaborate, but she didn't. After an uncomfortably long silence, she said, "That's too bad. Well, don't forget I have a reservation at the Villa Aurora for us. It's a real coup. I hope you'll be able to make it."

Heather glanced around again, as if she were looking for way to escape. "I don't think so, Faye."

"Why not?"

Heather sighed. "Look, Faye, I like you. You know that. But this doesn't really feel like a good time to be out and about sightseeing, does it? People are saying you put the poison in Rowena's drink."

Faye felt like she'd been slapped. It must have shown, because Heather hurried on, "They don't think you meant to kill Rowena. They say it was just as a bid for attention that went wrong. Like Munchausen syndrome or something. I don't think that, obviously. It's just, you know, maybe it would be a good idea to lay low right now.

"Lilly came yesterday," Faye said with as much dignity as she could muster. "I guess she's not afraid of being seen with a suspect."

"Lilly?" Heather cocked her head. "She's the last person I'd expect. She's not even a regular at your parties. Why was she there?"

"I guess she was being supportive," Faye said. "Some people do that, you know. I'll see you later, Heather."

Faye left without her book, feeling like a fool. Here she was, a lifetime out of junior high school, and she still cared what people thought of her. It was silly and she knew it, but Faye couldn't do anything about it.

She arrived at the Basilica di Sant'Agostino ten minutes early. She'd considered skipping, but she held out hope that Heather didn't speak for the gang. Faye found a place to sit outside and watched the pigeons pounce on the bread scraps an elderly man tossed out to them.

"Faye!" She turned and saw Cliff jogging toward her. "Great day to be out. What are you up to?"

Cliff was dressed in full running kit, with lightweight short shorts, sleeveless t-shirt, tiny backpack, and a headband around his shaggy hair. His calves were muddy, and his shoes were a mess.

First Lilly, now Cliff. She would never have guessed this couple would be the only ones left standing with her. "I'm just about to go inside," Faye said. "Have you seen the *Madonna di Loreto*?"

"Oh, you're here for the Caravaggio? No, I'm just back from a run." Cliff began a series of calf stretches. "I was doing some hill sprints up the Janiculum with some of the guys."

Oh. She refused to let her disappointment show. "I was out earlier. I don't know how you do it in the heat."

"This kind of weather is great for building endurance." He paused. "What the heck, I'll come in with you."

"You don't have to. It's just one picture. You've probably seen it."

"Nope. It's been on my list, though. There's a Raphael in there, too. And the altar's by Bernini, right?" He said it casually, but something didn't sound right. He was a little too polished.

"That's what I read."

"Well, come on then. Let's check it out."

The interior was grand, like so many of the churches in Rome: massive pillars supporting giant red-marble arches, Renaissance paintings everywhere. They joined the small crowd around Caravaggio's painting. It showed Mary and toddler Jesus with two shabbily dressed men kneeling in front of them. The light in the picture lit up the mother and child, but the effect was nowhere near as impressive as the *Conversion of Saint Paul* she'd seen with Lilly a few days before.

Cliff did a standing stretch, shifting weight from one leg to another. His thighs were solid, not an ounce of jiggle on them. "Some of the guys, they said they got a message from someone saying she's a friend of Rowena's. That wasn't you by any chance, was it?" His tone was casual, but his focus was intense.

Faye swallowed. Okay, he wasn't here for the Caravaggio Società. That was fine. He was the man who had made Rowena's drink, but they were in a public place.

She'd been naïve to think the runners she messaged wouldn't get in touch with him. "It was." She stepped around a couple reading from a guidebook and moved toward the altar. "I'm realizing now that I never knew Rowena. I'm trying to understand her better." It wasn't a lie.

"It's a little late now. Take it from someone who's been there, Faye. Drop it. You can't change the past by putting yourself through the wringer. You can't control anyone else. Just commit to being your best self as you move forward."

"Mmmm." Faye's phone buzzed, and she turned it to silent.

Cliff stopped. "I'm serious, Faye. Leave it alone. No good will come of looking into Rowena's life."

Cliff wasn't menacing, not exactly. But why not take her response at face value and tell her all about his great friend, Rowena? She had to push. "Did Rowena say anything last week that was unusual? I know she opened up to you on the training runs." Flattery, in Faye's experience, was the best way to get people talking.

"No. Everything was normal."

"Oh." He wasn't giving her anything to work with. "And she didn't reach out to you about that picture for Adam? It was such a good idea you had. I thought she'd want to jump on it."

"No." His tone was bitter.

Too late, Faye remembered that Rowena was working with Esta's dealer, not Cliff. Well, being nice hadn't gotten her anywhere. She changed tack. "Why not? It was your idea. Why wouldn't she want to get you a commission?"

Cliff shook his head. "She wanted my help, but I said no."

"Why not?"

Cliff removed his hat and scratched his scalp all over. Faye could smell the odor of stale sweat. "It's none of your business, but if you really want to know, Rowena asked me to dig up some sales records. I told her they were confidential, and she didn't like it. When I refused, she gave me the cold shoulder. I can't say it didn't hurt, but I've done enough work on myself to know that it was her issue, not mine."

Cliff made a show of checking his watch, one of those fancy GPS tracking ones that could probably signal satellites in case of trouble. "I should be going. It was good talking to you, Faye."

"Wait. I wanted to ask you about the smoothie."

"You too? I've already told the police everything."

"But what happened to your glass? Maggie and I didn't find it when we were cleaning up."

Cliff shrugged. "I poured it out when the party ended. That stuff gets sticky if you let it sit. Seriously, Faye. Let it drop, okay? You and I, we don't need to be involved in any of this."

Faye made her way home through the old city, turning from one small street onto another. The Bougainvillea was in full bloom, with pink and purple flowers covering the sides of buildings, sometimes climbing up five stories. Faye breathed in the fragrance, sweet like honeysuckle.

Cliff was Rowena's closest friend, and he'd just told a story that didn't jibe with the picture of Rowena that Adam had painted. The rule follower wouldn't have asked her friend for inside information. And why had Cliff gone out of his way to find Faye that afternoon? He was the man who mixed the drink that led to Rowena's death, and Faye was sure he was hiding something. She just didn't know what.

Chapter Seventeen

Sensitive artist types would do well to learn from Caravaggio's hutzpah. Patrons with contracts for a given subject frequently rejected his first attempts. Rather than wilt under criticism, the artist would simply find another customer and start the commission again, thus generating two sales instead of one.
—Caravaggio: Brash, Brutish, and Brilliant

I t was time to face the mess the police had left in Faye's apartment. From the hall, there was no sign her home was under investigation. Faye slid her key into the lock and swung the door open. The air was stale and the flowers on her dining table had wilted.

She braced herself as she made her way to the kitchen. Cabinet doors were open, and all her bakeware, pots, pans, and measuring cups were piled on the counter. The expensive chocolates George's stepchildren had sent were nowhere to be found. The police had probably tested and tossed them with everything else.

Faye sighed and set about washing anything the police had handled. She thought about the events of the day as she gave a silicone spatula a dip in soapy water. Judging by the attendance at the Società, Heather had been telling the truth about the gang's suspicions.

Faye gave a cake pan a dip, then her measuring spoons. Only Lilly and Cliff seemed immune to the gang's gossip. She had been pleased at first, but now it suggested something else was going on. Faye rinsed the rest of her pans and began systematically drying and putting everything away.

Her phone buzzed. It was Tim, George's middle stepchild. "Olivia told me to call and cheer you up. Did the chocolates come?"

"I'm afraid the police took them along with everything else consumable."

He tsked. "That's a shame. They were really expensive. Oh, well. It's the thought that counts. Something funny did happen to me the other day. I was walking to the train and...." Tim launched into a complicated story about a hamburger and pack of dogs that followed him.

"Anyway," Tim said when he finished, "I've told everyone my stepmother is a suspect in a murder investigation. My friends think you should start a true-crime podcast. I can be your producer. Think about it. We could have fun."

It was sweet of him and a little flattering, even if he was mostly joking. He was a good man. If she lived closer, she could meet him for lunch, maybe get to know his friends. She could be a part of his life. The same for the other sort-of-steps.

No, Faye refused to go down that road. She needed to build her own identity, not glom onto these young people.

"Have you heard from Ronnie?" Tim asked. "Olivia wants her share of the chocolate money. George said something about meeting him for dinner. Maybe you can put in a good word?"

"I'm not exactly chatting with your stepfather these days." Faye leaned back in her chair. The cushion was full and soft, a nice change from the lumpy ones at Maggie and Burt's. Faye should feel at home here, but she found she missed the comfortable shabbiness of the Whites'. "Where are they meeting? Not in Rome?"

"I think so. George is there for that annual conference."

"Did he bring his girlfriend?"

"Not a clue." Faye could make out the sound of chewing in the background. "I try not to ask about her. She's younger than I am. It's embarrassing."

"For you?"

"For everyone." There was the sound of paper crumpling. The wrapper of something. An egg biscuit? "Take care of yourself, Faye. I'll talk to you soon. Maybe even try to make a trip out there in the fall."

Would Faye still be in Rome in September? She had no idea. She pushed the thought away and went into the bedroom to put on fresh clothes. Faye pulled on linen pants and a blouse, but she had an uneasy feeling that something wasn't right.

Faye studied the room. Her bed was made, the white bedspread with the navy border as neat as ever. Both bedside tables were bare, just the way she liked them. Faye pulled open the closet door and rifled through the clothes, feeling slightly foolish, as if she expected someone to jump out and shout "Boo!" Or worse. But it was all in order: her side nearly organized by color; George's side empty.

That was it. George's boxes were gone.

Bile rose in Faye's throat. George had let himself in and taken what he wanted, not even leaving a note. The idea of George coming and going as he pleased made her feel violated. It shattered the illusion that she was safe in her own home.

Was it possible that he was the one who had laced the peanut butter after all? *Get a grip,* she told herself. *Sneaking in for a few boxes of clothes is not the same as plotting to kill your wife.*

But Faye called Inspector Nardelli anyway. "It's Faye Masters," she said when the inspector came on the line. Her heart was pounding, and her words came out in a rush, "George has been here, in my apartment."

"Calm down, Signora Masters."

Calm down? Faye had thought she was calm except for her hand gripping the phone so tightly it was starting to cramp. She relaxed her hand and inhaled deeply. She held her breath for a count of three, then released it. Faye was aware of the blood pounding in her ears, but she felt better.

"What happened?" Nardelli continued. "Do you feel safe?"

"He's not here. He took some things when I was out."

Nardelli clicked her tongue. "And how do you know it was him?"

"They were his things. Boxes he'd asked me to mail back to the States that I hadn't gotten around to. He's taken everything but his damn golf clubs."

"Would you like me to send Officer Piras to you to write a report?"

The idea of waiting for that silent young man was too much. There wouldn't be a point, anyway. The police had already interviewed George. A report wouldn't change anything. "That's kind of you, but no thank you. I'll tell my lawyer. That's probably sufficient."

Faye's lawyer was not especially interested. "I'll make a note of it, Faye. We can send a letter to his attorney."

"I could interpret this as attempting to terrorize me when I'm already on edge," Faye said. "What if I'd been home?"

"My guess? He'd have rung the doorbell, asked for his things, and you'd have told him to get lost. He probably timed it when he knew you'd be out, Faye."

"I would have been happy to have the boxes out of the house if it was a matter of just handing them over. It was the mailing that was onerous." It was weak, and she knew it.

"My advice is to wrap things up, Faye. Dragging it out won't win you any points. I'll send the letter, though. Call me if anything else comes up."

Faye put a kettle on for tea and prowled around her apartment, tossing the dead flowers, opening windows, fluffing pillows, and generally trying to return it to its homey state. Nothing had changed. No one was trying to kill her. It was exactly what she'd been saying all along.

He could have poisoned the peanut butter any time. She pushed the thought away. George knew what Faye ate and what she didn't. He was not a suspect.

She thought about the objects that had gone missing in her apartment over the last few weeks, the picture frames that were moved, the general feeling that things weren't as they should be. Had George been coming in, just to toy with her? She didn't think he would go as far as murder, but messing with Faye's mental state wouldn't have been out of character.

Her lawyer was right about the boxes, though. Faye would have refused to hand them over. So how had George timed his collection so well? He might have been watching the apartment, but he should have been too busy with the conference to be staking out her house. Then she thought of Lilly, who had the entire Società schedule. She must have tipped him off.

The water boiled, and Faye realized too late that she had no tea in the apartment. The police had taken everything, including three containers of very nice Earl Grey she had received for her birthday. Faye would have to borrow some from the Masterpiece Tours kitchen. She let herself in and found Thomas alone in the sitting room, reading a novel.

"The others have all gone on a bonus tour," he reported. "With air conditioning. Jean wanted to see the Etruscan Museum, and the others all joined her." He put his book down. "They're a really keen group. Especially your friends Nan and Paul. A little too keen."

Faye flushed.

"I knew it!" He laughed, clearly delighted. "I told Ilaria they were too good to be true. They're plants, aren't they? You paid them?"

"Are they too much?"

He smiled. "Let's just say the Royal Court Theater isn't going to come calling for them. But they're so nice, I don't think anyone else has given it a second thought."

"It was important for the tour to get off to a good start. Make sure the guests left with glowing reviews."

"It was really kind of you, Faye." He ran a hand through his hair. It was spiky today, less the TV host and more the artist-in-residence vibe. "What are you up to?"

"I came to borrow some tea. The police cleaned me out."

"Fair play. We've borrowed enough things from you over the last few weeks."

"Join me?"

"Absolutely. I'll contribute the cookies Ilaria left."

"That sounds perfect." Faye sank into the soft sofa and closed her eyes while he prepared everything. It felt wonderful to just *be*.

Thomas bustled in with a tray loaded with cookies and tea. "Catch me up. What have you learned?"

Faye took a sip before answering. Thomas made it strong, just the way she liked it. "George has been in my apartment."

"No!"

"Yes." Faye told him about the boxes and was gratified by his indignance. "That beast. How'd he get in? You changed the code, didn't you?"

"I used my birthday." At the time, it felt like a statement of independence, but now she realized it had been a rookie mistake.

Thomas clucked. "He probably kept a key anyway. But I think it's a good sign. He wouldn't have done anything so obvious if he was the one who'd put the poison in, would he? He'd be lying low if he thought he had something to hide."

"I agree." Faye took another sip. "I'm not so sure the same logic applies to Cliff, though. He came to the Caravaggio Società today to warn me off a looking into Rowena's life."

Thomas whistled. "I asked around about him and didn't get anything useful. Everyone says he's doing great at work, happy in his marriage, everything hunky-dory. Other than talking about his addiction whenever anyone suggests going out for drinks, they like him."

"No chance he's had a relapse?" Faye asked hopefully. That sort of thing could trigger a spiral that ended in death—his or someone else's.

"No way." Thomas crossed his legs in a figure four. "Adam has to be suspect number one. He handed the drink to Rowena. We should be focusing in on him, yeah?"

"And his motive?" It was just like her conversation with Maggie and Burt. Adam could get a divorce if he was truly unhappy. Faye hadn't forgiven him for telling his wife about the bank accounts, but she just didn't see him as a killer.

"He and Rowena had a big fight last weekend, right?" Thomas leaned forward and began drumming his fingers against the coffee table. "He wanted that job, and Rowena said he couldn't take it."

"That's annoying, yes, but no motive to kill someone. Marriage is about compromise, and he decided to turn the job down rather than make waves. He didn't like it, but he made the decision willingly."

"Maybe he didn't like the compromise?"

"Then why kill her after turning the job down? If a job was worth killing for—which I am not saying it was—then the timing makes no sense."

Thomas tapped faster, building to a crescendo, then paused, fingers in mid-air. "Everything you're saying is from Adam's point of view. I'd like to hear someone else's version of the story."

"Well, his wife is dead, so that's not going to be easy."

A scooter buzzed down the street. When Faye first moved here, she had disliked the high-pitched zipping sound of people racing around the city, but now it sounded like home. She missed it when she visited the States. "There might be someone else," she said slowly. "I was in human resources before we moved here. The hiring manager could tell us what happened."

"Do you know anyone who would know the story?"

"Headhunting is a small world." Faye pulled out her phone and began scrolling until she found the name she was looking for. "My contacts are a few years out of date. Let's see."

Faye sent a message, and the response came back almost instantly. *Sure, I know that company. Here's the number for the senior recruiter.*

Faye showed the message to Thomas. "Should I?"

"Would they actually talk to you?"

Hiring information is highly confidential. Too much so, in Faye's opinion. If employees would just talk to each other about pay and vacation time, they'd all be better off. Somehow most companies convinced employees to keep it a secret. "Probably not. But let's try."

Faye dialed, and an American voice answered on the third ring. "James here."

The nice thing about calling from an Italian phone number was that Americans never screened your calls.

Faye put on her best version of an Italian accent. "*Ciao*, hello." Faye winked at Thomas. "This Flavia calling from Roma. You placed a Signor Burke, yes? The paperwork, it has some blanks." She stood up, getting into character. "I am planning the move, but there is no date listed. The senior executives, they do not think of the paperwork. You, I am sure, can understand, no?"

James murmured his agreement without asking what office "Flavia" was calling from. When talking with someone with an accent, many Americans just go with the flow, finding it easier than stopping to ask questions.

"You've got some bad information," James said. "Adam Burke isn't working for us."

Faye could make out the sounds of a coffee shop in the background. "No?

The paperwork, it is all mixed up." It was fun playing Flavia, the annoyed office manager. "What happened? We did not make a good enough offer? This company! You must pay to get the best, no?"

"It's a mess," James said. "We made a generous offer, and he accepted. Just a moment, Flavia—" Faye could make out James ordering an iced white chocolate mocha. "I'm back. Sorry about that. So, the guy accepts the job, we tell the hiring team, who are all delighted, then we find out he lied on the application so we've got to start all over again, this time with egg on our faces."

"He told you he lied?" Faye had let her accent drop, so she hurried to cover it up. "That is very unusual, no?"

James snorted. "He didn't tell us, someone else did. I got a message from my boss to look deeper into his history, and I found inconsistencies. It happens sometimes when another candidate wants to sandbag a frontrunner. But this time it came from higher up."

"But how did your boss know?"

"Beats me. She was told to look into it and passed the task on to me." There was the sound of a grinder buzzing in the background. "We had to take the offer back. The guy was furious, but he's the one who made me look bad. You know how it is. You can't verify every detail."

"When did this happen? The paperwork, it should have been fixed."

"Last Monday." There was a chime in the background. "I'm about to get into the elevator. Do you have everything you need?"

"Si. I will fix the paperwork. Ciao."

Faye turned to Thomas. "You were right. Adam was lying about the job."

He leaned forward, elbows on his knees. "Tell me."

"Adam didn't turn the job down. They withdrew the offer after someone tipped them off."

Thomas nodded. "Husband, just like I said." He was grinning now. "The tip came from Rowena, yeah?"

"The recruiter didn't know, but it could have been. Executives at different companies are all clubby. It would have been a simple thing to call one and tell them to check out the applicant's credentials. It doesn't prove anything."

"No, but it's a motive, a solid one."

Faye began pacing. "Adam would have been humiliated to be sold out like that. It's no surprise he said he turned the job down himself." Adam had put a good face on his marriage, but this would be an understandable last straw.

"No wonder Adam didn't go to Rowena's race," Thomas said. "He probably stayed home plotting ways to knock her off."

"No, they didn't take the offer back until Monday. Rowena must have taken the weekend to decide what to do." Lilly had heard the couple arguing on Monday. It must have been about this, not Faye's offer to sell in exchange for silence.

Thomas steepled his fingers. "Same thing. So, Monday or Tuesday he begins planning. It isn't easy to kill a wife. Or at least, not easy to kill her and get away with it. Everyone knows to look at the husband first. Poisoning your peanut butter so the police would think you were the target was rather brilliant. Deflecting attention and all that."

Thomas made it sound straightforward, but Adam hadn't told the police about the bank accounts she had hidden from George. That would have made the deflection more likely to succeed.

"You've got him, Faye." Thomas was practically bouncing on his toes. "You're going to tell that inspector, aren't you?"

Everything Thomas said made sense, but it didn't feel right. "The police have the same information we do. They won't thank us for doing their jobs for them."

Thomas frowned, deflated. "So, you're going to drop it? We found out something big, Faye."

"Let's sleep on it," Faye said. "We can call them in the morning."

Chapter Eighteen

Caravaggio seems to have had little compassion for his fellow worker. In one incident, he assaulted a waiter with a plate of artichokes, an attack serious enough to land him in magistrate's court.
—Caravaggio: Brash, Brutish, and Brilliant

F aye glanced up as she bent to fasten a heavy lock around the front wheel of her scooter. She'd ridden to the Palazzo Barberini for the next Caravaggio Società, and the sky was ominous. Rain would probably begin bucketing shortly. It would match Faye's mood. She'd been up all night trying to decide what to do about Adam. In the end, she'd decided nothing. She would put it off until the afternoon when she and Thomas could talk again.

Faye didn't hold out much hope that the gang would show up this morning. Lilly was the only one who'd respond to her reminder email—and that was only a short note. *Sorry! Work conflict!!*

The others had made themselves loud and clear without any words: Faye was a pariah until further notice.

That was fine. She would tour the museum on her own. The Palazzo Barberini was a hidden treasure, or so Faye had read. It didn't have any antiquities, so Faye had never made visiting a priority. And judging by the lack of crowds, not many other people did, either.

Faye bought her ticket and headed off in search of the Caravaggios. Most museums in Rome cram their art frame to frame, but this museum was delightfully spare, with just a few pictures on each wall, giving each space to breathe and be admired. Faye would normally appreciate the curator's less-is-more aesthetic, but today, she couldn't help feeling grouchy as she took two wrong turns and had to ask a guard where the three paintings by Caravaggio were.

He sorted her out, and soon enough she found herself standing in front of them, trying to feel something. But the paintings were just paintings. Completely fine, nothing more, nothing less.

One was of a monk holding a skull at arm's length, looking as if he were trying to have a conversation with it. It was St. Francis, who looked as miserable as Faye felt, and his conversation with some anonymous skeleton wasn't particularly inspiring.

Another was Narcissus, the handsome hunter who had fallen in love with his own image. The setting was brown and muddy looking, and there was nothing particularly sympathetic about the poor sap.

And, finally, there was the showstopper: *Judith Beheading Holofernes*. It was the most dramatic of the three and certainly famous, but it wasn't pretty. Caravaggio had captured a young woman mid-slice as she hacked the head off a bearded bad guy. Faye knew from her reading that the theatrical lighting and tortured figures were a triumph of the artist's skill, but that didn't make it any more pleasant to look at.

Faye turned away and tried to focus on the museum map, but she failed to generate enthusiasm to see anything else. She'd accomplished her mission. That would have to be enough today.

Faye made her way to the exit. With any luck she'd beat the rain. Would she have enjoyed the outing more if Lilly had been there? Probably. At least they could have talked about the women's dresses. It was strange that Lilly, Faye's most casual acquaintance, was the only one who was sticking by her. Perhaps being so close to the investigation, she knew better than to judge Faye's involvement.

Or maybe Lilly has an ulterior motive. Faye had wanted to use the tour as part of her investigation. If Lilly was worried about her husband, maybe she'd joined Faye at Santa Maria del Popolo to do the same. Faye thought back to their conversation. Lilly hadn't asked anything about Faye's relationship with Adam, but she had brought up Faye's relationship with George. And she was the one who'd said George was in town. Was there something more to her conversation?

Faye paused when she got to the museum exit. It was indeed pouring rain. She could stay and see more of the museum's collection, but she decided she'd rather get wet. Faye turned up her collar and dashed the two blocks to where she'd parked her scooter. Her feet were soaked, and she was glad, at least, that she wasn't wearing her new sandals.

This wasn't Faye's favorite part of the city. It was technically in the historic center, but at the very edge, unpleasantly close to Termini train station. Not seedy exactly, but it lacked cobblestones and quaint churches and, frankly, any kind of charm. The buildings were tall, the streets wide with racing cars, and pedestrians walked with purpose.

Even the piazza in front of the museum managed to be ugly. It had a nice enough statue of Neptune, but it was caged in by heavy traffic and unattractive buildings, so you'd never want to stay and linger, no matter how nice the weather.

Faye's wet hair clung to her scalp as she dashed past the *Quattro Fontane*, the busy intersection with Renaissance-era fountains located on each corner. No one was admiring them on a day like today, especially not Faye.

Feet wet, hair dripping, Faye finally came to the row of scooters where she'd parked her bike. She scanned the row. *Where was it?* She'd parked at the end, but others might have arrived. She sped up as she walked along the row. Two red, a black, another red, a yellow, and then she saw it: her shiny pink Vespa lying on its side.

It was like seeing an injured pet. She had bought that scooter when she first arrived in Rome and took special care of it. It didn't have so much of a scratch, an accomplishment in a rough and tumble city like Rome where most drivers parked their scooters anywhere there was an inch to spare.

Now she had to figure out how to get the machine back on its wheels. If anyone from the gang had shown up, they could have worked together. If she was still in George's good graces, she could have called him for help. Faye swallowed her frustration. Maggie and Burt would help her, so would

Thomas. But they were working, and she'd already asked them for too much.

Faye stopped a passerby, a suited man carrying an umbrella. She gave him her most appealing smile. *"Mi può aiutare?"* but he shook his head and kept walking. The next three people did the same thing. So much for Italian warmth.

Fine. She'd lift the three-hundred-pound bike herself. Faye had been the star of her cycle safety class. She could do this.

Faye made sure the kickstand was in position, then bent down and cupped her hands under the lower handlebar, rain dripping down her arms. She got a good grip and looked straight ahead, then used her legs to lift straight up and began walking the bike into a standing position. Miracle of miracles, it worked.

Faye felt a surge of relief. She had solved the problem herself. She was no helpless female. In ten minutes, she'd have her bike back home, and she'd be relaxing in a hot shower.

Faye pulled her helmet on, shivering as cold water ran down the back of her neck. The temperature must have dropped fifteen degrees, and she wished she'd brought a raincoat. Faye took her seat and turned the key. The motor started, but when she tested the brake handle, nothing happened. She squeezed again. *Hell.*

Faye took the helmet off for a closer look. The fall had broken the brake lever. She swore under her breath and smacked her hand on the bike's frame so hard her palm hurt.

She swallowed her frustration. There was nothing to do but call roadside assistance. Faye's skirt was sticking to her legs, and she began to shiver while she waited for them to answer.

"Yes, I need transportation for my scooter," she said when the call finally connected. She spoke in Italian and gave the address and all the membership information that seemed to take forever to process.

"I have put you on the roster," the receptionist said cheerfully.

"How long do you think?" Faye asked.

"Impossible to say," the receptionist said in a sing-song voice. "With this rain, we are swamped. It would be reckless to promise a time." Her accent was Sicilian, and she dropped vowels at the beginning of her words. "Just remember, you must be there when we arrive. Liability issues, yes?"

"Wait, that's—" But the receptionist had hung up.

Faye refused to give in to her frustration. She was wet. Her scooter was unrideable. None of the gang had bothered to show up at the Caravaggio Società, even though she'd hosted these people at dinners and parties numerous times over the years. She'd gone on more houseware shopping trips to help newcomers adjust than she could count. She'd even taken care of cats while their owners went away for a week. It was all fine. Totally fine. Fine, maybe, but certainly not good.

Faye sighed. She was fortunate, really. Most people in her situation would have pressing engagements that they would have to frantically reschedule while waiting for the tow truck. Faye didn't have anyone depending on her.

She decided to look for the cafe she'd identified for the gang to go to after the museum. It was supposed to be just around the corner, and she could enjoy a pastry and hot drink while drying off.

The cafe was packed, probably others with the same idea of waiting out the rain. She made her way across the peach-tiled floor, head down to spot the dripping umbrellas blocking the narrow spaces between tables.

"Faye! Come join me." It was Rowena's assistant, smiling and waving as if the sight of Faye made his day. Stefano rose as she approached, and her heart melted at the sight of someone genuinely pleased to see her. "What a good surprise. You are here for refuge? Please, sit with me."

Before she knew what had happened, Stefano moved his leather bag and newspaper to the floor under his chair and urged her to take the seat opposite. "What will you have? Pastry with your *caffe*? What brings you here? Not close to home, is it?"

Before Faye had time to think clearly, Stefano had waived a waiter over and she had a pastry and steaming coffee in front of her. Faye gripped her cup and inhaled the aroma of perfectly brewed coffee. She felt herself relax as the heat began to travel back through her limbs.

"I was visiting the Palazzo Barberini, and someone knocked over my scooter while I was out. I'm stuck here until emergency services can come to my rescue."

He frowned. "Knocked over? That is terrible. Maybe I can help you raise it up? I am not strong, but between the two of us…."

She shook her head. "No. The brake is broken. It's unsafe as it is now."

He flushed. "That is not good. I am so sorry. Can I call a taxi?"

"You're sweet. I have to wait for roadside services. The person didn't even leave a note."

Stefano began coughing. He took a sip of water and recovered after a moment. "The streets are so narrow, and there are not many places to leave vehicles. I am sure the driver did not realize the mistake."

"I'm tempted to file a police report. It's genuine damage."

He shook his head. "No, no. Do not waste your time."

"Italians always say that, don't they?" Since Faye had moved to Rome, the advice was always the same: keep your head down and stay as far from the bureaucracy machine as possible.

Stefano took a bite of his *sfogliatella*, the crunchy, flaky pastry leaving a trail of crumbs on his plate. He wiped a spot of vanilla cream from the corner of his mouth. "You would spend all day filling out forms, and they would not look into it. You are a busy woman. I would move on."

Adam and Cliff said that Rowena wasn't satisfied with Stefano's performance at work. Was it because of this Italian casualness?

"Unless you think it was intentional," he went on. "Your husband, would he have done something like this? I understand he is in Italy now?"

"Who told you that?"

He shrugged. "Esta. The police are keeping her informed of the investigation."

"George wouldn't be above knocking over my scooter in some sort of passive-aggressive burst. He was angry that I didn't return his clothes to him, and knocking over my scooter in revenge wouldn't be above him. But he's gotten what he wants. He snuck into my apartment and took what he wanted."

Stefano made a sympathetic face. "I am sorry."

Faye waved a hand. "It's fine." It wasn't, but she didn't want to come across like a vindictive woman. "There's been something I've been meaning to ask you."

He leaned back in his chair. "Anything."

"You mentioned that Rowena wanted to buy a picture from Esta's dealer. Why not ask Cliff? They were close friends, weren't they?" Thomas seemed convinced that they'd found the solution with Adam, but Cliff's story hadn't rung true.

Stefano shook his head. "I'm not sure they were so close. They ran together a lot. But when he came to the office on Friday, they were arguing about something."

This was new. "What was it about?"

"I don't know."

"Didn't the police look into it?" Faye could hear her voice trending toward shrill.

"I'm sure they did," Stefano said. "Esta says they are being thorough."

"Is the argument why Rowena wasn't working with Cliff to buy the picture?"

Stefano shook his head. "No, Rowena asked for the name of Esta's dealer before that."

"What day? Can you remember?"

"Does it matter?"

"I don't know." It seemed like Rowena had been unhappy with everyone the week she died. She'd picked a fight with Faye. She found out her husband had fudged a job application. And now she had a falling out with the man who said he'd been her spiritual guru.

Stefano screwed up his face in thought. "Tuesday, I think. She'd asked for a special meeting with Esta on Monday, and it was the day after that."

"Why a special meeting? Didn't they meet all the time?"

"They had a standing weekly meeting, but Rowena set up a special meeting on Monday. They were talking about the purchase of the final building for the hotel. Your building, yes?"

Faye took a bite of her *zeppola*. The fried dough topped with cherry jam was just as prone to messy flakes as Stefano's snack, but it had the benefit of being eaten with a fork. "What else did the police tell Esta?"

He shrugged. "Probably the same things they told you. They found an energy bar in her stomach, plus some of that energy drink, yes? But they have told Esta they are confident it was the smoothie that was the issue, because of the poison they found in the peanut butter."

He leaned forward confidentially, as if someone around them might be listening in. "It seems unreal, yes? If she were eating regular food, it might not have happened."

"She ate an energy bar? I thought those were just for the trail."

He frowned. "You caught me. Rowena's appetite, it was so big because of all her running. She was hungry all the time, and I kept her food in the kitchen. But on Friday, her friend Cliff, he stopped by and ate all the food I had put out. It was almost the weekend. I did not think to buy more. I do not feel guilty, that is not accurate. But I do wonder. If Cliff had not come by, maybe Rowena, she would not have died."

He took a sip of his coffee. "I am sorry. It must be distressing, have the poison in your kitchen, intended for you. I do not mean to minimize it."

Faye patted his hand. "That's all right." Faye took a sip of her coffee. "What was Cliff doing there? A training run?"

Stefano shook his head. "No, not a run. I do not know what they were discussing."

"The picture she was buying for Adam, maybe?" Faye said. "Cliff said she had some questions about it."

Stefano shrugged. "I did not hear." He brushed a stray crumb off the table. "Have you thought more about selling to Esta?"

"I'll make a decision soon."

"If money matters to you at all, you should sell. The offer will not be good for very long. Once they begin building, they will not change their plans, even if you agree to sell. As I said, Rowena already started the construction process. It will begin any day."

"And Esta's on board with this? She's not trying to delay her retirement any longer?"

"It will take several years before it's completed. I think she recognizes that she must begin now or see the hotel division sold immediately. Two choices she does not like, but what can she do?"

If Faye took his advice and sold, Stefano would have helped secure Esta's legacy. Esta could build the hotel on the entire block, making a big splash. Faye wanted to trust this young man. He seemed so earnest about helping Faye navigate the DiLorenzo politics, she couldn't help but like him. But Stefano's allegiance was to Esta, the woman who was helping him get back into his family's good graces. Faye couldn't shake the feeling she was being played.

"I appreciate that. The fact is, I don't need the money, and I don't like being bullied. I'm going to stay where I am." There, she'd said it. Without meaning to, she'd made her decision once and for all.

So what if everyone said Faye needed a fresh start? Faye was just fine where she was. They could bring on the bulldozers. She'd be just fine. And if the noise was too much for Masterpiece, Maggie could find a new place without the pressure of a demolition ball tearing through her own wall.

He frowned. "Are you sure? This is not a decision to make on a whim. You have a few days."

"I'm sure." She took another sip of coffee. "What brings you here today, anyway? Esta doesn't need you at the office?"

He shook his head. "I am my grandfather's driver today. He has several meetings and wants me to escort him. Some, he tells me to come to. Others, he tells me to wait outside like a good boy." He gave a wry smile. "I do not like it, but what can I do?"

"Maybe you're missing the dull ones."

Stefano shook his head. "No, they are tests for which I cannot study. We were earlier at his art dealer, and he said I must come. The art market, it is good for buyers now, and he was trying to decide whether to buy three pictures or four. They negotiate, and he asks for my opinion. I have none. You tell me a price, how do I know whether it is correct? The value of art, it is what someone is willing to pay for it, yes? But the meeting he is at now, it is with his bankers. It is about our business. I have opinions. But am I invited? No."

Stefano took a bite of his pastry. "But at least I get to enjoy your company. And my pastry. All is not so bad."

Stefano took another sip of his coffee. "My family, I think I have told you, does not have a high opinion of me. It is very important that I make a good impression on my grandfather if I am going to return to our business. An excellent report from Esta, it will help."

"Why worry about your family? You're standing on your own two feet now at DiLorenzo. You can do what you want."

"There are pleasant people at DiLorenzo, even a woman that I am dating, yes? And the work, it is interesting. But I do not want to live on an assistant's salary forever." His appearance was one of an affluent man. He had expensive taste, that was clear.

Faye took another bite of her sweet. The jam tasted like summer, and it was a perfect contrast to the crunchy pastry. The sugar and the caffeine were making her feel like herself again. Even her skirt was nearly dry.

"What kinds of things were you and Rowena working on? Anything that was a source of conflict? People disagreeing about strategy?"

He frowned. "Now you sound like the police again. It was all very interesting if you enjoy hotel management: a new advertising plan, some changes in the loyalty program, and the Via Pecora project. Everyone was in agreement. Business is good."

"But the brothers want to sell?"

"They want to sell because the business is too small, not because it is losing money. They might enjoy the challenge of a turnaround, a chance to be heroes. But the hotel business today, it is just a gnat, buzzing in the ear of a giant bear. Better to have it gone."

"What kind of boss was Rowena?"

People had hinted that Rowena was unhappy with Stefano's performance, but Stefano just shrugged. "She knew I was loyal to Esta before anything else."

A couple at the table next to them paid their bill, and a threesome who had been hovering pounced.

Stefano pushed his plate aside. "The question I find interesting is why did Adam not arrange for food his wife could eat? Did he not take enough interest in his wife to know? Or did he intend for there to be no food for her, so that she would be required to eat the poison?"

It was an argument in favor of telling the police what she and Thomas had learned about Adam. And good assistants always know more about their employers' private lives than anyone likes to admit. "Did Rowena mention anything to you about her marriage? About them fighting?"

He shook his head. "She was a private woman. She was agitated about something for one or two days, maybe? But then it was over. She was buying her husband a picture. She was happy in the marriage. But was Adam happy? That I cannot say."

Stefano's phone buzzed. "That is my grandfather. My services are required. Back to the art dealer. I hope I do better this time. It was a very good fortune to meet you here. I hope your service vehicle comes very soon."

"Your grandfather will come around sooner or later."

Stefano smiled. "We can hope, yes? Take care of yourself, Faye."

She watched as Stefano wove through the tables and out the door, then turned her attention back to her plate. She was taking the last bite when a middle-aged American approached.

He smiled. "Are you alone?" He was attractive, if a few years older than she was. She gestured to the empty place. A little company while she waited would be nice.

"Great, thanks," he said as he picked up the chair and made a move to take it to another table. "Oh, here's your bag." He handed her a briefcase that had been under the seat. Stefano's.

She forced a smile. "Oh, right, thank you."

Here she was, clothes a mess, sitting alone with nowhere to be. Faye sighed. This was her life now.

Chapter Nineteen

In addition to accusations of excessive drink and unsavory companions, one of Caravaggio's landlords complained that the artist cut a hole in his ceiling. Caravaggio's only defense was that he needed more light in his studio.
—Caravaggio: Brash, Brutish, and Brilliant

I t rained all night. Faye didn't mind being tucked inside the Whites' apartment. She'd learned nothing concrete, not yet. But she told herself she had tangible leads: Adam's job and Cliff's strange behavior seemed to argue there was more to Rowena's final week than everyone had let on. She'd convinced Thomas that they should wait another day before going to the police. It wasn't as if Inspector Nardelli was asking them for help.

Burt was out at a work dinner and Maggie was with the tour. Faye read a few chapters about Caravaggio before turning in. The artist's life became increasingly erratic with every chapter. He managed to escape Rome after he killed Ranuccio Tommasoni and stayed with benefactor after benefactor, painting all the while. He couldn't have been an easy guest, but people seemed to have put up with him.

The sun was out when Faye woke, and it looked like it would be one of Rome's glorious early summer days. She made high-protein breakfast muffins before taking an extra-long morning run—in well-populated areas—to give Burt and Maggie peace in their apartment. She planned her day as she lapped the park, dodging puddles and nodding to the others out on such a nice day. The Caravaggio Società was scheduled to visit the

Villa Aurora that morning. Afterward, she'd go to the market to restock her pantry and make a go at returning to her own home.

Faye was sweaty and tired as she approached the Whites. Her phone buzzed as she climbed the stairs. It was Stefano.

"I am sorry to be so slow in returning your call. You found my bag? You are a hero, thank you. I will send someone to pick it up. Are you at Via Pecora now?"

Faye glanced down Maggie and Burt's street. For some reason, she didn't want to tell Stefano where she was staying. "I'll come to you. Shall I drop it at the DiLorenzo offices?"

He paused. "*È perfetto*. What time, do you think?"

"About one?"

"*Ciao. A presto.*"

Faye braced herself to tour Villa Aurora alone. It was the private home that Faye had booked a very special, very expensive tour of for the Caravaggio Società. She didn't bother to send a reminder to the group. Her old friends had been clear enough that they didn't trust her.

Villa Aurora, officially named *Casino dell'Aurora di Villa Ludovisi Boncompagni*, was a thirty-thousand-square-foot private home just around the corner from the Borghese Gardens and owned by an honest-to-goodness princess. A Texan, actually, who Faye understood had married an Italian prince. There wasn't a royal family in Italy any longer, but somehow this branch managed to hold onto its title.

Faye announced herself and was buzzed through the gates. She fought back nerves as she walked up a steep gravel drive to the front door of an enormous house. She'd read it had been in total disrepair until about twenty years ago, when the prince and princess began a massive restoration project starting with the eviction of the birds and bats that had taken up residence.

The prince had died, and the princess was looking for a new owner. The seven-acre property was rumored to be located above the remains of Julius Caesar's villa. Archaeological questions aside, Faye couldn't wrap her head around the idea that historians weren't even certain where the home of Rome's most famous leader had been. How did such information get lost?

174

Faye was still pondering this when a young woman opened the door. The caretaker, who the princess had said would give the tour that day.

"Faye? Welcome. Are the others on their way?" Faye guessed the woman was an American, probably from the West Coast, based on her accent. She looked past Faye, as if expecting a vanload of visitors to materialize.

Faye shook her head. "It'll be an intimate gathering." She had tried to convince Maggie to bring the Masterpiece guests, but her friend said they already had a full schedule, and she didn't want to raise expectations for future tours.

The woman nodded, as if people paid the exorbitant fee for solo tours all the time. "No problem. One of your guests has already arrived. Through here, please."

Faye followed her into the foyer, wondering which member of the Caravaggio Società had come. Lilly?

It was Adam standing in the grand entry hall. He looked small in this great space, with its fourteen-foot painted ceiling covered with a painting of a chariot being pulled across the sky. "Where is everyone?"

"Turnout has not been good."

He seemed to deflate. "Oh. I thought everyone would be here."

"Would you like to start with the Caravaggio?" the woman asked. "I understand that's your primary interest, though you must see everything before you go. Restoration has been a passion for the princess and her late husband." She led the way up a stone staircase to the second floor.

"Why did you come?" Faye whispered. "You're in mourning."

"To see the Caravaggio, just like you."

What would Thomas say about that? It was either a sign of a guilty conscience that he was out looking at pictures a few days after his wife died, or an innocent desire for company.

"Here it is," their guide said, leading them into a small room. "It's Caravaggio's only painting directly onto plaster: *Jupiter, Neptune and Pluto*."

Faye looked up at the vaulted ceiling and caught her breath. Whatever she had been expecting, it wasn't this. A giant moon dominated the center third of the painting, with three burly bearded men looming over. The perspective was dizzying. She felt as if she were actually looking up at them, seeing the soles of their feet and, on one, full frontal nudity, all viewed from below.

"Can you believe someone covered it up?" the caretaker asked. "They forgot about it for centuries." Just like Caesar's villa and the bust of Commodus, Faye thought.

"This room was a cardinal's study, wasn't it?" Adam said. "I'm not sure how I'd feel having that lot looking down at me when I was working."

This picture wasn't about the play of light and dark, and it didn't have the theatrical feel of so many of Caravaggio's other paintings. This one was just a gathering of the gods plotting something. Faye rather liked it.

"What's with the bird?" she asked. It was hard to tell exactly, but it looked like one of the enormous men was actually riding an eagle. It made for an odd view, the big man's legs and arms stretched out while he balanced on the relatively small raptor.

"A symbol of Jupiter's authority," their guide said. "Eagles are king of the sky, fitting for Jupiter. Later, the Roman Empire adopted them as a symbol of courage, strength, and immortality."

Cerberus, the three-headed dog at Pluto's side, reminded Faye of Daisy: same black coat and white markings on the chest. Faye had always imagined the hound guarding the underworld as a snarling three-headed mastiff, but Caravaggio had painted this dog looking rather friendly, almost like a sheepdog standing in a three-sided mirror: left profile, right profile, and a straight-on view.

"It's one of Caravaggio's earlier works," Adam said. "Before he got all the sacred commissions. Right around the time he painted *The Fortune Teller*, I think. His critics said he didn't do perspectives, so he painted this to show them they were wrong." Adam was playing the role of Caravaggio expert, but Faye knew for a fact that he was even less knowledgeable about art history than she was. He had studied for this.

"I'm happy to have you enjoy it," their guide said. "May I leave you for a few moments? There are some things I must attend to."

"We must look trustworthy," Faye said when the woman was gone. "I guess no one told her we're suspects in a murder investigation." She paused, but Adam didn't laugh. "Why did you really come? And don't tell me it was to see the fresco."

Adam was silent for a moment. Finally, he spoke. "Do you know how many of our friends have stopped by? Zero. Just like you said, I'm a suspect. The prime suspect, judging from how the police are treating me. I thought if the gang saw me, they'd see how crazy that idea is."

Faye should be glad that she wasn't the only one who felt unfairly accused by their friends. Maybe it was just something that everyone went through in a situation like this. "Where did you find all that Caravaggio stuff, anyway? Your book sounds more informative than mine was."

"Scholarly articles on the Internet. You?"

Faye thought of her paperback *Caravaggio: Brash, Brutish, and Brilliant.* "About the same." She looked back up at the painting. "Did your reading explain why the moon's so big?"

"It's a crystal ball. The painting is about alchemy, somehow. Something to do with the patron's passion for the topic. Did you notice all the gods look the same? They're all supposed to be portraits Caravaggio painted of himself."

The men weren't Faye's taste, but preferences change. Who could say if Caravaggio made himself into the Baroque equivalent of a GQ model, or if he'd stuck true to life. He must have given himself more muscular legs, though. The diets back then had been terrible, and a painter wasn't exactly spending hours at the gym working on his quads.

"Are there any more versions of this?" Faye asked. Caravaggio seemed to have painted several copies of paintings he liked, or that had sold well. There were two versions of *The Fortune Teller*, which looked virtually identical on her computer screen, several *Boy Peeling Fruit*, two *Lute Player,* and the whole series of *John the Baptist.* It would be nice to see a version of this painting without having to strain her neck to look up.

"None as far as I've read," Adam said. "And it's painted right on the ceiling, so the family can't sell it off, even if they wanted to."

Faye had read that the princess did her morning yoga under this painting.

The woman had dedicated her life to restoring the house and the grounds and was successful at it. Art must give joy to the right type of person. Why else would Esta spend so much of her time and resources acquiring new works?

The guide returned and offered to show them the rest of the home. She moved the pair through quickly, then left them alone in the garden. Faye strolled with Adam through the grounds. She took in the usual busts and headless statues scattered about and paused in front of a statue of Pan, that half-man, half-goat god.

She'd never liked him, with his celebration of all things wild. Faye understood that the English word panic derived from his name. It was fitting. This sculpture, which the guide had said was by Michelangelo, didn't make him look any more reliable.

"I know that it wasn't your choice to give up that new job," Faye said. "I know that Rowena told them you lied. But I won't tell the police." Adam had stayed quiet about her bank accounts, and she owed him.

Adam swiveled toward her. "What are you talking about?"

"I know how humiliating it must have been to have your wife sell you out like that. It wouldn't look good if the police found out." It was coming out wrong. She was trying to tell him they were even, but she was muddling it up. "I'm just saying that I won't tell."

A cat darted across the yard, ducking behind a statue. "Even if this story is true, why are you telling me this?" Adam's tone was cold, and Faye regretted saying anything.

"I'm not sure. Forget all about it."

Adam grunted. "We should leave, the caretaker's watching us. I'll give you a ride home."

Adam was preoccupied during the drive, answering Faye's attempts at small talk with the minimum possible responses. She shouldn't have said anything about the job. Clearly, he was humiliated at her knowing the true state of his marriage. Faye wished she'd taken a taxi.

He maneuvered a tiny two-seater into a parking space near his house. "Daisy needs to go out. We'll walk you back."

Faye followed him upstairs and was gratified by the thwacking of Daisy's tail when they came into the apartment. Adam disappeared to get the dog's harness, and Faye glanced around. The food she'd brought sat on the counter, untouched. Everything was clean and tidy, with a laptop on the coffee table and a magazine open by the sofa. It didn't look like a house of mourning.

Faye regretted coming up. "I forgot I need to take something to the DiLorenzo offices," she called out. "I'll see you later."

Adam came down the hall, harness in hand. "You don't need to do that." Something about his expression wasn't right. He was frowning, eyes creased at the corners. "Aren't we still friends?"

He took a step closer, and she stepped back. "Sure we are."

He threw the harness down. "So what's this about? You suspect me too, is that it?"

She didn't know why it had suddenly been so important to get away, but Faye couldn't bring herself to stay a moment longer. She left without saying a word.

Chapter Twenty

With a short temper and willingness to fight, Caravaggio faced trial more than ten times for crimes ranging from swearing at a constable to scarring a guard. The only surprise, perhaps, is that he passed thirty-two years before actually killing someone.
—Caravaggio: Brash, Brutish, and Brilliant

Burt had his computer open on the kitchen counter, a cup of coffee and two empty muffin wrappers at his side, when Faye returned to the Whites'. "How was the tour?"

"Unique," Faye said. "You're working from home?"

"I'm golfing at Castel Gandolfo later and my last meeting just canceled. I've decided to play hooky. What are your plans?"

"Walking up to the DiLorenzo offices."

"A meeting with Esta?"

"No, Stefano left something in a café. I'm returning it."

Burt closed the laptop. "I'm not doing anything that can't wait until Monday. I'll come with you."

Faye ate a sandwich on the Whites' balcony before they set off. She was glad for the company. It was one of those June days that was more spring than summer: warm enough to wear a sleeveless top, but not so hot you needed to stay in the shade.

Walking down the street with Burt, Faye shook off the unease that had struck at Adam's apartment. It was only a matter of time before they figured out what happened to Rowena. She'd be back to her old life before she knew it.

They took a wandering route north along the Tiber toward Castel Sant'Angelo, the huge round mausoleum originally built for Hadrian, then turned into a prison, and later into a papal refuge connected to the Vatican by a special corridor.

They crossed the stone bridge and headed toward the center city. "Have you decided what you're going to do about 10 Via Pecora?" Burt asked.

They dodged a family taking a series of selfies. "I should stay put. I don't need the money, and I don't enjoy being bullied."

"Hmmm."

"You think it's a mistake?"

"I don't know," Burt said. "If someone is pressuring you, maybe there's more going on than they're letting on."

They paused at the end of the bridge, waiting for a group with enormous backpacks to move on, then continued north along the Lungotevere Tor di Nona, the boulevard snaking alongside the Tiber. Containing the Tiber was more accurate.

At one point, buildings lined the river, but the city tired of the regular flooding in the 1800s, and neighborhoods up and down the river were demolished to make room for high walls around the Tiber and impersonal roads next to those. It was a shame from an aesthetic point of view. The river, which had once been so important to the city, now felt separate and far away. Still, it was easy for Faye to take a sentimental view. She hadn't experienced the mayhem of a flood.

"It sounds like the DiLorenzos are going to move forward with or without my building. And quickly. It won't be fun living next to a construction site, but I can do it. I don't think it'll be good for Masterpiece, though. When the tour's over, I'll talk with Maggie about looking for another place." Faye shifted Stefano's leather bag to her other hand. "We'll find her something better."

Faye had been so worried about telling Maggie she was selling. She'd been afraid Maggie would be furious with her for forcing Masterpiece to move again so soon. But now with DiLorenzo Industries driving it, and the whole situation felt different. Faye could be a hero again, helping Maggie find a place that was even better. And Faye could wait out the construction. Maybe find a temporary apartment if things got really bad.

"I meant something going on with Esta," Burt said. "Why would she move forward with an incomplete vision?"

"I think she's being practical. Luca and Matteo could pull the plug while Esta waits for everything to be perfect."

"Esta's not going to like being disappointed. She's waited a long time for this project. Starting now, without your piece? It doesn't make sense to me."

"You make it sound sinister, Burt."

"The poison was in your home, Faye. You've got to take that seriously. You've found out a lot about Rowena, and things with Adam were bad. But between George and this building, there's still a chance the poison was for you."

Faye couldn't tell Burt that she'd already agreed to sell. No one needed to kill her to move the construction project forward. "Companies don't do things like that, Burt. Not in real life. And even if George wanted to kill me, which I don't think is the case, peanut butter wouldn't be his style. He'd look for a way to make it seem like an accident."

Something like a broken brake lever, maybe? Faye dismissed the idea.

They turned into the older part of the city, with its cobblestones and winding streets. Faye hadn't bothered to plan a specific route. The DiLorenzo offices were in the tony neighborhood near the Spanish Steps, and she knew the area well enough to adjust when she got closer.

Faye remembered George's last call before the party. He was furious over the investigation into his finances. Furious that Faye hadn't sent him his things. Furious that she was dragging her feet.

They turned onto a main street, and Faye took a moment to get her bearings. They were close to the Trevi Fountain, and tourists were out in force.

"I'm not sure the hotel would be so bad for the neighborhood," Burt said. "Your apartment is wonderful, but the rest of the block is looking a little down at the heels."

"Only because it's been in limbo. Don't you think it's wrong somehow, to turn old buildings that generations of families have called home into a soulless place that entices even more tourists to flood the city?"

"Since when are you the guardian of Rome's history?" Burt stepped aside to let two men with guidebooks stride by. "It's possible you're using the building to hold onto a life that's gone, Faye. Don't take this the wrong way, but things are constantly changing. It's the only universal truth."

George had called Faye controlling on many occasions. When he left, he said it had become intolerable. Faye forced a laugh. "Maybe you're right. Just look at Rome. When I came, I kept looking around for the famous seven hills. I was so disappointed to find out that the valleys had been filled in and the tops shaved off two thousand years ago." Burt hadn't been talking about geography and Faye knew it, but she didn't want to talk about fresh starts, even with this man who had been so kind.

A large tour group waited at the intersection with Via delle Convertite. The guests wore earpieces and clustered around a guide holding an umbrella in one hand and microphone in the other. Several other tourists holding guidebooks stood near them, and a group of European teenagers on some sort of school tour were being rowdy in the way teens in groups always were. It was just another day during the height of tourist season.

Faye stepped forward to make some room, then felt a hard shove from behind. She stumbled, lost her balance, and fell into the street.

Faye felt an explosion of pain as her chin hit the pavement and her shoulder twisted. There was a blare of horns and shouts and the screeching of brakes as the Number 100 bus screeched to a standstill just a few feet from her.

Faye felt the heat from the engine and the smell of the exhaust as she lay on the ground. Its enormous wheels were inches away from her head, and she felt like a trapped animal, waiting for a beast to open its jaws and swallow her whole.

For a moment, everything was silent as the world around her froze. No scooters raced by; no cars pulled past. Then a moment later, it all roared back to life with shouts and horns blaring and scooters zipping by, buzzing like angry hornets.

Faye fought back tears as she felt hands lifting her up and dragging her out of the way.

Burt squatted next to her. "Are you all right?"

Faye gingerly moved her arms, her hands, and her fingers. All appeared to be in proper working order, but it hurt. A lot. Her chin felt raw, and her right hand was scraped.

All she could think of was getting her heart rate back to normal. She breathed in, counted, then slowly exhaled. "I'm fine. Just help me find a place to sit."

Burt put an arm around her and helped her to a bench. She was wobbly, but she would be okay.

"Stay here," he said. "I'll get some water."

Faye closed her eyes and repeated her breathing. It didn't help. Her hands were still shaking, and she couldn't stop shivering, even on this eighty-degree day.

Burt returned soon enough and handed her a bottle of water. "What happened?"

"I'm not sure. It was so crowded." She tried to open the bottle, but her hands hurt too much. She passed it back to Burt to unscrew. "One minute, I was standing there. The next, I was being pushed. Hard."

Burt frowned. "Are you sure you were pushed? There were a lot of tourists. Americans, judging by the baseball hats. You know how impatient they get at intersections. Could it have been an accident?"

Heather said one rumor circulating was that Faye was an attention seeker who'd poisoned Rowena in a bid to insert herself into the center of things. Could Burt actually believe that?

"I don't know." Faye grimaced as she poured water over her hands, and her nerves rose in protest.

"Could it have been a mugging attempt?" Burt asked.

Faye had lived in Rome for a decade without any trouble. She was careful, the way you were in any big city. Stefano's bag, with its soft leather and discrete logo, could have marked it as a prize for an enterprising thief.

Then she spotted Stefano's bag on the ground not far away and pointed at it. "I don't think so." There was nothing inside of value. She knew. She'd had a look. Would a thief have thrown it away so quickly? Unlikely. They were supposed to grab the bag and run.

While Burt retrieved the bag, Faye tried to remember what exactly had happened. Had someone pulled it out of her hand? It had all happened so fast, she couldn't be sure. It was just a shove out of nowhere.

She asked herself if it could have been those teenagers monkeying around, or someone from the tour group stepping forward without looking. Things happened in crowds. People behaved differently when they were anonymous.

But no. The more she replayed the scene in her mind, the more sure she was that she had been pushed. Faye ignored the sinking feeling in her stomach. First, poisoned peanut butter, then George taking things from her apartment. Her scooter had been damaged, and now she was shoved in front of a bus.

"I'm calling Inspector Nardelli," Faye decided. "She may believe me, she may not. But I want this on record."

Adam's silence on the ride back from Villa Aurora had been unsettling. Faye had thought she was giving him a peace offering when she promised to keep quiet about Rowena's call to his would-be employer. Could he have interpreted it as a threat?

Faye had trouble catching her breath. For the first time, she felt scared. She took a sip of water and tried to regain control. "You didn't recognize anyone in the crowd, Burt?"

"You know I would have told you if I had," Burt said.

"Are you absolutely sure?"

"How can I be? I wasn't paying any attention until you fell."

Faye shook her head. This whole time, everyone was acting like she wasn't taking the threat against her seriously. Now, finally, when she was considering the possibility, it was as if Burt thought she was crazy.

"I'm calling." Faye's hands shook as she attempted to unlock her phone, and her fingers kept mixing up the numbers in her password. She tried to ignore the feeling that Burt was watching.

Before she got it right, the phone vibrated in her hand and she managed to accept the call. *"Pronto, sono Ispettrice Nardelli. Signora Masters?"*

Faye felt a wave of relief. It was as if Nardelli had read her mind and come to her rescue. All would be fine. "I was just trying to call you."

"Can you come to the station, please? We can send a car for you."

"Certainly." There had been a development. Nardelli was going to tell her they had sorted everything out. Faye glanced at Burt, who was frowning. "First, though, I need to tell you why I called. Or why I was trying to call. Someone attacked me. Just now. I think I might still be in shock."

"An attack?" It was noisy where Inspector Nardelli was. The station had been such an oasis of calm when Faye had been there before.

"I was on the Via delle Convertite and fell in front of a bus. Someone pushed me. There was a crowd of people, and I—"

"Are you well? Are safe?"

"I'm fine, yes, thank you. Just a little winded. But you were calling me. Have you learned something?"

Maybe they were on their way to arrest Adam right now. Maybe they'd learned the same things Faye had. There was a pause, then Inspector Nardelli exhaled a long sigh. "We are at the hospital. Signor Burke is in critical condition."

Faye's mind raced. Critical condition? Now? Had he run into the street after shoving her and landed in the very traffic he'd planned for her? "Did he get hit by a car?"

"A car? I am not understanding you, Signora Masters. He has been poisoned, the same as his wife. He arrived just a short while ago."

Burt was mouthing "what?" and Faye waved him off. Now she understood the noises in the background. They were those of a busy hospital: voices, announcements, beeping. "This afternoon?"

"A neighbor found him. It was, fortunately, a very small amount of poison. The doctors say he will recover. You understand I need to ask you questions. How soon can you come to the *questura*?"

An empty potato chip bag caught in the breeze danced toward Faye. She made a half-hearted attempt to catch it with her foot, but it drifted out of reach. "Fifteen minutes. Maybe twenty."

"Where are you? I will send a car."

"It's not necessary. I'll come there." Faye clicked off the phone. "Let's go to DiLorenzo and get rid of this bag." An extra ten minutes wouldn't make a difference, and she needed to get her head clear before she talked to the police again.

It didn't take long to catch Burt up: Adam had been poisoned; the police wanted to talk with Faye; that was all she knew.

"It was lucky the poison was such a small dose," Burt said.

"Yes." They paused at an intersection, well back from the curb. "Or it was planned that way."

"What do you mean?"

"A non-lethal dose of a very lethal poison?" Faye said. "It doesn't feel right."

"Someone wanted Adam sick, but not dead?" Burt asked. "Why? As a warning?"

"Maybe a distraction," Faye said. "Maybe he took a small dose himself to throw suspicion off."

"He couldn't have done that and pushed you, too."

The light changed, and they crossed. Faye's heart jumped as the engine of a waiting car revved.

"Are you sure you didn't just stumble?" Burt said.

"I'm sure. Pretty sure. Probably, sure, anyway."

Faye hated being this uncertain. She was not a woman who hesitated. She always knew which cards had been played, which ones were still out there, and calculated the right move.

Right now, she felt like she was playing a game with ten decks of cards, and no one had told her the rules. She couldn't get a handle on what was important and what wasn't. That had to change, and fast.

Chapter Twenty-One

In May 1606, Caravaggio murdered Ranuccio Tommasoni. The artist ran, fearing arrest and execution. He was convicted in absentia of murder and made subject to a capital sentence, meaning anyone in the Papal States had the right to kill him in exchange for a reward.
—Caravaggio: Brash, Brutish, and Brilliant

DiLorenzo Industries' Rome office was far from luxurious. A bored receptionist sat behind a small desk, keeping watch over two elevators and a sitting area barely large enough for five visitors to wait.

The receptionist spoke before Faye and George were more than a foot inside the space. "There is no public restroom. Use the McDonald's down the street."

Faye must look awful if she was being mistaken for a tourist. "We're here to see Stefano Ungaro. Faye Masters and Burt White."

The receptionist frowned and typed into his computer, then picked up the phone. He swiveled his chair away from Faye while he spoke, waited a few moments, then said a few more words. He swiveled his chair back toward Faye and Burt. "Have a seat, please."

Faye was supposed to be on her way to the police station. "That's all right. If it's not a good time, we can just leave this for him." She set Stefano's bag on the desk.

The receptionist eyed it as if it might contain a bomb. "They asked for you to wait, please."

Faye's hands stung from the fall. She was debating asking for the restroom to wash up when the elevator chimed. The doors opened, revealing Esta and another woman, younger, no more than mid-twenties. Their body language was all business. The younger woman was looking up at Esta in a deferential, slightly cowed manner that made Faye feel for her.

"Talk with Stefano," Esta was saying in Italian. Her tone was sharp. "He tracks those things."

"I tried, but he's not here. I'm not sure when he'll be back and—"

Esta turned toward the visitors and switched to English. "Faye! And your advisor. They told me you were here for Stefano, and I came myself. You have made your decision at last and wanted to inform us immediately? It's only by chance that I am in."

"Nothing like that," Faye said. "Just a courier service."

She explained about the forgotten bag, and Esta laughed. "Typical Stefano. He would forget his head if it were not attached to his body. That is the expression in English, no?"

The young woman stood off to the side, forgotten, but clearly still needing her boss's attention. Faye held out her hand, then noticed the woman's expression at the grime on it. "I'm sorry, I had an accident earlier. I'm Faye Masters. Stefano's not here? I spoke with him this morning."

"Paola," the young woman said, turning slightly pink. "I expected him, too. We had plans after work..."

"It is nothing," Esta said. "You know young people, they flit off without any notice. But tell me, how did you come to be with Stefano yesterday, Faye?" Esta's tone was light, but something in her eyes gave Faye the impression Esta cared very much about the answer.

"We ran into each other at a cafe. I needed a place to wait out the rain, and he was kind enough to share his table. He left the bag when his grandfather called for his ride."

Esta laughed. "Roberto is too cheap to pay for a driver. Instead, he takes my employee. Stefano's grandfather is my dear friend, so I can say as much, but Roberto would do better to hire a professional. Stefano is easily distracted, yes? The smallest thing and bump! Driving in Rome is not easy. It requires courage, but also finesse, yes?"

Faye thought of her scooter. She had always found riding in Rome a joy.

"You were very kind to help my young friend with his bag," Esta continued. "I will see that he gets it. My car is outside. It would be no problem to drop you on my way. You are going home, yes?"

"To the police station, actually."

Esta frowned. "There is news?"

"Adam Burke is in the hospital," Burt said. "Poison."

Esta sagged a little and said something under her breath. "This tragedy, it does not ever seem to end." Esta gripped the top rail of the chair next to her. "We will drive you. You would like to use the washroom first, perhaps?"

Faye glanced down. Her knee was bleeding, and her skirt had grit from the street on it. No wonder the receptionist had given them such a cool welcome. She was a wreck.

Paola led Faye up to the executive floor. It was quiet, and there was no evidence of the worker bees who must keep DiLorenzo running.

"You and Stefano are friends?" Paola asked. Her English was more heavily accented than Esta's. "He is very nice, isn't he?"

Faye washed her hands. It was as painful as she expected. There were lots of scrapes, but no active bleeding. "Have you worked together very long?"

Paola blushed. "Just a few months. I am in the accounting department, so we see each other often. DiLorenzo does things differently than my last company. I have many questions. And the people here, Esta and Rowena, they are so busy, it is difficult to ask."

"That must be hard."

Paola nodded. "It is! I do not like to say something bad about someone who has died, but Rowena, she could have a short temper. Once I had a question about a painting, and I didn't know which division it went with. She was very fierce."

Faye frowned. "A painting?"

Paola nodded. "Stefano explained it all to me, but how was I supposed to know if no one tells me? Am I a mind reader?"

Faye wet a paper towel and tried to ignore the stinging as she dabbed at her knee.

"Stefano helps me," Paola went on. "And he is sweet. We have the same taste in music, so we meet at lunch, sometimes, and share new favorites." Paola frowned. "We were supposed to go to a concert tonight."

Faye noted the past tense. "Is he all right? He said he'd be here today."

"I do not know. He has not been in, and he has not answered my calls." Paola bit her lip. "I wonder if he is staying with his grandfather. When he calls, Stefano asks how tall to climb. That is the expression?"

"How high to jump, yes. Maybe they are repairing their relationship?"

"I hope that is it," Paola said. "Stefano is eager to please his family. It is a good thing, in most situations."

But Faye felt a twinge of unease. Stefano had been the only person who knew Faye's plans to come to DiLorenzo Industries this afternoon. It would have been easy enough to follow her. And Stefano hadn't told Esta about Faye's decision not to sell. Was it because he hoped to change Faye's mind?

Or maybe he thought they could get the property another way. George would sell the building in a heartbeat if she died.

Faye didn't like where her mind was going. *Get a grip*, she told herself. Stefano was not the one shoved her. She would have noticed him. *But in a baseball hat holding a guidebook like an American tourist?*

She pushed the thought away and gave herself a final check in the mirror. Faye looked presentable, which would have to be good enough.

Right now, she was wasting an opportunity to talk to someone who knew Rowena. She smiled at Paola. "Was Rowena like that, too? Eager to please Esta?"

Paola took a moment before answering. "The job of an executive is not to please, it is to do the right thing, no? Rowena was diligent, that is the word? If there was something she was interested in, she would spend no end of hours learning about it."

"What sort of things?"

Paola shrugged. "All things, at one time or another. Return on marketing investments. Competitor advertising campaigns. Construction rules in different countries. Even the costs of decorating our hotels. She had me pull many years' worth of invoices to understand the cost of the paintings for the lobbies. But then, her interests changed. I saw an issue with the cost of carpeting in our new UK hotel, which was over budget, and she said it was a local concern. It is strange, no?"

It didn't seem strange to Faye. Rowena had probably been digging into something that she thought would help the business, learned what she needed to make an informed decision, then moved on. Faye nodded in agreement anyway.

"She was helping to make modern our processes," Paola went on.

"Oh?" Faye was only half-listening now, and she tried to remove the worst of the grit from her skirt.

"DiLorenzo Industries is a family-owned business, you understand, so things do not need to follow the same rules as in a public company. I found it difficult to adjust, and Rowena, too. She was adding structure."

"Mmmm." Faye had worked at both types of companies. The larger ones always had more processes.

Paola seemed to enjoy having an audience, because she went on, "Like Esta's art. If there is a picture she wants, she has the company buy it, then she buys it from us for her own personal collection."

"Why not buy the pictures directly?"

"Esta wants to keep her purchases out of the public eye. The media, they are interested in everything the family does. She wants to stay private when she can, yes?"

It did make sense, but it also felt like an invitation for trouble. Money sloshing back and forth in a company with loose controls was just asking for someone to take advantage.

Paola must have read the look on Faye's face, because she went on, "It is no problem. Esta pays the company back. There are invoices, it is easy to compare. It is just different from what I am used to."

"If everyone was happy with it, why was Rowena modernizing the systems?"

"It has to do with the future sale of the hotel division. When they are showing it to buyers, it will be important there is an accurate picture of the financials. Rowena said it was setting the stage, yes? Preparation for the future. Every bit counts for profitability, yes?"

"Didn't Esta mind?" The sale of the hotel division had always been discussed in the distant future.

"Mind? No. I think she had done it the old way for so long it did not occur to her to do anything else. No, I heard Esta just bought something new, and it was all through her own accounts, separate from the business. She and Rowena had a good relationship. They learned from each other. That is why it is so hard to believe Rowena died in such a way. She was tough, yes? But also fair. Everyone respected her." Paola inspected herself in the mirror and turned back to Faye. "Are you ready?"

When they returned to the lobby, Burt offered to escort Faye to the police station.

"There is no need for that," Esta said. "We will take good care of Faye."

Faye waved goodbye to her friend and leaned back on the car's soft leather seat. She closed her eyes, enjoying the smell of Esta's expensive car.

Esta broke into her thoughts. "If I may ask, what happened to you today? You did not look good when you entered."

"I fell. Right in front of a bus." Faye's voice cracked. "Silly, really." Faye was aware of the driver, but his head was facing forward, and he seemed totally uninterested in their conversation.

"That is terrible." Esta's voice was full of concern. "What happened?"

Faye told her about the crowded corner and finding herself on the ground. "It happened so fast, I didn't have time to do anything about it."

Faye felt helpless, and she hated it. That was what was so awful about this past week. She'd been floating along, not knowing where she stood, not able to get her feet under her. Events were carrying her instead of her directing them. It wasn't her way. She liked to know where she was and what she was going to do next.

Esta squeezed her hand. "And you think it was on purpose?"

"I don't know what to think."

The car paused at a light and a slew of tourists poured across the intersection. This was a city with more visitors at this time of year than its streets were able to handle. The accident could have been nothing. Or it was the perfect cover. There was anonymity in crowds, wasn't there?

"If it is any comfort, I have a report from the hospital," Esta said. "Adam is doing well."

It wasn't any comfort. It just was more evidence that Adam took the poison on purpose. But if that was true, it didn't explain what had happened on the corner.

"You are a smart woman with *buon fiuto*," Esta said. Good instincts. "What are you thinking?"

Faye considered telling Esta about Adam's job and Rowena taking it away from him, but there didn't seem to be any point in sullying the woman's memories of Rowena, at least not until Faye was certain.

"I just don't know." She decided to move to safer territory. "Paola was just telling me about Rowena's work updating the accounting systems."

"Rowena was very efficient," Esta said. She looked like she was about to say more, but Faye's phone chirped. It was a text from her sort-of-stepson Tim.

Just checking in. You still among the living? He'd included a clip of a 1950s Hollywood-style mummy walking out of a tomb. Faye smiled and showed it to Esta. "My family's sense of humor."

"You are lucky to have them. My family is more serious. They would hire bodyguards, but not call. It is different. Yours is better, I think."

Faye had heard from all of George's stepchildren except Ronnie. It wasn't surprising. Of them all, Ronnie was the most standoffish. He hadn't been in touch after she refused his request for money. Every family has a black sheep, and Ronnie was hers.

Faye looked out the window. They were passing the Palazzo del Quirinale, the grand old palace that is home to Italy's president. Twenty times the size of the U.S. White House, it was a testament to Italy's history and its present. "Well, there is my husband who might want me dead."

"I have not always been a good woman to live with," Esta said. "I have been through three divorces. If one of my ex-husbands did not try to murder me, I do not think your George would try to, either."

Esta's driver stopped when a light changed to amber and drivers behind them blared their horns in disapproval. A scooter raced around from behind.

"May I give you some advice?" Esta leaned close. Her perfume reminded Faye of her grandmother. "Give him what he wants."

It wasn't what Faye expected from this woman, whose family was famous for their toughness.

"Really, it is true," Esta said. "So many people, they want to win in a divorce. But there is no winning. There is just anger and sadness and too much money for the lawyers. It is faster and easier to move on with your life. It is hard to accept, but consider it, yes?"

Faye's own lawyer had said something similar, but that didn't make it any easier to swallow.

Esta rubbed her hands as if washing the topic away. "We will speak of something else, yes? What did you think of the Palazzo Barberini yesterday? A marvelous collection, if a bit old-fashioned. My taste is more modern."

"I didn't see much of it," Faye said. She explained about the Caravaggio Società.

"Ah, you are a fellow lover of art."

"Not really," Faye admitted. "I thought it would be a way to get everyone together, to stay involved, you know? I think I might have be too late, though."

Esta patted Faye's hand. "It can be so tiring keeping up appearances, can't it?"

Chapter Twenty-Two

While there is no doubt Caravaggio found his exile unpleasant, the artist enjoyed the hospitality of wealthy friends and patrons every step of the way.
—Caravaggio: Brash, Brutish, and Brilliant

T he staff at the police station were exceptionally friendly. Officer Piras led Faye into a private room and provided her with a cup of surprisingly good coffee. She smoothed her skirt and rolled her shoulders back. She had nothing to worry about.

When Inspector Nardelli arrived a few minutes later, the woman did not look her best. Her brown hair had not been brushed, and her shirt was untucked. And while the inspector's clothes appeared stain-free, they had not been ironed. She had been working hard on the case, that much was clear.

"Thank you for coming," Nardelli said, standing by the table, but not taking a seat. "You will wish to make a report, I think, yes? I will leave you with Officer Piras. Then we will talk. Good?"

It sounded very reasonable. Nardelli was a supervisor. She would let someone junior get the facts of the situation, then meet with Faye about the course forward.

Nardelli left, and Faye told everything she could remember. At the last moment, she included the knocked-down scooter. It might not be connected, but since she was here, she might as well get it on record. There were documents to sign, and it all felt very official.

Officer Piras departed, and Faye was alone. She glanced around the office, fighting the nerves that were bubbling up. The room was drab, just a table and three chairs. There was a mirror that Faye assumed from her television watching was two-way. It all felt very conventional, as if a set in a play rather than the real thing. Finally, Nardelli and Piras returned. "I have read the report. It has not been easy for you, Signora Masters. The scooter accident, I was unaware of that."

"I didn't want to trouble you before. But in the light of everything that's happened, it seemed like you should know."

Nardelli leaned forward. "Let me put your mind at ease first thing, yes? Signor Burke will be fine. He had too little poison to be very dangerous. A relief, yes?" It was what Esta had told her.

"Certainly." Why did Faye feel so nervous?

"Would it surprise you to learn the poison was in his cereal?"

Faye stared at Nardelli. Something about her tone had shifted. Faye glanced at Officer Piras, but his expression was blank. "You have lab results back already?"

"When a victim has only one thing in his stomach, it is very easy. I understand the cereal was a gift from you, is that right? You baked it, Signora Masters?"

Faye swallowed. The inspector wasn't being rude. But she sounded as if she knew the answers to the questions before Faye answered. It was as if she was looking to trap Faye. "That's right."

"We will be analyzing the remains along with the other things you brought to Signor Burke's home. Cakes, yes? They have not been touched. That could explain why he did not fall sick until today."

"The granola was just oats, honey, salt, cardamom, allspice, and poppy seeds," Faye said. "There's no peanut butter in it, the cakes either." But Faye understood what Nardelli was suggesting. She thought Faye had poisoned Rowena's husband.

Faye looked around the dingy room with its scuffed floor and these two officers, who, in the week since Rowena died, seemed to have come up with no one better to pin things on than her.

She was tired of it. She was tired of Heather's rumors. She was tired of doubting herself. She'd had enough. "If what you're asking is whether I poisoned Adam's food, the answer is no. I had no reason to want him dead, and if you are suggesting otherwise, I would appreciate you coming out and saying it."

Nardelli exchanged a look with Piras, then shrugged. "Fine. Signora Masters, did you poison the food of Adam Burke or Rowena Burke?"

"No." Faye leaned forward in her chair. "I'm a smart woman. You know that, right? I graduated summa cum laude from Smith College. I'm an excellent bridge player. If I wanted to kill Adam—which I don't—I wouldn't put anything in things I baked myself. Just like I wouldn't poison Rowena at my own party."

Piras was scribbling in his notebook. Good. Faye hoped he was getting all this, because she wasn't done. "I'd choose something else, something that couldn't be linked to me. And for the record, I don't even know how poison works."

Nardelli cocked her head. "Ah, but you are a smart woman, as you said. You could learn the chemistry. It is not so difficult. And the Internet makes things very easy, yes?"

"I majored in philosophy!" Faye realized her hands were clenched into fists and folded them in her lap. "Really, I understand the questions. You're doing your job. But look at my computer records. I've researched nothing like that."

"We take one step at a time, Signora Masters."

"You do realize that Adam is the obvious suspect, don't you? His wife treated him like dirt, and now he turns up sick? If that's not a smokescreen, I don't know what is."

"I, too, am a smart woman, Signora Masters. I see many possibilities, but I do not jump to any conclusions. This you can trust."

"You know he lied to get that job, right?" Faye said. "He fudged his credentials, and Rowena found out about it. She called them and told them to check his story. How humiliated do you think a husband would be to have a wife who did that? Can you imagine?"

There, she'd told the authorities exactly what she'd promised Adam she wouldn't. Thomas, at least, would be happy. "I'm ready to leave now."

Faye took the long route back to Via Pecora, fuming the entire way. She was angry at herself for being blindsided. She was angry at the police for having made so little progress. And she was angry at Adam for putting her in this position in the first place.

Maggie met her at the door. "Faye! We were worried sick. Burt told me about you being pushed. And then Adam in the hospital. What's going on? Are you all right?"

Faye was touched by Maggie's flood of words. "I'm fine, but food first. Do you have anything?" Faye was suddenly starving. Her nerves must be kicking in.

"Help yourself."

The guests were nowhere to be seen, but the remains of a buffet lunch were still in the kitchen. Faye filled a plate and joined Thomas and Maggie in the studio, where they were clipping pictures to a string along the back wall. Faye had forgotten that tonight was the tour's final evening. There would be a party, complete with a showcase of everyone's favorite creations from the week.

Faye recognized a series of Fontana di Santa Maria, which must be Paul's. They played with the perspective, some with the background piazza disappearing, others looming large. He had talent.

She took a bite of salad. Ilaria had paired slices of raw artichoke with arugula and fresh Parmesan, and the texture combination was perfect. Faye tore off a piece of bread to mop up some of the salad's peppery, lemony, olive oil dressing. She sighed.

Thomas turned to her. "It's good, isn't it? Ilaria has a magic touch." He picked up another picture from the stack, an awkward painting of a woman standing in a doorway. The shapes were all right, but the colors were bland. There was no sense of where the light was coming from. No feeling of drama. "So, what happened?"

"Adam ate the granola I brought him, then collapsed. There was too little poison to kill him."

"And you think it was a little too convenient," Thomas said.

"Exactly." She wanted to pump her fist in the air in triumph. Thomas come to the same conclusion she had. "I think Adam poisoned himself to divert suspicion."

"Then who pushed you?" Maggie said.

"I wish I knew." Faye had been going over it again and again, and she was still no closer.

Thomas broke into her thoughts. "Maybe you have it wrong."

"Someone pushed me, Thomas. I'm not trying to be a drama queen, but I—"

"I don't mean that," Thomas interrupted. "I'm saying maybe Adam didn't kill his wife. If the pieces don't fit, it means we're not there yet. We need to keep an open mind."

Faye sagged. Thomas had been the biggest proponent of the "it's always the husband" theory.

"What about Stefano?" Maggie said. "Burt says he knew exactly where you'd be this afternoon. And he wasn't even at the office."

"Why would he want Faye dead?" Thomas said, stepping back to admire his work. He'd covered the walls with the guests' paintings. Most of them were quite good, and some were very good. It was impressive what he and Maggie had helped the guests accomplish in such a short time.

"To get her building for Esta, of course." Maggie rubbed her sleeve against her forehead. "She's been after Faye to sell for years, and Faye keeps saying no. Maybe Stefano decides to poison Faye with her peanut butter, only botches the job and puts the poison in the one food in her refrigerator that she doesn't eat. He tries again with a shove. Everyone says he's not amazing at details. Isn't it possible?"

It would be possible if Faye hadn't already agreed to sell. She should set the record straight, but Faye couldn't bring herself to do it.

"I keep coming back to Cliff," Thomas said. "He went to the church to warn you off. And then what do you do? You keep digging around asking questions. Maybe it's no surprise that you suddenly took a nosedive into the street."

"You just don't like him because you worked together," Maggie said. She had a stack of tablecloths next to her and was wiping down the tables. "What motive would he have for killing Rowena?"

"The absence of evidence is not evidence of an absence," Thomas said.

"What's that?" Thomas made it sound like a quote, but it wasn't one Faye knew.

"It's something the history professors went on about. You can't conclude something didn't happen just because there's no evidence the other way. You might have just not found the evidence yet, or maybe there isn't any. In history, the record isn't perfect, you know?"

"So it's a long-winded way of saying that not having found a motive doesn't mean there isn't one, right?" Maggie shook one of the tablecloths and spread it out over a table, then moved on to a second. She was doing it all wrong. She hadn't smoothed the wrinkles and one side hung lopsided.

Faye set her plate aside, then took the table-setting duties over from her friend.

"Don't look so glum, Faye," Thomas said. "We'll get on the case tomorrow, right after the guests leave."

Faye wished she could share his optimism. "What's happening with the paperwork situation, Maggie?" Faye asked. "Is it sorted out?"

Maggie had come back from the municipal offices on Monday saying that she'd struck a dead end. After that, she'd spent at least thirty minutes on the phone each day trying to find someone who could tell her more.

Maggie sighed. "Nothing. I keep getting told to call a different office. I'm going to go in person when the guests are gone. At this point, though, it doesn't seem like anyone is going to shut us down over it."

If Masterpiece had to relocate—or *when*, Faye reminded herself—all the paperwork would just have to be redone.

"Ignore it," Thomas said. "Half the time someone issues a ticket, they never bother to finish the paperwork."

Italy was a country with a million laws but no rules. Italian train conductors were notorious for flexing their muscles when it came to minor violations of the rules: taking the wrong train or mistakenly forgetting to punch a ticket. They'd make a fuss, threaten to throw you off the train if you didn't comply. The thing was, Faye had never heard of anyone actually getting into trouble. It was all fuss, no meat.

Not that Faye was a *furbo*, those Italian foxes always looking for a loophole. But she wasn't a persnickety *pignolo* like Rowena, either.

Faye took her dishes to the kitchen and Maggie opened a drawer and handed Faye a whisk. "You'll want this back. We didn't mean to keep it so long."

"Is it mine?"

"Ilaria borrowed it, and it got mixed up in our things. We used some of your sugar, too. There's a replacement bag in the cupboard."

Faye had told Maggie to help herself to anything she needed to get the tour company set up. Faye had left a key in Maggie's desk drawer, so getting in and out was no issue.

"Have you told your lawyer about the police talking with you?" Maggie continued.

"No." It hadn't even occurred to Faye. "Do you think George would try to use it against me or something?"

"No, not for the divorce. Just, you know, as support? Maybe she could recommend someone local who could go with you if they call again?"

It took longer than it should have for Faye to understand what Maggie was getting at. "You're not listening to the gang, are you?" Faye couldn't keep the hurt out of her voice. She thought Maggie, at least, would always have her back. "They're just a bunch of gossips. I had nothing to do with any of this."

Maggie patted her shoulder. "I'm sure you didn't. But I don't want to see you getting railroaded. Things can go bad in a heartbeat."

Faye wanted to say she didn't need it, that this would blow over. But now, she wasn't so sure.

"Will you join us for the party tonight?" Maggie's tone was artificially bright. "You made a big impression on the guests. They'd love to see you."

Faye always made a good impression on people when they met her for the first time. It was after they got to know her that they started to slip away.

Chapter Twenty-Three

Caravaggio's time on the run was far from fruitless. He produced some of his greatest and most influential work during this period.
—Caravaggio: Brash, Brutish, and Brilliant

W innie Rogers called that afternoon. "I'm sorry I've been out of touch. Things have been crazy at work." Winnie was Faye's banker friend, the one who had helped set up the accounts that got her into the mess with Rowena. "How's the Caravaggio Società going?"

Winnie sounded the same as always: a little scattered, but warm and genuinely interested. If she'd heard the rumors Heather had mentioned, she didn't let on.

Normally Faye would lie and say everything was terrific. "Not so great."

"Oh no. Why not?" A dog was barking on Winnie's end of the phone. Anginetti—whose name came from her blonde-white coloring so similar to the lemon cookie popular in the south of Italy—was upset about something.

"Poor turnout. Just Adam, Cliff, and Lilly have shown up, and I'm pretty sure they only came to talk about Rowena's death. Plus Caravaggio was kind of a jerk, and I don't especially like his art."

Anginetti went on barking. "You can give up any time, you know. Just call it off." Like it or not, Faye would see this project through. Quitting wasn't something she did. "Listen, I'm calling to ask a favor," Winnie went on.

Faye braced herself. "Sure, anything."

"You heard about Adam being in the hospital, right? Well, the police asked me to take care of Daisy. Don't ask me how they got my name. But Daisy and Anginetti aren't getting along. Anginetti's great with other dogs, you've seen her, but the two are growling and barking at each other, and I've had to shut poor Daisy in our bedroom. I know you helped Adam out before. Can you take her?"

Faye was so relieved she said, "No problem," before she thought it through. Winnie should be asking someone not currently under suspicion for murder. Or faked victimhood. Or whatever else the gang suspected. But the fact was, Faye liked Daisy. And maybe with a dog on guard duty, she could finally spend the night back at her own apartment. "Want me to pick her up?"

Winnie had Daisy leashed and ready to go when Faye arrived. "You're a lifesaver," Winnie said over Anginetti's barking from deeper inside the apartment. "You might need some food, but I'll pay for it. Here." She tried to hand Faye a hundred euros, which Faye waved away.

"Listen, Winnie, you didn't mention those accounts you set up to George, did you?"

"Of course not. Or anyone else. Those are legitimate accounts, and I have no knowledge of what you are or are not disclosing to your husband. Let's keep it that way." She handed over a bag of Daisy's supplies. "I owe you one. Thanks, Faye. Anginetti, hush!" She smiled at Faye. "Dogs, what can you do? Bye Daisy."

Daisy seemed totally oblivious to the fact that she'd been kicked out. She sniffed the wall next to Winnie's building, then trotted along next to Faye. They made a good pair. Daisy chased a few pigeons, and Faye got more *"buon dì"*s in the thirty-minute walk home than she had gotten in the last week. Dog walkers were a friendly breed.

When she reached her building, Faye fumbled with the street door and nearly jumped out of her skin when she felt a hand on her shoulder.

"Cavolo!" She turned and found George. "You scared the life out of me."

Her husband's face was puffy and red, and damp sweat marks showed through on his shirt. "You just always have to be right, don't you, Faye?"

Her heart thumped as she glanced up the street. Other than a couple walking away from them, it was deserted. Faye instinctively pulled Daisy closer. "You shouldn't be here, George."

Faye made a move to go inside the building, but George pulled the door shut before she could get her foot inside. She felt his breath on her cheek.

"You're so used to getting everything your way you can't stand losing, is that it? You get your kicks making my life hell? No more."

Faye ducked away under his arm, and Daisy's leash got tangled around George's leg. He yelped, and Daisy barked as if it were playtime. Some guard dog.

George stepped back. "I'm tired of you ignoring my calls. My lawyer says you're dragging your feet. Get the paperwork in, and let's settle this."

"Or what?"

He frowned. "What do you mean?"

"Or you'll try to push me in front of another bus? You'll knock my scooter over again? You'll break into my house when I'm asleep this time? Or do you have something new planned?"

He looked completely and utterly baffled. "What are you talking about?" The menace in her husband was gone. It was just George. Unhappy, ineffectual, bumbling George. Faye suddenly couldn't remember why she'd been trying so hard to hold on to this man who'd fallen out of love with her so many years ago.

She didn't know whether to laugh or cry. She'd built her husband into some kind of bogeyman all day, but that was just a mirage. "Someone shoved me in front of a bus today," Faye said. "My scooter is broken. And you burgled my apartment."

George flushed. "I didn't break in."

"Fine, you used your key. But you had no right in there any longer."

Faye sat on the step, and Daisy lay down next to her. Faye thought of all the things that had moved over the past few weeks. Some shifting position, others disappearing and reappearing at odd times. "Were you trying to scare me? Make me think I was crazy?"

Daisy stretched all four legs, then flopped her head back onto the pavement.

George sat next to Faye. "I wasn't there, Faye. Ronnie took the boxes. A misguided attempt to be helpful. I'm sorry if it scared you."

"Ronnie?" Her sort-of-stepson was supposed to be launching his career as a social media influencer somewhere. Then she remembered Tim saying that his brother was supposed to be seeing George for dinner. "He's back in Rome?"

"He reached out and suggested we meet at the conference," George said. "Turns out he wanted a loan. It was a waste of time. I told him I'm broke until we get this divorce settled."

George had plenty of money when he left. "Girlfriend's been on a spending spree?"

George's face turned a deeper shade of crimson. "You have no idea. The book money's stopped rolling in, and the university powers that be aren't thrilled about our relationship. They can't prove anything, but—"

Just knowing George's life wasn't all roses was suddenly enough for her. Faye wasn't mad at George, she realized. She'd been jealous. He'd been moving to a shiny new life while hers was rolling downhill. If his wasn't perfect, it felt like the scales of karma were back in balance. "I'll talk with my lawyer."

"Really?" He looked pathetically grateful.

"I'll call this afternoon." Besides, if she delayed too long, someone might get the idea to dig into Faye's financials a little further. It was time to move on.

Faye led Daisy up the stairs to her apartment. The dog darted around Faye's living room, sniffing madly, then curled up in a sunny patch in front of the terrace doors. Faye read a bit more of the Caravaggio book, then picked up a crossword puzzle. She wasn't any closer to clearing her name. Someone still wanted her dead. But listening to Daisy's gentle snores, Faye felt at peace.

Faye turned in early and lay in bed telling herself that she was safe. She had a dog next to her, and George was cleared as a suspect once and for all. But after fifteen minutes of self-talk, she got up and stacked pots and pans in front of her front door so she'd at least know if someone broke in. She pushed aside the nagging question: *And then what?*

Faye's phone buzzed in the morning. She reached for it, hoping it was

Stefano, but it was only Nan confirming their plans to visit the Capuchin Museum after the tour's goodbye breakfast.

Faye wondered if she ought to worry about Stefano, but she put the thoughts aside as she organized Daisy for a morning walk. Back home, the dog interrupted her morning strength exercises, nudging her snout into Faye every time she tried to do a crunch, so Faye gave up and gave the dog a belly rub instead. She had trouble remembering the last time she'd had such a relaxed morning.

Faye left Daisy snoozing on the bed when she went to meet Nan and Paul. They were already in the vestibule of the "Bone Church" when she arrived. With the Masterpiece Tour complete, they were heading north to spend a week visiting Florence and Venice.

It was Faye's first visit to this church decorated with the bones of thousands of monks. Faye had always dismissed it as sensationalist tourist bait, but Nan wanted to see it. Besides, there was a Caravaggio Faye could check off in the process.

The Caravaggio Società wasn't scheduled to visit for another two days, but it was clear the gang wouldn't be joining. Faye would continue to see the pictures on her own and be happy, even if it wasn't the social success she'd hoped.

"Start with the art?" Paul asked.

"We may as well get it out of the way," Nan said. "I think the Caravaggio's over there." The museum wasn't at all what Faye expected. Many of Rome's museums are created from repurposed *palazzos*, but this one was purpose-built, and it had a sleek style that seemed more Danish modern than old Rome.

The three wandered through the exhibits, breezing past displays about the history of the Capuchin Order until they reached the Caravaggio. It looked just like the painting Faye had seen at Palazzo Barberini: a kneeling monk gazing at a skull, the scene illuminated from somewhere overhead. The painting itself was fine, but all brown and beige and lacking any dramatic tension that she could see. Certainly not a favorite.

"Hmmm, not my style," Nan said. "And you're seeing how many of these?"

"A lot," Faye said. "And reading a book. Caravaggio was crazy. Well, that's not fair." Crazy was not a term to throw around. "He had a tough childhood: both parents died in the plague, grandparents too. But he got into fights all the time. He threw artichokes at a waiter. He walked around with a sword. He killed someone and ran away before he could be arrested."

"A childhood like that would scar anyone," Nan said.

"Caravaggio wasn't the only impoverished plague orphan back then," Paul said. "Everyone else didn't go around killing people and throwing artichokes."

"Maybe they did," Nan said, "And they weren't famous enough for anyone to write the fact down."

"I think it's more likely that the others just got on with their lives," Paul said. "Caravaggio's celebrity gave him permission to act out."

"My husband has strongly held beliefs about right and wrong," Nan said, squeezing her husband's elbow. "It makes watching movies together very difficult."

Paul laughed. "You knew it when you married me. Should we go see the crypt?"

They followed the signs downstairs, and Faye caught her breath when she got her first glimpse. Thousands of bones were arranged to create arches, tree branches, even medallions. It was beautiful in a macabre sort of way.

She stepped closer. In many of the arrangements, the bones were grouped by type, with pelvic bones overlapping to create one design and finger bones to create another. In other places, towers of skulls covered the walls like crazy stonework. From a distance, you might mistake it for mere decoration. Except for the leering skeletons draped in robes. Those were unmistakably human.

Faye found herself in a small chapel in front of a plaque. *What you are now, we used to be. What we are now, you will become.* It was creepy. And humbling. And true. So easy to think of the figures of the past as just that: figures, unconnected with our lives today.

A family with two boys walked past. One boy asked how the monks had removed the human tissue from the bones, and his brother suggested it had been boiled off.

Rowena, like Paul, had had a strong sense of right and wrong. Growing up in a crazy world, a child could choose the always-angry path of Caravaggio or, perhaps, the black-and-white one of Rowena.

"Is there any word from the police?" Paul asked. "We didn't like to ask, but we've been worried."

Faye was surprised how cold it was in the crypt, despite the crowds jostling around them. "Worried?"

"We didn't want to leave until we knew you'd be safe," Nan said. "We know you didn't have anything to do with this, but you hear about police errors all the time. We have some friends who are super lawyers. We can put you in touch with them if it comes to that."

Faye squeezed her hand. These nice people had just met her, and they were ready to defend her. "That means so, so much to me. But everything's going to be fine."

"You think the police will make an arrest?"

She told them about Adam's poisoning. "I think it was a ploy to distract attention, make it look as though he's just a victim." Faye told them about Rowena pulling the rug out from under Adam's new job.

"Well, that's something," Nan said.

"More than something," Paul said. "What else do you have, Faye?"

"He didn't eat any of my baked good until I told him I knew about Rowena and his job. Not a single one, and then he suddenly decides to eat my cardamom granola, when he's snubbed my cinnamon rolls and scones? It doesn't make sense."

"Mmmmm," Nan said thoughtfully. "I see your point. But I'm afraid it doesn't really sound like evidence."

"I'm not so sure," Paul said. "Clearly, he suspected you of killing his wife. That's why he wasn't eating your food. And a guilty man wouldn't suspect someone else. Sure, he'd put on a show in public, but in the privacy of his own home? No, he'd eat the food."

"Paul, not everyone has your sweet tooth," Nan said.

"Adam does." Faye had seen it firsthand. He was a fiend for baked goods, especially cinnamon rolls. That's why Faye had made them.

"Then why eat the granola?" Nan said.

"Because Faye made it clear she suspected him," Paul said patiently. "When she left his apartment after that Villa Aurora tour. She wouldn't have had any reason to be afraid if she had poisoned his wife. It's circular as all get out, but they both suspect each other, so they're both innocent. Don't you see?"

Paul was right. Adam hadn't killed Rowena. The scooter, the fall, the poison in Faye's own home. This was about Faye, after all.

Chapter Twenty-Four

The Knights of Malta gave Caravaggio shelter when he was on the run, even
making him a member of their order. But true to form, the painter fought with a
fellow member and found himself exiled once again.
—Caravaggio: Brash, Brutish, and Brilliant

I t was nice coming home to Daisy. The dog began barking excitedly the moment Faye put her key in the lock, and when she had the door open, the dog raced to greet her, circling three times before flopping down for a tummy rub.

Faye laughed and found a tennis ball for Daisy to chase. A knock at the door interrupted their game, and Faye found Thomas holding a white bakery bag.

"Brain power, courtesy of Cafe Antica. The guests have departed, the studio is clean, and I am officially off the Masterpiece Tours' clock."

Thomas crouched down and gave Daisy a rub on the head. "What's our plan?"

Thomas said "we" like it was the most natural thing in the world. Faye got them drinks and notepads while he settled on the living room sofa and helped himself to a pastry. It was one of the cafe's strawberry *Pizzicati*, buttery cookies filled with jam and covered with powdered sugar.

"We focus on Cliff. I know your friends at the auction house say he's acting the same as always, but we need to learn more about him. Especially whatever was going on between him and Rowena."

"Makes sense." Thomas had a scattering of powdered sugar on his cheek, and Faye resisted the urge to brush it off like a mother hen.

"And Stefano," Faye said. "And Esta. They were at the party. They worked with Rowena. And Stefano has been MIA since Thursday night."

"Good thinking. What about the others at the party?"

"They all know my door code. I guess any of them could have snuck in." But other than cutting Faye socially, they had done nothing of interest. "But since they didn't touch Rowena's drink, they're no more suspects than anyone else who could have slipped into my apartment over the last month. Unless we're putting the plumber and all of my houseguests on the suspect list, I don't think we need to worry about them."

"Agreed," Thomas said. "Focus is what we need right now." Daisy stood up and stretched, then made her way to Thomas. She took care of the powdered sugar situation with a series of licks. Thomas gently pushed her away. "What about George?"

"He didn't do any of this."

"You're sure?"

Faye thought of George's face the other day. "He didn't know anything about it. He didn't even come in to take his things, that was Ronnie. George is out of it."

"And Adam?"

Faye flushed and told Thomas Paul's theory.

"Innocence by baked goods," Thomas said. "That's good enough for me. You take Cliff. I'll take Stefano and Esta."

They each began scrolling the Internet. Still no response from the runners Faye had pinged. She supposed Cliff had warned them off. Cliff was easy to find, though, and she went down a social media rabbit hole, clicking on photos and looking up people who commented on posts.

Faye took one of the cookies. It was light and buttery, almost as good as her own. She would have liked a more complex jelly, but they hit the spot. Faye reached for another, and Daisy trotted over expectantly.

Faye found herself on a website dedicated to training tips. There were posts about diet (some avidly in the plant-based camp, others just as adamant about animal protein), gear (the values of different anti-chafing ointments), and trailside etiquette (who knew riders on horseback have the right of way in nearly all situations?).

A post about cheating in ultra-marathons led Faye to a website dedicated to exposing cheaters. Why, in a sport with barely any prize money, barely any sponsorship, barely any anything, would someone bother cheating?

Faye felt Daisy's warm breath on her knee as she read about a man who'd posted a photo of himself on another site with a comment about how miserable a race had been, and someone had been interested enough to look up his bib number in the photo and realize it was registered to a different runner.

Apparently, the man in the photo used a friend's registration that the friend was unable to use, and both runners had been permanently barred from the sport. Why? Something to do with competing in the wrong age bracket and doing someone older out of his or her rightful place in the list of finishers by age group.

Daisy began snoring gently, and Faye was aware of how pleasant it was sitting here with Thomas and the dog. She'd left the doors to the balcony open, and the gentle breeze coming in was comfortably warm.

Faye stretched and turned back to the cheating site. She should go back to Cliff's posts, but it was hard to pull herself away from the exposés, and the squabbling among runners that they provoked. It was a mix of things that seemed like clear-cut cheating and innocent mistakes. Maybe Italy was rubbing off on her, seeing everything as a gray area.

Faye read a defensive comment from a woman saying it was unrealistic to expect runners to follow a trail with switchbacks up or down a hill. Straight lining was technically against the rules, but the woman writing the post said she did it, and so did many other runners. The woman argued organizers shouldn't try to over-regulate what was supposed to be a freewheeling sport.

There was an article about someone else, who was denied a result because he'd accepted water from a spectator, a story Faye remembered Lilly mentioning. Rowena had been against the runner, saying the rules were the rules.

There was a message from the organizer of Rowena's last race about the importance of self-regulation in the sport, and several runners had commented, including Rowena, whose message was friendly enough to suggest they knew each other. He wasn't in the original group Faye had pinged, so she sent him a private message. He'd probably be silent like the others, but it was worth a try.

Faye clicked back to the feel-good sites to read about Cliff. He was a big fish in this small pond of athletes. People commented on some of his blog posts with notes saying how much they'd enjoyed seeing him at a certain race, or how helpful he'd been in a tough spot. By all accounts, he was the nice guy he made himself out to be.

Church bells outside pulled Faye out of her research fog. They'd been at this for nearly an hour. "You having any luck?" she asked.

"Loads," Thomas said. "Stefano's all over social media. Trips, parties. He's a player."

"How does he afford it? His family's rich, but he says he's living off an assistant's salary."

"He seems to be a guest at all these things," Thomas said. "Friends with the right people and all that." Thomas clicked some more. "It's funny, isn't it? If you have lots of money, you're friends with people who also have lots of money, so they don't mind bringing you along for free. But if you don't have any money, you don't meet those folks, and so you would never get a free ride. Bit unfair, that."

"How long can someone sponge for, do you think?"

Thomas frowned. "Depends on his friends. If he's supposed to be working, he can't exactly drop everything to go to a house party on Capri. But if he keeps the nine to five gig, he drops off the radar, and people stop thinking to invite him. It's a bit of a doom spiral in the world of the spoiled rich." Thomas came from this world. Maggie had worried how long he'd stick it out at Masterpiece, but he seemed to genuinely enjoy working.

"Stefano was at DiLorenzo Industries Friday night and again on Saturday," Faye said. "Is he already in the doom spiral?"

"Maybe." Thomas clicked some more. "Definitely going out less and less. But it could be he's just getting serious about his job. That party life isn't for everyone."

Maybe not, but Stefano said that he didn't want to live on an assistant's salary forever, either. Once he had Esta's recommendation, he would go back to a bigger position at his family's company, presumably with a fat salary or allowance that came with being back in the family's good graces. "When did he last post?" Faye asked.

"Thursday morning," Thomas said. "He posted a picture of himself with his grandpa. Kind of sweet if you didn't know he was trying to make points with the old man."

"What are you finding on Esta?"

Thomas laughed. "She's not exactly all over social media. But she's photographed at posh events."

"At least we know she can pay her own way. No doom cycle for her."

"I'm not so sure about that. There was an article about DiLorenzo Industries with that Matteo fellow boasting how little salary the family took. It's less than many of their employees make, because the family is committed to keeping every penny in the company for the future generations. It's charming in an old-fashioned kind of way."

"It's charming if you have children you're saving the pennies for. Esta doesn't have any. She must be doing all right, though. I saw her house."

"Poverty is relative," Thomas said.

That was the truth. George was crying poor because his girlfriend was pushing for expensive gifts, but Faye knew his rental house was right on the beach.

"Still, her budget for her art isn't unlimited," Thomas said. "I'm not clear where the money comes from."

"I think it pays for itself," Faye said. "She showed me a picture she bought for a fraction of its value today. She probably supports her habit by selling the ones that appreciate so she can buy more."

"Maybe," Thomas says. "The art market is fickle, though. Lots of highs and lows. It's on a real low now. If someone's selling today, I hope they bought pretty cheap. Otherwise, they would be facing a huge loss. There are exceptions, but not many."

"That's a buyer's market, then. Esta said she just bought two new pictures. They were probably bargain-basement prices. It would fit her pattern. Have you come across the name of her art dealer?"

"No, why?"

"Rowena was supposed to be buying a painting for Adam. Maybe she said something about what was going on in her life." Faye thought of her conversations with Paul and Nan. "Sometimes people tell their casual acquaintances more than the people they know well."

"I'll look."

Faye settled back into reading some comments about Cliff and Rowena's most recent race. Someone named LGSL posted: *Unbelievable finish, man. You came out of nowhere.*

Cliff answered, *TY. It was touch and go when I lost the trail, but I was not about to let that stop me. When I got back on track, I fired up and drove it home.*

"I had no idea Cliff was such a big deal," Faye said. "He's all over these ultra sites."

"A giant among midgets?"

Faye's phone rang with an Italian number before she could respond. It was the race organizer she'd pinged. "*Pronto*, Faye? This is Bernard. I saw your message and thought it best to call."

He spoke in Italian, and she did the same. "*Ciao.* Thank you, that is wonderful. I am a friend of Rowena's. Your race was her last one, and she was so proud afterward, I just wondered—" Faye paused. Wondered what, exactly? It was difficult to ask questions when you didn't know what you didn't know.

But Bernard spoke anyway. "You are calling about her complaint?"

"Oh, ah, yes. The complaint." Faye didn't know what he was talking about, but she'd learned from moving around a lot as a child that the best way to catch up was to pretend she was already in the loop. She'd figure out the details as she went.

"I do not know what to say," Bernard said. "Rowena sent a message asking to meet. She wanted to file a complaint, but she provided no details. I proposed a time to talk, then nothing. It wasn't until I heard about her death that I understood her silence."

Faye gripped the phone. No one—not Cliff, not Lilly, not Adam—had mentioned Rowena lodging a complaint. "What did she say in the message?"

"That is just it. Nothing. No name, no details. I am at a loss. Are you a runner?"

"Not like Rowena," Faye said.

"Well, you may not know. But I am deeply concerned about the honor of the sport, and there have been some issues in the past, very troubling, which I have spoken out against. Rowena was a like-minded athlete. Others in our community fear over-regulation will spoil the sport. There is an individuality to ultra running that we all hold dear, me above anyone. I cherish it."

Faye murmured encouragement.

"But now, my hands are tied," Bernard said. "It is very difficult. I do not know if it was cheating or sportsmanship. It could have been anything."

Thomas looked up from what he was doing and shot Faye a questioning look. She shrugged. It was too soon to know what this meant. But her heart was beating harder. "When did she contact you?"

"Tuesday. I responded the next day but have heard nothing back. It is a shame."

"Have you heard any rumors?" Faye asked. "Anything at all?"

"Not a thing. More grumbles about the food provisions. I was hoping you might be able to help me."

"I'm sorry. I don't know anything."

He sighed. "Well, reach out if you do. And give Adam our condolences on behalf of the entire community. It's such a loss. *Ciao.*"

Thomas poured himself another cup of tea. "A lead?"

"It was the race organizer from the big event. It sounds like Rowena was preparing to file a complaint."

"What kind of complaint?"

"He didn't know."

Thomas leaned back. "That's a bit of a smoking gun. She was killed before she could spill the beans?"

Faye looked back at the race comments. "Cliff says he got lost on the course, but he still managed to beat Rowena." Faye stretched, and Daisy trotted over to her. Faye rubbed the dog's silky head. "Rowena never saw him."

"After a hundred miles in the woods, she could have missed him," Thomas said. "Especially sleep deprived. And if it was dark when he got back on track, maybe he took a different path."

"That would be against the rules. They're supposed to follow the trail."

"It's not like he won the race. No one would be hurt if he cut a few feet off by accident."

"I'm not sure the other runners feel the same way." Faye reached for another cookie and found the bag was empty. Thomas must have eaten six or seven without her noticing. "You'd kind of expect a lot of cheating in ultras, wouldn't you? When people are tired, they make decisions they wouldn't ever consider when they were fresh."

"I guess," Thomas said. "But who really cares? The sport's supposed to be fun, isn't it? They could put microchips on everyone's bibs if they really cared about regulating the heck out of it. The fact that they don't do that must mean something."

According to Cliff, races were about personal accomplishment. You didn't need microchips for that. Still, an article Faye had read on cheaters said most didn't acknowledge they were doing anything unfair.

Cheaters believed they were simply correctly a wrong. If someone had to stay late at work, he might think it was okay to skip out early the next afternoon, even if the office policies didn't allow it. Someone who lost her wallet might tell herself it's okay to take a soda from a store to make up for it. Someone who had trouble focusing might think it's okay to get help on a test. Again and again, the human mind can trick us into justifying our actions.

"Rowena sent the message about the complaint on Tuesday," Faye said. "The organizer offered to meet the next day, but she ghosted him."

"She was having second thoughts about screwing up some poor sod's life?" Thomas said. "That's about the first nice thing I've heard about her."

Rowena could have told George what she'd known about Faye, but she hadn't. She'd wanted Faye to come clean herself. "Maybe she wanted the runner to turn himself or herself in."

"And if the runner didn't want to?" Thomas said.

"Then he'd find another way to keep her quiet."

Chapter Twenty-Five

Caravaggio sent paintings to powerful friends in hopes that they would use their influence to win him a papal pardon for his crime. No pardon was ever given.
—Caravaggio: Brash, Brutish, and Brilliant

"Cliff got lost on the course," Faye said to Thomas. "It's public knowledge. And he might have felt justified in cutting some corners to get back on track. But Cliff's reputation is everything to him. If Rowena accused him of cheating, maybe he would do anything to keep his record clean."

"It's not a bad theory," Thomas said. "But there's no way to prove it."

The two had moved to Faye's terrace. It was the first time she'd sat out here since the interview with Nardelli and Piras. Usually, she came out every morning with a cup of coffee to watch the city come to life. Even in the winter, she'd bundle up with a blanket. Faye was a believer in the power of sunshine and fresh air.

"I think there is," Faye said. "Lilly told me that Rowena dropped by asking to see Cliff's watch with some story about buying one for herself. It was after the race, and I should have realized right then that something was off. Someone like Rowena would have sent Stefano or Adam out to do the research for her. She wasn't doing her own comparison shopping. She was looking for evidence."

Faye felt the way she did when her bridge partner laid out their cards for the dummy and she could see how she'd play the hand to victory. Faye knew the cards in play now, and she could see a path to success. "Cliff met with

Rowena on Friday. He ate all the snacks Stefano had for Rowena. It's why she was so hungry when she arrived at the party. He made up a story about her pressuring him for information about a painting, but that doesn't fit. This does."

"He killed her so she wouldn't tell anyone he'd been cheating. All so he could keep his qualifying points for the big race? Is the Valtellina 100 really such a big deal?"

"This wasn't about one race. Cliff's reputation is his entire identity. He'd do anything to protect it."

Thomas leaned back in his chair, hands laced behind his head. "And he comes to the party, knowing full well that Rowena is going to be a picky eater. He walks around waving that smoothie, probably just waiting for the right moment to pour it for her. I like it, Faye. There's just one problem: the poisoned jar of peanut butter. Why bother?"

"Cliff was trying to be clever. He knew the police had to search the kitchen eventually, so he put some poison in my things to confuse the issue. And he succeeded. The police have been going around in circles ever since they got that piece of evidence."

There was laughter in the street below. Students at the university heading to the bars, probably.

Thomas rubbed Daisy's ears. "I'm on board with the idea of St. Cliff being the villain in this whole thing. And he pushed you because you were asking questions?"

"It was risky, but he was getting desperate." Faye reached for a *crostino*. She'd grilled bread to eat with olive oil, cheese, and olives for dinner. She had enjoyed cooking for Burt, but she'd made things he would consider a proper dinner. Tonight, she was eating what she pleased, and told Thomas to take it or leave it. He'd opted to take it.

"So, what's our plan?" Thomas asked.

"We get the GPS data from Cliff's watch, just like Rowena did."

"Why not just tell the police what we know and have them dig into it?" Daisy had stretched out next to Thomas's chair and was snoring gently. "They can get a warrant or whatever."

"How will she feel if we come to her with a motive that she missed?"

"She'd be thrilled, I'd say, given that she's made no progress on the case on her own."

Faye crunched on another piece of toast while she considered this, enjoying the salty-savory aspect of something so simple. The residents of this city had eaten bread and oil for thousands of years. "She won't want to hear it from me. I'm a suspect." Faye took out her phone. "I'm calling Lilly."

Cliff's wife picked up right away. "Hi, Faye. How are the Caravaggios going? I'm so sorry I keep missing them. Things have been crazy at work, so I just—"

"It's fine," Faye said. "Listen, I was curious about something you said about watching the races and how you're able to see where the runners were. I need a birthday present for one of George's stepchildren. He's the sporty type, and the family would appreciate being able to keep track of him."

It wasn't a complete lie. Ronnie did have a birthday coming up, and the family would like to know where he was on his rambles. "Anyway, I thought it would be great to see how the tracking worked. Could I check it out tomorrow?"

There was a pause, and Faye wasn't sure Lilly was still on the phone, but finally, she spoke. "I'm sure Cliff is going to want it on his run tomorrow. But I can show it to you this afternoon. I was just going for a walk. Can you meet me at the Domine Quo Vadis in an hour? You know how to find the church?"

"Of course. I'll see you soon."

"Are you sure about this?" Thomas said when Faye explained the plan. "Going to a park at dusk with the suspect's wife? That's mad. Who's to say she won't tell Cliff? He already pushed you in front of a bus, Faye."

"There will be two of us. And Daisy." Daisy's feet twitched in her sleep, and she let out another snore. "It's a public place, Thomas."

"At dusk."

"The sun won't set for hours. You don't have to come if you don't want to."

Thomas raked his fingers through his hair. "Why is this so important to you? You haven't been arrested. You haven't done anything wrong. Let it go."

"This is going to hang over me forever if I don't clear my name. You get that, don't you? I'll always be the woman who got away with murder. Not because I did it, but because I might have."

"That's better than being the woman who was bumped off because she thought she could confront a killer."

"Killer's wife. And no confrontation. I'm just looking at a watch."

They arrived at Domine Quo Vadis ten minutes early. It was a tiny church at the edge of the Appian Way. Its name—literally, "Lord, where are you going?"—came from its location as the place where Peter had a vision of Christ. The apostle asked about Christ's destination and was told "to face crucifixion again." The vision disappeared, leaving behind an impression of his footprints on the road. A church was built on the spot and, at some point, the prints were packed off to one museum or another.

At least, that was one explanation for the ancient footprints. Another said they were a common Roman votive symbol for a successful journey. Faye liked that idea today, and hoped the good luck held for the meeting with Lilly.

Faye and Thomas positioned themselves next to the church and waited. "This is a bad idea, isn't it?" Thomas said. "Let's bail. The noble thing is to live to fight another day and all that."

"Caravaggio wouldn't have done that," Faye said. "He'd stay and fight no matter what."

"He's your hero, not mine," Thomas said. "I'd prefer a nice long life of anonymity than as a shining star who dies of syphilis."

Caravaggio was notorious for his drinking and gambling. He was arrested for carrying a sword without a permit, sued for beating a man with a stick, and went to prison for throwing stones at a policeman. Then he'd gone and killed a man, though it was unclear if the fight was over a tennis match or a love interest. Either way, the artist cut the rival's femoral artery, and the victim bled to death. Caravaggio ran, and after four years in exile, he died.

It was a nasty end to an artist who was, by all accounts, a nasty man.

"I read it was lead poisoning."

"Is that any better? Come on, Faye. This is madness. Lilly's going to be here any minute. Let's get out of here."

"Too late." Faye spotted Lilly walking toward them, five minutes early.

Chapter Twenty-Six

While on the run, Caravaggio's behavior became increasingly bizarre, with contemporaries reporting he slept fully armed and ripped up his paintings at the slightest word of criticism.
—Caravaggio: Brash, Brutish, and Brilliant

D aisy wagged her tail in a friendly greeting as Lilly made her way over. She was in her usual uniform of flowing skirt and sleeveless shirt. "You brought a friend."

"Hi, Lilly," Thomas said. "We met at an office party a year or two ago. I used to work with Cliff."

Lilly squinted. "Oh, sure. Nice to see you again."

Faye shot Thomas a smile. This was going to be fine. "Thanks for bringing the watch, Lilly. Can I take a look?"

"I didn't bring it." Lilly's tone was distinctly unfriendly.

"Oh?" Now it was Thomas's turn to catch Faye's eye. He shook his head slightly, but Faye ignored him. "You couldn't find it?"

"He got rid of it, Faye. Right after Rowena died." There was no question Lilly's voice had an edge to it. "Let's walk."

"We can talk just fine here," Thomas said.

"I don't think so," Lilly said. "Are you interested in what I have to say or not?"

"Of course," Faye said at the same moment Thomas said, "No."

Lilly shrugged and started down the tree-lined stretch of the ancient Appian Way. The original road, the "Queen of Highways," ran over three hundred miles all the way to Brindisi, that coastal city in the heel of the Italian boot that was a major port in Roman times. Now, two-thousand years later, the road was still clear and level. This section was part of a ten-mile archeological park complete with old cobblestones, mausoleums, and pastoral views that had hardly changed since Roman times.

Faye walked next to Lilly. Daisy trotted happily along on her leash, but it was unlikely she would provide any security assistance if the need arose. Faye did not want to believe that Lilly was involved in Cliff's mess, but she remembered Lilly leading her away from the kitchen during the party with questions about a weekend trip to Bolsena that, later, she seemed to have forgotten all about.

Where is Thomas? He had lagged behind, but in a moment he caught up, apologizing as he slid his phone into his pocket.

Lilly walked fast, and Faye had to almost jog to keep up. The sun was still high in the sky, and Faye felt a trickle of sweat roll down her back.

"Cliff and I took a tour through here once," Lilly said. "Some of the inscriptions on the mausoleums were really funny. One says, 'I advise you to enjoy life more than I did.' And another one is 'Beware of doctors, they were the ones who killed me.' You don't think about the Romans having a sense of humor."

Faye certainly didn't. Not when they had crucified six thousand enslaved people along one hundred twenty miles of this very road. That averaged fifty humans strung up every mile.

At the Empire's peak, about one-third of this city's residents had been enslaved. One-third! And if one of those people killed a member of the owner's family, all the household's enslaved people would be killed as punishment. It was ugly stuff, to put it mildly.

Lilly avoided most of the cobblestones and took the worn dirt path on the side instead. "Cliff said you were talking to other runners. What did you find out?"

"Do you really not know?" Faye asked.

"Tell me."

"You know Cliff got lost out on the course, then seemed to finish out of nowhere."

"And?"

Faye knew how to play any hand in any game of bridge, but she didn't know what Lilly hoped for at this meeting. Maybe Lilly was in the dark. Maybe she had suspicions about her husband and genuinely wanted to hear what Faye had learned. Faye glanced at Thomas, but he was no help. "Rowena told the race director she wanted to talk. Then she died."

"My husband is a good man. He's been a mentor to more people in crisis than I can count. He's made a real difference in the world." Three women rode past on rental bikes. There was nothing to be concerned about. They were in a very public place. "If you think he pulled a Rosie Ruiz, you've got it wrong. He didn't even land in the top twenty."

Rosie Ruiz was the runner who had claimed victory in the Boston Marathon in the 1980s, sneaking onto the course close to the finish. Apparently, she hadn't intended to win, but she misjudged her entry point and came in before the other women. Faye remembered the runner went to jail for unrelated crimes that included embezzling and maybe even a drug deal. Her life was a mess, and the marathon had been just one symptom of a troubled mind.

"No one's saying that." Faye hadn't said Cliff cheated, but it was clear Lilly had already gone down that path.

"Cliff says he got lost in the dark," Thomas chimed in. "Maybe he just didn't bother to backtrack when he figured out where he was. He probably saw the headlamps up a hill or something, right? He was exhausted and just cut up toward them. I don't blame him. No one would." Thomas was doing his best to be chummy, but Faye could tell from the set of Lilly's jaw that she was gritting her teeth.

They passed the Catacombs of Callisto. Roman public health policies had prohibited dead bodies within the city walls, and this entire stretch of road had once been a burial ground.

"Cliff logged one hundred four miles that day, if you're really interested," Lilly said. "He got lost at the turn by the river and had the misfortune to be alone. It was terribly marked, and he went the wrong way. Didn't realize it until the trail fizzled out in the woods. He had to turn back, right when his energy was at its lowest."

Faye hated it when people complained about something totally self-indulgent going wrong. It reminded her of the time a friend got cosmetic surgery—against Faye's advice—and then whined about the pain when Faye dropped off some coffee cake. But she had kept her mouth shut then, and she did so now.

"He went up through the bracken," Lilly went on. "Rowena didn't see him pass her, so she confronted him and accused him of cheating."

It was just as Faye had thought. She didn't mean to smile, but she must have.

"You've just always got to be right, don't you, Faye?" Lilly said.

Faye was taken aback. This was about Cliff and Rowena, not her. "That's your problem, Faye," Lilly continued. "It's why no one's stuck by you. You've got to be in control all the times. That's why George left. It's why no one has come to that Caravaggio Società of yours. Well, you know what? That gets old."

If Daisy noticed the change in Lilly's tone, she didn't show it. The dog was absorbed in sniffing a tuft of grass, oblivious to the rising tension around her.

"Really, Lilly, that's not fair," Thomas said. "Your husband dumped Faye into a right mess."

Faye made a conscious effort to imagine a string attached to the top of her head pulling her body up, lightening the weight on her spine, rolling her shoulders back as she walked. She was not going to let this aging hippie put her on the defensive. "So, set me right, Lilly. Why are you here?"

"To tell you that I know everything. You can leave my husband alone now."

Thomas coughed. "It's not quite that simple, Lilly. If Cliff poisoned Rowena—"

Lilly turned on him. "He didn't! Do you have any idea how much courage it took for Cliff to tell me what was going on? He doesn't care about his race records. Not even the Valtellina 100, not really. He wouldn't have hurt Rowena."

It felt very much like Lilly was trying to convince herself. "Did he tell you all this before Rowena died?" Faye asked.

"No." Lilly said it so quietly Faye could barely hear her.

They passed the Catacombs of San Sebastiano and then the Villa of Maxentius, the country home of an emperor who had his own racetrack. They moved around an American family in front of them. The two girls were whining that they wanted to return to the hotel, while a boy was asking when they were getting ice cream.

"But Rowena knew," Faye said.

"She figured it out, just like you did. Anyone else would just stop hanging out with Cliff if they really cared. Snub him or something. But not Rowena. She wanted him to come clean. She insisted on it."

They were still walking, moving through a more scenic area now. Tall pines lined the road, and there was a faint aroma of wild mint. And fewer tourists. They weren't alone, but they were exiting the most visited section of the route.

Faye thought about Cliff and Rowena out in the countryside for miles on end. They'd be in places much more remote than this lonely stretch. Sometimes they even met up in the middle of the night to practice running in the dark.

If Cliff had any sense, that's when he'd have killed her. A push into a river in the middle of the night, a slip down a ravine. Even tampering with her liquids out on a long run could be enough. He would have no reason at all to poison her in front of a crowd of people. Damn it. Faye had been wrong, again. "We don't think Cliff killed Rowena, Lilly."

"We don't?" Thomas squeaked. He cleared his throat. "No, of course not."

"No," Faye said. "He'd have killed her out on a run." Cliff wasn't a man to sit around tinkering with poisons when he had nature's bounty of accidents at his fingertips.

"He never would have done any of that," Lilly said. But she sounded relieved. Faye didn't know how much Lilly suspected, but she was sure the woman hadn't been a hundred percent convinced of her husband's innocence. That was why she'd wanted to meet, and why she'd gone to the first Caravaggio Società meeting. She'd been looking for clues, just like Faye.

"I agree," Faye said. "He could have killed her, but he didn't. He's not that man."

Lilly shook her head. "I'm going to take a taxi home. I'll see you later, Faye. Thomas."

Lilly turned onto a side path that would take her to a busy road. Faye wished she could feel sorry for the woman, but she didn't. Lilly had pretended to be her friend, then said no one liked her. Faye should be above it all, but she wasn't. Faye and Thomas turned and began a slow walk back.

"We were sort of right," Thomas said finally. "Cliff did cheat."

"We weren't looking at the crime. That's been our problem all along. Forget motive, why would anyone kill Rowena the way they did?"

"Because they were after you, Faye. Rowena was collateral damage, end of story," Thomas said.

"I'm not so sure." Before Faye could elaborate, two motorcycles raced toward them. Two drivers dressed in black from head to toe pulled up to a stop inches away. Daisy took refuge behind Faye. Faye's heart was pounding, but she was frozen in place, unable to even consider running.

One of the thugs removed his helmet. "Thomas Evans? Ilaria sent us."

"Good lord," Faye said. "What does Ilaria's family do?"

Chapter Twenty-Seven

Four men set upon Caravaggio while he was in exile, beating the artist until he was at death's door. His attackers' motive is uncertain, with theories ranging from bounty hunting to revenge by the Knights of Malta, and, more mundane, simple theft.
—Caravaggio: Brash, Brutish, and Brilliant

Thomas grinned. "I knew she'd come through. You're a little late, lads. We're safe and sound."

The men eyed Faye, as if she were the threat they were supposed to be protecting Thomas against. "*Va bene,*" one said. "But we cannot leave without authorization." He dialed a number and handed Thomas the phone.

"Ilaria, that was bloody amazing," Thomas said. His face was practically glowing. "They rolled up out of nowhere. If we'd been in danger, they would have taken care of it, no questions asked." He laughed about something. "No, no, it was fine. A misunderstanding. I'll catch you up later. But seriously, I'm agog." Another pause. "Yes, Faye's here. Hold a sec." Thomas held out the phone. "Ilaria wants to talk to you."

Faye took it. "It was really kind of you to send them, Ilaria, but we're perfectly safe."

"My men would have been too late if Lilly had intended you any harm," Ilaria said, her voice commanding through the device. "They are more effective if they are actually with you when the danger comes, no? I can tell them to stay with you."

Faye considered it. What would it be like to have those two men

231

accompanying her everywhere she went? She'd be like Esta with her handlers. Safe, but caged.

"It is not weakness to accept assistance," Ilaria continued.

Faye was used to being the one offering support. It was a much more comfortable place to be. "I'm fine. If things change, I'll call."

Faye handed the phone back to its owner, who spoke to Ilaria for a moment before giving his partner a signal to depart. "That was amazing," Faye said as the pair zipped off, leaving a cloud of dust in their wake. "But how did Ilaria know to send them?"

Thomas grinned. "I sent an SOS when Lilly asked us to go for a walk. I thought Cliff might be lurking around the corner. You know, a trap about to spring."

Faye squeezed his hand. "Good thinking."

"I'm a believer in outsourcing. It's how I was raised." Thomas' family was wealthy. Maybe growing up with servants made it easier to ask for help. "So, what now? With Cliff, Lilly, George, and Adam in the clear, we seem to be left with just Stefano, right?"

Faye didn't want to suspect Stefano. She wanted to believe she could trust her gut about the young man. She gripped Daisy's leash as the dog lunged after a rabbit. "I just wish we knew where he was," Faye said.

"He's done a runner, just like Caravaggio when he killed that man," Thomas said.

"I thought you knew nothing about Caravaggio." Faye stepped aside to make room for two walkers.

"I believe I said I didn't like his work, that's not the same thing," Thomas said. "Besides, I do like art history trivia. Makes me look sharp in front of the guests."

"Stefano has a history of running away," Faye said. "Esta's nephews said that. But kill Rowena? Or me? I don't see it."

"Esta's his ticket back to the good life with his family," Thomas said. "Maybe he was trying to get her approval."

"By killing her hand-selected successor?"

"The successor who was angling to get a different job. Maybe he was angry on Esta's behalf."

"I don't see it," Faye said.

Faye remembered the time she and George had mixed two jig-saw puzzles together to increase the challenge. When you picked up a piece, you never knew which picture it was part of. Someone poisoned Rowena. Someone poisoned Adam. Someone shoved Faye in front of a bus. She had no idea what it meant.

"You keep saying that," Thomas said. "But there's got to be something there."

It had been a long day. Faye needed a shower and a good night's sleep, and they could come up with a plan in the morning.

She said goodbye to Thomas at Via Pecora. He wanted to stay, but she told him go have dinner with Ilaria. Faye half-expected Maggie to be inside catching up on emails or putting her marketing plans into action, but the building was deserted.

Faye pushed aside her unease as she climbed the stairs. She stumbled at the turn, catching her foot on a step and had to put her hands out for support, but not before she banged her shin, hard. George had always said the stairs were an accident waiting to happen.

She brushed her hands on her skirt, succeeding only in spreading the grime from her hands. It was strange how silent the hall was. With the thick walls of the old building, you'd never guess there were hundreds of people within a five-block area. *Was the window in the hall always open?* The dust caked on it said yes. She should have someone come look at it. Improve the lighting too.

Faye unlocked her door, and Daisy raced ahead into the apartment. Faye left the dog sniffing every corner while she headed straight for a shower. Faye ran the water, then pulled out her biggest, fluffiest towel. She hesitated before stepping under the water. She pulled her towel tighter and padded to her door, double-checking it was locked. She was halfway to the bathroom when she decided to lock the balcony doors, as well. Silly, of course. No cat burglar was going to leap down from the roof to her balcony. But still, why invite trouble?

Daisy was stretched out, leaning against the wall next to the sofa. She opened one eye as Faye passed, then let it close without even raising her head.

Faye had just rubbed shampoo into her hair when she heard a squeak from the hall. Not loud, but the distinctive sound of her front door. She froze, heart pounding. She had no idea what she was supposed to do.

Why had she told Ilaria she didn't need protection? If she got through this, she would accept help, stop being so independent, admit weakness. *Get a grip*, Faye told herself. *You can figure that out later.*

Faye listened for the jingle of Daisy's tags, but there was nothing. She left the water running and grabbed her towel, then her phone. She tiptoed into the hall. Her front door was open, and there was the sound of drawers sliding in the kitchen. Faye hesitated. Go down the street and call the police, or stay and find out what was going on?

Her brain said to leave, but she couldn't move. She thought of the rabbits Daisy sniffed out in the park who froze when they should be dashing away. Soapy water ran down Faye's cheek, and she lost her grip on the phone. The sound it made as it clattered to the floor might as well have been a gunshot. Faye grabbed for it.

"Yikes!" A woman's voice squeaked. "You nearly gave me a heart attack." It was Maggie, standing in the kitchen holding a panini press.

"You? I was in the shower and heard someone in here. What was I supposed to think?"

Maggie leaned against the counter and laughed. "What a pair we make."

A panini press and a slippery cell phone would have been very poor defenses against an actual assassin. "I'll just rinse off. Can you stay for tea?"

"It's half-past eight. I'll take some wine, though." Daisy's tail thumped against the floor. "Is that you, Daisy? Lazy girl. Come and say hello."

Daisy yawned, then pushed herself to her feet and ambled toward Maggie, who began rubbing her head. "It must be the heat. Not much of a guard dog, is she?"

Faye found Maggie and Daisy on the terrace when she finally emerged from the bathroom. Faye had taken her time, enjoying using her own hair dryer and having her own cabinet of lotions to choose from after all those nights camped out at the Whites.

Maggie had opened a bottle of red wine and set out a plate of peanut butter cookies. "Where did those come from?"

"Leftovers from the tour," Maggie said. "They're the last ones. The guests devoured them."

Maggie had sent a form to all the guests before they arrived asking about likes and dislikes. Ilaria had offered Faye the cookies earlier.

"They're Jean's favorites. I think she ate at least a dozen." Maggie reached for a cookie. "I'm sorry for scaring you, Faye. We seem to have borrowed a lot of things from you over this last week. We tried to return them as we went along, but we got behind."

A cat was making its way along a roof a few doors down. It crossed two buildings, paused, then jumped onto a balcony with an open door. The cat disappeared inside.

"It's no problem. What all did you borrow?"

"It's hard to even remember," Maggie said. "That panini press. A knife. We would have asked, but we were in a rush, and you'd said to help ourselves to anything...."

"A corkscrew?" Faye asked.

"I think so," Maggie said. "I've kept a list so I can be better prepared for the next tour."

Faye had been blind. There hadn't been a ghost moving things around in her apartment. Or George, trying to throw her off balance. It had been Maggie and Ilaria, borrowing and returning items, and never getting them back exactly right. Even knocking a few picture frames over on that table by the door.

If Faye were playing bridge, her partner would have dumped her for being so slow on the uptake. Faye had seen one plus one and jumped straight to eleven.

Maggie must have noticed her expression. "I didn't mean to overstep; we were just so frantic getting ready—"

235

"No, no, it's fine. Great, even. I'm glad to have been able to help. I'm just kicking myself for something, that's all."

Maggie smiled. "Don't be so hard on yourself, Faye. It's hard work keeping it all together."

Easier said than done. Faye took a bite of peanut butter cookie so she didn't have to answer. It was salty and sweet, and the bite of chocolate in the middle was a little piece of heaven. "I'll have to ask Ilaria for the recipe. These really are wonderful."

Maggie nodded. "I want it, too. It uses tons of peanut butter. She didn't buy enough, so she had to borrow a cup of yours. I hope you don't mind."

Ilaria had said she made the cookies Saturday afternoon and that she'd had to raid Faye's kitchen for some of the ingredients. Faye put her cookie down. "And Jean's eaten them?"

Maggie tilted her head. "I just said she did. So did everyone else. What's the problem, Faye?"

"And Ilaria returned the jar she borrowed?" Faye asked.

"I guess so. What's wrong?"

Faye did the math. "Can you call Ilaria? Right now?"

Maggie shrugged and dialed her phone, then put Ilaria on speaker.

Faye took charge. "I'm here with Maggie. We have a question for you about the peanut butter cookies."

"Delicious, yes? I am sorry I have not sent the recipe to Maggie yet. Tomorrow."

"What did you do with the jar of peanut butter you borrowed?"

"I put it back in the refrigerator. If it's a problem, I can—"

"No, that's fine. Enjoy your dinner. Tell Thomas everything's fine."

"What's going on?" Maggie asked.

Faye blew out her breath. "Don't you see? Ilaria made these cookies with peanut butter from my house after the party. After Rowena supposedly died from the peanut butter in her smoothie."

Maggie dropped her cookie. "The peanut butter? I didn't even think…." The two women looked down at the cookies. "Is it possible that baking changed its effects? Made the poison inactive or something?"

Faye shook her head. "The police said it was stable. It would have affected Rowena no matter how she'd taken it."

"Well, maybe it didn't get mixed in," Maggie said. "Maybe the poison was just in the top layer, and that all went into the smoothie. The peanut butter Ilaria used was lower down, and that's why no one got sick."

"If that were true, there would have been no poison left for the police to find," Faye said. "The peanut butter was fine on Friday night. Someone doctored it later to confuse everything."

This time, finally, she knew she had proof. She picked up a cookie and ate the entire thing. Then she made a choking gesture, a show of hands around her neck, and tried to cross her eyes, but was smiling too much to pull it off.

"Not funny," Maggie said. "What about the granola that was poisoned? What was that about?"

"I think it was a mistake."

"What kind of mistake?"

"The only other ingredient in the smoothie that came from my kitchen other than bananas was cinnamon. The Italian word for cinnamon is *cannella*. Ilaria mixed it up with cardamom and grabbed the wrong jar last week. I think someone else did the same."

"They poisoned the cardamom thinking it was cinnamon?" Maggie said.

"I think so. Then Ilaria borrowed it before the police took everything for testing."

"And why did they have to poison all these things?" Maggie asked.

Faye tapped her finger on the arm of her chair, willing Maggie to catch up. "Because they wanted the police to think the poison was in the smoothie. Don't you see? Someone poisoned Rowena, then had to backtrack. They came in while I was out and planted the poison for the police to find."

"That was a bit reckless," Maggie said. "They must have been desperate."

A pigeon landed on the railing and Daisy eyed it a moment before getting to her feet. She stalked it inch by inch, getting within a foot before the bird flapped lazily away.

"I don't know," Faye said. "The police took everything. If Ilaria hadn't taken that bottle of cardamom away, no one else would have gotten sick. It probably felt like a safe bet."

"It feels sloppy," Maggie said.

"Rowena's murder didn't happen the way it was supposed to. Someone was rushing around covering their tracks, and they slipped up."

Chapter Twenty-Eight

Caravaggio died at age thirty-eight. Whether it was from syphilis, malaria, lead poisoning, or an infected wound remains the subject of debate.
—Caravaggio: Brash, Brutish, and Brilliant

Faye texted Stefano three times on Sunday morning but heard nothing back. His social media accounts hadn't been updated, and she had no inkling of whether the young man was missing, or just offline for the weekend.

Faye wondered if Paola had heard from him, but she didn't have the accountant's number. Esta would know how to reach the woman. Faye didn't have her number either, but she did know where the *donna* lived. Faye decided to try.

She had sent Maggie home last night insisting she would be fine. And she was. It felt good to be on her own turf. She still didn't have a plan, but she had the feeling of the cards sliding into place. All she needed was Stefano.

Faye wrestled Daisy into her harness and stepped outside, careful to lock the door behind her. The air was green and clean with a hint of freshly brewed coffee. It was a glorious morning, and Romans were out in force. Faye wished she felt as carefree as the couples and families laughing as they walked past.

Faye was a moment late in tugging Daisy away from a group of teenagers lounging in the shade, and the dog got a taste of strawberry gelato. She refused to feel guilty. The boy shouldn't have been eating ice cream before noon anyway.

Esta didn't answer her door, and Faye was surprised at how let down she felt. She hadn't realized she'd been pinning so much hope on Esta, who would either know Stefano's whereabouts or put her in touch with Paola, who could confirm if he was still missing.

Faye should have known better. A woman like Esta wouldn't be at home on a day like this. She'd be at a baptism, enjoying a pastry with a friend, or visiting an art gallery eyeing a new work. Something other than sitting home alone just waiting for Faye to drop by.

She rummaged in her purse and found a pen and scrap of paper. She didn't have room for a full explanation, so she kept it simple: *Please call me – Faye.* She included her phone number and slipped the paper through the mail slot. With any luck, Esta would see it and be in touch.

There was nothing more she could do here. Faye and Daisy turned toward home. They walked along the Tiber, greeting other dogs and their owners along the way. It was surprising, really, how quickly the simple act of smiling and saying hello to strangers told her brain to buck up. She would go to DiLorenzo Industries tomorrow and see if there was word from Stefano. One day would not make a difference.

Faye was passing Castel Sant'Angelo when her phone buzzed with a call from Thomas. "Where are you?" His voice radiated excitement.

"Out with Daisy."

"Great. Pop her home, then meet me near the Pantheon in twenty minutes. Maggie's coming, too."

"I can't. I'm still a half-hour walk from home."

"Bring her then. Chiara Moretti is expecting us." He rattled off an address and hung up before Faye could ask anything more. The Pantheon neighborhood was refined and elegant, and very expensive. Faye and Daisy arrived at the address just as Thomas pulled up on his scooter with Maggie clinging to the back.

"You promised not to weave between cars," Maggie said after removing her helmet. "There was no need to rush. We're still early. Oh, hi, Faye." Maggie frowned. "I thought we agreed you wouldn't go out alone?"

"Daisy needed a walk. Thomas, what's this about?"

Thomas grinned and gestured to a door. "Behold, the mysterious art dealer."

"Esta's? She's mysterious?" Faye stepped aside as two women in the type of casual clothing that was astronomically expensive strolled by deep in conversation.

"That's the one. Chiara Moretti. We know Rowena was trying to buy a picture for Adam, but where's the picture? I tracked her down so we can find out." Thomas looked exceedingly pleased with himself. "I asked some friends which dealer Esta uses for her purchases. It took all of two phone calls. Come on, Chiara's expecting us."

They were buzzed into a tidy building and trooped up the stairs to a sun-filled room on the second floor. Daisy wagged her tail, excited at the prospect of a new room to sniff.

Chiara greeted them at the door. "Welcome. It is always a pleasure to meet a new client. Oh, and you brought your pet. How nice."

If Faye was asked to imagine an art dealer's office, she would have conjured up the opposite of Chiara's space. The room was practically bare, with just two pieces of art on the wall and no big wooden boxes hinting at treasures within. It had a nakedness to it.

Chiara took a seat behind a large desk and waved them to the guest chairs. She didn't bend down to pet Daisy, but they couldn't be the first group to bring a dog here. "Signor Evans said you are building a collection. What is it you are looking for?" Her accent was light, but Faye couldn't place it. Somewhere in the north?

Thomas leaned forward. "I'm assisting Signora Masters. She's come into some money and wants to invest." He lied with an ease Faye hadn't expected.

"That's right." Faye tried to follow his lead. "I was at Esta's the other day. Her collection is so unique, I wanted to meet the woman who advised her."

Chiara tipped her head. "And Signora DiLorenzo gave my name?"

"Rowena Burke, actually," Faye said. "She was excited about making a purchase herself."

"What exactly are you looking for?" It might have been Faye's imagination, but Chiara's tone seemed a shade cooler.

"I'm not very knowledgeable." Faye gave a little laugh, not minding that it made her sound a little ditzy. Ditzy clients would generate as much in commissions as intelligent ones. "What did Rowena want? She has good taste."

Chiara leaned back in her chair. "Ah, you are like Rowena. Just curious, not really serious? My business is hard enough without people wasting my time."

"I'm sorry, we didn't—"

Chiara ignored her. "I'm afraid a lot of the people who contact me are the same. You mentioned Rowena Burke. She comes in, thinking she knows about art. She says she wants to buy a piece; then she finds out the price, and poof!"

Faye nodded along, expecting Chiara to continue, but the dealer stopped.

"I'm sorry," Maggie said. "I'm a little lost. Poof, what?"

Chiara seemed to notice Maggie for the first time. She frowned. "What is your role?"

Maggie flushed. "Friend. The price of the picture Rowena was interested in was too high?"

"Too low. *Pazzo*, yes?" Crazy indeed.

Who wouldn't be happy with a price lower than what they expected to pay? "Rowena didn't mention price to me," Faye said. "What artist was she talking about? I don't mind a bargain."

"If you've seen Esta's collection, then you've seen the artist's work. They are worth a fraction of what she paid for them. But then, Esta bought at the height of the market. I advised against it, but she insisted. And one can never tell. In time, they could go back up. Or not." Chiara shrugged, as if the price was of no interest to her.

If Esta loved a piece, the current value should not interest her, either. "The child in the sailboat, the one that looks like an insect on a leaf. Is that one of them?"

"Ah, no, that was an excellent purchase. The value has increased at least a hundred, maybe a thousand times. That is the way with gambling. You make some good bets, you make some bad ones." Chiara took a sip of tea, warming to her theme. "Esta, she keeps teasing me with that picture. Some days, she says she will sell at last, take the profit to cover her losses. Then the next, she says no, she will hold on longer. For years it has been like that, back and forth. Just last week she says, 'Yes, sell it.' Then this week, 'No, do not.' It is tiring, but she is a good customer, so I am patient."

The dealer eyed her visitors, and Faye knew they didn't fit the profile of collectors with a limitless budget. On paper, they might check the boxes: middle-aged woman with a dog, attractive young man, and hanger-on in tow, but the details were all wrong: Daisy was hardly a purse-size purebred, Thomas's hands were spattered with paint, and Maggie was Maggie.

"I am surprised that Signora Burke sent you to me. I did not feel I was the right dealer to assist her."

Faye coughed. "It might have been Stefano Ungaro, now that I think about it."

Chiara nodded. "Ah, that is more logical. He is a good young man. The Ungaro collection, it is marvelous. His grandfather has a very good eye."

"He was here last week, wasn't he? Was his grandfather was taking advantage of the market?"

"Buy low and sell high," Thomas said.

"*Proprio così.*" Chiara nodded. "His home is not so very far, but he treats it like a journey to come to *Roma*. An event, yes? He made some excellent selections."

"And Esta, too. She just bought two pictures, didn't she?"

Chiara glanced at her watch. "If there is a piece of art you want, I can find it for you. If you can pay, we should continue our conversation. If not, I have many messages waiting for my attention."

She said it in such a nice way, Faye almost missed the fact that Chiara was giving them the boot. Faye stood up. "We'll let you get back to it."

"Come by any time." Chiara swiveled back toward her computer and had her eyes on the screen. "My door is always open."

"You've got to admire Chiara's spirit," Thomas said when they returned to the sidewalk. "Pay up or get out. It must save a lot of client-service headaches."

He unlocked the chain around his scooter. "Glad we were able to clear up one mystery. We haven't heard anything about Adam's picture because Rowena didn't buy one. Sorry it didn't get us any closer to clearing things up, though."

He held a helmet out to Maggie. "You all right getting home, Faye? When do you pick your scooter up, anyway?"

"This afternoon." The shop had promised it would be as good as new. She hoped they didn't buff the character out when they fixed the brake. It was approaching middle age and had earned its scrapes, just the Faye had.

"I'll walk with you," Maggie said. "You go on ahead, Thomas." They waved, and Thomas sped off, zipping between three cars and a delivery truck. "Is Thomas right?" Maggie asked. "Was this a waste of time?"

"No," Faye said. "I thought it was very helpful. Didn't you?"

"I'm not sure. Stefano is the grandson of a collector. Rowena was misinformed about the price of art. Is there more?"

"DiLorenzo Industries had poor accounting procedures when Rowena came in. Paola told me that Esta used to make her purchases through the corporate account, then reimburse the company. It was about privacy or something."

Maggie frowned. "That doesn't sound like a good idea."

"No, but I guess with family-owned businesses things get lax. The company exists for the owners. In this case, the owners are Esta and her relatives, so you can see why she might have done it."

"What now?" Maggie asked.

Stefano was still MIA. Esta hadn't called her back yet, and Faye had no other way of getting in touch with Paola on a Sunday. "I don't think we can do anything until tomorrow when we can go to the DiLorenzo offices."

Maggie looked at her. "So what now?"

"There are three Caravaggios at San Luigi dei Francesi. It's not too far. Would you mind holding Daisy while I dash in?"

"Dash in? You're still doing that?"

"I've given up the schedule," Faye said. "But I do still want to see them all, if only to say I did it."

Maggie shrugged. Faye left her on a bench with Daisy at her side. Even the loveliest, most beautiful churches become tedious when you see them in excess, so she made a quick circle and exited, mission accomplished.

Maggie handed the leash back and stretched. "This is about Esta's art, isn't it? Embezzling 101. Someone could have added an extra zero to the invoices going through the company and pocketed the difference."

Faye thought about Stefano, with his expensive taste and sudden loss of his family's allowance. He wouldn't be the first person to be tempted by vast sums of money just there for the taking. Skimming a little off the top as he was processing invoices might not even feel like stealing. He might think he was just taking what was owed to him for grinding it out in a low-paying job.

"Paola said Rowena was going through invoices," Faye said. They had entered the maze of streets south of the Pantheon and made their way toward the river. It seemed half of Rome had the same idea, and Faye half hoped that they'd see Stefano in one of the piazzas enjoying a meal with Paola. But she knew she wouldn't. He was on the run.

"And this is why Chiara said Rowena expected it to be more expensive," Maggie said. "She knew how much Esta had paid, but she didn't know the market had cratered. You said we needed to know what was happening with Rowena in her last week, and you were right."

Faye didn't feel like she'd been right about much. She hadn't believed Cliff when he said Rowena was asking about the art market. But it looked like he was telling the truth after all. Something Chiara had told Rowena had set an alarm bell off, and Rowena had been trying to dig into it.

"We're talking about Stefano, aren't we?" Maggie said. "He was embezzling, and Rowena figured it out, so he killed her?"

They entered the Piazza di Pietra. The "Piazza of Stone" was flanked on one side by the massive columned wall of the ancient Temple of Hadrian, one of the largest of its day. The rest of the building had been dismantled by scavengers in the Middle Ages who took everything from the granite blocks to the metal pins that held the stones together.

It was one of Faye's favorite places in the city. The ancient facade had been incorporated into a more modern building—modern, at least, on a European timeline—and became the home of the stock exchange in the 1800s. Esta was right about incorporating old into new when she explained her vision for the hotel. It gave life and meaning to this square. The difference was that Faye's street had been full of life before DiLorenzo Industries started buying things up. It was after the purchases that it lost its spark.

"He knew I was going to be out visiting Esta last week," Faye said. "He's the one who set the appointment. He could have easily gone in to dose my peanut butter and the cinnamon. It wouldn't be out of character to make a mistake, but it's just a theory."

They paused in front of a fluted column. The base alone, before any decoration began, was taller than Faye. They were chipped and worn, not surprising after two thousand years of service. Faye leaned against a railing and looked down into an empty moat surrounding the building's façade. It was the ancient street level, a good ten or fifteen feet lower than today.

Faye wished she could share Maggie's enthusiasm, but the explanation didn't feel right. If Stefano were fiddling with the invoices, why help Rowena find Esta's dealer. Without Chiara, Rowena wouldn't have known the prices were off.For all his faults, Stefano was smart. He would have kept Rowena and Chiara apart.

Maggie's theory just didn't fit.

Chapter Twenty-Nine

Disease, famine, and accidents took the lives of many of Caravaggio's countrymen. Life expectancy in Europe was a mere thirty to forty years in the 17th Century. Perhaps the greatest surprise is not that the artist died young, but that he lived as long as he did.
—Caravaggio: Brash, Brutish, and Brilliant

Faye spotted her beloved pink scooter parked in a place of honor in front of the repair shop. It shone from fresh polish.

"There are a few scratches from the fall, but she's safe to ride," Lorenzo said in Italian. He had been taking care of Faye's scooter since she bought it ten years ago.

"*Sta benissimo,*" Faye answered as she ran her hand over the machine. Lifting the bike up herself was a small thing, maybe, but it was an accomplishment Faye was proud of. The bike's scratches from its tumble were a badge of honor that she would treasure. "How much do I owe you?"

Lorenzo shook his head. "Not a thing, Faye. You can take it now."

"Absolutely not," Faye said. She'd been a good customer and referred all her friends to Lorenzo, but the last thing she wanted was for him to be doing her work for free. She handed him a credit card, but he didn't touch it.

"A man paid for it. He called on Thursday, just as we were closing. He asked if we had a pink scooter with a broken brake. I told him yes, and he gave his card."

For a moment, Faye wondered if George could have done it as some kind of peace offering. But such a gesture would never have occurred to him,

247

even if he had known about the accident. Only one man had known the details. "Stefano Ungaro?"

Lorenzo nodded. "That sounds right. Take care of her now, yes?" He handed Faye the keys, and she wheeled the scooter out onto the street.

"I don't know what to think." Maggie held Daisy's leash, and the dog made a dash for a flock of pigeons. "Come back here, Daisy. Is he trying to buy your silence by paying your bills?"

"I think he's apologizing," Faye said.

"Apologizing for what?"

"For being the one who knocked it over. He was driving an unfamiliar car in the rain, and his grandfather makes him nervous. Esta said Stefano's a terrible driver when he's distracted. He probably bumped it, then didn't have the courage to tell me it was him when I met him at the café."

Maggie stopped and turned to face Faye. "Did you know?"

"I wondered." Faye sighed. "At first I thought it was an attempt to threaten me, but I think it was just an accident."

"Same for your fall in front of the bus?"

"No," Faye said. "That was real. Do you mind taking Daisy back to Masterpiece for a few hours? I have a call I need to make."

"You don't want company?"

Faye shook her head. She was happy to be alone, and she didn't want Maggie to know the details of the call. "You must have work to do."

"I do have some reservations to catch up on. Word of mouth has been terrific, and the next three tours are fully booked." Maggie paused. "This might not be the best time for this, but I'm thinking we're going to need to move. We just need more space, and I can't see a way around it. You've been so generous, but if we expanded, we could—"

Faye held up her hand. "Say no more. Just let me know if I can help you look."

She watched Maggie and Daisy meander down the street. Buying or selling Via Pecora was completely up to her now. She didn't have to worry about letting Maggie down. She didn't have to worry about Rowena's pressure campaign. But she did have to decide whether she was staying in Rome, or if she was going to start a new life.

Faye pulled out her phone and dialed. Winnie Rogers answered on the first ring. "How's Daisy?"

"She's fine. I need to ask a favor."

"Anything. Except taking Daisy back. Anginetti would eat my shoes."

"No, nothing like that. I wanted some professional advice."

"Let's talk in person. The Caravaggio Società's going to the Doria Pamphili Gallery today, isn't it? How about meeting there in thirty? Is that enough time before the others arrive?"

Winnie was probably the only member of the gang who still knew the schedule. Faye hadn't even bothered sending out a note canceling. She'd just assumed that no one would want to be seen in public with her. "I don't think it'll be a problem. I'll see you then."

Faye rode her scooter for the sheer pleasure of it. She zipped south along the Tiber before doubling back and heading north and east, then west again to park near the museum. It was a roundabout route just for the fun of it.

Winnie met her out front. "Never talk on the phone, Faye. Rule number one. Let's go in."

The museum was a delight, plain and simple. Housed in a 17th Century palace still owned by a powerful Italian family, it was packed with treasures. But it was the building itself Faye loved. Every inch of the walls and ceilings was covered with frescos, tapestries, and chandeliers. "The owners once roller-skated through here as children," Faye said. "Can you imagine?"

"A brother and sister," Winnie said. "I've read about them. They live in different wings. Some kind of feud."

"What kind of feud?"

"The usual: a court case over who will inherit," Winnie said. "That's why estate planning is so important."

Ancient sculptures were arranged on pedestals, one in front of each window. Beautiful youths frozen in a moment in time two thousand years ago. Faye paused in front of a mirror, taking in the slightly sweaty version of herself. Her pants were wrinkled, and her top didn't match as well as she'd thought this morning. The lines around her eyes were looking more prominent than usual, and her hair was mussed from the helmet.

Faye realized she didn't care. She'd been busy. She'd been taking care of a dog, helping Maggie with Masterpiece, and trying, really trying, to understand why someone had died. Right now, that was enough.

"You'd think half a fortune would be plenty," Faye said.

"If it were, it would put people like me out of business." Winnie studied the map. "Come on, the Caravaggio's this way."

Faye let her mind wander as she trailed Winnie through a covered walkway created by a series of Renaissance arches enclosing a peaceful courtyard of trees and a tinkling fountain. It was sad to think of the two children growing up here, roller skating down the halls, and now at odds over a fortune.

It took Faye a moment to realize what was so strange here. It was the total lack of crowds. Right now, thousands of visitors were muscling their way through the Vatican and the Colosseum, and here it was quiet enough for her to hear a fountain.

"We want the second wing," Winnie said. "Through the Hall of Mirrors."

Faye felt like she was walking through Versailles as she moved through the gallery with gold-framed mirrors covering every inch of wall space, broken up only by tall windows and detailed moldings. The ceiling was a riot of cavorting pink cupids and barely-clothed men striding heroically. Ornate didn't even begin to describe it.

"Now, what can I do for you?" Winnie said.

"If you were going to embezzle money from a company, how would you do it?"

"Is this theoretical or specific?"

They had arrived in front of Caravaggio's *The Rest on the Flight into Egypt*. It was one of Caravaggio's earlier works, and Faye was surprised to realize that she could tell. It didn't have the dramatic lighting of his later art. It didn't carry any deep insights into life. The picture was just a fairly ordinary painting of a woman holding a baby in the middle of a lush landscape.

Faye had read that it depicted the holy family escaping King Herod's planned massacre of baby boys. The family didn't look particularly stressed. Joseph was enjoying some music played by an angel. Had Caravaggio thought of this painting when he'd made his own escape? It must have been a more rushed departure. Faye decided she was officially over Caravaggio. He was a thuggish man who had painted well. Groundbreaking, probably, but not her taste.

"Does it matter?" Faye asked.

"Not really," Winnie said. "Setting up fake suppliers is one of the most common tricks. An employee dummies up some invoices for services never rendered, gets the company to pay them, and pockets the lot. End of story."

"And how do they catch that?"

"Someone finally checks the invoices. They realize they didn't get the services or the products or raw materials or whatever."

"What else do people do?"

"All kinds of things. Employees make up people to put on the payroll who don't exist. They sell things that don't belong to them. They take out loans and use corporate assets as collateral. Does any of that help?"

Faye felt a glimmer of recognition. "What do you mean about selling things that don't belong to them?"

Winnie shrugged. "Exactly that. I had a client with a refuse hauling business. An employee sold some old dumpsters that are sitting around not being used, socking away the money the company didn't even know they were entitled to."

"How do people get caught?"

"In this case, someone at the company had the same idea to sell the dumpsters—on the up and up this time—and found out they were gone. Usually, though, it's when someone looks a little deeper into the paperwork that they see something doesn't fit. They need to know enough to catch it, though. The problem is that companies get lazy. No, strike that. Companies aren't lazy. The people who run companies are lazy. Or, to be generous, they are focused on running the business and don't get bogged down in the details that they should."

"Or they trust the people who work for them," Faye said.

"Big mistake. Happens all the time in partnerships. They don't want to imagine that someone they are in business with would cheat them."

"So, when do they find out?"

"When they write a check that doesn't clear and find out their partner has made off with the money," Winnie said. "Or when they go to sell an asset and find out they don't own it anymore."

They began walking back toward the museum entrance. "I won't ask why you're thinking about all this," Winnie said. "A pathological lack of curiosity is part of my job description. But if you need help with something, you know you can ask me, right?"

Faye had thought she needed to solve this case to get her friends back, but she'd had it wrong. The right people believed in her whether the police made an arrest or not.

On Monday morning, Faye planted herself across from the DiLorenzo offices at seven a.m. There was still no word from Stefano, so she was waiting for Paola. Faye didn't know what time the woman came to work, and she thought it was easier to wait outside than try to convince the security guard to let her linger in the lobby. Finally, close to eight, she spotted Paola coming down the street.

"Paola!" Faye waved, and Paola's face brightened.

"Faye, yes? It is nice to see you again. You are here early. A meeting with Esta?"

"Do you have time for a coffee?"

Paola frowned. Of course she didn't. It was Monday morning, a time when people were in a hurry to start the week. "I wanted to talk about Stefano. Is there any word?"

Paola shifted her bag to the other shoulder. "Nothing. I am being ghosted. That is the word? He is not responding to my texts. He's gone away somewhere." Paola blushed. "I spoke with his neighbor. They saw him put a suitcase in the car on Thursday night and leave."

"Maybe he's been back since you stopped by."

"I have been there every day." Paola shifted her bag again and looked down. "It's close to a shop I like."

"That makes sense," Faye said. The woman was a little obsessive, but that was probably a useful quality in an accountant. "But he said he'd be here on

Friday to get his bag. Isn't Esta worried?"

"Worried? No, she says he sometimes does this, disappears."

If Faye disappeared, she liked to think someone would call the hospitals for a Jane Doe. "He could have had an accident."

"I should really go in," Paola said. "It's a busy day and—"

"Just a minute," Faye said. "I know it's none of my business, but you mentioned Rowena was looking through old records. Is there any chance that she found something not right?" Faye would have liked to have eased into this topic over coffee, but the woman wasn't giving her any time, so she had no choice but to barrel on. "Any hint of numbers not matching on invoices? Maybe things being paid twice?"

Paola flushed. *"Assolutamente no."*

The young woman probably took the question as a slight on her professionalism. Faye backtracked. "You're relatively new, aren't you? Could there have been something going on with the previous accountant?"

"No. Rowena looked at the invoices. She found nothing." Two men walking up the street waved at Paola. Coworkers, probably. "I was curious, and I looked too. It is something we learned in school, to be on the alert for. The amount Esta paid for her paintings matched what the company paid for them. The other purchases for the hotels, they matched actual items. There is nothing there, Faye."

Faye considered this young woman. She was an outsider. She was a tad obsessive. Faye believed her. Maggie's suggestion that Stefano was using Esta's art purchases to skim from the company was fine, but it was wrong. "Could you look something up for me?" Faye said. "Some ownership records?"

Paola was too polite to say, "Are you crazy?" but her expression communicated it loud and clear. "I must go, Faye."

"Wait." Faye put a hand on the woman's arm. "Stefano needs our help. He's missing, and Esta doesn't even seem to care. That's a red flag, don't you think?"

Paola bit her lip. "I can't give you any confidential information."

"No, of course not." Faye made a few notes and handed a paper to Paola.

"Just look at the history of these. That's all. Then you can decide what to do."

Paola hesitated, but finally accepted the note. "I'm very busy today. I'll need to see."

It was all Faye could do. She rode her scooter back to Trastevere and took Daisy for a walk, trying not to check her phone every few minutes. Paola would come through, Faye was sure of it. Finally, just after three, the accountant called.

"I have the information. But I do not understand it."

Faye fought a smile. "Can you take the afternoon off? I'll pick you up in twenty minutes." It wasn't over yet, but it would be soon.

Chapter Thirty

Historians agree that Caravaggio was arrogant and reckless. A more considered and careful approach to life might have led to a less stressful existence. But one must ask whether such a cautious man would have had the genius that characterized Caravaggio's work.
—Caravaggio: Brash, Brutish, and Brilliant

T homas insisted on driving when Faye asked to borrow Ilaria's car. He and Maggie were in the Masterpiece offices going over spreadsheets when Faye stopped in, and Faye suspected he might have agreed to anything to get out of the meeting.

"Ilaria has an exam today, but I know she won't mind," Thomas said. "Where are we headed?"

"Paola and I are going to see Stefano."

"A confrontation?" Maggie said. "Absolutely not. Take whatever it is you've learned to the police and let them sort it out."

"I don't have any proof without Stefano." Faye met Maggie's gaze. "It'll be fine."

"Famous last words and all that," Thomas said. "We'll bring Daisy, won't we, old girl? You'll keep us safe and sound?"

Daisy thumped her tail, as clear a sign as any that she did not understand a word of what Thomas had said apart from her own name.

"Stefano didn't kill Rowena," Faye said.

"Then who did?" Maggie took off her reading glasses and looked at Thomas. "Do you know?"

He shook his head. "She hasn't told me any more than you."

"Let's let Stefano tell us," Faye said. "You don't have to come, Maggie. Stay here, and Thomas and I can report back."

Maggie looked torn, then closed the laptop. "You'll need a navigator. Let's go."

They met Paola in front of the DiLorenzo offices. Paola eyed Daisy before climbing in. "Does the dog get vehicle sick?"

"Never," Faye said, though in truth she had no idea.

Paola nodded and squeezed into the back with Faye and Daisy. Ilaria's shiny sports car would have looked more at home careening through the curving streets of a mountain village in a Bond film than in the stop-and-go traffic they hit on their way out of the city. Soon enough, they were on the A1 highway, and Thomas gunned the engine for the hills. He really was a very good driver, despite the speed. In three hours, they were on a smaller road, then turned onto a private drive protected by heavy iron gates.

A disembodied voice buzzed them through the moment they said they were friends of Stefano. Unlike Caravaggio's flight from Rome, which had probably involved weeks on horses and untold discomforts, Stefano's escape had been a mere three-hour drive to his grandfather's estate.

A woman in a starched uniform glanced at Daisy, then directed them around the house to a pool, where they found Stefano lying under an umbrella, eyes closed, with a book open on his lap and a glass of something icy by his side.

Not Rowena's killer, but he'd known who was long before anyone else. If he'd spoken up, Adam's life would never have been in danger. Paola walked up and poured the drink over him.

Stefano sprang to his feet, knocking over his book and the side table.

"Paola! And Faye? And...." He trailed off.

"Maggie and Thomas," Faye said.

Stefano turned to Paola and spoke to her in Italian. "I'm sorry for not returning your calls. I've been busy entertaining my grandfather." It was a blatant lie and he had the decency to blush before addressing the group in English. "How did you find me?"

Faye felt everyone's gaze on her. Maggie, Thomas, Paola, and even Daisy waited. "Your grandfather's address was easy enough to find. We've come to bring you back to Rome. You need to tell the police about the energy bar."

Stefano shook his head. "No. That is not possible."

If he'd said, "What energy bar?" she might have doubted herself. But Stefano's answer made it clear he knew what Faye was talking about, and why it mattered. It was as if she'd put out an aggressive bid in a hand of bridge and had just turned the corner when she saw it was going to pay off.

"You're an honest man, Stefano. Paying for the scooter, you didn't have to do that. You did it because you're a good person." This did not seem the moment to mention that Stefano had suggested George might have been behind the scooter's fall. "Everyone will understand. All you need to do is tell the police that Esta knew Rowena ate an energy bar. That's all. No one will be mad."

Thomas cleared his throat. "I'm having a little trouble keeping up. Energy bar?"

"Rowena ate one at the office," Faye said. "Before coming to the party. The poison was in the energy bar, not the smoothie."

"I know nothing for certain," Stefano said. "This is nothing to do with me."

It was ridiculous crowding around Stefano like this. "Let's all go sit down," Faye said.

They took the wicker chairs positioned around a glass table. The woman in the starched uniform who had let them in hovered. *"Bevande,"* Stefano ordered. Drinks.

"And a bowl of water for Daisy, please," Faye added. The woman nodded and returned to the house. This estate was the type of place Faye saw in glossy travel magazines, with its lush lawn, manicured hedges, gravel paths and, of course, the pool. She understood why Stefano wanted to hide from his responsibilities here.

"Let's go back to the beginning," Faye said. "You knew the energy bar was important to Esta. You put the pieces together after Rowena collapsed."

Stefano nodded miserably. "Rowena, she never ate energy bars at the office. It was my job to supply high-quality food, yes? But her friend Cliff, he came, he ate everything. She and Esta were working late, so Rowena took a bar from her running pack. She ate it. I held nothing back. The police, they asked me about the energy bar. They knew she had eaten one. The medical exam, they saw it in her stomach, yes?"

He must have heard the crunch of the housekeeper's feet on the gravel path, because he paused. The woman put a tray with glasses and a pitcher of lemonade on the table, then returned to the house.

Faye watched the woman go. "The police didn't know about Esta's reaction, though."

He shook his head miserably. "She saw me with the empty packaging, and she asked where it had come from. I told her, and she became agitated. I have not seen her like that. She said we must leave. Immediately. 'Get Rowena to the party.' 'Find her food. A drink.' It was–" He paused. "Unusual."

It was suspicious. And he hadn't shared the information with the police. "But how did you know, Faye?" Maggie said.

She hadn't. Some would call it guesswork, but Faye called it deduction. "Esta's behavior was 'unusual' all along," Faye said. "Why did she bother coming to a party that she hadn't been invited to? Esta wasn't friends with Rowena. She went to make sure there was something in Rowena's stomach other than the energy bar."

"You were tipped off because of an uninvited party guest?" Thomas said.

"No, it was because nothing else fit. It's been strange all along, the idea that someone would kill Rowena in such a public way. No one would have planned it like that. It shouldn't have taken me so long to realize that what happened was a cover up. Someone scrambling because Rowena took the poison at the wrong time."

The housekeeper returned with Daisy's water, and the dog began lapping it up, showering Faye's ankle in the process. "Esta poisoned Rowena's energy bar assuming she'd eat it on a run miles away from help," Faye went on. "Rowena would have collapsed and had her death written off to the rigors of her training."

Thomas tapped the table. "Then Cliff comes in and eats his friend's food, so the plan goes wrong. I did say there was something suspicious about him."

Faye ignored him. "When Esta saw the wrapper, she knew she had to act fast. She got Rowena out of there and made sure she ate something else. The next day, when she had a chance to plan, she invited me to her apartment to find out exactly what had been in the smoothie so it could be laced with the same poison."

"Burt said she was a nice old lady, and he's a terrible judge of character," Maggie said. "I did wonder before if she was targeting you, Faye, to get your building. But how would she know how to manage poison?"

"Her security," Stefano said glumly. "Her driver, yes? Eduardo can arrange anything that needs to be done. But evidence? No. It is all theory. This is why I did not talk to the police. They would ask why Esta would want Rowena dead, and I would have no answer." He took a sip of his lemonade. "With Esta's endorsement, I will be back with my family. Big job, lots of money. It's what I have been working for. To give up all this," he waved a hand, "on a guess? It is madness."

"That's why Paola is here." Faye turned to the accountant. "Do you want to explain?"

Paola pulled out a file folder. "Esta didn't want construction to begin on the Via Pecora project because DiLorenzo Industries does not own the properties there. At least, they do not have a clear title. Esta mortgaged them."

"Mortgages?" Thomas drummed his fingers on the table. "That's hardly a smoking gun. Companies mortgage buildings all the time. It's financial jigging. Totally legal."

"Yes," Paola said. "And when they do this, the money from the loan, it goes back to the company. But not here. The money from the loans, it has not come through to DiLorenzo Industries. Someone took it for themselves."

It was one of the classic scams Winnie had described: take a loan out on a company's property and pocket the money yourself. Daisy nudged against Faye's knee, looking for a rub. Faye obliged, stroking her under the chin the way she liked.

"So, these loans—this theft, if you will—they would have come out anyway," Thomas said. "When the loans came due, or when construction started, whichever was first."

"She wouldn't have planned for them to be permanent," Faye said. "I think she treated them like a revolving line of credit. She was a gambler with a good eye for art. She was known for buying low and selling high. When she wanted to add to her collection, she took a loan out on one of the Via Pecora properties, telling herself she'd sell something when the time came to pay it back. Paola checked. The timing matches with her big investments."

"But she's rich," Maggie said.

Stefano shook his head. "Not rich enough. The DiLorenzo family, they keep their profits in the company. They pay each other low salaries. They take pride in their economies, yes? It was always the same, growing up." He adjusted his expensive watch. "I prefer my family, which enjoys the results of our labor."

"Esta could have just paid off the loans and no one would have been the wiser," Faye said. "That was probably her plan when she started. She'd spoken with the dealer about selling some pieces, do you remember? Chiara said Esta kept going back and forth. But when the time came, Esta didn't want to give her pictures up, so she took out another mortgage. She bought more art, took out more mortgages. She probably told herself she could stop any time." Addicts, Cliff would have been sure to tell them, believe that lie time and time again.

"It might have been fine if the art market hadn't cratered," Thomas said. "Selling her favorites to cover the loans would have been painful."

"My grandfather, he has wondered at Esta's collection," Stefano said. "He asked where she got the money. She said good business sense, but the math, my grandfather says, it does not add up."

"When was this?" Paola asked.

A lawnmower growled in the distance. There was a pause before Stefano answered. "Thursday afternoon." That conversation with his grandfather about the price of art must have been what sent Stefano running. He knew she'd killed Rowena, and this information about her collection would have

260

been the explanation of motive that he'd been missing. Instead of telling what he knew, Stefano had run.

"This is all a bit pedantic," Thomas complained. "How did Rowena find out about the mortgages? Did she go looking for something to hold over Esta to get a promotion with?"

"I told her," Paola said. "She began the paperwork for the construction and the forms required the titles. I told her there were liens on them. It did not occur to me that there should not have been any. Not until Faye asked me to confirm the payments."

Thomas whistled. "But Rowena knew the significance. Did she pull the same trick she did on Cliff? A 'Confess to your nephews, or I'll tell them myself' type of thing?"

"If I may," Paola said. "I do not believe that is correct. Rowena asked me a question about the title, and I asked Esta. She said she would explain it to Rowena. Rowena is not an accountant. I think she believed whatever it was Esta told her."

"So…." Thomas began. He coughed, then started again. "So, why is Rowena dead?"

"Because I agreed to sell Via Pecora," Faye said. She glanced at Maggie and Thomas, then down to Daisy, who looked up at her with adoring eyes. The dog would love her, even if Maggie and Thomas didn't. "Rowena made me an offer I couldn't refuse." She paused. "Well, that's not exactly fair. She wanted to me to tell George something, and I offered to sell instead."

Faye flushed, waiting for her friends to slam their fists on the table or hurl accusations at her, but they didn't.

"Sounds like Rowena," Thomas said. "She caught you in a grey area, yeah?"

"Something like that," Faye said. She turned to Maggie. "I didn't want to sell out from under you, just when you were getting set up. I just couldn't think what else to do."

"Oh Faye," Maggie said, reaching out a hand. "How awful for you. Your peace of mind is more important than a lease, Faye. We're friends, whether Masterpiece is renting space from you or not."

Maggie and Thomas weren't asking what her secret was. They didn't seem to care. Faye felt, finally, relief.

"We're good, yes?" Thomas said. "Now, connect the dots for me, please."

"I get it," Maggie said slowly. "Rowena might have believed Esta's explanation about the titles, but the nephews wouldn't. Esta needed time to sell her art and pay it all back. It's what she would have done if Faye had ever agreed to a deal over all the years Esta was pitching the sale, but the timing now was bad."

"I think the final straw was when Esta found out that Rowena set up a meeting with the nephews to present the Via Pecora sale as a done deal," Faye said. "But if Esta could get Rowena out of the picture, she could come up with more delays. Slow the negations with me down, at least until she sold her artwork and repaid the loans."

"She even told Chaira she was finally going to sell," Thomas said. "But why not transfer Rowena? Fire her? It would be simpler, and more humane, if you care about things like that."

"Because of Adam's picture," Faye said. "Rowena went to Chiara and found out the market had cratered and probably said something innocent to Esta. I don't know if Rowena put it together with the mortgages or not, but Esta couldn't risk it. She had to act before Rowena could."

"She was a gambler through and through," Thomas said.

Stefano stood. "Now that you know everything, you have no need for me. Paola, I apologize for missing a date. I will make it up to you, yes?"

"Keeping your head in the sand won't help, Stefano," Maggie said in a commanding voice. She had two grown children, and Faye could imagine Maggie using the same tone with them as teenagers if they came home after curfew. "It's going to come out, and if your family sees that you're ahead of it, they'll see you as a leader, not a follower."

Stefano laughed. "You do not know my grandfather. He and Esta, they are good friends. No—" he pointed a finger. "No, not quite like Esta. He is more careful, yes? But reputation, it is very important to my family, and to Esta. It is more than important. It is everything. It is all she has. It cannot take that away from her."

Esta had killed Rowena to maintain face. Faye would never admit that she understood that impulse, that she and Esta were not so very different, but it was true.

Stefano looked to Paola, as if hoping she would save him, but she remained impassive. "All right, first thing tomorrow, yes?"

"Better come back with us, old man," Thomas said.

No one felt like talking on the drive back to the city. Daisy slept most of the way home with her head in Faye's lap. She drooled slightly, which Faye didn't mind at all. Her leg was asleep from the weight of Daisy's head, though, and she imagined Stefano's would be worse. They'd given him the middle seat and Daisy on his lap. It wasn't sufficient punishment, but it was a start.

As the lights of Rome started to show on the horizon, Thomas spoke. "This bodyguard fellow. Did he push Faye in front of the bus, too?"

"No," Faye said. "That was Ronnie."

Chapter Thirty-One

Is it possible to separate the art from the artist? Fans of pop stars wrestle with this question. Caravaggio's adherents would do well to do the same.
—Caravaggio: Brash, Brutish, and Brilliant

"Ronnie pushed you?" Thomas turned back to look at Faye, veering out of his lane on the highway. He swerved back. "The stepson who sent you chocolates?"

"His brother," Faye said. "The one who's been asking George for money. I shouldn't have been so slow to realize it."

"But why Ronnie?" Thomas asked. Seeming to realize there were two people in the car who didn't have the back story, Thomas went on. "Faye has loads of stepchildren, and they all get a piece of the pie when she dies, so to speak. She's also in the middle of a rather nasty divorce. When the peanut butter came up poisoned, we all thought someone intended it for her." He coughed. "Clearly, we were wrong."

"And Ronnie is one of these children?" Paola said. "Why would he want to kill you, Faye? Just for the money? How much is it?"

As if any amount would make taking a life worthwhile. People killed for whatever they thought they needed. Muggers had murdered for twenty dollars. Faye should have realized sooner that the money Ronnie wanted was an actual motive.

"It's George's fault," Faye said. "Ronnie wants help with some venture, and George told him he couldn't because of the divorce."

Ronnie had broken into Faye's apartment—well, used the key he'd walked off with on his last visit —to try to get into George's good graces. When that failed, he'd followed Faye and Burt. Pushing Faye in front of traffic for pocket change, and failing, was exactly the type of thing Ronnie would do. Daisy yawned and adjusted position, digging her shoulder into Faye as she moved.

"Is there any evidence?" Maggie asked.

"None," Faye said. "I'm going to ask Nardelli to talk with him, scare him straight."

"Right after she makes headlines with the arrest of Esta DiLorenzo," Thomas said. "I'm sure she'll jump on it. Why don't we ask Ilaria to send some men to give him a talking to?"

"Vigilante justice?" Faye said. "Olivia would never forgive me. Let's see what Inspector Nardelli can do."

Thomas pulled to a stop at 10 Via Pecora. "I'll come up. Check the apartment and all that."

The night air was a relief after the heat of the day. The streets were filled with couples and groups of friends. Some might be heading home, but others were still be on their way out for the evening. It would be a good two hours before the neighborhood finally went to sleep.

"We're fine." They'd agreed that Stefano would spend the night at Faye's. She didn't want him getting cold feet, and he was drawn by the offer of a home-cooked breakfast. "Between Stefano and Daisy, Ronnie wouldn't stand a chance."

Faye slid her key into the entry door, and Daisy snuffled around, then followed Faye and Stefano up the stairs. Faye would be sorry to return the dog to Adam. She'd have to consider a pet of her own when she got her life settled.

"I should go in first," Stefano said. "Just in case."

"I appreciate the chivalry," Faye said, "but Ronnie's hardly going to be inside holding a gun. He doesn't have any idea I'm on to him." Faye opened the door to her dark apartment, and Daisy trotted inside. "See, it's—" Faye began as she flipped on the lights.

Ronnie wasn't inside holding a gun; Esta's bodyguard was. Faye felt her stomach drop as she took in the man's calm face.

"Daisy, attack!" But Daisy ignored her. She moved past the gunman to the living room, where Faye could make out Esta on the sofa. "Bite, Daisy! Bite!" Daisy wagged her tail. "Daisy, come!" Faye's voice was shrill now, but the dog ignored her.

"I told you animals love me," Esta said.

Faye swallowed, trying to get her bearings as the situation sank in. Esta was here. In her apartment. With the lights off and the door locked. With a man holding a gun. Faye felt her pulse pounding in her ears.

"Ah, Stefano and Faye. This is very efficient, finding you together. Come in." Esta sounded for all the world as if this were a business meeting. No hint that there was anything odd about her sitting in the dark with her armed bodyguard.

Faye looked at Stefano, whose face had turned white. "Esta. There's no need for this. I would never—"

Esta shook her head. "But you have. Your grandfather's housekeeper, she always liked me."

"Gabriella?"

"I asked her to tell me if you had any visitors. I was surprised, yes? When she tells me you had not one but four. Such a crowd. And this nice dog. I did not expect you to be together here, but no matter."

"There's no need for a gun," Faye said. "We can talk."

"Talk?" Esta said. "Is that why you put a note in my door asking me to call you? A little advice, Faye: do not try to blackmail a woman who has already killed. It will not end well."

"Blackmail? No, I was trying to find Stefano."

"And you found him. And you are, what? Together for company? No. My entire life, people have misjudged me, undervalued me. I will not risk it happening again."

"Thomas and Maggie and Paola, they will notice if we are missing." Faye glanced at the bodyguard, whose expression was impassive. Was he following the conversation, or was Esta speaking in English to keep him in the dark?"

"You believe that?" Esta said. "Stefano, you have a history of disappearing, no? You left work without any notice. Then you were seen leaving your grandfather's house in the company of two women. You could be anywhere, yes? Having fun? That is typical. No reason to believe any harm has come of you." She nodded at Faye. "And this one? I understand she has been in fear for her life for some time."

Faye forced herself to sound calm. "No one would believe it." But even as she said it, she knew Esta was right. Everyone would believe it, especially with the power of Esta's influence with the police. "It's a big risk."

"Perhaps. But I have nothing to lose." Ever the gambler.

Faye glanced at Stefano, hoping for some sort of telepathic message with a plan, but he looked terrified. Guns were rare in Italy. Did that make the bodyguard more or less likely to use it? Faye had no idea.

She turned to the bodyguard and addressed him in Italian. "Your loyalty is impressive, but you must see that Esta has delusions. You've done nothing wrong yet, but if you help her here, it will be too late."

The man just stared ahead.

"Do you know what this is about? It's about money. Esta was stealing from her relatives. This has nothing to do with you."

Esta slapped Faye. It stung more than she would have expected.

"You know nothing of me, of my life. You and Rowena, you think that you get to decide right and wrong. You know nothing of the world."

Esta would never let them go. They knew too much. Faye tried to remember her self-defense classes. Her instructors had said the biggest mistake was to adopt some kind of karate stance that tells the assailant you're going to fight back. Faye put her hands up. "You're right, Esta, of course. You win."

She turned to the gunman and stomped on his foot, hard. He winced and let his hand down for a moment. Faye tried to grab his gun, but he held on to it, pulling Faye down to the ground. She twisted in his grip, reaching desperately for the gun again. He had her face pressed up against her beautiful hardwood floor when suddenly he stopped and slammed onto the ground next to her.

Faye heard Esta scream, then the clicking of high heels as she lay on the ground, taking in the blood trickling from the bodyguard's nose. He'd been hit by something.

George's golf club was on the ground. His driver with the light handle and powerful head. Perfect for knocking the life out of an attacker. The clubs had been in her bedroom. How had Stefano gotten to them?

Faye pushed herself to her knees and saw Stefano racing toward the door. Esta was ahead of him, heels clattering on the stairs. Then there was a sickening change in tempo, followed by a thump-thump-thump and then silence.

Faye felt her stomach bile rise, even before she joined Stefano at the railing and saw Esta at the bottom, neck twisted at an impossible angle. There was no question she was dead.

Stefano cleared his throat, but his voice was raspy. "We should—" He stopped, then started again. "We must call the police. They may be able to catch him."

"Him?"

"The young man with the golf club."

Daisy nudged against Faye's knee. "What young man?" Faye said. "Didn't you hit the bodyguard?"

Stefano looked taken aback. "Me, do that? No, a man came out of the bedroom swinging. He hit Eduardo, then went down the stairs. He was ahead of Esta."

Faye felt limp. "Thomas was right. Ronnie was waiting."

"Thank God for that."

Poor Ronnie. Poor Olivia. Poor Paul. Poor George. What a waste. Ronnie had saved her life tonight, but his presence would be evidence he'd also tried to take it. Twice. Once on the street corner, and again here in her own home.

They would get him a good defense lawyer, who would probably argue Ronnie was acting like a guardian angel. Stalkerish, maybe, but nothing more. The family would ensure he got counseling, but even if that worked, it would never be the same.

Maybe this was how Cliff had felt when he began his recovery: that he would never be trusted again. And then, when he was tested, he had failed. Lilly seemed to love him anyway. There was a lesson in that, but Faye was in no mood to contemplate it.

Chapter Thirty-Two

Caravaggio faded into obscurity after his death. It wasn't until the early 20th Century that art lovers rediscovered the power of his work. Would anything have irked this painter more than being ignored for two hundred years?
—Caravaggio: Brash, Brutish, and Brilliant

Stefano sat next to Faye with his back to the banister. "Why did Esta run? She could never have escaped."

Faye thought of the loose step, the steep stairs, Esta's heels. "She had nothing to lose. Esta couldn't have planned her fatal fall, but Faye suspected she would have chosen it over arrest and public humiliation.

If Faye hadn't been so worried about people finding out about her secret, she would have spent less time running around in circles. She leaned against the wall, uncomfortably aware that while it was easy to judge Stefano, the police could have solved the case if she'd told them all she'd known. Faye dialed emergency services and waited in the hall. She was shaking, and Stefano put his arm around her.

"Are you still seeing all those Caravaggios?"

"I'm done," Faye said. What was it Thomas had said? *Important as all get out, but hardly full of sunshine and unicorns.* She was ready for some sunshine and unicorns. "I'm not sure I could have figured it out without him, though."

"No?" Stefano said. "Which is the painting with bank loans and poisoned energy bars? I will look for it."

Faye laughed. "It was his swagger. Here's this man who pulled himself up out of obscurity to become a superstar. And he took himself so seriously.

He was always getting into fights."

"Okay…."

Faye sighed. "Same as Rowena. She pulled herself up from this really crummy childhood, and it left her with a chip on her shoulder that made her—" Faye paused, searching for the word. Sanctimonious? Priggish? "Prickly. It was like she was walking around, looking for trouble. What kind of person turns her running partner in for cheating? Or her husband? Someone with something to prove. That was what got her killed."

The evening passed in a blur. Faye remembered the bodies being removed by an efficient team from the coroner's office. Inspector Nardelli took her statement and promised to trace Ronnie.

Faye's eyes welled up with relief when she was finally released to the *questura* lobby and found the Burt and Maggie waiting. Faye was glad to collapse into their guest bed with Daisy snoring gently beside her.

The next morning, Faye woke to the smell of coffee brewing and something sweet. She couldn't remember the last time someone else had prepared breakfast for her.

"Pancakes," Maggie said when Faye came into the living room. "With bananas and strawberries. It's nearly ten. It took all of Burt and my restraint to save some for you."

"But it's Tuesday."

"Burt's working from home. Said he couldn't go to work with Ronnie out there, though Nardelli called an hour ago and said they have him." Maggie passed Faye a cup and lowered her voice. "To be honest, I'm not sure exactly what Burt would have done if Ronnie showed up here, but it was a nice gesture all the same."

Faye sat at the table and took in the stack of golden pancakes with fruit sprinkled over top. Not as fluffy as her own, and the fruit was cut a little too large, but delicious none-the-less. Maggie had used a hint of lemon zest that Faye decided to incorporate into her own recipe.

"The gang's all been around this morning," Maggie said. "Winnie brought flowers, Heather brought some cookies, and Jessica had a bottle of wine. They're all asking when the next bridge party is, by the way. Burt too. Says his brain is atrophying without it."

Faye took another bite of pancake. Two weeks ago, she would have responded by pulling out her calendar and setting a date then and there. But this morning, the idea of hosting the gang as if nothing had happened held little appeal. "Vultures," she said.

"True. Word's out that you're not just innocent, but the woman who cracked the case. They're riveted. Winnie seemed genuinely concerned, though."

"No word from Adam?"

Maggie frowned. "He called. He said he was well enough to take care of Daisy whenever it's convenient to drop her by."

"It was rude," Burt said. He had wandered in from the bedroom and was wearing a headset that made him look like a TV producer. "If it weren't for you, a cloud would still be over him."

Maggie coughed. "I gather he's not entirely convinced the cardamom in the granola was an accident. He said he's moving back to the States as soon as he gets things sorted here."

Faye was relieved. It would have been nice if Adam had shown some gratitude, but having him out of the city was what she really wanted. She'd miss Daisy, though.

Stefano came by in the afternoon. "Luca called me this morning," Stefano said. "The hotel business will go up for sale immediately. He offered me a job at headquarters. Paola too. There was mention of gratitude for our discretion."

"You told the police everything?"

"I did. My grandfather, too. It is, as Maggie suggested. My grandfather said he was proud of me. I am astonished."

News coverage of Esta's death was vague, reporting only that she had fallen at the site of a proposed hotel project. A casual reader would assume it was a workplace accident. Tragic, but nothing more.

Did her nephews know their aunt had killed to maintain face? Despite everything, part of Faye hoped not. She understood that desire to keep up appearances.

CHAPTER THIRTY-TWO

"And you, Faye?" Stefano said. "What will you do?"

"There's no need to make any decisions now," Maggie said. "It's been less than twelve hours."

"It's all right," Faye said. "I'm selling the building."

"Now?" Stefano said. "The price, it will be very low if the DiLorenzos are selling their properties there, too. Can you not wait?"

"I can, but why?" Faye was tired of living with vacant buildings on her block. She wanted to be somewhere alive where she could make new memories, not wallow in her old ones. "Besides, George will go crazy when he finds out the price. It will be a fraction of the proposed fair market value with the other properties going up for sale."

Faye would wrap up the divorce. She had briefly considered coming clean with her soon-to-be-ex-husband about the scale of her outside investments. But to what end? She didn't have to live her life according to an arbitrary law.

Daisy came up and leaned against her. "Beyond that, I have made no plans." And for once, that felt right.

A Note from the Author

This is a work of fiction, but most of the places in it are real, including the magnificent Villa Aurora. As recently as 2020, Princess Rita Boncompagni-Ludovisi really did sell private tours of her home, and I created a caretaker to escort Faye on her visit. While revising this book, I learned that the Princess put the home up for sale and moved out. At the time of this writing, it can still be had for the purchase price of $534 million.

Acknowledgements

This book would not exist without the wonderful readers who asked when there would be another "Maggie mystery." You encouraged me to write this one, and I hope you enjoy seeing Maggie's world from a new perspective as much as I enjoyed writing it.

I could not have completed this book without the support of my family—my number one cheerleader Pete, my parents, Holly and David, my sister, Holly Storck, and my patient children, Harry and Gus, who kindly ask how my writing is going.

A huge shout out to my early readers Jaclyn Hamer, Lisa Rothstein, and Dan Finnen, who saw a very rough draft and were kind and helpful in their feedback, and to my later readers, Dorothy Lam and Roberta Levin, who helped me take it over the finish line, and to Raegan O'Lone for reading pages and responding to plot ideas. Thank you to Jen Sinclair Johnson for being my accountability partner, and to Len Joy and Cameria Granstra for sharing insights about the world of ultra sports. The characterization of the sport in this story, though, is all my own.

I am beyond indebted to the magnificent women behind Sleuths and Sidekicks, Tina deBellegarde, Carol Pouliot, and Lida Sideris, who are wonderful boosters and role models for how to be a professional author. I'm so glad that we connected and can share this writing journey together.

Thank you to the wonderful mystery writing community of Sisters in Crime and Mystery Writers of America, and all the writers who make time to participate in the panels, articles, craft events, and honest conversations hosted by these organizations over the years.

Finally, thank you to my agent, Dawn Dowdle, my editor, Shawn Reilly Simmons, and everyone at Level Best Books for making this a reality. The mystery community is a wonderful group, and I'm grateful to be part of it.

About the Author

Jen Collins Moore transports readers to Rome in the Roman Holiday Mysteries. Her short fiction has appeared in *Mystery Weekly* and *Masthead: The Best New England Crime Stories*. She is president of Sisters in Crime Chicagoland and a founding member of Sleuths and Sidekicks. A transplanted New Englander, she lives in Chicago with her husband and two boys.

SOCIAL MEDIA HANDLES:
  www.jennifercollinsmoore.com
  www.sleuthsandsidekicks.com
  www.facebook.com/jencollinsmoore

AUTHOR WEBSITE:
  www.jennifercollinsmoore.com

Also by Jen Collins Moore

Murder in the Piazza

Masthead: The Best New England Crime Stories

The Secret Ingredient: The Mystery Writers' Cookbook